LOUISE ALLEN

Unlacing The Forbidden

Quills

Two classic historical stories

CONTENTS

LOUISE ALLEN

has been immersing herself in history, real and fictional, for as long as she can remember. She finds landscapes and places evoke powerful images of the past—Venice, Burgundy and the Greek Islands are favorite atmospheric destinations. Louise lives on the North Norfolk coast, where she shares with her husband the cottage they have renovated. She spends her spare time gardening, researching family history or traveling in the U.K. and abroad in search of inspiration. Please visit Louise's website, www.louiseallenregency.com, for the latest news, or find her on Twitter, @LouiseRegency, and on Facebook.

UNLACING LADY THEA

The Hussies,
with thanks for all the support, advice and laughter.

Author Note

Last year I spent a wonderful fortnight traveling along the Italian coast from Venice to Sicily on board a small boat. The whole trip was so interesting, and the scenery so beautiful that I knew I had to put it into a novel.

Unlacing Lady Thea is the result, and it is set in that short space of peace before Napoleon escaped from Elba and it seemed that the whole of Europe was going to be consumed by war again.

I knew Thea immediately—practical, funny, loving and brave—but I had no idea who she was going to share this adventure with, until Rhys Denham, rather the worse for wear after an evening out, appeared on the page and began discussing Life with the kitchen cat.

It was enormous fun to revisit some of my favorite places in France and Italy in the course of this novel, and I hope you enjoy the journey as much as Thea and Rhys did—although hopefully with fewer accidents along the way!

Chapter One

London—June 3, 1814

The skeleton clock on the overmantel struck four. No point in going to bed. Besides, he was thoroughly foxed, although not drunk enough to keep him from lying awake, wondering what had possessed him to make this insane plan. And worse, to follow through with organisation so ruthlessly efficient that to cancel now would throw his entire staff, financial team, estate management and social life into disorder—and make it seem he did not know his own mind.

'Which I do not,' Rhys Denham informed the ragged-eared ginger tom that sat on the hearthrug eyeing him with the disdain that only a feline or a dowager duchess could muster. 'Know my own mind, that is. Always do, just not this time.'

The appearance of the kitchen mouser on the principal floor, let alone in the study of the third Earl of Palgrave, was unheard of. The household must be stirring already, too distracted by their master's imminent departure for the Continent to notice an open door at the head of the servants' stair.

'It seemed a good plan at the time,' Rhys mused. The brandy at the bottom of the glass glowed in the candlelight, and he splashed in more and tossed the lot back. 'I'm drunk. Haven't been this drunk in years.' Not since he had woken up one afternoon and realised that drink was never going to blot out the disaster of his wedding day, restore his faith in friendship or his delusions about romantic love.

The cat switched its attention to the plate with the remains of the cold beef, cheese and bread that had been left out with the decanters. 'And you can stop licking your whiskers.' Rhys reached for the food. 'I need this more than you do. I have to be more or less sober in three hours.' That seemed improbable, even to his fogged brain.

'You have to admit, I deserve a holiday. The estate is in order, my finances could hardly be better, I am bored to the back teeth with town and Bonaparte has been out of harm's way on Elba for a month,' he informed the cat around a mouthful of beef. 'You think I am a trifle old for the Grand Tour? I disagree. At twenty-eight I will appreciate things more.' The cat sneered, lifted one hind leg and began to groom itself intimately.

'Stop that. A gentleman does not wash his balls in the study.' He tossed it a scrap of fat and the cat pounced. 'But a year? What was I thinking of?' *Escape.*

Of course, he could come back at any time and his staff would adjust to his demands with their usual smooth efficiency. After all, if there was some kind of crisis, he would return immediately. But to cancel on a whim was not responsible behaviour. It put people out, it let them down, and Rhys Denham despised people who let others down.

'No, I am going to go through with this,' he declared. 'It will do me good to have a complete change of scene, and then I'll be in the mood to find a pretty, modest, well-bred girl with a stay-at-home temperament and good child-bearing hips. I will be married by the time I am thirty.' *And bored out of my skull.* A vision of the succession of prime bits of muslin who had worked their magic in preventing just such boredom flitted across his memory. They had never expected dutiful monogamy. A wife would. Rhys sighed.

The friends who had deposited him on his doorstep an hour ago after a convivial farewell night at the club were all married, or about to be. Some even had children. And, to a man, they seemed cheered by the thought of someone else falling into parson's mousetrap. As Fred Herrick had put it, 'About time a rake like you stops nibbling the cheese, takes a proper bite at it and springs the trap, Denham.'

'And why is that such a damnably depressing thought?'

'I could not say, my lord.' Griffin stood in the doorway, his face set in the expressionless mask that signified deep disapproval.

What the devil had his butler got to be disapproving about? Rhys levered himself upright in his chair. A man was entitled to be in his cups in his own house, damn it. 'I was speaking to the cat, Griffin.'

'If you say so, my lord.'

Rhys glanced down at the rug. The ginger beast had vanished, leaving behind it only a faint grease stain on the silk pile.

'There is a person to see you, my lord.' From his tone it was clear this was the cause of the stone face, rather than his master's maudlin conversations with an invisible cat.

'What kind of person?'

'A young person, my lord.'

'A boy? I am not up to guessing games just at the moment, Griffin.'

'As you say, my lord. It *appears* to be a youth. Beyond that I am not prepared to commit myself.'

Appears? Does Griffin mean what I think he means? 'Well, where is it…. Him?' *Her?* 'Below stairs?'

'In the small reception room. It came to the front door, refused to go down to the tradesman's entrance and said it was certain your lordship would wish to see it.'

Rhys blinked at the decanter. How much had he drunk since he got back from White's? A lot, yes, but surely not enough to have imagined that faint hint of desperation in Griffin's voice. The man was capable of dealing with anything without turning a hair, whether it was pilfering footmen or furious discarded mistresses throwing the china.

A faint trickle of unease ran down his spine. *Mistresses.* Had Georgina failed to take her *congé* as calmly as she had appeared to do yesterday? Surely she was satisfied with a very nice diamond necklace and the lease on her little house for a further year? Rhys got to his feet and tugged off his already loosened neckcloth, leaving his coat where it was on the sofa. Ridiculous. He might seek pleasure without emotional entanglement, but he was no Lord Byron with hysterical females dressed as boys dogging his footsteps. He was careful to stick to professionals and fast married women who knew what they were about, not single ladies and certainly not unstable cross-dressing ones.

'Very well, let us see this mysterious youth.' His feet seemed to be obeying him, which was gratifying, considering the way the furniture swayed as Griffin preceded him down the hallway. Tomorrow—no, this morning—promised a hangover of monumental proportions.

Griffin opened the door to the room reserved for visitors who did not meet his exacting standards for admission to the Chinese Drawing Room. The figure seated on a hard chair against the far wall came to its feet. Short, bundled into an ill-fitting dark suit of clothes that said 'junior clerk' to Rhys's unfocused eye, it had a pair of portmanteaux at its feet and a battered beaver hat on the chair by its side.

Rhys blinked. He wasn't *that* drunk. 'Griffin, if that is male, then you and I are eunuchs in the Great Chan's court.'

The girl in the youth's clothes gave an exasperated sigh, set her fists on the curving hips that betrayed her sex and said, 'Rhys Denham, you are drunk—just when I was counting on you to be reliable.'

Thea? Lady Althea Curtiss, daughter of the Earl of Wellingstone by his scandalous first wife, the plain little brat who had dogged his heels throughout his boyhood, the loyal friend he had scarcely seen since the day his world fell apart. Here, in the early hours of the morning in his bachelor household, dressed as a boy. A walking scandal waiting to explode like a smouldering shell. He could almost hear the fuse fizzing.

Rhys was bigger than she had remembered. More solid. More…*male* as he loomed in the doorway in his shirt-sleeves, his chin darkened by his morning beard, the black hair that came from his Welsh mother in his eyes, that blue gaze blurred by drink and lack of sleep. A dangerous stranger. And then she blinked and remembered that it was six years since she had seen him close to. Of course he had changed.

'Thea?' He stalked across the room and took her by the shoulders, his focus sharp now, despite the smell of brandy on his breath. 'What the blazes are you doing here? And dressed like that.' He reached round and pulled the plait of mouse-brown hair out of the back of her coat. 'Who were you attempting to fool, you little idiot? Have you run away from home?'

Rhys was thin lipped with anger. Thea stepped back out of his grip, which made it easier to breathe, although it did nothing for her knocking knees. 'I am dressed like this because on a stagecoach in the dark it is enough to deceive lecherous men. I am perfectly aware that I do not pass muster as a youth in good light. And I have *left* home, I am not *running away*.'

Rhys's lips moved. He was silently counting up to ten in Welsh, she could tell. When he had been a boy he would say it out loud and she had learned the numbers. *Un, dau, tri...* 'Griffin. More brandy. Tea and something to eat for Lady Althea. Who is not, of course, here.'

Thea allowed herself to be shepherded into the study. Rhys dumped her bags on the hearthrug and pushed an ugly ginger cat off one of the chairs that flanked the fire. 'Sit. The cat hairs can't make that suit any worse than it is.' The cat swore at both of them, battered ears flat to its skull.

When she clicked her fingers, it curled its tail into a question mark and stalked off. Hopefully this was not an omen for how her reception was going to be. 'Is it your pet?'

Rhys narrowed his eyes at her. 'It is the kitchen cat and appears to think it owns the place.' He dropped into the opposite chair and ran his hands through his hair. 'Tell me this is not about a man. *Please.* I am leaving for Dover at seven o'clock and I would prefer not to postpone it in order to fight a duel with some scoundrel you fancy yourself in love with.'

If he was sober, it would help. As for duelling, she wondered if he was capable of hitting a barn door with a blunderbuss in this state. 'Of course it is not a man.' *Of course it is, but if I tell you the details we'll never get anywhere.* 'Don't be ridiculous. And why would you be fighting duels on my behalf, pray?' It was surprising how difficult it was to keep her voice steady. She must be more tired than she had realised.

'I always used to be,' Rhys said with a sudden grin and drew his index finger down the line of his nose. Its perfect Grecian profile had been lost in a scrap with some village boys who had called her names when she was six and he was twelve. The smile vanished as quickly as it had appeared. 'So if it isn't a man…'

'It is, in a way.' She had rehearsed all this in the smelly darkness of the stagecoach through the long hours on the road. Not quite lies, not quite the truth. 'You recall I have had three Seasons. No, of course you do not—our paths never crossed in town. You weren't attending all the Marriage Mart ghastliness that I was expected to.'

His jaw set hard and she bit her lower lip. *Stupid, tactless, to mention marriage. He still cares; it must still hurt.* 'Anyway, Papa said I was wasting money and another Season with all the other girls so much younger would be even worse. So he sent me back to Longley Park and set about finding me a husband locally.'

'Do you mean you didn't have *any* offers—?' Rhys broke off as Griffin brought in a tray, then waved a hand for her to help herself as he sloshed dark liquid into his glass. 'I mean, I know that with your mother…'

'Oh, yes, several very eligible younger sons offered. My dowry is respectable and there's my trust fund, of course.' Both were considerable inducements to make up for the other things—her plain speaking, her intellectual enthusiasms, her very average looks. Not to mention a mother who had been an actress and her father's mistress before their impetuous marriage and her tragic death in childbirth. 'I turned them all down.'

'Why?' Rhys squinted at her over his glass, apparently in an effort to bring her into focus.

'I didn't love any of them.' *They didn't love me.... None of them.* 'Papa has settled upon Sir Anthony Meldreth.' Would Rhys understand if she explained why she felt so betrayed now? Why she had to leave? The old Rhys would have done, but this man, in this condition? No, better to fudge. 'We did not suit, but Papa says that either I marry Anthony or I must remain at Longley and be a companion for Stepmama for the rest of my days.'

'Hell.' Rhys obviously recalled her stepmother's capacity for hypochondria, vapours and utterly selfish behaviour all too well. He rubbed long fingers against his forehead as though to push away a headache, or perhaps push coherent thought in. 'I understand your problem.'

Does he understand? Probably not, a man like Rhys couldn't be expected to comprehend the sheer mind-numbing dullness a spinster daughter was supposed to dwindle into. It would be like being buried alive. Nor could she expect him to comprehend the horrors of finding herself married to a man she did not like or trust or have a thing in common with.

'I can see it would be tiresome,' he continued, confirming her belief in his lack of understanding. 'But running away...' He frowned at her. 'I do not have time to deal with this now. I am about to leave for a Continental tour.'

'I know, Papa told me. He considers it shows a commendable enthusiasm for culture he had hitherto not recognised in you. Please *listen*, Rhys. I am twenty-two and of age. I am not running away, I am taking control of my life.'

'Twenty-two? Rubbish. You don't look it.' It was not a compliment.

Thea gritted her teeth and ploughed on. 'All I need is the approval of two of my three trustees in order to take control of my money and be independent.' It wasn't a fortune, but it would give her freedom, give her choice. 'If I do not get consent, then I will receive nothing unless Papa approves my marriage.'

'One of the trustees is your father, I presume.' Rhys picked up the decanter, studied it for a moment then put it down. 'Tempting as complete oblivion is at this moment—'

'He is,' she interrupted. 'And Grandmother was quite well aware of what he is like.' There was no point in feigning filial piety. Her father had been a distant, shadowy figure throughout her childhood, only taking any notice when she was of an age where she could not be relegated to the nursery. A girl was bad enough. A girl without a glimmer of her mother's legendary beauty and charm was worthless unless she made a useful marriage. Thea felt she hardly knew him, and, regrettably, felt no desire to do so.

If this stratagem failed and Papa realised what she was about and put pressure on the third trustee, Mr Heale, then she was trapped. She shivered at the memory of her cold, loveless childhood home. The Season had been an escape, but now that had been snatched away the walls were closing in.

'Grandmother had to name Papa as a trustee, for it would have seemed very strange if she had not, but she put in the clause about me only needing the permission of two of them for major decisions in order to get around him.'

She poured another cup of tea, ravenous and thirsty now that her immediate worries about finding Rhys at home were laid to rest. 'One of the others is the younger Mr Heale, the son of Grandmother's solicitor. I have spoken to him and he is perfectly agreeable to my taking control. I have his letter to that effect. So long as Papa does not realise exactly what I am about and try to influence him...' She touched the packet over her heart and felt the crisp, reassuring crackle of parchment. Surely her father's bullying could not negate that letter? 'My other trustee is Godmama Agnes.'

'Godmama. Now, *she* would approve of you having control of your fortune.' The brandy seemed to be having no serious effect on Rhys's understanding, or perhaps the fumes were clearing. 'Although what you'll do with it at your age...'

He was paying attention, even if he still seemed to believe she was sixteen, or incapable of making decisions. Thea took a sustaining gulp of tea, then reached for another scone. It had been a long time since breakfast at Longley Park and a snatched bun at the midafternoon change of horses.

'Has it ever occurred to you how fortunate we have been in our godmother?' Rhys asked. The thought of Lady Hughson was enough to curve his lips into a smile.

'Daily,' Thea agreed fervently. 'When we were all children I never gave it a thought, but now I see how lucky we were that she turned her unhappiness into pleasure in caring for her godchildren.' Godmama's home had been the only place she had experienced love and warmth.

'The fifteen little lambs in Agnes's personal flock?'

'Exactly. She must have loved her husband very much, then she lost him so young, before they could have children.'

Rhys gave a grunt of agreement. 'But that is history and if you ran, sorry, *left*, home to go to her, she's not in London. Have you just discovered that? Is that why you came to me?' The sleepy blue eyes studied her over the rim of his glass.

'I knew she was not in town and I dared not write and risk her reply falling into Papa's hands. She's in Venice. That is why I came straight here. As soon as I discovered where she was and what you were planning…' This was the tricky part. Would it help that Rhys was castaway?

He was not drunk enough to miss her meaning or perhaps he just knew her too well. 'Oh, no. No, no, *no*. You are not coming with me to the Continent. It is impossible, impractical, outrageous.'

'Have you become such a conventional prude that you cannot help an old friend?' she demanded. The old Rhys would rise to that lure.

'I am not *conventional*.' Rightly taking her words as an insult, Rhys banged the glass down, slopping brandy onto the highly polished mahogany. The smell was a physical reminder of what she was dealing with. 'Nor am I a prude. Revolting word. Like prunes and…' He shook his head as though to jerk his thoughts back on course. 'You cannot go gallivanting about Europe with a man you are not married to. Think of the scandal.'

'A scandal only if I am recognised, and who is going to do that? I will be veiled and anyone who sees us will assume I am your mistress.' He rolled his eyes, as well he might. She was hardly mistress material, veil or no veil. 'Frankly, I do not care if I am ruined. It can't make things any worse.

Rhys, I am not asking to be taken about as though I was on an expedition of pleasure, merely to be transported. I cannot go by myself, not easily, although if you do not help me then I will hire a courier and a maid and attempt it.'

'Using what for money?' he demanded. 'Or do you expect me to lend you the funds to ruin yourself with?'

'Certainly not. But my life will be wrecked if I have to stay.' He looked decidedly unconvinced. 'I have eighteen months' allowance with me.' The bundles of notes and the coins sewn into her underwear had kept her warm and comforted her with their solid presence throughout the long journey.

'I suppose your father handed it over without question?' There was the faintest hint of a twitch at the corner of his mouth. It gave her some hope that the old Rhys, the carefree, reckless boy who was up for any lark, was still lurking somewhere inside this rather formidable man.

'Of course not. I have not spent more than a few pounds of my allowance for three months. The rest I took from the money box in Papa's study. I left a proper receipt.'

'And who taught you to pick locks, madam?'

'You did.'

'The devil! I can't deny it.' He did grin then. 'You were very good at it, I recall. Remember the day when you opened Godmama's desk drawer and rescued my catapult? And I had a perfect alibi, clearing up under the nose of the head gardener after I broke three windows in the conservatory.'

'You said that you would be for ever in my debt.' She did not make the mistake of smiling triumphantly.

'I think I was thirteen at the time,' Rhys said. 'That is a very long time to remember a debt.'

'Surely a gentleman never forgets one, especially to a

lady.' His eyes flickered over her appalling clothes, but he refrained from comment. 'You have three choices, Rhys. Take me with you, leave me to my own devices in London or send me back to Papa.' Thea smiled to reduce the bluntness of her demand. 'Think of it as one last adventure. Or don't you dare?'

He shook his head at her, then winced as his eyes crossed. 'Do not think you are going to provoke me that way. I am twenty-eight, Thea, much too old for that nonsense.'

Rhys was not too old for anything, she thought as she concentrated on keeping her face open and ingenuous. He looked perfect for one last adventure, one last dream. 'Please?'

It had never failed before. She had no idea why, of all the group of godchildren who had spent their long summers with Lady Hughson, she was the one who could always wheedle Rhys into doing anything she asked. Her, ordinary little Althea, not the other boys, not even Serena, the blue-eyed beauty he had fallen in love with.

'I must be mad.' She held her breath as he took a long swallow of brandy, his Adam's apple moving in the muscled column of his throat. 'I'll take you. But you had better behave, brat, or you'll be on the first boat home.'

Chapter Two

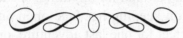

Rhys might have been foxed, but he could still organise his affairs with an autocratic authority. Hurrying upstairs to get changed, a sleepy maid at her heels, Thea recognised the development of the charm she remembered from years before. Then he would smile, explain, persuade—and things happened as the young Earl of Palgrave desired them. Everything except his marriage.

As an adult he still smiled, but he had no need for persuasion, it seemed. What his lordship ordered, happened. Now a travelling carriage was waiting behind the chaise in which she sat, clad in the plain, crumpled gown and cloak she had pulled from her portmanteau. A startled housemaid had received an unexpected promotion to lady's attendant and was chattering excitedly with Rhys's valet, Hodge, while the remainder of the luggage was packed into the carriage.

Thea twitched the side blind to make certain it was securely down, although there was no one in the dawn-lit street to see her inside the vehicle, let alone recognise her with the thick veil that covered her face. She yawned and wriggled her toes, relishing the thick carpet and the comfortable squabs after the Spartan stagecoach. Her new maid— Molly, Polly?—would join her in the chaise and Rhys would travel in the carriage with his valet, she assumed.

That was a good thing. She had not realised quite what a shock to the system this fully grown Rhys would be. Other than some distant glimpses when their paths had crossed while she was doing the Season, her last memories were of a youthful, trusting twenty-two-year-old standing white-faced at the altar as his world fell about his ears. After that he had been in London and, even when she was there, too, following her come-out, the paths of a wealthy, sophisticated man about town with no interest in finding a bride did not cross those of a young lady in the midst of the Marriage Mart.

The door opened and a footman leaned in. 'Excuse me, ma'am, but shall I put your seat into the sleeping position?' As he spoke he tugged a section of the padded facing panel away to reveal the darkness of the compartment that jutted out at the front of the vehicle, then he fitted the panel into the gap in front of the seat. She had heard about sleeping chaises, but had never travelled in one before.

'No, thank you.' She felt too tense to lie down. The maid deserved some rest after being dragged from her sleep to attend to her so she could use the facility.

The door opened again, the chaise dipped to the side as someone put their foot on the step. 'Rhys?'

'Not sleeping?' Shaven but heavy-eyed, he climbed past her, shrugged out of his coat and slid down the bed the footman had created, his booted feet disappearing into the void. 'Wake me when we stop for breakfast.' He closed his eyes and curled up on his side. 'Or for highwaymen.'

Without his coat Thea had an unimpeded view of the back of his head, his broad shoulders, the quite admirable lines of long thigh muscles and—she made no effort to avert her eyes—a firm, trim backside.

She stared for a long minute, being only human and female, then fixed her gaze on the postilions as the chaise lurched into motion. Oh, yes, indeed, her childhood friend had grown up. She felt rather as if she had whistled for a friendly hound to come to her side and had found instead she had summoned a wolf. He might be Rhys, but he was also a *male*. An adult male. With, she recalled, a reputation.

She brought to mind the sight of him in a box at Covent Garden Theatre, plying a beautiful woman with champagne, and hearing the whispers of the married ladies in her party. He had snatched that ladybird from the keeping of Lord Hepplethwaite and the displaced lord had blustered about calling him out—and had then recalled Rhys's reputation with a rapier.

After a few minutes Thea lowered the blind. It was easier on her nerves to see where they were and, if she was looking out of the window, then she was not watching the man slumbering by her side. He was snoring a little, which was not surprising after all he had drunk, she supposed. The sound was oddly comforting.

A glint of water showed her they were crossing Westminster Bridge, the new gaslights disappointingly extinguished. But the view downriver was as dramatic as when Wordsworth had written about it. 'The City now doth like a garment wear the beauty of the morning...' she murmured.

Beside her Rhys sighed as if in protest at the sound of her voice and turned over, his eyes tightly closed in sleep. His hair was fashionably cropped, but one dark lock fell over his forehead, a vivid reminder of the youth she had known. Thea reached out to brush it back, then stopped, her ungloved hand a fraction above the slightly waving strands. They rose to meet her fingertips like the pelt of a cat that had been stroked until its fur crackled.

Thea folded her hands in her lap. Some things were better left as dreams and memories. Some things were safer as girlhood follies. After a few minutes she drew the road guide from her reticule, where she had placed it in case she had needed to set out by herself, and unfolded the map.

They were heading into Southwark. As she had since she had begun this journey, she began to count off milestones in her head. Gathering everything she needed, undetected. Escaping from the house to the King's Head—not the closest inn, but one where she would not be recognised, despite the extra hour's walking it added to her flight. Taking the stage. Finding a hackney carriage to Rhys's house and then, the most difficult part of all, persuading him to take her with him.

Would he have agreed if he had not been drinking or if he had recognised that she was a grown woman now? She glanced down at his face, pillowed on his bent arm. Those blue eyes were closed, the veiling lashes a dark fringe. The bend in his nose was more visible from this angle and his lips moved slightly with his soft snores. There was a small scar just below his ear. That was new.

Thea wrenched her attention back to the map and the view from the window. Houses were thinning out; ahead was Deptford, full of history. According to her guidebook, it was where Sir Francis Drake was knighted and where Tsar Peter the Great stayed when he visited England. She watched eagerly for signs of the glamorous past and was sadly disappointed by crowded, dirty streets. They rattled over cobbles, the chaise jerked to a halt several times but Rhys slept on, much to her relief. When he woke, sobered and doubtless with a crashing hangover, would he change his mind about her?

The road began to climb towards Blackheath. *Wake me for highwaymen,* Rhys had instructed. Well, if they were to find any, this was a likely spot. She found she could not become very apprehensive, not on a clear June morning. More worrying was wondering where he had given the order for the first change. If it was too close to London, then there was the risk he would send her back. They rattled past the Sun in the Sands, the Fox under the Hill and the Earl of Moira as the road kept climbing. Shooter's Hill, she supposed, and relaxed a little.

Now they were slowing. Ahead she could see buildings, swinging inn signs. The postilions turned into the Red Lion's courtyard and ostlers ran out to make the change as the landlord strode across the yard towards them, attracted no doubt by the coat of arms emblazoned on the carriage doors.

Thea dropped the window. 'Shh! His lordship is sleeping,' she whispered to the man. Hodge appeared beside him and she murmured, 'Please have something if you need to, but don't wake his lordship.'

Hodge showed no surprise, but then, he must have been aware of the state his master had been in when he boarded the chaise. He nodded and went into the inn, her maid on his heels. Thea closed the window and sat on guard, her veil in place, jealously watching for anyone who might disturb Rhys's sleep. But after the arrival of a stagecoach, an altercation between two stable dogs and the shrill laughter of a kitchen maid flirting with an ostler all failed to do more than make him bury his head more firmly in his arms, she began to think he might sleep all morning, and began to doze herself.

Hodge opening the door woke her with a start. He passed her a mug of coffee and a napkin wrapped around a bread roll stuffed with bacon and glanced at his unconscious master.

'Does he always sleep like this?' Thea whispered.

The valet shook his head. 'No, my lady.' He took the mug when she had gulped the cooling coffee and closed the door softly, leaving her more than a little disturbed. Did Hodge mean he always drank that much and therefore slept heavily?

It had shocked her to find Rhys castaway and to see him toss off brandy as though it were lemonade. The rumours immediately after the fiasco of his wedding day were that he was a man who did not care, who had been glad to lose the responsibility of a wife and that he had plunged into a life of rakish dissipation.

He *had* cared, of course. She had seen his face in that first shock of betrayal; she had felt his fingers shake as she had pressed her pocket handkerchief into them, had felt his body rigid with pain when she had risked a brief hug. But then he had turned from the altar rail, a rueful smile on his lips, confessed that he had suspected the impending elopement all along and that he wished the scandalous couple happy.

For a man not given to falsehood, it was an impressive performance. It confused the gossipmongers, deflected some of the opprobrium from Serena and Paul and, she supposed, it salved Rhys's pride not to appear a victim, someone to be sorry for.

When she had been in London for her first Season the

only news she could discover of him was that he had steadied, taken his seat in the House of Lords and was managing his estates with a firm hand—but that he had a shocking reputation with women. Far from seeking a new bride, he flirted as if it was a form of elegant warfare, while keeping a string of mistresses who were, she gathered from the whispers, both beautiful and expensive. He was either not invited to the entertainments thought suitable for innocent young ladies, or he chose not to attend them.

The mothers of hopeful daughters were outraged: a young, wealthy, handsome earl should be setting up his nursery. Preferably with one of their girls, any of whom had been better brought up than that flighty Lady Serena Haslow. If Lord Denham would stop indulging in the pleasures of the flesh and the gaming room long enough, he would soon come to his senses and marry one of them.

The chaise rattled out of the yard and turned east towards Dartford. No one was forcing Rhys to go on this European trip. A few months ago, with the Continent at war, he could not even have contemplated it. So why was he going now, and why had she sensed such equivocal feelings about it the night before?

The bed, unaccountably bumpy, suddenly tipped. Half awake, Rhys grabbed for the edge, missed it and slid down until his booted feet hit some obstacle. *Boots in bed? A gentleman always takes his boots off, at the very least.* 'Where in Hades…?'

'This is the West Hill down into Dartford. The route guide warns it is uncommonly steep.' The matter-of-fact voice jolted him into a wakefulness that the discomforts of his bed had not achieved.

'Thea?' Rhys sat up, shoved the hair out of his eyes and groaned at the sunlight. If this was a dream, it was an uncommonly uncomfortable one. 'What the devil are you doing in my chaise?'

'You said I might come with you to the Continent. Surely you weren't so foxed last night that you cannot recall promising?' Pin neat, drab in mud-brown wool, as ordinary as a London sparrow and three times as real, she regarded him with what appeared to be disapproval.

'I'd hoped it was a nightmare. And what are you looking at me like that for?' He lifted the section of padded board and slotted it back into position so he could sit. 'My mouth feels like the floor of a cockpit.'

'I am not surprised—you were positively castaway last night. I suggest you tell the postilions to stop here and have some breakfast. The rest of us ate at Shooter's Hill.'

To retort that he was in charge of this journey and would make the decisions where to stop was to plunge back into the bickering of their childhood. Not that Thea had ever bickered. Or whined, come to that. She merely widened those unremarkable hazel eyes until he felt he had somehow disappointed her. And he did want something to eat and a quart of black coffee and then, with any luck, someone would hit him over the head so he could forget this headache in merciful oblivion.

Rhys dropped the window, leaned out and yelled, 'Next decent inn!'

'That will be the Bull.' Thea frowned at her road book.

'Never mind inn names, what the devil am I going to do about you?' He must have been beyond foxed to give in to the girl. Vague memories of an awful suit of male clothing swam into his memory.

'Take me to Godmama.' She regarded him through eyes suddenly narrowed with suspicion. 'As you promised.'

'You took advantage of me,' Rhys retorted.

'Do women often take advantage of you?' she enquired sweetly.

'When my luck's in,' Rhys muttered and Thea laughed. How could he have forgotten that wicked gurgle of laughter? He bit his lip to stop himself smiling back at her. 'This is an improper conversation and an utterly improper situation. If it ever gets out, you'll be ruined.' He squinted at her. 'You aren't a child any longer.' Was she? She looked about seventeen, if he was generous.

'No, I am not. And as for being ruined—' Thea shrugged as the chaise slowed. 'Good. Then Papa will stop trying to marry me off to devious, fortune-hunting… I mean, then I can have the freedom to live my life as I want to and not dwindle into an old maid.'

What is the matter with her? Every other girl wants a husband, full stop. Why must Thea be so contrary? 'Is that before or after your father shoots me?' he enquired as they stopped and an ostler hurried up. Rhys opened the door. 'No, we do not need a change of horses, but I want breakfast.'

'So do I, now I think about it.' Thea hopped down before he could offer his hand. 'A bacon roll and warm coffee were not very sustaining.'

She had her thick veil down, so he could find no reason to object, but when she returned from, he presumed, finding the privy, he wedged a chair under the door handle of the private parlour.

'Very wise,' Thea observed, taking her seat. 'If this was a stage farce, someone would burst through the door just as I removed my veil to eat. And, of course, by hideous co-incidence they would know me very well and have a fatal penchant for gossip. Papa would arrive with a horsewhip....'

'Do you see many farces?' Rhys refilled his cup and added sugar. He needed all the strength he could get.

'Not these days,' Thea said, and sliced the top off an egg with undue force. Eggshell fragments splintered, Rhys winced. 'Papa knows perfectly well that being kept away from London and the galleries and the theatres and the libraries is a torture. I am *so* looking forward to Paris.'

Rhys told himself that it was unmanly to whimper. 'Perhaps you have a friend somewhere in Kent or Sussex? Someone you can stay with?'

'You promised.' And he had. Being drunk was no excuse; a gentleman should be able to hold his liquor. A gentleman never broke his word. And he owed her. Not for that lock-picking incident that he vaguely recalled coming up last night, but for years of friendship culminating in that moment in the church when she had slipped him her handkerchief, had looked at him with a world of understanding in her eyes for his pain, had given him a brief hug.

Thea had said nothing and had broken the contact almost immediately, as though she knew that too much sympathy would break him. The sixteen-year-old girl had offered him the only thing she could: her understanding and a calm presence that stopped him falling apart. That clear-eyed look told him that she trusted him to do the right thing and, somehow, he had.

What would have happened if she had not been there? Would he have given chase, called out his best friend? Put a bullet in him and left three lives in ruin instead of just his own?

'Yes, I did, didn't I? All right, I won't go back on it.'

'Thank you.' Her hand shook a little as she lifted her cup, but otherwise she gave no sign that she had feared his refusal.

She always was a courageous little thing. Rhys poured more coffee so she wouldn't know he'd noticed that tremble and felt a pang of guilt. He should have kept in touch. But gentlemen did not write to young girls.

'Why were you—?' Thea broke off. 'Nothing.'

'Why was I so drunk last night? Damned if I know. Twelve months suddenly seemed a hell of a long time to be away and I started having doubts about whether I really wanted to do it, whether it was just a whim. I'd told myself I deserve a holiday before—' he almost did not finish the sentence, but then this was Thea and he'd always been able to tell her anything '—before I look for a wife next Season.'

And I despise myself for snatching at Bonaparte's defeat as an excuse to put off that search for another year, and that's why I was drinking. Coward. You should have dealt with those memories. There was little risk history would repeat itself; it was safe enough to seek to marry. His reason knew it, but apparently his emotions did not. It seemed there were some things he could not confess to Thea after all.

'You always have a plan,' she said, so coolly that he was taken aback. But what did he expect? That she would gasp in shock that he could forget Serena?

'And that involves getting back on the road now. I expect to be in Dover at half past four. That will give us an hour to get the carriages loaded and still catch the tide.'

'You are taking the carriages to France? How?' Her voice was oddly muffled behind the veil as she replaced her bonnet. Had he upset her somehow?

'I've hired a ship. I do not intend roughing it.'

'Excellent.' Thea's voice held nothing but approval. He had obviously been mistaken. 'I do so approve of luxury. And that means much more room for the shopping.'

'Shopping?' The Thea he remembered had no interest in shopping. But then, she had only been a girl and a tomboy at that. Looking at that disastrous gown, he shuddered to think what her idea of shopping entailed. Oh, well, her stepmother would soon sort out her wardrobe before her come-out. The vague memory of her saying she had been out for several Seasons floated into his aching head. And offers, and some man she was supposed to marry... No, surely not.

'Of course. Shopping is the entire point of Paris.'

This time he did not care how weak it sounded. Rhys whimpered.

Chapter Three

Dartford, Greenhithe, Northfleet. They travelled the next five miles in virtual silence, both of them, it seemed to Thea, adapting to their new relationship as travelling companions. Rhys had the excuse of his hangover as well, of course. She almost suggested they stop at the next apothecary's shop for a headache remedy, but this was a grown man beside her, not a boy. The very last thing she wanted to do was mother him.

'What has put you to the blush?' he asked without preamble.

She wished she had resumed her veil, but it hardly seemed friendly, not while they were travelling through open country. 'I was thinking about a man.' After all, she had always been able to tell Rhys everything. *Almost everything.*

'Really?' Rhys stopped slouching in his corner and regarded her quizzically. 'A very romantic man, by the look of those pink cheeks. Fallen in love with the drawing master?'

'No.' He obviously could not stop thinking of her as a

sixteen-year-old. 'Not the drawing master and no one romantic. Men do not woo me romantically. They check that I am not a complete ninny-hammer, assure themselves that I have all my own teeth and do not giggle and then they trot off and talk to Papa about the size of my dowry and whether he can assure them my mother's family will never make themselves known.'

'Thea, give it a chance. Just because you haven't taken yet it doesn't mean you won't get a perfectly reasonable proposal or two.'

'Rhys, I have not *taken* in three Seasons. I am not a beauty. I am not pretty. I am not even interestingly eccentric in my looks. I am perfectly ordinary. Average height, average face, ordinary eyes, mouse-brown hair which does *not* cascade into tumultuous waves to my waist when I take it down.

'If any man wrote poetry to my eyebrows I would fall about laughing and suggest he bought eyeglasses. When I do laugh no one compares it to the trill of a lark or the ripple of running water. I can sing and play the piano adequately and no one is so foolish as to ask for an encore.'

Rhys looked rather daunted. 'But you—'

'If you say I have a wonderful sense of humour, I will lose all respect for you,' she warned. 'Such a cliché.'

'Well, you do have. But what I was going to say is that you have a talent for friendship.'

'Oh.' Now he had surprised her. What a very lovely thing to say. He had always been generous with his friendship— to her, to Paul who had betrayed him. She had not realised he had valued that in her and she was touched he recalled it now. 'You have made me blush in earnest now,' Thea said as lightly as she knew how. 'I hope I am a good friend. But I do have a talent, and you will see what it is in Paris.'

'Shopping?'

'Not quite. Where are we now?'

'Gravesend. We will change horses again at Strood. But you have evaded the subject. Who is this man that the mere thought of him makes you blush? Did he break your heart?'

He was teasing, that was all. Thea found her smile from somewhere. 'Not deliberately. He had no idea of my feelings, you see, and besides, he was in love with someone else.'

'He *was*?'

'Is, I am sure. He was never the fickle sort. But don't look so indignant on my behalf. It was ages ago.'

Simply a youthful *tendre*, the delicious, painful quivering of first love. Puppy love. That was behind her now, thank goodness. That girl and that young man no longer existed. Except in dreams, sometimes, but it would be too cruel to give up on dreams of love.

But they were dangerous things to hold on to. If she had realised that then, she would never have believed Anthony sincere when he began to court her, never have thought that she could find an adult love, prosaic and sensible perhaps, but true and honest nevertheless. It had made the disillusion even greater when she had overheard her father discussing the terms of her dowry, the extra lands he was adding to compensate Anthony for taking his plain, awkward daughter off his hands.

Rhys had the tact to stop questioning her, which was a relief because she was not certain how long she could maintain a mask of indifference in the face of direct interrogation. She should never have said as much as she had. 'Look,' she said as she drew down her veil. 'This must be Strood.'

They arrived in Dover at a quarter to five and Rhys ushered his small party into private rooms at the Queen's Head on the quayside. 'I'll go along to the ship and send for you in about an hour.'

Thea balked at the threshold. 'I will come with you.' The prospect of sitting in a stuffy parlour with a yawning maid and a ramrod-backed valet perched on the edge of his chair had no appeal. 'You go and lie down and get some sleep, Polly.'

One of the things she had always liked about Rhys was the way he would never try to persuade her out of the harmless things that stuffy convention decreed girls were not supposed to do. She tucked her hand under his arm and walked along the quayside. The wind flipped her veil back from her face, but there was no one around who might recognise her.

'The wind is quite strong.' Waves slapped high against the stonework. 'And the sea looks rather rough, even in the shelter of the harbour.'

'Do you get seasick?'

'I don't know. I am fine in a rowing boat on the lake and as cool as a cucumber in a punt on the river.'

'They do not have waves.'

'No.' Thea took a deep breath of bracing sea air and found it was composed of an equally bracing mix of rotting seaweed and drains. 'I am sure it is all a case of mind over matter.'

'Or stomach. Perhaps I should acquire a basin.' Rhys nodded towards a chandler's shop. 'They probably have some.'

'We should write a book together. A practical guide to

elopement. You do it from the male point of view, I will do the hints for the ladies. It should have a list of things to take that can fit in a small valise....'

'*Very* small. No cabin trunks,' Rhys said with feeling. 'A rope ladder.'

'Sensible shoes for climbing down a ladder. Smelling salts.'

'A road book and plenty of money. A good team of horses to start with and close-mouthed postilions.'

'A compass to make certain the gentleman really is heading for the Border.'

'Cynic! And that obviates the need for a basin. No sea crossing.'

'So it does. Oh, dear,' Thea said mournfully. 'I was so enjoying the vision of an amorous young gentleman, tiptoeing around the corner at the dead of night, lantern in his teeth, rope ladder tripping him up, basin under one arm.'

Rhys chuckled. 'Why would he take the basin with him for the ladder-climbing part of the proceedings?'

'Because he is young and romantic and silly. Of course,' she added hopefully, 'his true love may be overcome with nerves and need it. Or he could use it to knock out a pursuing parent.'

Rhys disentangled himself from her grasp and caught her hand in his. 'You,' he said with a grin, 'are a bad girl.'

'I wish I was. I fear I am simply too prosaic.'

'If leaving home disguised as a boy, bullying a half-cut gentleman into escorting you across the Channel and spinning fantasies about elopements is prosaic, then I hope I may never meet an adventurous lady.' He looked down at her, more intently. 'Thea, *how* old did you say you are now?'

Having Rhys smile at her was such a relief it affected her

like one glass of champagne too many. It was going to be all right. He really would take her, not change his mind at the last moment. 'Twenty-two. I am six years younger than you, just as I have always been.' She laughed up at him and, distracted, tripped over a mooring rope.

Rhys spun her round and caught her up in his arms before she fell on the rough cobbles. 'Steady! Are you all right?'

'Oh, yes.' Tight in his embrace, close against his body and breathless with laughter, Thea looked up into intent blue eyes and smiled.

And then he went very still and his arms tightened around her as his eyes went dark. It lasted a second. It lasted an hour. Heat, strength, intensity. A hard, very adult, body against hers. A body that was becoming aroused.

Then he let her go, stepped back, stared at her in horror. 'God! I am sorry. Hell, Thea… I never meant for a moment to…manhandle you like that.'

Rhys was more shaken than she had ever seen him. *It was that bad, holding me in your arms, was it?* 'Please, do not regard it. I most certainly do not, you merely steadied me.' *Once I would have paid with everything I owned to be in your arms.*

'Of course you should regard it,' he snapped. *As though it was my fault, as though I had flung myself into his embrace on purpose...* 'I beg your pardon. Let me escort you back to the inn.' He offered his arm and she slid her fingers under his elbow. Through the kid leather of her glove she could feel his warmth and the thud of his heart against his ribs. *So agitated by discovering I am female!*

'There is no need. I would like to see the ship and the carriages being loaded.' Anything to stop her thinking about how the body that had pressed against hers had been so… A man's body, not a youth's.

Rhys ignored her, as though intent only on setting a brisk pace towards the Queen's Head. Then, just as she was on the point of jerking her hand free, he said, 'You are right not to regard it. Men are creatures of instinct, I am afraid. To find one's arms suddenly full of woman… It is no excuse, but you must not take it personally. It does not mean I do not hold you in the highest respect.' He cleared his throat.

As well he might, he has probably just heard how pompous he sounds. The rake lecturing on propriety, indeed! And he has just admitted that he was aroused and that I would have recognised that, so now he is thoroughly embarrassed and it is all my fault.

'I should regard it in the light of a cat who cannot resist catching a trailing ball of wool or a hound chasing a rabbit?' Thea enquired with all the sweetness of a lemon drop. She could not decide who she was more angry with: Rhys for making it so very clear that never again, if he was in a position to give it a moment's thought, would he take her in his arms, or herself for finding that attitude wounding. She should know better than to care. Caresses were betrayals; Anthony had taught her that.

'I am afraid so, hence the rules young ladies are sheltered by. But please, do not fear that it will ever happen again. You will have severe doubts about travelling with me now, of course. I will change places with your maid for the rest of the journey. Or I could escort you to a friend. Are you sure you do not have one in the area?'

There is no need to sound quite so hopeful, you exasperating man. 'There is no one and, besides, I am so desperate to reach Godmama that I would risk travelling with a carriage full of rakehells if need be. I could not bear to be taken back.' She sensed his frowning sideways glance, but kept her own gaze firmly forward, focused on the uneven stone setts. He really had no idea of what an emotional prison she faced. Men had so much freedom, unmarried women, none. 'You may rest easy. I have no intention of casting myself upon your manly bosom a second time.'

Delivered with punctilious formality to the custody of her maid, Thea waited until the parlour door had closed, then threw bonnet, reticule and finally herself onto the plush-covered sofa.

'Did the sight of the sea upset you, my lady?' Polly scooped up the scattered things and began to roll the bonnet ribbons neatly. 'I'm used to it, but I know many folks get proper queasy just looking at it.' Thea's silence seemed to make no impression as she chatted on. 'Mr Hodge says as how his lordship's taking the carriages over on deck. Now, that'll be the place for you to sleep, my lady. The chaise with the window open. Fresh air's what you need. Me, I like it nice and snug down below and I'm used to the smell of the bilges, what with being brought up on me dad's sailing barge on the Thames.'

'Really?' Thea made herself listen. It was ridiculous to sit there panicking—besides, what Polly said made sense. 'I'll do that, then. The chaise seats convert into a bed.'

'If you'll take my advice, my lady, you have a nice wash now and leave off your stays when you dress again. That way you can lie down and be properly comfy.'

No stays? It sounded rather…loose. A huff of laughter escaped her at the unintended pun. Loose or not, it also sounded exceedingly sensible, and she could always wrap her cloak around her so any lack of support was not noticeable. Not that there was anything wrong with her figure that made stays a necessity. It was a perfectly nice, perfectly ordinary figure that went in and out where it should. Nothing jiggled unnecessarily, there were no scrawny bits. *Perfectly ordinary...*

'That was a big sigh, my lady. You'll be tired, I'll wager. I'll ring for the hot water and you have a little rest.'

Polly bustled out and Thea sat quite still and kept her hands folded in her lap, nowhere near her lips that tingled as though Rhys's mouth had touched them.

Of all the damn-fool things to have done, embracing Thea came top of the list by a country mile. What had possessed him? The only consolation was that he had not kissed her. Rhys strode along the quayside past a group of loitering labourers who stepped back sharply at his approach.

He was scowling. Rhys unclenched his teeth and slowed his pace. Poor girl, she must have been appalled to find herself being clutched like that by her old friend, the man she so obviously trusted. No wonder Thea had snapped at him. It had never occurred to him to think of her in that light and then, suddenly, there she was in his arms, laughing up at him, and all he was conscious of was warm soft curves pressed against him and smiling lips and the faint scent of roses, and his treacherous body had reacted.

And she had felt it and had understood what was happening. Twenty-two! He still could not get his head around the fact that she was an adult—although when she was in his arms he'd had no trouble with the concept.

Thea had been too shocked to move, he thought, heaping hot coals on his conscience. Why, she hadn't even turned her head away. Her mouth had been… *Stop it!* Even now, thinking about it, he was growing hard, to his shame. *Thea.* Hell, he might have kissed her. He might be an arrant flirt, but he never trifled with virgins. Never.

'My lord?'

Rhys found himself at the foot of a crane alongside a sturdy hoy. With the tide full, its deck was on the level of the quayside and a blue-coated man with his hat pushed to the back of his head was standing, hands on hips, studying him. Men were leading away the teams from the carriages and removing the shafts under the watchful eye of Tom Felling, the coachman.

'I am Lord Palgrave. Are you Captain Wilmott?'

'I am, my lord, and this is the *Nancy Rose* all ready to take you to Dieppe in an hour.'

'How long will the crossing take?'

The captain squinted up at the sky. 'Twenty-four hours, give or take.'

'Give or take what?' Rhys demanded. Twenty-four hours cooped up on a boat with an embarrassed, angry woman was probably fitting penance, but he could do without the uncertainty.

'Give or take sudden changes in the weather, accidents to the sails or rigging or getting stopped and searched by the coastguard,' Harris said. 'Acts of God, men overboard, collisions with whales…'

Rhys bit his tongue. The man was master of his own vessel and wouldn't take kindly to imperious orders to get a move on. 'Try to avoid the whales,' he said with a smile to show he knew it was a joke. *I hope it was,* he thought as he strolled over to watch the men fixing ropes to the chaise to attach it to the crane.

There was something very compelling about watching experts working. Within half an hour the carriages were on deck and were being lashed down and the harness and shafts stowed. Rhys, temper restored, walked back to collect his party. The only possible approach was to act as though nothing had happened.

Thea, he found, was at least as good an actor as he was. 'Polly is an experienced sailor,' she remarked as they left the inn, a lad with a barrow trundling their hand luggage behind them. 'She advises that I sleep in the chaise in order to benefit from the fresh air. Will that inconvenience you, my lord?'

He echoed her tone of careful formality in front of the servants. 'Not at all, Lady Althea. She will be joining you, I collect?'

'She says she prefers to be below decks. There are no other passengers on board, are there? Surely I will be quite safe alone.'

'I will sleep in the carriage with Hodge. You have only to call out if you feel alarmed, but you will be quite secure.'

'Begging your pardon, my lord, but if I might spend the night below decks I would appreciate it. I don't rightly fancy being up on the top like that.' The valet was wearing his usual poker face and Rhys wondered whether it was fear of the sea or the company of Polly that motivated him.

'As you will, Hodge. Make certain there are blankets and pillows for Lady Althea.'

He helped Thea to the foot of the gangplank, then let the sailor stationed on deck take her hand to guide her safely onto the deck. *Same old Thea,* he thought with a rush of affection. Sensible, level-headed, brave enough not to flinch at the narrow bridge of wooden planks, rising and falling over the drop to the water.

Ridiculous to worry that she would be affected by that moment on the quayside. In six years he had forgotten what she was like—intelligent, loyal, full of fun and thoroughly rational. Until she was seized by some madcap idea, and then she was unstoppable.

Even during those awkward years when all the little girls he knew suddenly transformed into mystifying, alarming, thrilling creatures who left him hot, bothered and, ultimately, falling in love with one of them, Thea had stayed an honorary boy, even with her hems down and her hair up.

She had never giggled at him or ruthlessly used him to practise the arts of flirtation or reduced him to stammering incoherence with one look from beneath fluttering lashes. *Good old tomboy Thea. No wonder she never received an offer.* Rhys rested his elbows on the rail next to her. 'Off we go on our adventure.'

Her answering smile was not the carefree grin of the young Thea. There were layers he could not read, a tension about her that he supposed was partly anxiety and partly tiredness. But she would be all right when they were safely across the Channel and she'd had a good night's sleep. Plain little brown mouse—what the devil was the matter with him that she could send that shock of arousal through him? Must be the hangover, that was it.

Thea studied Rhys's profile as he watched the crew working the hoy away from the quayside and into the harbour. He was a trifle heavy-eyed still—hung-over, she supposed.

How long ago had it been when she had first realised how her feelings were changing for the boy who had been a part of her childhood for so long? And how had he, who had always understood her so well, failed to notice that she had tumbled into love with him with all the disastrous suddenness of their fall out of Squire Gravestock's pear tree, the time he broke his arm?

It must have been almost eight years ago. So long! Rhys always told her she was stubborn and she supposed he must be correct. Certainly her adoration was stubborn, for it had lived for months, flourished in the barren soil of his cheerful, friendly ignorance and then the desert of his total absence. Eventually she'd come to her senses and had grown up and out of love.

It had seemed such a good idea to go to Rhys when she'd heard he was going to the Continent, for any Grand Tour worth the name must include the great cities of Italy. It had not occurred to her for a moment that there was any danger in being alone with him. That girlish infatuation was long over and she could never forget that this was a man who loved another woman. If he did not, then surely he would have married by now.

But she had not taken the passing years into account. She had grown up and so, inevitably, had Rhys. And her mind might be cool and sensible, but her body was having a perfectly outrageous conversation with his, clamouring at her to look at him, admire him, let it explore this fascinating, frightening man. Her entire skin felt sensitive, her fingers itched to touch his....

She had never felt in the slightest danger from any of the dull, dutiful men who had asked for her hand when she was undertaking the Season. Even Anthony... *No, do not think about him.*

Now, alone with a man who was not dull and who was

probably anything but dutiful, it was not Rhys who presented a threat, it was her own sensual self, startled into awareness when all she had ever expected to feel for a man again was a dull ache, like an old bruise.

And then she remembered his rejection just now when he had found her in his arms. No, she was quite safe. The only danger was of embarrassing herself thoroughly by allowing him to glimpse her new consciousness of him as a man.

Chapter Four

Being at sea was more pleasant than Thea had anticipated. The sun shone, her heavy cloak kept the wind at bay and seeing how the ship worked was entertaining. The captain took them straight out into the Channel where they met the large waves head on, so, once she had got used to the motion, Thea felt quite comfortable.

'Take my arm,' Rhys urged.

It was a foolish indulgence to cling to him, feel his strength expended just to keep her safe, to be looked after, the sole focus of his attentions. This was how beautiful women felt all the time: cared for, fussed over, treated as though they were fragile and valuable.

'We can stagger drunkenly up and down the deck together,' he added as they set off, surprising a gasp of laughter from her. No, Rhys didn't think of her as a delicate flower. *Good old tomboy Thea, that's me.*

It was difficult to speak, the wind whipping the words from their mouths, so they fell silent, occasionally pointing things out to each other—the famous White Cliffs, shining in the afternoon sun, the ship's boy scampering amidst the rigging like a monkey, the gulls following their wake.

It made it all too easy to think and to remember.

She had been fourteen, a woman for only a few months, still awkward with her changing body and her strange shifting moods. Rhys had just turned twenty and for two years he had spent most of the summers with his male friends. Still, when he came back he treated her just the same, as a younger friend, not as a little girl or a nuisance. Looking back, she supposed that was because he simply did not think of her as female, a lowering conclusion.

She could recall thinking with relief that he hadn't changed at all in the five months since she had last seen him. And then Serena Halstow had walked into the room, seventeen, blonde and pretty, and Rhys was looking at her in a way she had never seen him look at anyone before. Thea had not quite understood what was happening, but she did recognise her own feelings. She'd been violently jealous. In fact, she could have slapped Serena simply for lowering that sweep of dark lashes over her big blue eyes and then biting her lower lip as she peeped up at Rhys, who was looking, Thea had thought viciously, like a stunned cod.

They had taken no notice when she'd stamped off to sulk in the summerhouse, but when she'd calmed down a little she'd applied her brain to the situation and realised that Rhys was besotted with Serena and Serena was by no means averse to that. It had also become clear that her perception of Rhys as her best friend had shifted into something else entirely. She loved him. She was not sure what that meant, she simply knew that she had given her heart. When you are fourteen, love is for ever. She knew better now.

The butterfly-fluttering, pulse-quickening wonder of that feeling had lasted until supper when she'd stood next to Serena and saw them both reflected in the long glass. Her emotions might have decided they wanted to grow up, her body had started the uncomfortable, embarrassing process of doing so, but she was still a girl while Serena, there was no doubt, was already a young lady.

Thea had resented the approach of womanhood. She'd dug her heels in and fought every step, hating her changing shape, the monthly misery of her courses, the restrictions and the rules. But Serena had run towards it, arms wide, thrilled with her transformation into a beautiful young woman.

Looks had never mattered to Thea, who was far more interested in character. Her stepmother was constantly lecturing. 'Stand up straight. Rinse your hair in vinegar, it might make it shine. Put this cream on those freckles.' But most of the time she would just stare at Thea and sigh.

Gazing into the mirror beside Serena, she'd realised why. She was ordinary. Not ugly, not even interestingly plain. Just run-of-the-mill ordinary. Dull. Men were not attracted to ordinary—not that she wanted men in general, just her Rhys. And her Rhys had eyes only for Serena.

In one evening Thea came to terms with the truth: that she was not fit for the handsome, eligible young man she wanted because handsome, eligible men deserved beautiful wives. She was a disappointment to Papa, which was why he did not love her and she was invisible as a female to Rhys—and so he did not want her, either.

She'd stayed very quiet all that summer and even Godmama, usually so perceptive, put it down to her being at an *awkward stage*. By the time she'd met Rhys again she had conquered that foolish puppy love and had learned to live with reality. It was better in the end—daydreams only led to hurt.

'Penny for your thoughts?' Rhys bent to her ear, his breath hot on her wind-chilled skin.

'Only one penny?' Her laugh sounded as shrill as the gulls' cries to her, but he did not appear to notice. 'Ten guineas at the very least, my lord. They are very deep thoughts about ancient history.'

'Are you a bluestocking, Thea?' he teased.

'I fear I am not serious enough.'

'Thank goodness,' Rhys said. 'That's what I always loved about you, Thea. You are so bright and yet such fun to be with.'

Her stomach swooped with a sensation that had nothing to do with the waves beneath the hull. 'Is that what it was? And I had always assumed it was because I would tell the most outrageous fibs to get you out of scrapes.'

Love me? As a friend, there was no doubt. Rhys had always been a loyal friend. What would it be like to hear him say those words and mean them, as he must have said them to Serena?

He had fallen in love with Serena Halstow, had wooed and won her, so everyone thought. And then Serena had run away on her wedding day with Paul Weston, Rhys's best friend, leaving Rhys to receive a note on the altar steps. In one shocked moment both Thea and Rhys had realised that Serena had been using Rhys's courtship as a disguise for her love affair with the other man, who had little money and smaller prospects.

Paul, Thea had thought as she stood clutching the bride's useless bouquet until the stems bent in her fingers. *Of course.* Paul, who Lord Halstow had been so vocal in dismissing as a rake and a wastrel.

For a second, a shameful second, her heart had leapt. Rhys was free. Then she realised he might be free, but he was also broken-hearted, however well he covered it up. The last thing he needed was his gawky little friend. Thea had bitten her lip and slammed the door firmly on the silly, romantic girl she had been.

She was grown-up now. When she'd come out, the men who did court her confirmed everything her stepmother had said. Men were not interested in ordinary girls unless they had connections and wealth. She had those in abundance, but her suitors were careless enough to let her see that was all the value she had for them. They were not interested in her sense of humour, her mind, her gift for friendship.

She would never have asked Rhys to let her travel with him if she had not believed those foolish feelings for him were safely in the past. And, of course, they were. Only, she never dreamt he would touch her on the first day like that.

Oh, well, as the Duke of Wellington said, I must tie a knot and carry on. Although she rather doubted whether the duke, famous for his *amours*, ever found such things disturbing his plans.

'Tired?' Rhys was leaning against the rail, supported on both elbows. His coat fell back, exposing the length of those well-muscled horseman's legs, the breadth of his chest, the flat stomach under the watch chain curving across the subdued silk of his waistcoat. 'You look very heavy-eyed.'

Her body felt achy, her lids heavy. She knew the cause, but it was hard to fight it. She was tired, that was the problem. Once she'd had a good night's sleep in a proper bed she would be able to control these infuriating animal urges perfectly easily. She was an intelligent woman, after all. Sensible. That was all it needed—common sense.

'It must be this sea air,' Thea murmured. The same sea air that blew Rhys's shirt tight against his body and tugged his hair back from his face. The young man she had known had grown into the breadth of his shoulders and the strong bones of his face as a hound puppy grew into its big feet and suddenly changed from a friendly, ungainly plaything into a sleek, muscled killing machine.

And it was not just physical. There was an assurance about him. He knew who he was, what he was. He existed in his world with complete confidence. No, his *worlds*, she realised. Even castaway he was master of his household and received only respect. His reputation as a landowner was unblemished. He had a full social life in a shark pool where there was no tolerance for anyone who was less than polished, assured, courageous, physically and mentally adept. How did a young man acquire those attributes? she wondered. He surely never had a doubt, never felt the fear and uncertainty that she was constantly having to suppress.

As for the way he unsettled her, well, she was not a girl any longer. She had read a lot of books, watched from the sidelines many a flirtation and courtship, allowed Anthony liberties that had gone too far, even if they had been disappointing and had taught her little.

What she was feeling was physical desire and telling herself that ladies did not permit such feelings was no help whatsoever. Either she was the single wanton exception to the rule or well-bred young women were fed a pack of lies about sex. Thea strongly suspected the latter.

'Sea air and the fact that you haven't had a decent night's sleep for at least two days,' Rhys diagnosed. Apparently he could read some of her thoughts, but hopefully not all of them. 'Still, this swell doesn't appear to be upsetting you, so you might manage a few hours tonight.'

'I agree, it is a positively pleasant motion, dip and rise. Very smooth.' She ran her tongue over salty lips.

'My lord, Lady Althea. There is dinner below if you would care to come down,' Hodge announced.

Polly had been right, there was a distinct odour of something unpleasant below decks and the motion of the ship, when one couldn't see the horizon, was far more noticeable than when she had been leaning on the rail. Thea took a plate of bread and cheese, a mug of tea, and went back on deck with a sigh of relief both for the fresh air and the interruption.

Rhys joined her as she perched on a barrel and sipped cautiously at the black brew. 'Definitely better than down there,' he said with a shudder, and bit into a slice of meat pie.

'Rhys, why not find a wife now?' He looked across, the pie still in his hand, and a chunk of pastry fell unheeded to the deck. *Oh, goodness, whatever possessed me to blurt that out?* Too late now to go back on the question. Thea ploughed on. 'It will be the house-party season very soon, or you could go to Brighton. There would be plenty of opportunities to find an eligible young lady and then you could honeymoon on the Continent.'

'It is too soon,' he said. His expression did not invite her to continue.

Too soon? Six years? How long does it take to get over a broken heart? *But if Rhys jilted me on the altar steps, would I feel able to marry another man even six years later? Probably not. He still loves her, then.*

* * *

It felt like kicking his favourite hound, Rhys thought. Thea didn't snap back or even show any sign that he had snubbed her, although he had an indefinable sense that she had withdrawn from him.

'Of course, it was insensitive of me to ask,' she said, each word laid down so carefully it might have been made of spun glass. 'You are not fickle. You still love Serena. Marrying again, out of duty, will be difficult.'

Still love Serena? Of course not. He almost said it out loud before he realised that would shock Thea. She believed him faithful, steadfast, the sort of man who would love loyally until death, and somehow he couldn't face the risk that she would think less of him if he admitted the truth.

It had taken six months, not six years, to come to his senses. Six months of heavy drinking, a succession of utterly unsatisfying amatory encounters and the crushing sense that if he wasn't worthy of being loved, then he wasn't worthy to behave like a gentleman, to care about his estates, to bother with his friends.

And then he had woken up one morning and asked why he was punishing himself. He had not driven Serena into Paul's arms; she had been there all the time. She had deceived him, lied to him, used him. He knew then he was not going to drink himself into an early grave for the sake of a woman who had never loved him.

'I meant that I need a holiday. I've been working hard on the estate with the new model farm, the changes to the tenants' cottages, the improvements we've been making to the cropping and livestock systems. I just want a break, something completely different.' He had also been burning the candle at both ends all Season and he was feeling utterly jaded with women, gaming… Not that he could tell Thea that.

Rhys took a swig of ale and watched Thea out of the corner of his eye as she chewed on her bread, apparently intent on digesting his words as thoroughly as her food.

What would she say if he told her the truth? *I want all my wits about me before I select a woman who will not betray me, who will fulfil her part of the bargain, will prove to be the bland, undemanding countess that I will be able to coexist with for the rest of my life. But the whole damn thing feels so cold, so…mechanical, that I'm clutching at excuses to put it off.*

He didn't need to ask Thea's opinion; he knew what it would be. She would frown a little, making a crease between the brows that were a shade darker than her hair. Then she would twiddle a strand of flyaway brown hair while she thought about it and finally she would tell him that he must wait until he found a woman to love and who loved him. Her obsession with love matches was the only irrational thing he had ever discovered about Thea.

If he waited to stray into the path of Cupid's arrows, he would die a bachelor. No, he would decide on a wife on the basis of her suitability as a countess and the mother of his heir. She would have to be intelligent enough to be a pleasant companion and a good parent, of course. And she would be attractive enough to make sharing a bed no penance—he intended to take his marriage vows seriously—but really, beyond that, he was prepared to be flexible and business-like about the matter.

The women he would be deciding between—or, rather, their fathers—would make *their* decision based on his title, his bloodlines and his estate. It would be rational, calm and safe on both sides. No messy emotions. No pretence of love. He had no intention of laying his own heart out to be trampled on again and he was wary of doing anything that would make an impressionable young woman fancy herself in love with him.

'Yes, I see.' Thea nodded at last, a firm little jerk of her head. 'It is very sensible to take a holiday if you need a change.'

'Are you cold? You shivered just then.' They were both well wrapped up, but the wind was cutting across the deck, sending tendrils of her hair dancing. It was rather pretty, that soft brown. Not obvious, just…nice. He'd never noticed before. Rhys leaned forward and tucked a strand back behind her ear, and she shivered again. He really should not touch her, not until he was feeling more himself, he thought, and frowned.

'I must be tired. I think I'll retire for the night.'

'Hodge has made up the chaise, by the look of it.' The valet was pulling down the blinds as he backed out of the vehicle.

'I'll just have a word with Polly.' Thea stood up and brushed at the skirts of the serviceable walking dress she was wearing. 'Goodnight, Rhys.' She leaned forward and, before he could react, planted a chaste kiss on his cheek. 'Thank you for bringing me. I'll try not to be a nuisance.'

He must be forgiven for that idiotic moment on the quayside, he decided as he watched her making her way across the gently heaving deck, her skirts caught up tight to stop the wind tossing them.

She had developed some very feminine curves since he had last seen her, he realised as she vanished into the companionway. The memory of them pressed against his body was…stimulating.

Ridiculous chit. What on earth had possessed her to think those boy's clothes would have been any protection at all once it had become light? It was fortunate that he had been home and she had not been out on the streets in the morning.

With a muttered curse Rhys got to his feet and went to see what Hodge was doing to make the carriage habitable for the night. This was Thea, for goodness' sake! What was the matter with him? He was going to have to find some obliging female company when they reached Paris if a few days' celibacy had this effect on him. *Thea, indeed!*

Hodge had created a snug nest for her with pillows and rugs. Thea took off her shoes and stockings, folded her cloak and lay down. How clever of Polly to suggest she take off her stays, she thought as she wriggled into a comfortable position. There was absolutely no reason why she could not get a perfectly good night's sleep with the boat moving in such a soothing rhythm.

No reason at all, except that her foolish brain decided to worry about Rhys and his marriage plans. Not that he was going about finding a bride differently from most eligible gentlemen, she supposed, punching a pillow into shape. But this was Rhys, and he was too passionate, too involved, too…alive, to settle for a bland marriage of mutual convenience, surely?

If he would only take an interest in the young women themselves and not in their parentage and dowries, then he might find a soulmate, someone who could heal the wounds Serena had inflicted.

She tried to think what sort of young lady would suit him.

Not blonde, of course. But she'd have to be pretty. And...
Warm, rocked by the waves, Thea drifted off to sleep.

'Ow!' Thea let out a startled cry, more of confusion than
pain. It was dark, her whole left side hurt from colliding
with something hard and she had no idea where on earth
she was. The surface she was lying on rose and fell and she
thumped down again, her limbs tangled in blankets.

*The chaise. I'm in the chaise on the deck of the ship
and we must have hit a rock or something. Get out....* She
scrabbled at the door catch but it wouldn't open. *I'm going
to drown....* 'Rhys!'

Chapter Five

'Thea?' The door swung open and Rhys landed on top of her with more force than grace, a shadowy form in the dark. 'Are you all right? I heard you cry out.'

'Are we sinking?' She grabbed for him and found a handful of linen shirt. He must have shed coat and waistcoat before settling for the night.

'No, nothing like that, we are quite safe.' The words ended on a grunt of pain as they were jolted up again. 'Damn, I bit my tongue.' He wedged himself into a corner and pulled Thea across his lap, his arms safe and sure around her as the panic drained away.

'The captain has altered course and we're running across some very choppy waves, something to do with the set of the wind and the way the tide is running. Do you feel sick?'

'I was asleep, and when I was thrown into the air I had no idea where I was or what was happening, so I was alarmed, but I don't feel ill, which must be a miracle. This is like being in a butter churn pulled across cobbles.' She clutched at his arms. 'How will we ever sleep?'

'Stay there a moment.' Rhys began to rummage around in the dark, heaping up blankets by the sound of it. 'If I lie down diagonally, I can wedge myself pretty well. You lie down in front of me.'

He reached for her hand and tugged and Thea half slid, half tumbled, across his body.

'*Ugh*. Turn your back and try not to elbow me in the stomach again.'

'Sorry.' It was a very firm stomach. Thea gave herself a brisk mental shake. 'Like this?' He was warm and hard and, when his arms came around her to anchor her in place, she stopped sliding about. It did nothing for the up-and-down jolting.

'Just like this.' His voice in her ear trembled on the edge of a laugh.

'What is so funny?' she enquired tartly.

'This is. I was imagining our eloping couple—the ones from the book you think we should write. Here they are, alone at last, and Neptune has decided to act as chaperon.'

'Of course! He is on the seabed, poking up irritably with his trident. Here he goes…again. Ouch.'

'Try to relax.' Rhys ignored her snort of derision. 'We'll get used to it. Just let go. You need the sleep.'

'Impossible! How can I sleep like this?'

'Count dolphins jumping over rocks,' Rhys murmured in her ear. 'Sheep would get too wet.'

'Idiot,' she murmured. *One, two, three…here comes a porpoise….*

Rhys sighed and moved his mouth gently against the head of the woman in his arms. This was the way to wake up. Warm, rocking gently, arms full of soft, curvaceous femininity.

She smelled of roses, whoever she was. He must try to recall her name in a minute; it was ungentlemanly to forget in the morning. Not that he could recall the night before either, but he supposed it must have been good. His body was certainly awake and interested.

When he pulled her more tightly against his groin she snuggled back with an erotic little wriggle that inflamed an already insistent erection to aching point.

'Mmm.' Rhys nuzzled the silky fine hair and let his right hand stray lightly across her body. They were both dressed, after a fashion, although their bare feet had obviously made friends in the night. Perhaps she had pulled on her gown again afterwards for warmth, because under the fine wool he could feel uncorseted curves and the sweet weight of an unfettered breast. As his thumb moved across the nipple it hardened and he smiled.

His companion stirred, stretched, her feet sliding down against his. She yawned and he came completely awake. He was in the chaise, on the ship, heading for France and in his arms, pressed against his insistent erection, her breast cupped in his hand, was Lady Althea Curtiss.

Rhys bit back the word that sprang to his lips and went very still. Was she awake? Had she realised? Probably not or she'd be screaming the place down, or, given that this was Thea, applying that sharp elbow where it would do most harm. He let his hand fall away from her breast, lifted the other from her hip, arched his mid-section as far back as he could. If he tried to slide his arm from under her, she would probably wake.

Damn it. *Thea*, the innocent, respectable friend whom

he had already shocked with that embrace. If his wretched wedding tackle would only take the hint and calm down, that would be a help; he was as hard as teak.

Rhys thought about Almack's, tripe and onions, Latin verbs, tailors' accounts. It didn't work. His brain, apparently having lost all its blood in a mad southwards dash, was disobediently musing on just where Thea had acquired those curves from and when she had begun to smell of roses and how that mousey mane of hair could be so silky.

'Rhys?' His name was muffled in a yawn.

'Yes. Roll off my arm, would you? I've got pins and needles.'

'Sorry.'

Merciful relief. In the dim morning light Rhys grabbed for a blanket and hauled it across his lap as he sat up.

Thea sat up, too, stretching her arms in a way that made him moan as her bosom rose and fell. 'Are you all right? Shall I rub it better?'

'No! I mean, no, my arm is fine now.' Rhys gave it a shake to demonstrate and grabbed for the door handle. 'I'll get out and let you get…get ready. Yes.' He landed on the deck and bundled the blanket back into the chaise. Damn it, he sounded like a gauche seventeen-year-old. 'I can see the shore clearly. We'll be landing soon, I expect.'

'Oh, good.' Thea's voice came faintly through the closed door. 'I won't be long.'

Hell's teeth. Rhys tottered to the main mast, took a firm grip on a rope and dragged cold sea air down into his lungs. *What have I agreed to? That isn't little Thea in there, that is Lady Althea, all grown up…and out and… Stop it.* He was, for Heaven's sake, a sophisticated man with considerable sexual experience. He was a notorious flirt. His wits were normally perfectly capable of dealing with any female. So why couldn't he cope with this one? It would be better when she was up and dressed and looking like Thea again in that drab dress with her cheerful, intelligent, blessedly ordinary face smiling at him. *And her corset on, please, God.*

Thea pulled on her stockings, tied her garters and searched for her shoes, all ordinary, every-morning tasks. Only this was not every morning. Today she had woken up plastered against the body of a virile, aroused man. Which was *interesting,* if ruinous for her peace of mind. She suspected that Rhys had no idea how awake she had been, or that she knew why he had bundled out of the carriage in such haste with a blanket clutched to his midriff.

After her first encounter with an overamorous rake at a ball during her first Season, she had resolved to discover exactly what physical love involved, if only to avoid unwanted advances.

Her researches had involved a fair amount of eavesdropping on her married acquaintances and discreet rummaging in the library, to say nothing of a survey of some Greek vases that had been pushed right to the back of a high shelf. And there was the Home Farm, of course. No country-bred girl could be completely ignorant, although one hoped one's husband, if one did ever marry, had more...*finesse* than Hector, the stud bull. Or Anthony, she thought with a shudder.

Thea felt she was reasonably well informed about the mechanics of the thing and had even gleaned the interesting snippet that men tended to wake up in a state of readiness for the act. That was obviously what had happened this morning. All perfectly natural and normal. Nothing to feel hot and bothered about. It had been quite impersonal, just as Rhys's hand on her breast had been the unintentional result of sleeping so close together. And presumably her own physical reaction to that sleepy caress was automatic and natural, too. *Goodness, he was large....* Even yesterday on the quayside she had not quite realised.

She spared a wistful thought for their innocent childhood as there was a tap on the door and Polly looked in.

'I've got your brushes here, my lady, and some water and a towel. Would you like your breakfast in here or on deck? The ship's cook's got some nice fried herring.'

'Just tea and bread and butter please, Polly. I'll take it outside. Were you all right last night?'

The motion of the boat was gentle enough now for the water in the deep bowl to lap safely at the sides when she wedged it in a corner. She washed her face.

'I was fine, my lady, but Mr Hodge isn't at all happy this morning.' Polly flapped blankets vigorously as she tidied the interior of the chaise. 'Green as pea soup, he is, and properly on his dignity when I twitted him about it. There, all that needs is the seats putting back. And did you manage any sleep, my lady?'

Thea glanced at the maid. Was that a snide question or a perfectly genuine one? She was not going to put herself in the position of appearing defensive. 'I was very alarmed when we started to toss so,' she said. 'In fact, I think I cried out, because his lordship came and wedged me in with the blankets.'

'Oh. Wasn't he...?' The maid caught herself up and bit her lip.

'Wasn't he in here the entire time? Do you assume that I am his lordship's mistress, Polly?'

'Oh! My lady, I wouldn't… I mean, it isn't my place.'

Thea raised one eyebrow and waited.

'Well, yes, my lady. At least, I thought you must be elop-ing, like. Getting married abroad. Only he's never brought women—ladies, that's to say, home before.' She trailed off. 'I'm sorry, my lady. You won't dismiss me for impertinence, will you?'

'No, of course not. I am not his lordship's lover, nor are we eloping. I have left home and he is accompanying me to Venice where I will join my godmother. We are old friends, that is all. It makes it quite unexceptional for him to have spent the night in the chaise under the circumstances. Why, he might be my brother.'

It sounded to her own ears like a rehearsed explanation and Polly's pursed lips indicated that she was less than con-vinced. 'Of course, my lady.' She gathered up the pillows. 'I'm very discreet, my lady.'

'I am glad to hear it. If you wish to become a lady's maid on a permanent basis, then that is essential.' Thea would not stoop to giving the girl money for silence, for that would convince her there really was something to hide, but the subtle hint that good behaviour might result in the privileged position of personal attendant being assured was probably just as effective.

She followed the maid out onto the deck, wrapped se-curely into the concealing folds of the cloak. Rhys was lean-ing against the main mast, hands clasped round a steaming mug, watching the coastline slip past. *France, the next part of the adventure.*

'I didn't realise there would be cliffs,' Thea observed as she reached his side. Thankfully her voice sounded per-fectly normal, although she suspected she was blushing. It was strange to have intimate knowledge of his body like that, even more disconcerting than the fact that he had caressed her breast.

'They are not as high as at Dover. We'll be in Dieppe soon.' Rhys sounded perfectly normal, too. He could not have realised that she had been awake as long as she had, or perhaps men were completely blasé about that kind of thing.

But he had not been indifferent about that hectic moment on the quayside in Dover. A sharp pain made her realise that she was biting her lower lip. The only thing to be done was to seem entirely unconscious of any reaction on either of their parts, and Rhys would soon realise that she had no interest in him as anything but an old friend.

Polly brought her tea and she leaned on the other side of the mast, scanning the coast for anything particularly foreign and exotic. 'It looks just like England,' she complained as they swung into the harbour.

'That doesn't.' Rhys nodded to a life-sized crucifix set up to dominate the quayside. 'And look at the costumes. Do you think they are fishwives?'

'They are exceptionally clean if they are,' Thea observed as the crowd on the quay came into focus. 'Not like Billingsgate at all!' The women had tight-waisted bodices with vast skirts billowing out and finishing well above their white-stockinged ankles. They wore snow-white caps with flaps hanging down to their shoulders and, as the sails came down and the ship lost way, Thea could see the glint of gold in every ear.

'So many soldiers,' she added as they glided closer. The crowd was full of men in greatcoats, military-looking jackets, cocked hats—all studying the ship and its human cargo with sullen faces. Thea was suddenly very grateful that she was not attempting this journey by herself. They had been at war with these people for years and, it seemed, peace had not made much difference. 'I thought the army would have been disbanded,' she added, trying for a note of bright interest and not apprehension. She had fought down her fears about leaving home, but it had never occurred to her to worry about dangers beyond escaping the shores of England.

'It has, by and large. Those aren't soldiers, at least not anymore. These are just conscripts who have returned home. Look around, virtually everyone is wearing some piece of cast-off uniform, even some of the women. They've been at war for years, poor devils, and they probably don't have much else.'

'Is there a hotel we will go to?' Thea saw jostling porters, lads with barrows, and tried to start thinking in French. It had never been her best subject, much to the disapproval of her governess.

'Of course. It is all arranged. We will be met—in fact, that must be the agent there.' Rhys raised a hand and a tall, thin man in a dark suit of clothes lifted his hat in acknowledgement.

The ship bumped alongside, almost level with the top of the quay. Ropes were thrown and tied, a ladder let down the few feet to the deck and Rhys went up, then reached out to help Thea, who twitched her veil into place.

'Monsieur le comte!' The man was pushing his way to their side.

'No earls in France,' Rhys observed to Thea. 'With or without their heads. It appears I have become a count.'

'François le Brun, at your service, *monsieur le comte.*' He whipped his hat off again as he saw Thea. 'And *madame la comtesse*! I had not expected the honour.'

'Non, monsieur. Je suis...'

'This is Madame Smith,' Rhys said firmly in French that was considerably better than hers. 'A family friend I am escorting to Paris.'

'But of course!' Le Brun's hands fluttered in urgent signals to indicate his total willingness to oblige. He was desperate to please, Thea realised. The returning English must offer employment and hope after difficult times. 'It is as *monsieur le comte* says. Another chamber will be no problem. I have taken the entire *hôtel* for the convenience of *monsieur le comte*.'

He clicked his fingers and half a dozen men lined up beside him. 'These will unload your carriages. I have engaged two post boys and hired horses of the best quality.' He grimaced. 'At least, of the best quality that is available these days.

'If you will follow me.' He turned, apparently unconcerned by the fight that had broken out between porters over who would load their luggage onto whose barrows. Hodge, in French almost as good as his master's, was laying down the law to some effect and Rhys did not appear concerned, so Thea took his arm and allowed herself to be led through the crowd.

'They are staring,' she muttered in English.

'Of course. We are still a novelty and no doubt they are studying us for the latest in English fashions.'

'Then they will be sadly disappointed in me,' she retorted. 'How long are we staying? I must buy one new gown at the very least. I cannot bear this drab old thing for much longer.'

'It is fine, surely?' Rhys glanced down at her skirts, protruding limply between the openings of her cloak.

Either he was completely indifferent to fashion or he simply expected her to wear something dowdy. Probably the latter. 'No, it is not fine. I chose it because it is so dull and worn. I had no wish to draw attention to myself in England. It is my gardening dress and the last thing Papa would expect me to be seen out in. I took the precaution of hiding some of my newest gowns so the description of what I was wearing would be wrong.'

'You would make an excellent spy,' Rhys observed. 'But can you not endure your limp brown skirts until Rouen? I was intending to spend just the one night here, but two there. The shops should be better, too.'

'Very well, it does seem sensible. But you are going to disappoint Monsieur le Brun when he has taken over an entire hotel just for one night.' The Frenchman paused to wave them on with a flourish. Behind them, she could hear Hodge nagging the porters to take care with his lordship's luggage. She had seen less dramatic circus processions.

'Monsieur le Brun has been promised a generous fee, so he will be advised to put a good face on it whether I stay ten minutes or ten days.' Rhys regarded their French guide's flamboyant gestures through narrowed eyes. 'This hotel had better be a good one.'

'He did not believe I was just a friend,' Thea murmured, tweaking her veil. 'Perhaps the hotelier will not approve....'

'The hotelier will approve even if we choose to hold an orgy for two, import every one of the Regent's mistresses or spend the evening playing whist,' Rhys said with an edge that startled her. 'It is none of his damn business. I am Palgrave, and if he does not know what that means then he will discover a startling shortage of English visitors of rank over the next few years.'

I am Palgrave. He would never have said that six years ago, and certainly not with that cool threat behind it. He had never spoken to her in that way and suddenly she saw him as others did: an earl, a powerful man by inheritance and his own force of will. Unnerved by his irritation, she stammered, 'I-it is just that I had not regarded what people might think, provided no one recognised me. And now I feel a trifle… I would not wish to cause you embarrassment.'

'Cause *me* embarrassment?' Rhys stopped dead and frowned down at her, six foot plus of exasperated masculinity. 'I doubt anything would put me to the blush, but you are my responsibility now.'

'Th-thank you.' Thea had to take a little run to catch up with him as he strode off across the cobbles. 'I had no intention of being a nuisance.'

'We will talk when we are alone,' Rhys said. 'Here, give me your arm, these stones will turn your ankle.'

In other words, I am *a nuisance.* It felt very much like being summoned to Papa's study for a lecture. Behind the sheltering veil, Thea grimaced at the haughty profile, fell obediently silent and wished very hard that she had the young Rhys back again.

Chapter Six

The hotel, when they reached it, was large, but half seemed in ruin with windows boarded up. There was even a small tree sprouting in the gutters.

'This looks a wreck,' Rhys said to le Brun.

'It is too big these days, too expensive to keep it all in repair. Before the Revolution it belonged to…a family. They no longer needed it, so part was taken over by a *citoyen*, a citizen of the Revolution, you understand? The same has happened all over the town.' He shrugged. 'All over France.'

'No longer needed it? You mean they were guillotined?' A citizen. *Citoyen*, one of the people. Had the landlord been part of the mob who bayed for *the death of aristocrats*? Thea shivered.

'*Madame*, such an unpleasant subject.' He pursed his lips as though she had made a remark in bad taste. Perhaps she had.

'The half that is in use seems decent enough,' Thea said to placate him as he ushered them inside.

He exchanged a flurry of rapid French with the short man who came out to greet them and two maids were despatched upstairs, arms full of linens. 'They prepare another bedchamber for *madame*,' le Brun explained. 'I show you now to the salon of the suite.' The landlord was swept aside. 'There is a chef, a proper man cook,' le Brun announced with a gesture towards a door at the rear. 'Not a female cook as so often is the case in England, I understand.'

They followed him upstairs, leaving the porters and Hodge in energetic dispute over how much extra it would cost to have the luggage carried up.

'Voilà!' Le Brun flung open a door with a flourish.

They were on the principal floor of the house, in a chamber that had once been an elegant reception room. It was whitewashed now and worn rugs were scattered over a floor of soft red brick, but the fireplace was magnificent and marble. The walls were hung with huge mirrors, damp spotted, their ornate frames bearing faint traces of their original gilding, and the assortment of furniture had once seen far better days.

'Monsieur le comte, your chamber is here.' Le Brun opened a door on the far side. *'Madame*, they prepare yours there.'

On the far side, thank goodness. 'I trust the beds are aired.' Thea had practised the sentence in French in her head all the way up the stairs.

Le Brun shot her a look of deep reproach. 'But of course!'

'We will need hot baths immediately, and then breakfast.' She threw back her veil and produced a smile. 'If you please.'

The effect on the Frenchman was curious. He smiled back at her with more genuine warmth than he had shown before, then he glanced at Rhys with a faint smirk. 'I see to it at once, *madame.*'

Thea snorted as he closed the door behind himself. 'He has realised that I am not, after all, your mistress. He will treat *me* with slightly more respect and he feels rather less for *you* now.'

'How did you work that out?' Rhys turned from the window and his contemplation of the street outside.

'He saw me unveiled. I told you, I am not mistress material. So he decides I am respectable and you are to be pitied for having the chore of escorting me.'

'Oh, for goodness' sake! As if the suitability of a woman for that role has anything to do with looks.' Rhys's brain appeared to catch up with his mouth and he shut it with a snap.

'What *does* it have to do with?' Thea asked, overcome with curiosity.

'Never mind! Will you please stop talking about mistresses?'

'Certainly! Perhaps, while you are lecturing me, you can tell me what it is we have to discuss in private?'

'Lecturing?' Rhys narrowed his eyes at her. 'Please sit down, Thea.' This was not the just-awakened man who had made her smile with his precipitous exit from the chaise. It was certainly not the inebriated old friend, sprawled in a chair and harassed by the kitchen cat. This was every inch the adult half stranger she had caught unsettling glimpses of on their journey.

'Very well.' She swept cloak and skirts around her with a flourish and sat in a chair that had probably once graced the town house of some now-executed aristocrat. The idea made her shiver.

'You are cold.' From his frown, that appeared to be a fault on her part.

'No, I am…unsettled. Please say what it is you wish to say and then I will go and change.'

'You should never have come to me and I should never have brought you with me,' Rhys stated without preamble.

'I was obviously mistaken in thinking I could rely on an old friend to help me.'

'You should have been able to rely on an old friend to do the right thing. If I had been halfway sober, I would never have brought you. But it is done now and there is no going back from it. I will get you to Godmama safely.'

'Thank—'

'I have not finished. Your position is open to misinterpretation from everyone we meet, servants or otherwise. I will not have a lady under my protection insulted or embarrassed, and I would therefore be grateful if you would do nothing to draw attention to yourself, or our journey is likely to be a turbulent one.'

'Indeed?' Thea got to her feet with a swirl of skirts that would have been considerably more effective if they had not been overwashed old wool. 'Other than being female, I do not believe I have done anything that might be said to draw attention to my person. I regret that I am not able to rectify that grievous fault—unless you wish me to dress as a boy? I still have the clothes.'

'You make an appalling boy—you do not have the figure for it.' Rhys appeared to find the carved overmantel fascinating.

'I could bind my—'

'It is not your… Not the parts that need binding that are

the problem. No youth has hips like that, and those can't be bound.'

'Hips? Are you saying that I have a fat posterior?'

'No! Thea, this is a highly improper conversation.' Rhys glared at her. 'You have curves, that is all I am saying.'

'So I should hope.'

'You never had them before.' Rhys's lips twitched into a reluctant smile. 'You used to be all skin and bone and angles. You still have the elbows. I have the bruises from last night.'

'I was sixteen the last time we met face-to-face, for goodness' sake! I was a late developer,' she added mutinously.

'Well, you've developed now, and that's a problem.'

'Not according to Stepmama. She considers that I finally have an adequate figure.' Rhys appeared to be grinding his teeth. 'Anyway, I have no intention of flaunting anything, or of flirting with passing rakes, leaning over the balcony *en negligée* or otherwise drawing attention to myself. Does that reassure you?'

'It does. Thank you, Thea.' They watched each other in wary silence for a minute, then Rhys said, 'I am not used to having to look after an unmarried girl.'

'I am not a girl.' His words might have been intended as a small flag of truce, but her precarious hold on her temper was slipping again. 'If I am old enough to be married, and to inherit my own money, I think that makes me a woman, don't you?' Even to her own ears she sounded remarkably tart. What was the matter with her? She never lost her temper—she was known for cheerful common sense, everyone said so.

'No doubt it does. And that is the problem. At least we understand each other now.'

We do? She opened her mouth to ask that very question as Polly bustled in.

'The room's all ready for you, my lady, and the bath's being filled, although I had a bit of a problem with the servants here to start with. Cobwebs like you wouldn't believe and no proper pillows, just nasty, hard bolster things.' She picked up Thea's discarded bonnet. 'Amazing how they understand if you speak nice and loud and slow, isn't it?'

'French servants or Englishmen?' Thea murmured as she followed the maid out. From the corner of her eye she saw Rhys's mouth quirk up at the corner. So he had heard her. Ah well, so long as that half smile meant they were back on their old footing and he stopped that nonsense about drawing attention to herself. And wanting to fight anyone who insulted her.

It was rather charming, she decided as she rolled down her stockings. Gallant. Up to now gentlemen had not seemed to consider that she might need helping down gangplanks or rescuing from embarrassment. Even when Anthony was making his pretence of courting her so ardently he had never tried the 'fragile flower' treatment.

Not that she did *need* assistance, of course. She would hate to be a helpless female, but it was pleasant to be looked after once in a while. The memory of just how safe Rhys's body had made her feel sent a shiver shimmering across her skin. Odd, she must be tired, or perhaps she was coming down with a chill.

And perhaps *safe* was not the right word, not when she remembered the shocking pressure of his arousal against her buttocks, or the heat of his body. But that was just a male reflex, nothing to be worried about. Everything would be fine, provided Rhys stopped lecturing her. Even discovery and ruin hardly mattered. Nothing did, provided she was not forced back home into a grey nothingness of an existence. She shivered again. That would be so bad she might even agree to marriage and find herself tied to someone like Anthony.

Polly lifted her gown over her head and Thea shed shift and petticoats before stepping into the bath. 'Heaven.' This would stop the shivers. 'A hot soak and a soft bed that doesn't move. It is soft, I hope?'

'The sort that swallows you,' Polly said cheerfully, and passed the soap. 'They've put me in there.' She pointed at a door. 'Great big room. And Mr Hodge is on the other side next to his lordship. Not exactly cosy, though, is it?'

'Not at all. I think it was a quite grand town house once and this was the main reception floor. These are not really bedchambers.'

'And the owner's come down in the world? He doesn't look much like a gentleman.' Polly began to shake out Thea's clothes. The corset had reappeared, she noticed.

'I suspect the real owner and his family went to the guillotine,' Thea said, repressing another shiver.

'Ooh! I was forgetting that.' Polly's eyes were huge. 'Murdering Frenchies. Why, they're probably eyeing up his lordship and sharpening the blade even now….'

'We are at peace with France,' Thea soothed. 'There is a king on the throne again and Bonaparte is safely banished to Elba in the middle of the Mediterranean.'

'And quite right, too,' Polly muttered. 'Now, I suppose it will have to be the blue gown tonight.' She prodded the limp garment with disfavour while Thea made herself focus on the immediate crisis of her inadequate wardrobe and pushed other, more disturbing, thoughts back into the shadows.

* * *

Rhys folded his long legs into the bath and bent his head for Hodge to pour over a jug of hot water. *Thea and that tongue of hers, as sharp as ever.* But she never used it to wound. Only to tease, to create laughter, to press home a point.

He'd missed that laughter and teasing from a woman. There was laughter enough with his male friends, but his mistresses were always more intent on being seductive than on amusing him, which he supposed was fair enough, that was what he wanted from them—beauty, sensual expertise in bed and sophisticated conversation beforehand.

They were an expensive luxury, but Rhys was prepared to pay for quality. But some things could not be bought from a woman: friendship, laughter, loyalty. For a few weeks he would have those with Thea, he supposed, and felt the smile curve his mouth.

'More hot water, my lord?'

'Hmm?' He must have fallen into a trance. 'Yes. More hot water, more soap.' *Thea. Just as long as you remember that she's an innocent. A bright, clever, independent innocent. It is a good thing she's been stubborn enough to turn down those marriage offers—she isn't cut out for matrimony and they'd only make her miserable, forcing her into the mould of a perfect wife.*

Hodge passed him a back brush and Rhys began to scrub, shifting his shoulders under the pleasurable rasp of the bristles.

But she'd have to be careful, he realised as he considered it further. Life as a single woman would be made smoother with wealth, but it would be all too easy to slip into eccentricity, or worse, if she failed to find a manner of living that met with the approval of society. He would have to talk to her about it, make certain she made the right decisions, just as he had.

'So what are you planning to do with all this money when you have control of it?' Rhys asked.

The wind on the cliff top was blowing her veil in all directions and he could not see her face. With an irritated *'Tsk'*, Thea gave up wrestling with her veil and threw it back over her bonnet. 'There is no one up here to see,' she said, as though expecting him to demand that she lower it again. 'What am I planning? Why, to be independent.'

'I know that, but independently doing what, exactly?' Rhys hitched one hip onto a tumbledown stone wall and half turned as though watching the town and harbour below. Out of the corner of his eye he studied Thea as she paced back and forth over the rabbit-cropped turf.

'Living, of course! What a ridiculous question.'

'Where? With whom? Who will be managing your investments? What will you be spending your money on?' He swivelled to face her and she stopped, a furrow between her brows as she frowned at him. 'What will be your purpose in life?'

'To enjoy myself. To be free.'

'Selfish,' Rhys commented, with the intent of provoking her. Down in the harbour, fishing boats were running out on the tide, and he pretended to watch them. 'That's not like you.' Or perhaps it was. Six years was a long time. He had changed, she must have, too.

'I don't mean mindless frivolity,' Thea protested. 'I mean doing things that I consider worthwhile. Something that will tell me I am alive,' she added so softly he thought he must have misheard her. Surely life in her father's house was not so stifling? 'I will set up a charity—that would be satisfying….'

'To be Lady Bountiful to the grateful poor?' He let the corner of his mouth curl into a sneer. As it had in the past, his goading worked. Thea glared at him, but he had loosened her tongue.

'No, certainly not. People do not need to be patronised, to be done good to. I will find something worthwhile and invest in it. Perhaps set some enterprising women up in small businesses, or provide apprenticeships for bright boys. I have a brain with some ideas in it, Rhys. I will suffocate if I don't use it, if I am not free.'

He hid both his approval and his unease at her vehemence. 'It does not sound as though you have planned it out.'

'Of course I have not.' Thea marched round to stand in front of him, cutting off his view of the harbour. 'I need to find out exactly what my income is, learn how to manage it and, I hope, increase it. I have to find a suitable companion and somewhere to live. I need to work out all those things and then I can see where I am.

'Anyway,' she demanded, 'what is so important about planning? You used to do things on the spur of the moment. Improvise.'

'I do not any longer.' He stood up, rather too close for her comfort, it seemed. Thea cast a harried glance over her shoulder, apparently decided that the cliff edge was a safe distance from her heels and took a long step backwards. 'These days I plan—the estate, my investments, my political life, the way I live.'

'Predictable,' Thea retorted. 'Boring. Do you schedule your mistresses according to a timetable?'

'Responsible,' he flung back, ignoring that last jibe. Rhys planned so that nothing, nobody would have the chance to let him down again, but he saw no reason to justify himself. He caught at the ragged edge of his temper and said coolly, 'Grow up, Thea.'

'I have.' Annoyance was bringing out the colour to her cheeks. 'But I do not understand why being a responsible adult involves losing spontaneity, joy, surprise. Adventure.' The look she shot him held reproach. 'Have you any concept what it would be like to have to dwindle into an old maid or be married off to a man whom you cannot like, let alone respect?'

No, he could not, and it made him damnably uncomfortable that Thea of all people feared those things. His conscience nudged him. She had been his friend and he had all but forgotten her as he had rebuilt his life. But what did he know about respectable women and their emotional needs? Perhaps some practical common sense would help—it was all he had to offer. 'This is not about me. It is about you, Thea. You have two assets that must last you your lifetime, if you are not to marry.'

She tipped her head to one side, instantly curious. She had never been able to hold on to a bad mood for long. The only time he had seen her stay angry was two hours after the fiasco of his wedding ceremony when he had found her wringing the neck of Serena's bouquet. And even then, when she had seen him, she had smiled ruefully. 'Poor flowers, it isn't their fault.'

'I have my inheritance, that is all,' she said now.

'You have that, and you will need to choose your financial and legal advisers with great care, for those funds must last to finance your independence.'

'So what is the other asset?' Intelligent hazel eyes fringed with dark lashes narrowed in thought.

'Your reputation. Respectable single women with wealth and breeding and a certain interesting eccentricity will be accepted anywhere—look at Godmama. But get a shady reputation, just the hint of loose behaviour, and you will find doors close in your face.'

'Loose behaviour? Me?' Thea gave an unladylike snort of derision.

'Like gadding about the Continent unchaperoned with a man to whom you are not related, for example?'

The charming blush faded. 'Nonsense. No one is going to find out. Godmama and I will concoct a suitable story involving a courier and a suitable female companion, you'll see.' There it was again, just that flash of emotion behind the confidence. Surely it could not be fear of what would await her if she had to return home?

'I hope so. It is getting cold—let's go down and see what there is for dinner.' He stood and offered his arm and she slipped her hand under his elbow. He was apparently forgiven. But then, Thea always did forgive. Rhys felt another twinge of guilt, this time for goading her and, at the same time, for entertaining Gothic imaginings about her father. The earl might not be the best parent in the world, but he would not mistreat Thea, surely?

'Scallops, I hope. Dieppe is famous for them, I believe.'

'That sounds good,' Rhys agreed. 'I was thinking of a fat lobster, personally.'

He waited until they had left the slippery cliff-top turf for the worn path before he asked, 'Would it not be better to find a husband after all? Someone to take care of you—and your inheritance?'

'*His* inheritance, you mean. Once I marry, I lose all control of my money.'

'Is that why you are so set against marriage?' A group of soldiers lounged by a checkpoint on the road out of town. They glanced over at them, then went back to their game of dice. There was something she was not telling him, and he was going to winkle it out of her, however hard she resisted.

Chapter Seven

'I am not set against marriage, as such,' Thea protested. 'But it is such a risk. A woman hazards so much. I am resolved not to marry unless I fall in love, which seems to me to be the only reason for taking the plunge. And I can tell you, that is highly unlikely.'

'What about Sir Anthony Meldreth?'

'As I said, we found we did not suit.'

Perhaps she had sounded unconvincing, for Rhys stopped and looked at her sharply. 'What happened?'

Bother and blast, I am blushing. 'Nothing.'

'Thea…' Rhys's tone told her he would not let this go now. 'Sit down here and tell me.' He gestured to a bench by the side of the path.

'Oh, well, if you must pry into every last detail!' Thea sat down with an inelegant thump and stared at her toes. 'He led me to believe he loved me, that he was interested in the things that I enjoyed, that he respected my opinions, that he wanted a wife who would be an equal.'

'And did you love him?'

'In a way, yes. I thought he would be a good companion and I trusted him when he said he wanted only me, for myself.'

'And he did not?' Rhys's voice was softer now.

'I overheard him discussing settlements with my father. They had agreed on his approach together so that Papa could get me off his hands and Anthony would gain my inheritance and a piece of land he had been wanting for a long time that Papa had previously refused to sell.'

'That must have been…difficult to cope with. What did you do? Confront them?'

'No. I told Anthony that I had changed my mind and I did not think we would suit. He told me I was frigid and not worth what my father offered him.'

'*Frigid?* Did he force you?'

'No.' It was apparently possible to blush this hard without bursting into flames. 'I allowed him certain…liberties. When I thought we were in love, you understand.' Thea fixed her gaze on her clasped hands.

'*Certain liberties?* What the blazes does that mean?' Rhys sounded furious. Thea flickered a glance in his direction and saw his face. He *was* furious.

'Rhys, for goodness' sake, I cannot discuss this with you!'

'Why not? You are under my protection. The man's a bastard to trifle with you. I will deal with him when I get back to England.'

'Call him out? For pity's sake, Rhys—on what pretext?'

'I'll find one. I am certain I can take offence at his hat, or his face or the way he laughs.'

'Oh, Rhys.' There was no point in arguing and, besides,

Sir Anthony was a long way away. Rhys's temper would have cooled by the time he got home. He fired up when he saw her predicament as a matter of honour, but he did not truly understand her horror of returning to that life where she was either a pawn or a tool, where her true *self* would simply dwindle and vanish. A man simply would not comprehend how a woman's powerlessness could make her feel.

'Love's an illusion,' Rhys said abruptly. 'You realise that now, I presume?'

'No, I don't. I was mistaken in him and my own sentiments, that is all. You know that love does exist,' Thea said softly. She reached out and curled her fingers around his forearm for a moment. 'If it did not, you would not be so set on making a loveless, *suitable* marriage this time. Love hurts—that is how we know it is real.'

Rhys moved abruptly, but she kept looking straight ahead so all he would be able to see was the top of her plain straw bonnet. 'Put your veil down,' he ordered.

'Oh. Yes, of course.'

She arranged it carefully, then let him take her hand and help her to her feet. Now that she had satisfied his curiosity, perhaps Rhys would drop the subject and allow her to nurse her battered emotions in peace. Her fears she dared not contemplate.

'Tomorrow I shop,' Thea said firmly three days later as dinner was laid out on the table in their private salon in the Plume d'Or inn near the Louvre. 'Rouen was all very well, but one day was not enough.' All she and Polly had achieved was fresh linen, a pair of stockings apiece and some handkerchiefs.

'You are not tired by the journey?' Rhys took up the carving knife and began to dismember a chicken with forensic skill. He sounded hopeful. Why were men so anxious when women went shopping? It was not *his* money after all.

'Tired? Not at all. I love travelling. There was so much to look at and the roads are very good.'

'All the better for marching troops along,' Rhys said with a wry smile.

'It seems so strange to be at peace. All my life we have been at war with France. Thank goodness it is over now.' Thea accepted the meat he laid on her plate and began to investigate the steaming dishes that filled the table. 'How many people do they think they are feeding! This looks delicious. I am going to put on pounds if I am not careful.' She chewed a delicious morsel and took a sip of wine. 'Rhys...'

'Yes? That sounds like the start of a question I should be wary of.'

'Nothing of the kind. I just wondered if you could ask the innkeeper to recommend a guide for me tomorrow. My French is not equal to finding my way about and I have no idea where to discover the best shops.'

'I should escort you.'

'Thank you, but I am certain you have your time already planned out.' She studied his expression. 'I should give you credit for managing to look perfectly calm when I know you are filled with dread at the very idea of being dragged around Paris's shops in the wake of a female.'

'Very true. I am quaking, so the offer is one of great heroism on my part.' She opened her mouth to protest, but Rhys grinned. 'No, I will not inflict myself on you—take Hodge. His French is excellent and he was in Paris during the last peace.'

There, Thea told herself as she ate her dinner with good

appetite. *I am safely settled in a good hotel without any scandal or fuss, Rhys and I are conversing quite on our old terms. There is nothing at all to worry about.* But she never had been very anxious about scandal or fuss, so it must be Rhys that she was relieved about....

'What are you frowning about now?' he asked, the old teasing note back in his voice. 'Afraid there are frogs in the casserole again?'

'Provided they are not live ones hidden under the lid, like your birthday surprise for me when I was ten, I am not at all worried, you wretch,' she retorted. *You see? Nothing to worry about at all.*

'Please tell me there is more than a single item left in the shops of Paris.'

Thea followed Hodge, Polly and two hotel footmen into the private sitting room and peered around the piles of parcels at Rhys. He was dressed to go out, immaculate in black evening breeches and a midnight-blue swallowtail coat.

'Of course there is. These are just some essentials to tide me over until I can pick up the gowns that are being altered for me.' He rolled his eyes as Thea placed two hatboxes on the table. 'You look very elegant, I do admire your neckcloth. Where are you off to?'

'Thank you. I have tickets for the *Opéra*. There is a spectacular soprano I have been hearing about whom I would like to see in action. I was about to leave you a note to say order dinner without me.'

'Have a good time,' Thea called after him as he picked up hat and cane and left. 'Now what are we going to do with ourselves all evening?'

'Us, my lady?' Hodge asked as he came back from carrying the last of the parcels into her bedchamber.

'Are you tired, or shall we go out again after dinner, all three of us?'

'Where to, my lady? I'm not at all tired, I must confess. It is very stimulating, being back in Paris, but his lordship might not like…'

'Oh, pish! What harm is there in going to one of the more popular localities—the Palais Royale, for example?'

'It used to be rather, er…racy, my lady.'

'I am not suggesting going into one of the gaming houses, Hodge. But there are all those lovely coffee shops with tables outside—ladies seem to find it quite acceptable to sit there.'

'*Cafés*, my lady?'

'Yes, we will find a nice *café* and watch the world go by.'

'You could wear the new peacock-blue gown and that little black chip-straw headpiece with the veil,' Polly suggested. 'Perfect, my lady.'

Perfect, indeed. This was what being an independent woman was all about.

The opera singer known as *La Belle Seraphina* moved slightly in her chair and set her elbows tight together on the tiny *café* table, presenting Rhys with an even more spectacular view of her cleavage, its creamy shadows enhanced by a hint of lace in their depths.

He shifted in his seat, time enough to admire those very generous assets after he had discussed the possibility of her appearing at the London Opera House next season. His cousin Gregory had an interest in the place and Rhys had promised to keep his eye open for promising singers. After their negotiations, perhaps he would open discussions about a transaction of an altogether different kind. She certainly appeared to be sending out signals that such a suggestion might be welcome.

And a night spent in mutual pleasure would be more than welcome to him, Rhys acknowledged, wondering what was making him so damned randy. Anyone would think he had parted from his mistress a month ago, not just over a week. He moved again, restless, his body's automatic urging at odds with a surprisingly fastidious unwillingness to come to the point and make the proposition that he was certain the woman at his side was expecting.

Across the clipped box hedges and shorn grass of the central strip of garden, a small party arrived at the *café* opposite. A veiled woman seated herself in a flurry of peacock-blue skirts. *Very nice,* he thought absently, noting the trim figure and the grace with which she sat down between her companions, a plainly dressed maid and a man in sombre black.

'Hodge?'

'*Monseigneur?*' the woman at his side purred as she laid a hand on his forearm, the lush curve of her breast pressed against him in a blatant attempt to regain his attention.

'I beg your… *Excusez-moi.*' Rhys scrambled after his French. He might, strangely, be finding her uninteresting, but that was no excuse for bad manners. 'I just saw someone I know.' His valet, Thea's maid and…the elegant figure, her face hidden under a veil of figured lace that just reached her top lip in a way that was pure provocation… that must be Thea. *Thea?*

'I thought I saw someone I knew.' Rhys forced himself to think coherently in French again as he settled back in his chair, contriving to turn it slightly as he did so to bring the other table fully into his line of sight.

What the blazes was Hodge thinking of, to bring Thea here of all places? It was innocuous enough during the day, except for the effect on the wallet of the numerous tiny shops selling exquisite trinkets, jewellery and *objets de vertu*, but at night it was a playground. *And not for infants*, Rhys fumed inwardly.

The place was a very grown-up playground indeed, an ant heap of gaming hells, high-class brothels and intimate eating places. For respectable French couples who were sophisticated enough to know what they were doing it was safe enough, likewise for an escorted lady in a small party, but for an innocent like Thea it was fraught with perils.

He kept the discussion about London theatres going while he fought the instinct to march across, toss Thea over his shoulder and deposit her unceremoniously back at the hotel, sacking Hodge while he was at it. Making a scene was not the way to protect Thea's reputation and, to be fair, he had told Hodge to escort her wherever she wanted to go.

He realised the moment she recognised him. Her whole body stiffened, then her head tilted to one side as she studied him, and, doubtless, the woman at his table. It was strange seeing such a typical Thea pose from an elegant lady, dressed in the height of Parisian fashion and with her face hidden.

'Rhys!'

'I beg your pardon, my lady?' Hodge, standing stiffly behind her, leaned down.

'That is Lord Palgrave over there.'

She thought he muttered, 'Oh, my God,' but the music

and laughter and Polly's appreciative, 'That's a looker he's with, and no mistake,' made it hard to hear.

Rhys's companion most certainly was stunning. Thea assumed she was a courtesan, although she had never knowingly observed one before. Her gown was in the height of fashion, cut daringly to the limits of decency. Her hair, her teeth, her gems—all had an expensive gleam to them and she exuded a sensual confidence that was drawing male attention for yards around.

Thea chided herself firmly for having judgemental thoughts; she had spent all day shopping, Rhys was entitled to his…diversions. And this, she knew, was what men did— they sought out beautiful, elegant, sophisticated women and enjoyed them. There was nothing to feel upset about, not if one was a mature, sophisticated, intelligent woman oneself. Which she was.

But really, did he have to make such an obvious choice? The woman pressing her very ample curves against Rhys had tumbling blonde curls, big blue eyes and a quite spectacular amount of exposed cleavage. As Thea watched she touched her fingertips to his cheek and turned his head so she could whisper something in his ear.

A startlingly explicit image filled Thea's imagination. The woman was shedding that amber silk gown and falling back onto a wide bed, gesturing to Rhys, who…

'Oh! Order me a glass of champagne, Hodge, if you please.'

'My lady?' The valet sounded faintly scandalised.

Well, *she* felt scandalised, so that was two of them, and it was very annoying that she was letting herself be affected like this. She had never realised what a prude she must be. 'And for you and Polly, too.'

'But, my lady…'

'Stop dithering! *Garçon!*' She snapped her fingers and the man hurried over. *'Champagne, s'il vouz plaît. Pour trois.* Sit down, Hodge. This is a holiday.'

'I don't know what his lordship would say,' the man said, but he sat, perched on the edge of the little metal chair. Rhys had not seen them, or surely he would have made some sign?

'I am sure his lordship is entertaining himself very well, just at the moment.' *Nibbling that hussy's fingertips, by the look of it.*

The champagne and glasses arrived. 'Please pour, Hodge.' The wine fizzed into the flutes and Thea raised her glass. 'To Paris!'

'To beauty,' said a deep voice in English at her shoulder. The liquid splashed over her hand as she twisted round. A tall, saturnine man was watching her, his lips curved into an appreciative smile. He raised the wine glass in his hand in a toast. An Englishman, but not, thank Heavens, one she recognised. Hodge's chair scraped on the stone as he got to his feet, a slight figure against the stranger's bulk.

'Sir, we are not acquainted,' Thea said, coolly dismissive as she turned her shoulder, her mouth dry with apprehension. In all her chaperoned life she had never been accosted like this.

'But we have all evening to become so, *madame.*'

'Sir, my lady has told you—' Hodge began, but the stranger slid easily into his empty seat, sending the valet stumbling with a neat shove to the shoulder.

'Will you kindly remove yourself, sir!'

And then there was a swirl of black evening cloak, the table was sent rocking and the man gave a grunt of surprise as he was hoisted out of the chair.

Polly gave a little scream, but Thea could only stare as Rhys caught the stranger a sharp blow on the chin that felled him accurately into a gap between the tables. It was appalling, a brawl in one of the most public places in Paris, involving two Englishmen—and all she could think, she realised, shocked at herself, was how magnificent Rhys looked.

He towered, lean, muscled…fearless. Thea clutched the table with one hand and Polly's shaking arm with the other.

'The lady told you she did not wish for your acquaintance. Do you need me to explain that any more clearly?' Rhys's calm tone sounded utterly lethal.

'Just a misunderstanding.' The man got to his feet, rubbed his jaw and backed away.

Rhys turned back to the three of them. 'Time to go home,' he said between gritted teeth.

'Of course, my lord. I'll just call a cab….' Hodge began.

'You take Polly. I will look after her ladyship.' Rhys's expression had the maid recoiling towards the valet. 'Get yourselves back to the hotel or I may well reconsider my first impulse, which was to dismiss you here and now.'

'My lady?' To do him justice, Hodge looked to her for confirmation.

'Do as his lordship says.' Thea stood up. Over his shoulder she could see his table was empty. 'Your…friend has left. I am sorry.'

'Are you?' He swept a hard stare around the nearby tables and their gawking occupants found something else to interest them. Conversation started again, then became general when no more excitement was forthcoming.

'Yes, of course. She looked…expensive.' As soon as she spoke Thea regretted it. Never mind that it exposed the shocking fact that she knew what manner of woman the blonde must be, but it sounded like a jealous barb. And what had she to be jealous about, for goodness' sake? Or shocked. Rhys was a virile man, of course he wanted…needed…

'That lady,' he said with a curl of his lips which might, to the charitable, be construed as a smile, 'is an opera singer. A soprano known as *La Belle Seraphina*, with whom I was discussing, on behalf of my cousin Gregory, the possibility of her appearance next season on the London stage.' He took her cloak from the back of her chair where it had been draped and flipped it around her shoulders.

'I didn't mean— Oh, yes, I did,' Thea admitted as she fastened the bow at her neck with stiff fingers. 'And I am sorry, I should not have mentioned such a thing, or have leapt to that conclusion in the first place.'

'It was a perfectly correct conclusion,' Rhys said with ominous calm as he took her arm and steered her towards one of the narrow archways leading out of the gardens. 'But we had not reached that stage in the negotiations yet.' Even in the gloom of the passage he must have been aware of her instinctive reaction. 'Why so indignant, my dear? You raised the topic in the first place, and you must know what manner of place this is at night.'

Thea dug her heels in and he stopped. 'No, I did not know! Hodge told me it was lively, that there was a degree of licence in behaviour—it sounded like an evening at Vauxhall, not the antechamber to a brothel!' When Rhys did not speak she added, 'I will be more aware in future.'

'There will be no *future*, you little idiot. This will not happen again. Don't you know what danger you put yourself in?'

The awareness that she was in the wrong and the reaction to the violence, which had ceased now to be anything but frightening, left her close to tears. And she would *not* finish this disastrous evening by weeping all over Rhys, which left the alternative of losing her temper with him. And this was a Rhys she hardly recognised. He had rescued her from scrapes often enough when they were young, but this possessive aggression, this physical confidence, was new. Something in her responded to it and she recoiled from how primitive that reaction was. 'You mean, in danger from gentlemen like you?'

'No, not like me. A gentleman takes no for an answer. A buck like your friend back there is quite capable of taking other things. What might have happened if Hodge had gone to find the waiter, or to relieve himself? Do you think that maid of yours would have been any protection?'

'Against what?' Thea protested. 'There are people all around.'

'Against this,' Rhys said as he jerked her off balance, out of the archway and into the deserted alleyway beyond.

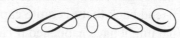

Chapter Eight

Thea found herself trapped in a corner, her back against the brickwork, her body caged by Rhys's. His hands were on the wall on either side of her head, his big feet bracketing hers in their fragile satin evening slippers. As she drew a trembling breath, her breasts touched his chest.

'Let me go—you are hurting me.' She tipped up her chin, a mistake. His mouth was just above her own.

'I am not touching you,' he pointed out, his voice reasonable. Only the brush of wine-scented air on her lips betrayed that his breathing had quickened.

Thea jerked up her knee, but he was too close and it merely pushed futilely against his leg. She ducked to get under his arm and he closed his elbows tightly. 'I'll scream,' she threatened.

'I have only to kiss you to stop that,' Rhys pointed out. 'And do you know what your buck would do after that?' She tried to worm backwards into the unyielding wall. 'He would flip up your skirts and take you here where we stand.'

His knee pushed against her, separating her legs. She felt her skirt ride up, felt the pressure of his thigh against her where a flutter of arousal was shameful acknowledgement that her body wanted this, and more. *He can feel how hot I am. How...wet.*

'You do not frighten me.' But he did, she realised. This was Rhys, who would never hurt her, and yet it was also an angry man, aroused by frustrated lust, the violence of that brief fight and anger with her, the cause of all of it.

'Then I am not trying hard enough,' he said and she saw the glint of white teeth as he lowered his head.

As he moved, so did his imprisoning leg. Thea dropped down between his arms, slid against his thighs and then rolled free to scramble to her feet as he turned and lunged for her. 'I wouldn't,' she warned, yanking the long hatpin from her elaborate hairpiece. As she brandished it, the light from the lantern at the end of the alley glinted off the metal.

There was silence, dangerous. The man she had thought she knew so well shifted on the balls of his feet as though ready to spring, a threatening stranger. *What has happened to us?*

Then Rhys spoke, amusement threading through his deep voice. 'I taught you that trick.'

'I know.' *It was going to be all right. He has not turned into someone else entirely.* 'When I was twelve and that horrible youth staying at the Wilkinsons' tried to pin me against the stable wall. I had no idea then what he wanted.'

'You do now.' Was he really amused or was this simply a trick so she would allow him close again? She wished she could make out his expression. 'I am impressed by your speed, but I wish I could be convinced you could escape another man so easily.' Perhaps his anger had subsided. The fluttering panic under her breastbone eased a little. 'Are you going to put the skewer away now?' Rhys asked. 'You could kill someone with that thing.'

'It was instinct, I would never have used it on you.' Thea jammed the pin back in and tried to sort out her emotions. Rhys had ruined her evening, had completely overreacted and had unsettled her to an alarming extent. But he had rescued her from the importunate rake and by doing so had spoiled his own evening. She supposed they were even.

'You would not have had the chance,' Rhys said, coming closer.

'I do wish you would stop looming over me like that.' They might be even, but she was having to hold on hard to her self-control. Rhys had meant to frighten her and, although she would die rather than admit it, he had succeeded and that was infuriating. And he had aroused feelings she simply did not want to acknowledge. 'Oh, Lord, my new gown.' She brushed at the skirts with all the force she could not apply to boxing his ears. 'At least the ground is dry.'

'If you allow me to walk you home in a ladylike manner, I will show you how to use your hatpin for self-defence without littering the streets of Paris with wounded admirers. Which does not mean,' he added as they crossed the road behind the Louvre, 'that I'll tolerate you putting yourself in a position where you might need it again. Do you understand me?'

'Yes, Rhys, thank you,' Thea said, striving for meekness and managing to sound at least biddable, she supposed. The flare of temper had subsided, but her heart was hammering and her blood seemed to be singing in her veins. It was the same way she felt after a long, hard gallop across country, or when she heard a beautiful piece of music…and yet, different. She was restless, there was an ache inside. Reaction, she told herself. And physical desire. She discovered that she was, perversely, happy.

'I am sorry about your singer,' she said. She had promised not to interfere with his enjoyment, she recalled guiltily. 'Is she nice?'

'Nice?' Rhys chuckled, amused, it seemed by the foolish word. 'I have no idea. But she is very beautiful.'

Of course. Beautiful. Thea felt the champagne fizz of happiness go flat. For a brief few moments, veiled, elegantly gowned, she had been fought over and pressed against a man's body as though he lusted for her. But, of course, it was no such thing. Her old friend Rhys had simply been protecting plain, ordinary Thea who had got herself into a pickle and had taught her a hard lesson. The air of Paris must be a drug, making her think she wanted something that, of course, she did not desire in the slightest.

'Here we are,' she said as the lamps outside their hotel came into sight. 'You must promise me you will not be angry with Hodge. It was all my fault.'

And most of all, my pleasure.

'Good morning!' Thea sounded quite disgustingly cheerful as she went to the buffet to inspect the chafing dishes.

Rhys scarcely glanced up as he rose to his feet, the French newspaper crumpled in his grasp, then sank back onto his chair to bury himself behind its pages. 'Morning.'

He was not good at mornings and especially not after a restless night filled with highly charged, and highly confusing, erotic dreams. For some reason the woman he had been chasing, futilely, had brown hair, not blonde, and as he reached for her over and over again he was shaken by feelings of unfamiliar guilt.

In broad daylight the dreams blurred into a half-remembered, discomforting muddle that he was doing his best to forget. He had completely overreacted with Thea last night; he could see that now in the bright light of morning. He could have rescued her from the importunate stranger and packed the lot of them back in a hackney carriage and brought his own evening to its probable outcome. As it was, he found he could not regret the missed encounter, which was strange.

His mood was not helped by Hodge, who started nervously every time Rhys spoke and obviously found it hard to believe that he was not about to be instantly dismissed for allowing Thea to go to the Palais Royale. As if the man had a hope of stopping her once she got an idea into her head.

'More coffee, Rhys?'

'Please.' With half his attention he was conscious of her bustling about while he wrestled with smudged newsprint and colloquial French. A waft of fresh coffee, the clink of china, the rustle of fabric as Thea settled herself at the table, a faint drift of subtle rose scent.

Rustling? Scented? Thea? Rhys folded the newssheet and laid it beside his plate so he could study her. The soft mouse-brown hair was gathered into a neat arrangement of plaits and pleats, her hazel eyes regarded him with slight wariness and small pearl earrings dangled from her lobes. Her face, which was developing a puzzled frown as he stared, was the familiar oval, unadorned by so much as a smudge of lamp black or a grain of rice powder.

And yet…she was curiously *soignée*. The French word, one that he would never have thought of before in connection with Thea, swam up from somewhere and he realised it was perfect. She was groomed, elegant and perfectly... plain. If plain could be applied to the soft gleam of fine wool cloth, to the narrow edge of Brussels lace around the muslin fichu at her neck, the glow of the little pearls. Or creamy skin that was developing a blush as he stared.

Under his scrutiny she shifted slightly and there was that soft rustle again—silk against linen, he guessed. Good Lord, what was she wearing under that elegantly simple morning gown?

'You have been shopping,' he accused. It was bad enough having to make conversation at breakfast without being confronted by a disturbingly different Thea.

Thea rolled her eyes. 'You know I have. You saw one of the evening gowns last night.'

'I was in no mood to notice anything but your hatpin,' he growled.

'I left home with the smallest portmanteaux I could find and only two old gowns. I have bought two morning dresses, three walking dresses, two evening gowns, several pairs of shoes and all the, um...associated linen.'

'Just linen?'

A dimple appeared at the corner of her mouth, unfamiliar and utterly feminine. 'You cannot believe the luxury of silk petticoats.'

'No, I cannot,' Rhys said repressively, as much to his own imagination as to her. 'You look extremely...elegant.'

'Thank you.' Thea reached for the butter, apparently unflustered by the compliment. 'I came to the conclusion when I first came out, and Stepmama was making such a fuss about my looks and figure and everything else, that frills and ornament do not suit me. I am never going to be pretty, but I knew I could achieve *elegant* if I put my mind to it. And I confess to loving luxury. Beautiful fabrics, well-made clothes, soft leather gloves and shoes, lovely scents and soaps...' She gave a little wriggle of pleasure and applied herself to her omelette.

'How did you find so much in only one day?' *How did you turn from a tomboy into such a feminine creature? But she is still plain,* he argued with himself. *No, she isn't... exactly.* He struggled to superimpose this elegant creature onto his image of Thea.

'Ready-to-wear gowns seem to be much more easily obtained in Paris than in London. Not everything has been delivered yet—some had to be altered slightly—but I am not out of the common way in any dimension, which appears to help.'

Rhys took a tactical mouthful of coffee to avoid any form of comment on Thea's *dimensions.*

'The only thing I am not happy with is the riding habit. It was foolish of me not to pack my own.'

'You are unlikely to do any riding.' Rhys, on the other hand, was strongly considering hiring a hack and removing himself from the chaise as much as possible. If he'd had sisters he would have been better fitted to deal with this, he acknowledged. But the only women he spent any time in private with were from the muslin company and that was no help at all in negotiating the shark pool of life with an unmarried, virtuous woman who was not related to him.

'No?' She wrinkled her nose, the expression so at odds with her ladylike appearance that Rhys laughed. Yes, *his* Thea was still there. She grinned back. 'That's better! I was thinking how serious you looked. I have spoken to

Hodge, by the by. Thank you for not blaming him for yesterday evening.'

Rhys shrugged and reached for the butter. 'I should not have expected him to be able to influence you when you had made up your mind to anything. *I* certainly never could. I have told the hotel to place a large footman at your disposal when you go out. With Hodge, Polly *and* a bodyguard you should be safe from unwanted attention.'

'Thank you.' The smile she flashed at him was warm, with just a hint of mischief. Rhys relaxed. 'I hope you have a very pleasant day today.'

'I intend to visit an antiquities dealer who has a pair of globes that sound as if they would suit the library at Palgrave Hall, then I will do some shopping on my own account—Hodge has recovered sufficiently to observe that his lordship requires at least half a dozen more shirts and several more neckcloths if he is to present even a passable appearance in Paris.'

'And will you see if you can persuade your opera singer to oblige you?' Thea regarded him with clear, innocent eyes above her coffee cup.

'Does nothing put you to the blush?' Rhys demanded hoarsely through a throat full of croissant crumbs inhaled on a sharp indrawn breath.

'I meant oblige with her agreement to travel to England to appear at the Opera House. If you are put out of countenance because of anything else you want from her, well, you told me about her yourself last night,' Thea pointed out prosaically while he spluttered. 'Would you like me to slap you on the back or would a glass of water help, do you think?'

'Thank you, no. I will certainly send her a note of apology for abandoning her so abruptly.' And that was all. Rhys mopped his streaming eyes and attempted to sound repressive. He had been mistaken in finding Thea the slightest bit alluring. The chit was as unmanageable as she had been at sixteen.

Thea pursed her lips over what he suspected was an unrepentant smirk. 'I expect it is the prospect of shopping that puts you in such a grumpy mood—men always seem to hate it.'

'Grumpy!' Rhys dug his knife into the butter and recovered his sense of humour. This was Thea, for goodness' sake. A few silk fal-lals and fine plumage were no reason to get hot under the collar. She hadn't changed in any way that mattered—certainly not for the better—but she *was* in Paris for the first time. 'Shall I get tickets for the opera tonight?'

'For us?' The excitement lit up her face and made him feel like a toad for the way he had reacted the night before.

'Wear something discreet and a veil and we'll sit in the stalls. No point in drawing attention to ourselves.'

'Thank you.' Thea jumped to her feet and came to plant a kiss on his cheek. 'You are an angel. Now I will go and leave you in peace with your newspaper.'

That was positively sisterly. Rhys turned a page and tried to feel like an indulgent brother. Even so, he was definitely going to ride tomorrow.

Thea gazed out of the window onto the Burgundian countryside. Three days from Paris and Rhys had ridden every mile while she sat in solitary state in the chaise.

It was not as though having the leisure to observe an athletically built gentleman in well-cut breeches was in any way a hardship, of course. Even the fact that the horses available from the posting stations were far below the standard Rhys would normally ride in no way diminished the sight, for it only showed his skill to advantage. As a boy and a young man he had been gangly. Now he had filled out and most of it appeared to be well-coordinated muscle. What did a gentleman do to keep fit, she wondered, other than bed sport? Sporting pursuits, she supposed, firmly instructing her imagination to cover that body with clothing.

A modest gentlewoman would not stare, let alone permit speculation to run wild through her daydreams. Which doubtless meant that she fell far short of the standards of breeding expected of her. Thea contemplated this lowering conclusion for a moment, then decided that she did not care.

Rhys's amorous interest was fixed, as it had always been, on curvaceous, tall, blue-eyed blondes of a coming disposition, and he would be thoroughly embarrassed to discover that his childhood friend had rediscovered the youthful attraction that—thank Heavens!—he had been blind to before.

The problem now was that the innocent adoration of her fourteen-year-old self had been replaced by the more mature understanding of a curious and uninhibited young lady. She understood what her body wanted and she was coming to regret, very much, that it was not going to experience it.

Still, it did no harm to fantasise. She was sure now that she was not going to find a man to love and who would love her in return, which meant she was not prepared to marry, even if Papa did find her and drag her back.

Thea stamped on the stirring of panic and made herself think of the present. If she did not marry, then that inexorably led her to the conclusion that she was never going to know what it would be like to lie naked with a man. She could not find the slightest shame in her for wishing to experience lovemaking, not after her experience with Sir Anthony. But it was certainly inconvenient for her composure that, if she had to choose a gentleman from a fairly wide acquaintance for the experiment, it had to be this one.

The vine-clad slopes of the Côte d'Or rolled past to the right of the chaise. The stop at Beaune for a change of horses had been regrettably short. The town had looked intriguing and the vast, bustling market colourful and exotic, but Rhys wanted to reach Lyon that evening, for some reason. When she had asked him the reason for his haste he'd simply closed his lips into an implacable line and strode off to talk to Tom Felling, the coach driver.

The horse Rhys had chosen at the livery stables was rather better than the previous one, Thea mused, her attention drawn back from the passing scene to the rider on the wide grass verge. He guided his mount to the side to jump a fallen tree and her breath caught at the fluid beauty of man and animal as they cleared the obstacle.

How would his skin slide under her hands—like silk or would it feel more like kidskin? How would his weight be, over her? He was so much larger than she was that it must be a matter of technique, she supposed. How would it feel when he sheathed himself within her? Would it hurt? Probably, it had with Anthony. She was less clear what happened then in bed, when lovemaking was a leisurely matter of mutual pleasure giving—movement, obviously, with that hard, strong body and her own soft, lesser strength somehow finding a rhythm and a unity.

She had seen Rhys naked as a child, swimming in the lake, but a man's body was different. Did he have a hairy chest? Would that chafe against her breasts or tickle? They tingled at the thought. She would run her fingertips through—

'Whoa!' From behind, Tom Felling shouted at his team. The chaise juddered and skidded as the postilions reined back their horses and Thea jerked her attention to the window at the front and the view beyond the be-capped boys and their waving whips.

A *diligence*, one of the lumbering French stagecoaches, had overturned, its bulk teetering over the deep ditch that bordered the road. In the road half a dozen passengers seemed stunned with shock and the driver and guard were struggling with the team as they thrashed in panic in the tangled traces.

Thea pushed open the door and jumped down as Rhys dismounted, shouting at the postilions, 'Hold our horses. Felling, go and help them free the team.' He saw her. 'Thea, get back in the chaise, this is no place for you.'

'I will do no such thing. There are people hurt.' She ran to help a stout woman to her feet, then pulled off the fichu around her neck to hold to the forehead of a slender young man who was slumped against the bank, blood pouring down his face. *This is no time to have missish vapours about blood*, she told herself firmly, swallowing hard.

'It is just a cut,' she began in English. 'They always bleed dramatically from the head. Oh, *pardon, c'est—*'

'I am English,' he said faintly and lifted his hand to hold the pad in place. 'Thank you, ma'am. I will do well enough. Please, see if anyone else is in need of your help.'

A young woman was screaming, in shock more than pain, Thea thought as she ran to her. Then she saw the girl was pointing a trembling finger towards the wide ditch. *'Mon fils, mon fils!'*

The *diligence* had been stopped from sliding down only by the spokes of one broken wheel and a scrubby thorn bush growing up from the side of the drain. It was slowly collapsing under the weight, the wheel making ominous cracking noises.

For a moment Thea could not see what the girl was panicking about, then she heard a faint wail and saw movement from a bundle of white cloth in the mud, directly under the collapsing carriage.

'Rhys! There is a baby!'

'I see it.' He slid down into the ditch, ducked under the edge of the coach and braced his back to it, his feet dug into the bank. The cracking stopped, but how much longer could he hold it? Thea scrambled down at the other end and crouched to look. The veins stood out of Rhys's forehead, his hands were white where the load pressed down, his body was bent double like Atlas under the weight of the globe. She wriggled closer and grabbed for the baby in the narrow space.

'Get out,' Rhys hissed between gritted teeth. 'I don't know how long I can hold this.'

'You can hold it,' she said, utterly confident as she got onto her stomach and wormed closer. This was Rhys: in that moment she trusted him to hold the world up if lives depended on him. Her fingers touched, gripped, pulled. The baby howled as she dragged him towards her. The wheel slid down with a jerk, Rhys cursed, shifted and it stopped.

There was movement at her feet, someone trod on her leg, apologised in English. 'Sorry. Can you slide out under me?' It was the injured Englishman, supporting the other end of the coach.

Thea wormed her way back with all the speed she could muster.

'She's out!' the Englishman shouted as hands reached down to haul her and her burden up the bank.

'Then roll free, this is about to go,' Rhys called, his voice strained to the point of being almost unrecognisable. 'On my mark. One, two, three—'

The young man landed in an ungainly heap in a patch of nettles as Thea thrust the baby into the arms of its sobbing mother and the *diligence* subsided into the ditch with the sound of splintering wood. 'Rhys!'

It seemed to take minutes, not seconds, to reach the side of the coach he had been supporting. Now he lay clear of it, on his back in the mud, eyes closed, hands bleeding, face white. Thea hurled herself down beside him and pressed her ear to his chest. Surely he hadn't broken his neck?

Under her hands she felt him drag air down to his diaphragm. Not dead, then. 'Rhys! Rhys, wake up.'

'Thea?' He seemed to come to with a jolt and she scrambled to her knees as he reached for her, his eyes opening wide and dark in his pale face, his grip on her wrists painful. 'You aren't hurt?'

'No, just terribly muddy. I thought you were under that when it fell.' She collapsed back onto his chest and hugged as much as she could of him.

'Mmm,' Rhys murmured. 'Much as I appreciate being cuddled, I prefer not to be sinking into the mire at the same time. I seem to be squashing a frog.'

'*Idiot!* I thought… I feared…'

'Don't you dare cry on me,' he said mildly. 'How do you think I felt when I saw you wriggling into that death trap, you madcap creature?'

Thea got to her feet, trying not to tread on him. He was battered enough without squashing what breath remained in him. 'Well, who else did you think was going to go in?'

she said belligerently to cover her reaction. 'The passengers were too shocked or too large. Are you hurt?'

Rhys sat up, winced and uncoiled himself from the ditch. 'Other than feeling as though our esteemed Prince Regent has been sitting on me, and kicking while he was at it, I am perfectly all right.'

Thea repressed the urge to fuss. 'I'll see how the Englishman is, then. He had a nasty cut to the head before he joined us in the ditch.'

She found him retrieving his baggage from the piles strewn along the road. 'Sir? Should you be on your feet?'

He had tied her fichu into a lopsided bandage which gave his pleasant, regular features an alarmingly piratical cast at odds with his severe pallor, and he was moving with great care as though all his joints hurt. Which, she supposed, they did.

'Ma'am, I thank you for your concern. They tell me there is an inn a mile or so along the road. I will find myself a room there.'

'At least allow us to carry you that far. Tom!' She gestured to the coachman who hurried over. 'Place this gentleman's luggage up behind the chaise.'

Rhys made his way towards them through the French passengers who were sorting themselves out amidst much weeping and waving of arms. No one appeared seriously injured.

'My lord, this is the gentleman who supported the other end of the coach. He needs to get to an inn where he can rest.'

'The lady is too kind, I trust I do not inconvenience you? My name is Giles Benton. I should have a card.' He dug into his breast pocket and produced one.

'The *Reverend* Benton,' Rhys looked up from his study of the rectangle of pasteboard. 'I am Palgrave.'

'My lord. I recognise you, of course, from the House....'

'Never mind the politics. And call me Denham,' Rhys said, offering his hand. 'May I present my cousin, Miss Smith.' He blandly ignored Thea's raised eyebrows, opened the door of the chaise for them then swung up on his horse, calling instructions to the postilions.

Now she was closeted with an Englishman, one who was a gentleman and a vicar to boot. He was probably even now working his way mentally through the *Peerage* and coming to the conclusion that the Earl of Palgrave had no cousins named Smith, certainly not young female ones without a wedding ring on their finger. If his mathematics was any good, he was putting two and two together and coming up with a thoroughly scandalous six.

But what other option did they have but to take him up? They could hardly leave him bleeding by the roadside. For the first time since her flight Thea faced the fact that a scandal would be humiliating, sordid and decidedly unamusing.

Chapter Nine

Thea took a deep breath and willed herself to calm. Panicking would only make her appear self-conscious and that would raise Mr Benton's suspicions about her scandalous status, even if he had none now.

She cast a harried glance out of the window at Rhys, who at least seemed capable of sitting a horse without collapse, and studied her new companion. 'You are travelling far, sir?' That was a safe sort of question and put the focus on him.

'To the Mediterranean coast.' He smiled. 'I have no very clear destination. I am taking advantage of the recent peace to indulge myself with a journey south to the sun before I take up a new position.'

'A new parish?'

'No. After I was ordained I realised I was not cut out for the ministry. I desired to put my talents, such as they are, in the service of the reform of society. I have taken a post as secretary to Lord Carstairs.'

'He has interested himself in the abolition of slavery, has

he not?' It was a cause she had read much about, much to the disapproval of her father, who had interests in the West Indies. 'It must be a great satisfaction to assist in that endeavour.'

'Yes, of course, I should have realised you would be knowledgeable on the subject,' he said, puzzling Thea. But Mr Benton swept on before she could query it. 'He is also interested in prison reform, and his wife, Lady Carstairs, is active in advancing the education of women. I hope I may make some contribution to all three causes. I was very fortunate that my elder brother, Lord Fulgrove, knows Lord Carstairs well and was able to recommend me to him.'

'Lord Fulgrove?' Thea faltered before she could gather her wits.

Mr Benton shifted on his seat. 'But do I not know you? I thought your face familiar, but I cannot place… I know, I have seen you talking to my sisters Jane and Elspeth in the park.'

Thea stared at him, struggling to find something intelligently evasive to say. 'I have met them a few times.' First the risk of scandal, now the danger that word would get back to Papa.

'I shall make a point of telling them how you aided me,' Mr Benton said. 'I write to them almost daily. They will be delighted to know their friend Miss Smith is such a Good Samaritan.'

'Ah. I, um… We have arrived at the inn. It seems exceedingly shabby.' She lowered the window as Rhys walked over. 'I do not like the look of this place. See how dirty the windows are, and the yard is full of rubbish.'

'Indeed, the merest country drinking house and none too well equipped for travellers by the look of it.'

'We cannot abandon Mr Benton here.' The sooner they parted company the better, but she could not allow his health to be jeopardised to conceal her guilty secrets. A blow to the head was potentially very serious, and he had lost a lot of blood, even before his heroic efforts with the *diligence*. 'He is travelling south. We can carry him to Lyon and find a doctor to attend to his head.' She turned to study his pale face. 'I fear you may require stitches, sir.'

Both men began to speak, but Polly, opening the opposite door to place a small bag on the floor, cut across them both. 'Here's the bag with the medical supplies. Mr Hodge thought the gentleman might need a fresh bandage, Lady Althea.'

Mr Benton shot Thea a glance and closed his lips firmly in a gesture that spoke far louder than any words. Rhys rolled his eyes upwards. 'Devil take it.'

Thea looked from one to the other, her heart sinking. He was a clergyman; he would not condone what he thought to be immorality. 'May I trust your discretion, Mr Benton?'

'This is an elopement, I collect?' he enquired stiffly. 'Naturally, it is none of my business.'

'No, we are not eloping!'

'Perish the thought,' Rhys added with what Thea felt was unflattering emphasis. 'I am escorting Lady Althea to our godmother, Lady Hughson, in Venice. We are childhood friends.'

Mr Benton's poker face softened into a smile. 'Lady Hughson? I know her well. What a relief! I should have realised nothing untoward was happening after observing your gallant and selfless actions at the scene of the accident. I do apologise! Lady Althea…?'

'Curtiss,' she supplied, her conscience giving her a decided pang. They might not be sinning in fact, but her imagination was scandalous enough to condemn her in the eyes of any minister. 'Because circumstances have led us to travel in a manner which is so open to misunderstanding, I hope you will understand if I ask you not to mention that we met along the way.'

'But of course,' Mr Benton assured her. 'My lips are sealed.'

'In that case,' Thea said, 'I will dress your head with a proper bandage and then we will be on our way to Lyon. Lord Palgrave, would you be so good as to have the sleeping couch put in place for Mr Benton? I am sure he should be lying down.'

'By no means, Lady Althea,' he protested. 'I assure you I will be quite well sitting up—and in any case, I should be travelling with your servants in the coach, should I not? After all, a lady alone in a chaise...'

'I have been travelling in the chaise with Lord Palgrave for most of this journey,' Thea said, unwinding the makeshift dressing from his head. 'I may as well be hanged for a sheep as a lamb. Besides, I doubt the presence of a clergyman will harm my reputation.' She peered at the cut. 'The bleeding has stopped, and I will not risk starting it again by washing your head with the water from this dirty inn. If you will just sit quite still...'

By the time they reached Lyon at seven o'clock that evening Rhys was convinced that he would never get off the horse, let alone walk to his bedchamber. The bruising and strains from holding up the coach had coalesced into one blaze of pain, and his hands, cut and pierced with splinters, were cramped on the reins.

'Hodge,' he called as the valet stepped down from the coach, 'see her ladyship and Mr Benton into the inn. I need to talk to Felling.'

He waited until they had vanished through the impressive front door of the Chapeau Rouge before he called to the coachman, 'Tom, come and give me a hand, I'm damned if I'm going to fall flat on my face in front of a gaggle of French ostlers.'

It was inelegant and exceedingly painful, but they managed the manoeuvre with a lot of swearing on Rhys's part. 'Say nothing to her ladyship or that maid of hers, do you understand?'

'Yes, my lord. You need some liniment on your back, I reckon. Got just the thing in my baggage.'

'Horse liniment? Do you want to take the skin off my back, man?'

'If it'll do for your thoroughbreds, I reckon it won't do you much harm, my lord,' the coachman said. 'But they'll be getting a doctor to the other gentleman and he'll prescribe some fancy French potions for you that'll set you back a bit of gold, I reckon.'

'Hot bath is all I need,' Rhys muttered. It took him the width of the courtyard before he could walk with the appearance of ease, but he managed the stairs and found Althea and Mr Benton in the private salon he had written ahead to reserve.

They were, it seemed, on first-name terms already. 'The landlord has sent for a doctor and is making up the spare bedchamber in this suite for Giles. Is it not fortunate that they gave us such a spacious one?' Thea did not turn round as she attempted to press Benton into a chair while she stayed on her feet. 'Giles, it is foolish to stand on ceremony.

You must take care and, really, I am such good friends with your sisters that you may treat me quite as one of them.'

Rhys cast a swift glance at Benton, whose faint air of dizziness seemed to owe at least as much to the effect of being organised by Thea as it did to his head wound. Or perhaps, he thought, narrowing his eyes at the other man, it was more than that. *Thea, enchanting a clergyman? Surely not.*

'What are you laughing about?' Thea demanded, her attention still on her patient. Apparently his huff of amusement had been audible.

'Just relief at the thought of a hot bath. I'll see you both at dinner,' he added, and caught sight of his own grey face in a mirror. Lord, he'd better be out of there before she noticed he was looking like death warmed over.

'Your chamber is here, my lord.' Hodge at least had the sense not to exclaim at the sight of him until the door was closed behind them. 'I'll send the doctor to you when he arrives.'

'Certainly not. There is nothing wrong with me that a good soak and basilicum powder will not put to rights. Which is probably more than can be said for that coat,' he added as Hodge eased him out of it and then held it up to inspect its battered back.

The sting of the hot water had made him hiss between his teeth as he lowered himself into it, but half an hour's soak had loosened the abused muscles, and he felt rather more human when he climbed out of the tub and wrapped a vast bath sheet around his waist.

Hodge began to dab cautiously at his back with a towel while Rhys hitched one hip on the edge of the table and contemplated his bruised and splinter-stuck hands. 'I need a needle to get these out, Hodge. Can you find one?'

'In my baggage next door, my lord. I won't be a moment.'

The door behind Rhys opened and he added, 'Tweezers might be a good thing, too.'

'Rhys Denham! Look at the state of your back!'

'I can't, can I?' he said reasonably, without turning. 'Thea, you should not be in here. I am not dressed.' In fact, he was damn near naked. Rhys reached for a towel to toss around his shoulders.

'Don't do that,' Thea said sharply. 'It needs dressing properly. Why on earth didn't you say it was this bad?'

'Hate fuss,' Rhys muttered. 'Will you please—?'

'Hodge, kindly tell the doctor to come in here as soon as he has finished stitching Mr Benton's head.'

Rhys took a deep breath. Unfortunately, getting the man out of the room was essential before this went any further. 'Hodge, go and see if you can assist Mr Benton.' He waited until the door was closed behind the valet before he added, 'Thea, go away.'

'You always were dreadful about admitting you were sick or hurt,' she said, deaf to both orders and propriety. Rhys heard the rustle of her skirts and then a towel was pressed gently over his back. 'I'll just get this dry and then you can get half dressed at least before the doctor comes in.'

He should get up and put her outside, but, clad in only a thin towel, Rhys had no confidence in maintaining even a vestige of decency. 'If I promise to let the doctor see to my back, will you leave?'

'Of course.' Thea came round to face him, her eyes sharp as she studied his naked torso. 'Your front does not appear to be injured.'

Rhys clutched a towel to his chest before she saw his nipples tightening. He did not dare look down to see how effective the towel around his waist was at concealing his sudden arousal. 'All I need is a light dressing on my back,' he began, but she reached out and took his hands in hers.

'Oh, look at these! How could you have held the reins? I will get a needle and some tweezers and take those splinters out while the doctor sees to your back.' To Rhys's enormous relief she released him. 'I'll leave you in peace to put your pantaloons on and come back when he has finished with Giles.'

'Thea, has no one told you that a young lady should faint before mentioning a man's nether garments?' Rhys demanded as she bustled away. He was not certain whether he was more relieved that she had taken no notice of his near-naked state—let alone the effect she was having on him—or whether he was indignant at being bossed around by her. The temptation to get up and let his draperies fall where they might was considerable. That would stop her ever trying such tricks again.

'Of course,' she said with a gurgle of laughter. 'Oh, poor Rhys, am I embarrassing you?'

'Shocking me, more like.' But she had gone.

It was quite obvious that she regarded him in no other light than the friend of her childhood. Grown-up to be sure, but no more to be treated with reserve than his fourteen-year-old self had been.

The only positive aspect to this trusting innocence, he concluded as he reached for his trousers, was that he was alone in the unfortunate physical attraction that being close to her provoked. If she felt the slightest awareness of him as a sexual being she would never be so open and so unselfconscious.

* * *

The doctor was ushered in ten minutes later. Monsieur Benton needed only a little rest. He had not even felt it necessary to bleed him. Ah, but *monsieur le comte* required a dressing on those abrasions and to rest for two or three days.

'Be damned to that,' Rhys said in English and was tutted at by Thea, who sat in front of him wielding a darning needle and tweezers to efficient, but painful, effect on his hands.

'Do listen to reason,' she scolded, her eyes fixed on what she was doing.

Rhys tried to sit still while the doctor prodded his bruised back and fixed his eyes on her bowed head, the neat centre parting of her hair and the intricate twists that secured it. *How long is it?* he wondered. *If I pull out those pins...*

Thea was still lecturing. '...or I will tell him to bleed you. Besides, Lyon looks delightful—what is the rush to get south?' She did not wait for his reply. 'May we suggest to Giles that he travel with us? I do not think he should travel on the *diligence* until he is well again, do you?'

Rhys almost told her that his vehicles were neither a public carrier nor a mobile hospital unit, then bit his tongue. 'You like him?' he asked warily.

'Very much. He is intelligent and good company and he was very brave back there on the road. Not as brave as you, of course,' she finished, matter-of-factly.

'Thank you.' She thought him brave? He had acted without considering the dangers because it was obvious what would happen if he did not stop the vehicle's slide downwards. A flutter of something absurdly like pride surprised him. *Popinjay*, he reproved himself. A gentleman simply did what was necessary without having to think about it, that was all.

But Benton, who'd had the opportunity to assess the dangers, and who was hurt into the bargain, was obviously a man of courage and resolution. *And good birth, even if he is a younger son.* An idea, probably absurd, was beginning to form. Thea ought to be married to someone of her own choosing. The man should be someone of principle who would value her for what she was, not for her connections and wealth. The nonsense about wanting to fall in love was just that, nonsense, and she would realise it soon enough once she found someone congenial and eligible she could trust. Someone who would steady her wild starts.

Rhys would give Benton some subtle encouragement. It was, if he said it himself, a brilliant plan. Thea eligibly, if not spectacularly, married, no risk of scandal—Godmama could put it about that Thea and Benton had met when Thea was staying with her in Venice—and the fact that she had travelled there so scandalously would be conveniently hidden.

The doctor finished and Hodge ushered him out. Thea dropped her tweezers on the table and peered at his hands closely. 'There! That should do perfectly,' she exclaimed, tipping her head back to study his face. 'And just what are you looking so smug about, my lord?'

'Just relief that it is over.' Rhys tried to turn the smirk into something innocuous. Relief no one was prodding his injuries any longer and relief that, as Thea said, he always had a plan.

Chapter Ten

'And you will rest for at least two days?'

Rhys gave a heavy sigh. Thea watched him suspiciously. He sounded as though he was reluctantly allowing himself to be persuaded. 'Two nights, certainly. And you and Benton can explore the city, if he feels well enough. I'll spend tomorrow lying down,' Rhys added. 'I'll probably go mad with boredom, but it is no doubt sensible.'

That was so unlike Rhys. Perhaps he really had changed with the years, for she would have sworn he would do anything rather than admit to weakness.

'Giles says his headache is better already and the doctor does not think he has a concussion, so if you do not need us, it will be amusing to explore.' She reached for a towel and tried to pat his hands dry.

Rhys twitched it out of her grasp. 'Don't fuss, Thea. I'm indestructible—you should know that by now.'

And yet you meekly agree to rest? 'Don't say that and tempt fate.' She met his eyes, saw thoughts there she could not decipher and felt the colour rise to her cheeks. 'I am sorry I burst in here when you were…had just got out of your bath. I had no wish to put you to the blush.' Rhys raised one eyebrow and she laughed. 'I suppose managing that is quite a challenge! But I made you uncomfortable, I know that.'

It had certainly made her uncomfortable. The shock of seeing his elegant, muscled back, and then the realisation of how much those vicious bruises and splits across the skin must hurt, had left her dizzy with a mixture of desire, horror and admiration for Rhys's stoicism.

Thea got up and walked across to the bed where his shirt was laid ready. She found she was shivering. Perhaps it was delayed shock after the accident, or perhaps the realisation of just how much danger they had been in under that carriage. She let her fingertips trail over the soft linen. Yes, both those things, but most of all, the impact of finding herself alone with Rhys when he was almost naked.

'You had better put this on. I'll help you so you do not dislodge the dressings.' She gathered it up in her hands as fiercely as she gathered her self-control and turned, her expression schooled into the one of slightly harassed practicality she knew he'd recognise.

Rhys still sat on the edge of the table, which brought them almost eye to eye. He bent his head for her to drop the shirt over, then threaded his hands into the sleeves, a little clumsy because of the strapping. For some reason that made her vision blur with sudden tears. *I might have lost him.*

Thea swallowed and reached to straighten the collar where it had rucked up at the back of his neck. With Rhys so close she could feel the warmth of his skin against her chest, see the laughter lines at the corner of his eyes, paler against his faintly tanned skin. What joys had caused that laughter? And what concerns had etched the faint lines between his brows and at the corners of his lips? Rhys had an entire, adult life she knew nothing of. Her fingers brushed the ends of his hair as she fussed with the collar.

Her composure seemed to unravel as though he had tugged a string, and yet he had not moved or spoken. 'I was worried about you,' Thea said abruptly. Before she could think she was clinging to him, her arms tight around his neck, her face buried in his shirtfront. 'I'm sorry,' she mumbled into the cloth. 'But when the *diligence* collapsed I thought you were still under it.'

Rhys closed his arms around her body and held her close. *It must hurt him to hold me so,* she thought, her senses filled with the scent of his damp skin, the Castile soap he had used in the bath, the smell of the liniment the doctor had applied. She felt him rest his cheek on the crown of her head and closed her eyes.

When he spoke softly against her hair it was as though his voice resonated through to the soles of her feet. 'You told me, when you were burrowing through the mud beneath my feet, that you trusted me to hold it up.'

'I did. For as long as there was anyone under it, I knew you would, somehow. I knew I was safe, and the baby, too. But when we were out...'

'Hush now.' Rhys rocked her back and forth, gentler than she could ever remember him being. All her will-power seemed to ebb as his tenderness sapped it. She would weep in a moment, and she had to be strong. 'We are all safe. Don't think about what might have been or you will have nightmares.'

'I know.' Thea sniffed, determined not to let him see how

affected she was by the touch of his body, the strength of his embrace.

She felt his mouth move against her hair and knew he smiled. 'Don't you go crying on me now, Thea.'

'I'm not.'

'You are sniffing.' He chuckled. 'Any other woman I have had in my arms would die rather than do anything so prosaic.' *Any other woman would be in his arms because he desired them.* 'No other woman I can think of would be so brave. All right now?'

'Mmm.' She loosened her stranglehold on his neck and leaned back against his linked arms to look up into his face, almost undone by that tribute. She had thought him angry with her, or, at the very least, that he had considered her foolhardy. She blinked back unshed tears, glad now she had not given in to them. 'Thank you.'

His lips were very close to hers. How had that happened? His breath was sweet—coffee and honey—and his lips were parted, his eyes intent and bright. She swayed closer as he lifted one hand to her hair, fumbled for the pins. What was he doing? His cut, bruised fingers lacked finesse, strands catching as the pins fell to the floor with tiny metallic sounds, and she felt the whole elegant construction unravel before the sliding weight was caught up in his palms.

'Soft, brown, scented silk,' he murmured.

'Rhys?'

'Thea.' She saw the movement of his throat as he swallowed and his voice roughened as he said, 'I wanted to see what it was like down. It is lovely, a living thing.'

'Mousy,' she protested.

'Pretty mouse.'

She took a deep breath and realised that she had been

holding it ever since he had touched her hair. *What is happening? One of us has to be sensible.* 'I think we have both had a shock today and probably we are not ourselves. Perhaps we should lie down before dinner.'

For a moment she saw the thoughts behind his eyes quite clearly. He had interpreted that as an euphemism, believed for a moment that she was suggesting they lie down on his bed and... *Please.* Had she said that out loud?

Then Rhys's face became an expressionless mask. She stepped back and he opened his fingers, letting her hair fall around her shoulders.

'That is a good idea.' Rhys said. 'Will you give Hodge whatever orders you think best about dinner? Tell him I am going to rest now and will not need him until just before it is served.'

'Yes, of course.' Thea stooped and raked together the little pile of pins, swinging the mass of hair over her shoulder. *Pretty mouse... What is this? Is he flirting because there is another man with us now? Men are so foolish like that, so possessive and territorial. Oh, Rhys.*

What would he have done if she had not stepped back, if she had lifted her lips to his and claimed a kiss?

He stood when she got to her feet, but did not turn as she left the room. Thea made herself walk with dignity, not take to her heels and flee as every instinct of self-preservation screamed at her to do.

Dinner was oddly unsettling. Perhaps it was because she had never eaten with Rhys in company like this. It felt as though they were a couple entertaining a guest, and that was too close to her foolish daydreams to be comfortable. Thea compensated by paying most of her attention to

Giles, on whom a rest and the attentions of the doctor had worked wonders.

No one, Thea decided as they exchanged impressions of Paris, would think he had been in an accident, hit on the head and half squashed under a stagecoach. He must be tougher than his slender frame suggested.

'Is your post with Carstairs a permanent position, Benton?' Rhys asked during a lull in conversation while the soup tureen was removed. He was a trifle paler than usual, and his hands were disfigured by the emerging bruises, but otherwise he seemed recovered. Perhaps she was imagining the strange watchfulness in his demeanour.

'Yes, to my great good fortune. I spent some time assisting him last year, so he knows I will suit.' Giles passed Thea the butter.

'He will be an influential patron. Do you have ambitions in politics yourself?'

'I hope for a seat in Parliament in a year or two, if I can convince his lordship and the party that I would be an asset. As you know yourself—'

'Oh, let us not discuss me.' Thea could have sworn Rhys threw Giles a warning glance. What was that about? 'And you will reside in the household?'

Thea shook her head slightly, but Rhys did not seem to notice. Really, he was interrogating poor Giles as though interviewing him for a position!

'I have my own small town house, although Lady Carstairs has made a suite available for me in both the town house and at their country seat.'

'How wonderful that both Lord and Lady Carstairs have such similar interests,' Thea remarked before Rhys could enquire how much Giles was being paid or something equally intrusive. 'So many couples in society appear to be completely distanced from each other.'

'And that is a bad thing?' Rhys enquired. 'Most marriages are ones of convenience, not of shared interests. Or passions,' he added sardonically. 'I would not expect a wife to want to live in my pocket.'

'I do not agree,' Thea retorted. 'That is another reason why I will not marry without lo—without affection. Do you not agree, Giles?'

'I am completely in accord with you, Althea. Take the question of prison reform, which greatly interests Lady Carstairs…'

Ten minutes later, when the servants came in to clear for dessert, Thea realised they had been in earnest dialogue the entire time. Giles had tried to draw Rhys in from time to time, but, after a few near snubs, had apparently accepted that he did not want to talk about social policy.

Guiltily she glanced across at Rhys and caught him with a look almost of approval on his face. It was odd, because Rhys must be completely bored by the conversation. As soon as he saw her watching him he raised a brow and assumed such an expression of innocence that she almost burst out laughing.

He was up to something, the rogue—she remembered that look all too well. But what could he be plotting? A mystery. She contented herself with giving Rhys a reproving shake of the head. 'Is there any shopping we can do for you tomorrow? Giles and I intend to visit the cathedral and then explore the town.'

'And the shops by the sound of it.'

'But, Rhys, this is *Lyon*. Silk! Surely you do not expect me to ignore the finest silk in France, if not in Europe?'

'I expect Benton to return virtually on his knees, staggering under the weight of your purchases.' He addressed Giles earnestly. 'I recommend you take at least one sturdy footman with you unless you wish to set back your recovery by days.'

'I will follow your advice, Denham, but I confess to finding industry of any sort of interest. I intend to take notes while Lady Althea makes her purchases.'

'I would have thought you better employed advising her on the best green to suit the colour of her eyes,' Rhys said, surprising Thea into silence and earning a startled look from Giles.

After Rhys's haste to reach Lyon, he had slowed their journey to what seemed to Thea to be a crawl by contrast. At first she could not understand it, but after the first day from Lyon, as they set out for Valence and she quizzed him about it, he confessed with reluctance that he was feeling sore and battered and preferred to take it easy.

'If you did not ride, you would be more rested,' she said, wishing she dared ask him to let her check his back, or call the doctor. This willingness to admit weakness was so unlike Rhys.

'You want me to act as gooseberry?' he enquired.

'Whatever do you mean? You are most welcome to ride in the chaise! I hardly feel that I am on such terms with Giles as to lead you to think you would be intruding upon anything.'

'Whoa!' He held up a hand to ward off the vehemence of her protests. 'I am not suggesting you have set up a flirtation with Benton and require a chaperon.' He studied her face and Thea felt her colour rising under the scrutiny. 'Hmm… on second thought, are you perhaps protesting too much?'

'Ridiculous man,' Thea muttered. 'Of course I am not flirting with Giles, merely enjoying his conversation and company. I do not flirt and, even if I did, Giles is too serious for that. Thank goodness,' she added.

Giles was indeed rather serious and, although intelligent, he lacked Rhys's sharp wit, but she was coming to like him very much. But surely neither man thought she was *falling* for Giles? She shot Rhys an anxious look from beneath her lashes. How could any woman fall for Giles Benton when there was Rhys Denham riding beside their carriage? Though she could hardly put forward that argument.

'You are blushing,' Rhys remarked. 'I will say no more. I have no wish to squash up in the chaise with you. The couple I was referring to are your maid and my valet—I foresee a wedding in the offing. At least, I trust one will be forthcoming.'

'Polly and Hodge? My goodness.' How had she not seen that developing? 'It would probably be a good idea if they were not alone for so long, in that case.' *Hypocrite. Why can't my maid enjoy a flirtation—it is what I want for myself after all. Flirtation and rather more.* But how reliable was Hodge where women were concerned?

'You may go and chaperon them if you wish,' Rhys said with a shrug. 'But I prefer the fresh air. Besides, my back may be stiff, but the exercise is good for it.'

Rhys's teasing made Thea self-conscious for a while, but Giles appeared not to find any awkwardness in being alone with her, and the unrolling countryside and the drama of the Rhone flowing beside the road were so engrossing that she forgot to be distant with him.

'*À Valence le midi commence,*' Giles said as they clattered though the gates of the town. 'That is all I recall from my lessons, I am afraid, but it is true—I think we are finally in the south. Look how shallow the pitch of the roofs is now—no need to shed the snow here.'

'And the air is warm, even though it is evening.' They climbed down and waited for the coach to pull up alongside in the inn courtyard. Thea drew a welcome breath of warm, scented air deep into her lungs and watched Rhys with what she hoped was well-concealed anxiety, but he swung down out of the saddle without any sign of discomfort.

'I cannot wait to explore,' she said as he walked across. 'There is the river and a Roman amphitheatre….' The joy of this freedom to experience new things, to form opinions, to share impressions, made her feel like a hot-air balloon, soaring free. *I am never going back, I am never going to accept I am fit for nothing but blind convention and obedience.*

'Fascinating, I am sure, but I have a letter of invitation from an old friend of my family, a French *émigré* who returned once things became stable. I was going to drop in and see if I could take pot luck on dinner. Why don't you and Benton explore the town this evening?'

'Of course, if Giles would like to do that.' Thea did her best to sound enthusiastic, but it was a disappointment. She and Rhys never seemed to spend any time together now. Since Paris, he had ridden, and it was almost as though he was using Giles as an excuse not to be alone with her.

But she had promised not to expect to be entertained, not to want to be taken about in the evening. No doubt Rhys was delighted she had some company and a reliable escort.

'If I could have a word with you before you go out, Denham,' she heard Giles say as Polly came up with her dressing case.

'Let us go in,' Thea urged her. Probably Giles wanted to discuss paying his share of the expenses. He had mentioned it in the carriage and she knew he felt awkward about accepting Rhys's hospitality to this extent. She just hoped Rhys had the tact to allow him to pay a share.

Giles was unusually silent that evening as they made their way along the riverbank under the spreading lime trees. Thea hugged her shawl tighter around her shoulders against the cool breeze from the water and hoped Rhys had not snubbed Giles's efforts to pay his way. Perhaps she should say something. 'Rhys can be a trifle…lordly,' she began and then wondered how to go on.

'I have not found him so,' Giles said. 'He has surprised me by how encouraging he has been.'

Thea had not noticed any encouragement. Perhaps the two men talked into the night after she had retired. 'Indeed?' she said with what she hoped was an encouraging intonation.

'Normally I would not presume…certainly not after such a brief acquaintance.' He stopped midsentence in front of a bench. 'This may be too soon and yet… Perhaps you could sit down, Althea. Let me brush these dead leaves away.'

Mystified, she did as he asked, although a hard wooden bench after hours sitting in the carriage was not what she had hoped for. 'Is there a problem? Forgive me for mentioning it, but is it money that is concerning you?'

'Money?' He seemed completely thrown off his stride. 'No indeed. I am more than capable of maintaining a wife and a household. As well as my salary I have a private income sufficient to keep a separate household from Lord Carstairs. Lord Palgrave was quite satisfied about that.'

'A wife? Lord Palgrave satisfied?' A horrible sinking feeling took possession of Thea's stomach. There could be no mistaking Giles's intent: this was a proposal of marriage. How on earth had she not realised Giles had become so attached to her? And how, without wounding him, was she going to get out of this?

Chapter Eleven

'Why, yes, a wife. Let me start again. I am making a dreadful mull of this,' Giles said with a rueful smile. 'Lady Althea, you cannot be unaware of the esteem in which I hold you. Both you and Lord Palgrave have shown me the greatest trust in admitting me into your confidence, and I am aware of your difficult circumstances.'

'My—?'

'You having left home without your father's consent, I mean.' He cleared his throat and embarked on what, through her state of befuddlement, she supposed was a prepared speech. 'My birth, although not the equal of yours, is respectable. I believe my prospects are good, and you already know my sisters.' He went down on one knee and took her unresisting hand. 'Lady Althea, will you do me the honour of becoming my wife? I will ensure that not the slightest scandal attaches to your name as a result of this journey and—'

'No! I mean... Mr Benton. Giles. I regret if anything I

have said or done has aroused expectations which… I am sorry. I hold you in the highest regard and I am sensible of the honour which you do me by your proposal.' *That is what one says, isn't it?* 'But I cannot accept you. Do, please, get up. Look, someone is coming.'

A couple were strolling along the bank towards them, a small dog at their heels. Giles sprang to his feet and assumed a rapt interest in the water tumbling over rocks at the waterside while Thea fiddled with her reticule and tried to make sense of what had just happened.

As soon as the couple had passed she asked, 'What led you to imagine I would accept a proposal of marriage? I realise my behaviour in travelling alone with you in the chaise is unconventional, but I hope I have done nothing to give you the impression that I expected a display of…affection or that I consider that you have in any way compromised me.'

'Certainly not.' Giles looked appalled. 'Your deportment has been, in every way, that of a lady of breeding. But I am aware of your circumstances, and Lord Palgrave was so encouraging when we spoke of this—in fact, he urged me not to waste time in securing your affections.'

'*Lord Palgrave?* Rhys encouraged you to propose to me?' *How could he?* Thea felt quite sick. *He wants to get me off his hands so badly that he would thrust me into the arms of a virtual stranger?* 'Lord Palgrave has no right to speak for me.' Somehow she kept her voice steady. 'He is no relation of mine and certainly no trustee or guardian. He knows little of my mind or he would understand that I will only marry when I fall in love with a man who can love me as deeply.'

She stood up. 'Please, will you walk me back to the inn, Giles? Your heart is not engaged in this, is it? I would not hurt you for any consideration.'

He shook his head as she took his arm. 'My deep regard, but, no, not my heart. That, I hoped, would follow our union, which I saw as a most advantageous one for both of us.' He sounded subdued, but not, thank goodness, hurt, Thea thought.

'Then no harm has been done.' *Except for my trust in Rhys.* 'Can we put the awkwardness of this behind us and return for dinner, do you think?'

'Of course.'

They walked back in the gathering gloom. Giles, like the gentleman he was, made light conversation on indifferent topics. Thea responded automatically while all she could think was, *How could he? How could he fail to understand me so very badly?*

Rhys strolled into his bedchamber, tugged off his neckcloth and stretched with a certain degree of caution. Not too bad—his muscles responded almost without a twinge now. He contemplated ringing for Hodge, then dismissed the idea. Let the poor devil sleep—whomever's bed he was in. Who was he to spoil the man's fun, if he was getting any?

Sharing a couple of bottles of good Burgundy and the old *vicomte*'s brandy had left him feeling more mellow than he had since Thea had reentered his life. Cunning old devil, to hide it behind a false wall in the cellar before he fled the country.

He took off his coat and threw it over the wing chair that stood with its back to him in front of the hearth. It was flung back at him with considerable force.

'How could you?' Thea erupted out of the chair and swung round to face him, her index finger pointed to jab, painfully, at his breastbone. 'How—could—you? I trusted you, Rhys Denham. I thought you were my friend. I thought, Heaven help me for being such an idiot, that you still had a trace of sensitivity and sympathy somewhere under that expensive tailoring.'

Another sharp jab and Rhys stepped back, mind working in frantic calculation. He could hardly pretend he had no idea what she was talking about. Somehow Benton had rushed his fences, managed to make a mull of a perfectly simple proposal and apparently it was all his fault.

'Stop poking me,' he protested mildly. 'It hurts.' Strategic retreat to the other side of the bed seemed advisable, but Thea stalked after him.

'Good. Excellent, in fact. I am delighted it hurts. If I had something more painful, like a blunderbuss, I would use it. What the blazes did you think you were doing, encouraging Giles to propose to me?'

'Don't swear.'

She bared her teeth at him.

'I thought you liked him,' Rhys protested.

'I do like him. I like your coachman. I like the Archbishop of Canterbury, who is a very nice man. I liked Byron on the one occasion I met him. I even like the Prince Regent because he makes me laugh. It does *not* mean I want to marry any of them!'

'You have to marry somebody.' Rhys wondered whether vaulting across the bed would be undignified or cowardly. Probably both, he decided with regret.

'No, I do not! Why did you do it?' Thea demanded, toe to toe with him now. 'I told you my plans—why did you have to go and incite poor Giles to propose to me?'

There were tears sparkling in her eyes, catching the candle flame. Rhys hoped they were tears of anger. 'I told you why I think this scheme of living by yourself is a bad idea. You would be much happier with a husband who shares your interests, your social circle. Benton will probably end up a government minister one day. He's well bred, has excellent connections, enjoys a comfortable private income as well as his salary, he's hard-working—' He broke off when she did not reply and just stood there, her mouth pressed into a hard line. He had a horrible feeling that was all that prevented it from trembling.

'Thea, for goodness' sake, say something.' It was so long since he had seen her this upset, and never because of something he had done. He felt a toad, despite his good motives. And he realised with something like horror that he was becoming aroused. Her eyes were sparkling, her bosom was heaving, the colour stained her cheeks and all that passion was directed at him. She was no longer ordinary little Thea. What she was, he had no idea, except that he wanted to have her under him so badly it was painful.

'Giles is everything you say. I cannot marry him.'

'Why?' he flung at her, furious that she made him feel bad in so many ways. 'Because of this idiotic *love* you are cherishing for some man long ago in your past?'

'No. Not that. I know that is impossible, otherwise I would never have allowed myself to be so foolish as to think I could marry Anthony.' She dragged the back of her hand clumsily across her eyes and his heart turned over.

'What is it, Thea?' Rhys made himself gentle his tone. 'Why won't you let a decent man make you secure and happy?'

'Because…because as well as not loving him, I do not *desire* Giles. There! You would have it.' Thea turned on her heel, marched back to the cold hearth and stood staring down at the jug of flowers that stood on the flagstones.

'Desire? Oh, for goodness' sake, Thea.' Exasperation won over compassion. 'What do you know about desire? A sheltered virgin—'

She muttered something, then lifted her head and stared defiantly back at him. 'I am not a virgin.'

'Not? That bastard Meldreth ravished you?' For a moment a wash of red coloured his vision. 'When I get back to England I'm calling him out and I'll make the swine sorry he was ever within a mile of you. I'll castrate—'

'I was willing,' Thea said and sat down in the wing chair, her back straight, her hands folded in her lap as though perfect posture would make this conversation somehow less shocking. 'I thought I was going to marry him and I wanted to know what it was like to make love, so when it was obvious that was what he hoped, I agreed. He did not ravish me.'

'I see.' Rhys told himself that she was an adult, that she had a right to make her own decisions about things like that. He picked his way carefully into his next sentence. 'Just because you experienced pleasure with Meldreth does not mean that you cannot experience it again with another man. Benton, for example...' The thought, he realised, made him queasy.

'Pleasure?' she exclaimed. 'What pleasure? It was thoroughly *un*pleasant. He is selfish, clumsy and has the finesse of a bull at stud.'

'I see.' Somehow he had to make this right, although shooting Meldreth because he was a poor lover was hardly honourable, not if she had consented.

'And then he had the nerve to say I was frigid!' She sniffed. 'Have you got a handkerchief?' Rhys produced one and she blew her nose. 'Thank you. I had read all about it—sex, I mean. I know what happens, I know it should be pleasurable for the woman.' Thea swept on, ignoring his faint moan of protest at these confidences. 'I am *not* going to find myself married to a man with whom I cannot enjoy making love.'

Thea making love, Thea studying an erotic text she had somehow got hold of, Thea's slender pale body writhing on cool linen sheets, that soft brown hair fanned out around her. Thea.

Rhys got a grip on himself and cleared his throat. Fleeing the room was not an option. 'Perhaps if Benton kissed you, you would feel more attracted,' he suggested. *What am I saying? I want her.* Thea shot him a withering look. 'Look, you think you know about desire, but, after all, you have only read about it. You might not be a virgin...' *Oh, good God,* I'm *blushing now. Ten years of sexual experience and this girl—woman—is putting me to the blush.* Doggedly he ploughed on. 'A woman needs arousing, and Meldreth is obviously an insensitive boor.'

'I know exactly what it is to desire a man physically.' Thea's face was as red as he suspected his own was.

'Who?' he demanded. *Another money-grubbing rake trying to seduce her?* She turned her head and stared out of the window, her lower lip caught hard between her teeth. 'Tell me, Thea.'

'You.' It was a whisper.

'What did you say? Don't mumble. For a moment I thought you said it was me.'

'It is. I do. I don't want to, for goodness' sake! It crept up on me,' she added wildly. 'Like a cold. You know how it is. One day the back of your nose feels odd and the next morning you are sneezing and then you've a sore throat and before you know it, you have a streaming cold.'

'Desiring me is like catching a cold?' What the devil had been in that brandy? This had to be a bad dream.

'It is about as welcome,' Thea snapped. 'You hold me. You wrap yourself round me at night on the boat. You rescue me from that rake, looking all masterful, and you were so strong and heroic at the accident and then you sit around with no clothes on and cuddle me.'

She glared at him as though he had drowned a basketful of kittens, Rhys thought, unable to take in this stream of accusations.

'You ride all day looking magnificent and you are so heroic and strong…. Do you wonder a poor female falls for you? Yes, that's better, stand there looking like a stunned cod, I don't want you at all when you look like that.' A choked laugh escaped her as she walked unsteadily to the window.

'Are you saying you have fallen in love with me?' Rhys sounded utterly incredulous.

'No, of course not.' *I haven't fallen. I was there years ago.* 'I am saying I desire you. That I want to make love with you.' Thea slapped the flat of her hand against the wall in frustration with herself. How had she stumbled into this— and how on earth was she going to get out of it?

'I want us to go to bed,' she added with desperate honesty. He would throw her out of the room in a moment, or the floor would open up, or lightning would strike. Something would save her from the looming humiliation of his rejection. 'Have sex,' she said, just in case Rhys had not entirely grasped the enormity of what she was saying. 'You may laugh now. I realise perfectly well that I am not the sort of woman you desire.'

There was silence. No natural disaster occurred to save her. Thea stared blankly out of the window and waited for Rhys to laugh. He would not take her at her word and mock her, of course not. Rhys, whatever else she felt for him, was her friend. He would turn it into a joke, pretend he thought she was teasing him. Yes, Rhys would think of something tactful and they could pretend this had never happened.

'There's coincidence for you,' Rhys said. 'Or fate? I didn't believe in fate, but here it comes and slaps me in the face.'

'What do you mean?' Thea made herself turn and look at him. He no longer looked stunned. He was studying her with rapt attention, his face starkly beautiful in the candle-light, his mouth, so often a hard line, relaxing into a sensual curve.

'I mean that I desire you. That I want to make love to you, go to bed with you. Have sex with you. Interesting coincidence, is it not? Damnably awkward, of course. But interesting.'

'You… You're drunk,' Thea said, suddenly certain. Relief swept through her. If she could get more brandy into him, he might, just might, wake up in the morning convinced he had imagined the whole episode.

'I am not.' He shook his head. 'Just a trifle mellow, nothing like far enough gone to think this is a dream when I wake in the morning, which is what you are hoping, is it not? I'm sorry, Thea, but we are just going to have to deal with this.'

'How?' She wanted, so much, to sound calm and sophisticated. The word escaped in a bat squeak.

'We could pretend it did not happen, but I would know

and you would know and every time we looked at one another there it would be.' Rhys walked away to the far side of the room, leaving the path to the door clear as though giving her room to escape. 'Or we could act on it. Make love. See if we get it out of our system.'

'But I—' Thea found her feet had rooted themselves to the wide chestnut floorboards. 'What if I became pregnant?' *What am I saying? I should say no and leave this instant. I should not be thinking of problems that might arise if we do make love!* 'But there are ways to avoid that, aren't there?'

'There are and, believe me, I'd use them. Nothing is infallible, of course,' Rhys said slowly, 'but there is always marriage.' He did not appear to notice her wince. 'You have been reading somewhat widely for an unmarried lady, have you not?'

'And talking to married friends,' Thea admitted. 'Rhys, it is all right, you do not have to make me feel better by pretending to want me. I know I am ordinary and mousy and not...alluring. Not what you are used to, in fact. If you had not made me so angry and hurt by encouraging Giles to propose, I would never have lost my temper and told you how I feel. I can pretend this never happened, I really can. You do not have to be kind.'

'Kind?' Rhys ran both hands through his hair. 'Making love to you, Thea, would be many things. Kind is not one of them.'

'But you do not want to marry me, do you?' she ventured. Better to get that firmly out of the way. 'I do not want to marry you, of course,' she added hastily in case he misunderstood.

'Good God, no!' He looked at her face and backtracked rapidly. 'I mean, I would be the worst sort of husband for you. I want… I *need* a wife who won't interfere with me, who won't expect me to fall in love with her, or dance attendance on her. I want, to be frank, a well-bred, well-dowered, moderately intelligent mother for my children and chatelaine for my homes. I'd make you miserable.'

And I, you, apparently. 'You do not want to find someone like Serena?'

'A deceitful, faithless little madam who expects every man for a mile around to worship at her pretty little feet? No. I want a wife who will be meek, obedient, faithful, slightly dull and perfectly content with comfortable domesticity.'

She must have hurt him so badly, Thea thought with a wrenching sensation of misery. 'Not at all like me and not like Serena, either.'

'Exactly.'

'And I am not at all like the women you usually… I mean I am not blonde, or beautiful or curvaceous.'

'No. But I have discovered to my considerable discomfort that you are entirely and provokingly female and no longer sixteen years old,' Rhys said grimly.

'So what are we going to do?' The suspense was killing her. 'Pretend this conversation never happened or go to bed? Those appear to be the only options.'

'There is a third.' Rhys sat on the end of the bed and dragged his fingers through his already disordered hair. 'I hire another coach and a good driver, some armed outriders and ask my friend the Comte de Beauregard to recommend a chaperon. You can then proceed to Venice with your maid, and Benton as escort, and I will follow along a few days behind. No one will be tempted by anything then.'

That was the best thing, of course. What a relief that one of them was thinking clearly. 'Is that what you wish to do?'

'No,' Rhys said with a rueful shrug. 'But I will do whatever you want. Do you know what that is?' He raised an eyebrow and waited.

Thea stared at the big bed. She *should* say she would go with Giles. She *could* say she wanted to sleep on it and would decide in the morning. With the sense that she stood at a fork in the road of her life, with no idea which path would lead to regrets, she met his questioning gaze. 'Yes, I know what I want to do.'

Chapter Twelve

Rhys stood, the blue of his eyes like the flame deep in the heart of a log fire. 'Tell me.'

'I would like to go to bed with you. Tonight.' Thea felt a trifle dizzy. An abyss was opening up beneath her feet and she dare not look down into it. 'I do not expect anything else, you understand. Not more nights, not to be your lover—your mistress.'

He took the few steps to the door. 'There is no need to think of tomorrow, just tonight. Let me lock this.' The snick of the key made her jump, even though she was expecting it. Every nerve ending seemed to be on the surface of her skin, exposed, quivering in the cool draught from the window. Rhys took the tinder box and lit the candles, and the flare of light deepened the evening shadows into mystery.

'Polly has gone to bed. She was tired and I told her I would not want her until the morning.'

'You are trembling.' Rhys's big hands cupped her shoulders.

'Just shivering. The evening air…'

'Then the sooner we are in bed the better.'

He sounds so calm, so in control. But of course, she told herself, *Rhys has done this many times*. It was not as reassuring as it ought to have been. *He has never done it with* me *before*.

His fingers, healed now, had regained their usual dexterity. The fastenings of her gown seemed to melt away. *He was always good with knots and fishing lines and...* The fabric whispered down and pooled at her feet, and fleeting memories of childhood went with it.

'Turn around,' Rhys murmured.

It should have been easier when she could not see him, but his breath raised the hairs on the exposed skin of her nape and she could hear his breathing almost, but not quite, controlled. That slight betraying catch gave her an unexpected feeling of power and the last lingering fear that he was pretending desire in order to save her humiliation fled.

'Ah.' The bliss of loosened stay laces, the sense of freedom as her corset joined the gown on the floor. Her petticoat followed it, leaving her in chemise, stockings and a blush. 'I find I am shy,' Thea confessed.

'And I find I am somewhat overdressed,' Rhys murmured in her ear.

She had though he would kiss her, touch her, but only his breath stroked her skin. Thea turned. 'Should I undress you?'

'Don't you want to?' There was amusement in his eyes, but not mockery.

'I told you, I am shy.' She had never been shy with Rhys before. Once she could tell him anything, make a fool of herself in his company, call for his help when she was stuck in a tree or shriek with horror when they had been paddling in the lake and leeches had attached themselves to her legs. And Rhys always kept her confidences, never laughed at her. He would rescue her from trees and remove the leeches. Now she felt as though she had never known him at all.

'Don't worry.' He dragged his shirt over his head and sat on the edge of the bed to dispose of shoes and stockings. 'At least you have encountered a naked man before.'

'No, I haven't. Anthony just unfastened his falls and pushed me onto the *chaise*.' It had almost been exciting at first and then...not.

Rhys stopped with his hands on the fastenings of his evening breeches. 'The man is a clod. Shall I put out the candles?'

Thea shook her head. If this was going to be the only time she made love, then she wanted to see everything, know everything. And she was prepared; she had felt Rhys's aroused body pressed against her in the *chaise* on the ship.

Rhys pulled off his breeches and stood there, a faintly quizzical expression on his face as she stared. It seemed she'd had no idea quite what to expect after all.

Oh, my goodness. Thea said the first thing that came into her head. 'I think you look magnificent.' Quite unable to feel shy, afraid or even apprehensive, she reached out her right hand.

Rhys gasped as her grip closed around his erection. 'Thea! Hell's teeth, you are as curious and bold as a cage full of monkeys, you wicked girl.' He wasn't angry; she could tell by the way he hardened still more against her fingers and by the trace of laugher in his voice. 'Let go for a moment and I will take off your chemise and do my share of admiring.'

'My stockings,' she mumbled as the fine lawn was whisked over her head.

'Leave them. They are very arousing.' Rhys sat down on the edge of the bed and pulled her close between his parted thighs before she could realise just how exposed she was or wonder how stockings could be arousing. He held her still with one hand behind her waist and bent to kiss her breast.

The hairs on his legs were strangely stimulating against her bare skin, his lips were warm and sure on the curve of her breast and she moaned softly. *So gentle.* And then he took the nipple in his mouth, sucked, nipped lightly with his teeth and Thea almost jumped out of her skin. She caught his head in her hands and held him close, panting with the shock of the sensation that tugged a response from her womb, her thighs, deeply, intimately...

When Rhys lifted his head she thought she would sink to the floor if it were not for the pressure of his legs and his hand holding her.

He looked up, his eyes dark. 'You are so lovely, Thea. So sweet and so innocent, despite what that oaf did. If I am going to stop, I have to do it now.'

'You cannot stop now,' she gasped.

'I can. Barely. I should.'

'Sooner or later I will find a man to make love to me, because I am not going to live and die a spinster and not know how it should be. And I would very much rather it was you, Rhys.'

'That, my sweet, is blackmail.'

Thea bit her lip. He sounded so serious. Was she goading him to act against his honour? She would never do that to Rhys. 'I am sorry, it was, was it not? Rhys, you aren't being a rake or a seducer. I am not a virgin. I want this and I understand what we are doing.'

'And the consequences? If I do not prevent you becoming pregnant?'

'It will not happen.' He would keep her safe, she had total trust in him, just as she had under that *diligence*. She placed her hands flat on his chest and leaned in to kiss him, as if that would explain just how deep her trust was.

With a groan Rhys lay back and pulled her with him, rolling until she was beneath him. His face was buried in the angle of her neck, his heart beat over hers and her legs had opened of their own accord to cradle him intimately against the heat at the core of her. It was a kind of perfection, a moment of stillness, poised on the brink of the blissful abyss.

Thea closed her eyes and let herself absorb every sensation. Rhys's hair smelled faintly of woodsmoke and somewhere he must have brushed against a flowering bush, for a fragrance clung to the cropped curls. His skin was soft and smooth in some places, firm and roughened with hair in others. The weight of him was dominating, and yet he held himself in such control that it was not at all frightening. At the junction of her thighs she could feel the shape of him, beating with a pulse of its own, heating her flesh, moving as it strained against his will, wanting to thrust.

'Ah, Thea.' He lifted himself on his elbows and she opened her eyes to look up into his. 'I never—'

'My lord, are you awake?' A piercing whisper, the rap of knuckles on the door. *Polly?*

They froze, staring at each other, desire fled. 'What do you want?' Rhys snarled. 'What hour is this to be hammering on doors, for goodness' sake?'

'It is one o'clock, my lord. I'm sorry, but I got up to go to the necessary and peeped into Lady Althea's room and she isn't in her bed and it's not been slept in. Where can she be?'

'Blast the woman, she'll start a hue and cry,' Rhys whispered, then raised his voice. 'Perhaps she went into the garden for some air and slipped and hurt herself, or fell asleep. Go down and look, Polly, and be quiet about it, don't make a fuss. I'll dress and come and help.'

'Yes, my lord. But I've told Mr Hodge and the landlady, I was that worried—and Mr Benton woke up, too.'

'Go! And don't wake anyone else,' Rhys ordered. He rolled off the bed and reached for his breeches. 'Confound the wench, she's started a hue and cry. Get dressed, Thea, hurry. The garden slopes up past this window. I'll lower you down—go and find a bench to pretend to fall asleep on.'

It was as though someone had doused her in icy water. The heat of Rhys's body had gone, the enchantment of that perfect sensual moment fled and in their place was the sordid possibility of being discovered in a man's room by a search party.

She whipped her hair into a braid as Rhys tied her corset strings. 'Try to tie it as it was or Polly will notice,' she urged. He tossed her gown over her head and fastened it in urgent silence. 'Find the hairpins, hide them,' she whispered as she thrust her feet into her slippers.

The window had a low sill. She sat on it and swung her legs over, straining to hear. There was the sound of movement and people talking lower down, near the entrance to the inn. Rhys took her wrists and swung her down to the path some six feet below the window, just as he had in those long-ago days when they went scrambling over walls to pick illicit apples. 'Take care!'

Thea crept up through the tangled garden that clad the

slope, onto a terrace that, in daylight, commanded a view of the river. There had been a wide bench, she remembered, and groped towards it in the starlight. When she bumped against the cool stone she lay down and tried to arrange herself in a convincing pose for sleep. She realised she was panting and focused on taking deep, sleepy breaths.

'Lady Althea! Thea!' Giles, coming closer…

When she heard footsteps on the gravel she sat up, stretched her arms and gasped with what she hoped was realistic alarm for someone waking up, confused, in the dark. 'Giles! Where are you? What time is it? Oh, my goodness, I must have fallen asleep.'

He came out onto the terrace, his face eerily underlit by the lantern in his hand. 'Past one,' he said as he went down on one knee by the bench. 'Are you all right, Thea? We thought you might have fallen and hurt yourself.'

There were voices farther down, the sound of bodies crashing through the undergrowth. 'I am perfectly all right. How many people are searching? What a fuss—it was only that I was hot…'

'Polly is convinced you have been snatched by bloodthirsty revolutionaries or a gang of ruffians bent on kidnap and ransom. Lord Palgrave suggested we search the gardens first.' He twisted round. 'Here he is.'

'Idiotic woman,' Rhys said, as he strode onto the terrace with Polly and what looked like half the inn's staff on his heels. 'You'll catch your death of cold one day with this obsession with fresh air. Why the blazes didn't you tell anyone you were out here?'

He sounded thoroughly irritable and was probably not having to act in the slightest. If he felt anything like her, Rhys was aching with frustrated desire.

'I didn't mean to stay and fall asleep,' she protested. 'I went out after Polly left me because I couldn't drop off.' That was all technically true, at least, even if it barely touched the real facts in passing.

'You are frozen.' Rhys hauled her to her feet, despite a murmur of protest from Giles. He pulled off his coat and slung it around her shoulders. 'How the hell I let you persuade me to bring you along on this journey, I'll never know.'

Whatever else the onlookers were imagining, Thea doubted they envisaged any kind of romantic tryst. Rhys sounded like a man with a delinquent younger sister.

'And don't start crying,' he snapped.

Thea took her cue and flung herself sobbing into Polly's arms. The more fuss she made, the less likely the maid would notice anything untoward about the way she was dressed. Goodness knew what Rhys had done with her corset strings.

'Don't shout at me,' she pleaded from behind the large handkerchief that Giles had pressed into her hands.

'I'll get rid of the staff,' he said. 'This is turning into a circus.' He herded them before him, leaving Thea, Polly and Rhys on the terrace.

'Go and get warm bricks for your mistress's bed,' Rhys ordered. He prised Thea's arms from around the maid's neck and marched her towards the steps down to the front of the inn. 'Hurry up, girl.'

'Hell's teeth, that was a near miss,' Rhys said as Polly ran off to obey. He tipped Thea's face up and studied it in the light of the lantern he held. 'Are you all right?'

'Yes, of course. You know I don't cry.'

'That isn't what I meant,' Rhys murmured as they walked down the steps.

'I feel… I haven't the words for it, but it isn't comfortable.' Her skin was sensitive, she was unnaturally aware of Rhys's hand on her bare arm, her breasts ached and an insistent pulse beat intimately. She wanted to tear off all her clothes, all his clothes, and wrap herself around him.

'No,' he agreed sombrely. 'I think we scraped through without anyone suspecting, but my nerves may never be the same again. That is not the experience I wanted you to have, Thea, my sweet.'

'I know. And you had better stay angry with me tomorrow.'

'I'll try.' He stopped and pulled her into the shadow of the log store. 'This will probably only make things worse for both of us, but I can't leave you without at least a kiss.'

He was right, it would only make the aching longing worse, but how could she resist? Thea went into his arms and his mouth moved over hers, tender and yet a little rough from frustrated desire. She opened to him and his tongue took possession, its rhythms mimicking the act they had been denied, his hands holding her as though he would never let her go.

It could only have lasted a bare minute. Sixty precious seconds for the kiss she had waited all her life for. Thea stroked the back of her hand down Rhys's cheek. 'I wish…'

'This is where I start shouting at you again,' he said as he caught her fingers in his and kissed the tips before pulling her towards the front door. 'Come on, Thea! If you catch a cold and we are held up here for days, I am not going to be at all pleased.'

* * *

The next day Rhys managed to inflict his bad mood on her, their servants and the inn staff until he flung himself into the saddle and cantered off ahead of their little cavalcade.

'Phew.' Giles collapsed back into his corner of the chaise. 'Is Denham's temper always that bad?'

'I don't know,' Thea confessed. 'I have never seen him lose it like that before.' She pondered a moment. 'At least, not since he got into fights when he was a lad, and that was usually because someone was being bullied, or was cruel to animals or something.' She suspected that it went against the grain for Rhys to shout at servants, but it was probably all part of the act.

'Are you well this morning?' Giles regarded her, frowning. 'You do not look as though you slept well.' She grimaced and he hastened to apologise. 'I am sorry. I realise that a gentleman never notices that a lady is looking anything other than ravishing.'

'You are quite correct. I hardly slept a wink.' She had wrapped herself tightly around a bolster and tried to imagine it was Rhys and his arms held her, but it had done nothing to calm the ache of longing or the shock of their near discovery.

'It is doubtless my fault that you could not sleep in the first place,' Giles said penitently. 'If I had not made that gauche declaration, you would probably have dropped off to sleep easily and none of this would have happened.'

Thea snatched gratefully at the offered explanation for her behaviour. 'I confess, I felt very badly about refusing you, but please do not think I found your proposal gauche, simply unexpected.'

'And unwelcome.'

'Never that,' she protested. 'What lady would not be flattered and charmed by a proposal from a gentleman such as yourself? But we would not suit, you know.'

'I would have said we would suit very well,' Giles observed. 'I suspect the problem is more that you know another gentleman who would suit you even better. One who has already secured your heart.'

It was not fair to lie to him and the knowledge that she loved another man must surely be a salve to his pride. 'Yes,' Thea agreed. 'There is someone.'

'And he does not feel the same way?'

She nodded.

'A man who has known you so long that he fails to see you as you are now, I suspect,' Giles continued. 'Someone who has hurt you by the way he has changed, perhaps. He does not understand your need to be loved, so he tried to arrange a suitable marriage for you. His temper is not as you remember it, either—'

'Stop!' Thea regarded him with something like horror running through her. 'You think... You suspect I am in love with Rhys?'

Chapter Thirteen

'I mention no name and I would never do so. Nor would I give anyone the slightest hint that is what I conjecture,' Giles said calmly.

'Thank you.' Thea turned from him and stared out of the window, struggling to find some composure. If Giles was so clear-sighted, who else might suspect her feelings? *Please, not Rhys,* she prayed. She thought she had convinced him that what she felt was simple desire. What would he do if he believed her to be in love with him? Shun her company? Insist she marry him out of duty after last night? Tell Godmama? He would be kind, of course, and pitying. That would be worst of all.

'Has he…has he asked you whether you have made me a declaration?'

'No, we have hardly had a chance for private speech.' Giles leaned across and patted her hand. 'He may be in such a temper because he thinks you might have accepted me. It sounds irrational, but if, having done what he thought was best for you, he then discovered he was jealous, it reveals he has deeper feelings for you than you suspect.'

He sounded so pleased to have discovered a possibility for hope that it hurt to disabuse him of the notion. 'I told him last night,' Thea said baldly. 'I am sure he will have recovered his temper by luncheon. He is…fond of me, of course, and feels responsible. That is all.'

'If you do not mind me mentioning it, I find it strange that, given your shared interest in social reform, he is so reluctant to discuss it.'

'Rhys? Social reform? He has no interest in that, I am sure. Certainly, he is no High Tory and, despite his spending so much time in town, I believe he is an excellent landlord, but beyond that—'

'You do not know how important he is to the reformers' cause? Why, Lord Palgrave always supports every vote and speaks with passion and clarity of all those subjects you and I have discussed.' Thea simply goggled at him. 'And beyond that, he is the man that the party leaders send to, shall we say, persuade the doubters and the troublemakers. He has, I understand, the knack of getting his own way. They call him Hermes.'

'The messenger of the gods?' Yes, Rhys would be very good at persuasion and, when that did not work, even better at domination. And he had discouraged Giles from discussing it with him in her presence. Thea frowned. She recalled Rhys's jeering remarks when she confessed she had not thought through her plans for charitable works. She had skimmed over the Parliamentary reports in the papers too often, or she would have seen his name. It made her ashamed to think she had dismissed him as simply a pleasure-loving aristocrat. She should have known the adult Rhys would care as much for the underdog as the boy ever had.

This conversation, with its layers of deceit, was becoming too complex for either safety or her peace of mind. 'You have the road book—tell me, which is the next town of note we will encounter?'

Rhys dismounted at their luncheon halt and watched Giles Benton assist Thea from the chaise. They seemed to be on perfectly good terms, despite her refusal of his suit. It had been a mistake to try to matchmake, and Thea had been hurt by his lack of understanding, that was obvious now he was sober. The fire of unsatisfied desire had finally left him with nothing but an edgy awareness of her and a dull ache he was trying to ignore, which was probably a suitable penance for his meddling, he reflected as he studied Thea from a distance.

She looked unwell this morning. Her face was pale and there were smudges under her eyes, which were heavy with lack of sleep. He just hoped it was frustration that had kept her awake and not regret.

He should be repenting last night's actions, but he could not find it in himself to be sorry that he had discovered this passionate, sensual Thea. His childhood friend was still there, he thought, recalling the way she had launched herself into space from the window, trusting him to hold her safe as he always had during their ramshackle adventures.

She was independent, caring, reckless—and she knew herself too well. Thea recognised she was unsuited for the tight boundaries of marriage. To force her into them with the wrong man would be to kill that spirit.

What a contradiction she was, he thought, as she followed Benton into the shade of an arbour outside the inn, laughing at something he said. The reckless child somehow coexisted with the elegant young lady. The plain child was still plain, yet transformed into tantalising femininity. He had been stupidly unimaginative, assuming only conventional good looks gave a woman true beauty. For the first time since she had thrown his coat back at him in his room, Rhys smiled.

Thea saw him, waved, and the last of his ill humour, real and assumed, dropped away.

Benton, having settled her on the bench, strolled over and joined him as he went into the inn to order their meal. 'I've a fancy to ride this afternoon,' the other man remarked as the landlord went off to relay their requests to the kitchen.

'I doubt this place has riding horses for hire.' Rhys leaned back against the counter, crossed his ankles and moved his shoulders in a pleasurable stretch.

'I thought we might change places for a bit.' There were definite undertones of an order in the pleasant voice.

'Did you, indeed?'

'I have quite recovered from my head wound and I would appreciate the exercise and fresh air,' Benton said, and added, without changing his tone, 'and I think some bridge-building between you and Lady Althea might be in order.'

Rhys stared at him. The reticent, polite clergyman was showing an unexpected set of teeth. 'The devil you say!'

'You and I both made an error yesterday—you in thinking that Thea would marry where she does not love and me for proposing to her when I had no reason to suspect she favoured me,' Benton remarked calmly. 'She could probably do without my company for a bit, and that will allow you to make your peace.'

'I need to do that, do I?' Rhys swivelled to face the other man and unclenched his hands, which had balled into fists at his sides. For a moment he had thought Benton was hinting that he knew last night's events had been a farce.

'I think so.'

Rhys studied Benton's thoughtful frown. No, he was too straightforward to throw out hints.

'Thea hasn't slept. She looks unhappy.' Benton picked up the glass of red wine the innkeeper had put before them the moment they walked through the door and held it up to the light, squinting at the colour as he spoke. 'She does her best to hide it, of course. A very remarkable young lady. Some man is going to be very lucky to win her heart.'

'Yes,' Rhys agreed as he took up his own glass. A pity some undeserving idiot had already got Thea's heart and had no idea what a treasure he held unawares. 'All right, you take the horse this afternoon, but I warn you, the stupid thing is afraid of goats.'

The food that was brought out to them was simple but good. Thea breathed the herb-scented, dry air and leaned back against the upright of the pergola that supported a trellis of vines over their heads, filtering the sunshine through to dapple them with shadows. A lad came out and flicked a printed cloth over the table, then laid it with platters of bread studded with olives, goat's-and sheep's-milk cheeses, air-dried meats redolent of garlic, more olives and a pitcher of wine.

They all ate well, but conversation lagged. There was nothing she wanted to say to Rhys in company, she and Giles had talked themselves out, there was a faint air of tension between the two men and the effect of a disturbed night had dried up even a well-bred young lady's resources of small talk, she discovered. Their staff, cheerfully ensconced around another table, had no inhibitions, laughing and chatting and, from what Thea could hear, teaching the post boys some English cant terms.

When she came out of the inn after refreshing herself she found Giles mounted on the horse, which was demonstrating a skittish dislike of the flock of hens that scratched in the dusty road. Giles, who did not seem to have Rhys's skill on horseback, was cursing mildly as the animal backed and fussed.

'I thought you said it was goats it objected to,' he called to Rhys, who was standing by the step of the chaise to help her up.

'Those are the first chickens we've been close to,' Rhys said with a grin. 'I'd take care with cows and sheep, too, if I were you.' He followed her into the carriage. 'He would ride.' He shrugged.

'Are you all right?' she asked.

'I am fine.' Rhys shut the door and leaned back in the corner, apparently in order to study her face. 'Giles thinks we need to talk.' When she did not answer he added, 'He is probably correct, although I must admit, talking is not what I would prefer to be doing.'

As if I need reminding! To be alone like this with Rhys, surrounded by windows and perfectly visible to Giles as he trotted alongside, was more difficult than she had imagined it would be. With an instinct not to throw fuel on the fire, she ignored the end of Rhys's remark and asked, 'What does he suggest we should be discussing?'

'He says I should be apologising for urging him to propose to you, and I think he is right.' He reached to take her ungloved hand in his. The touch of his bare skin on hers sent the fine hairs shivering erect all along her arm. 'I am sorry, Thea. I should have listened when you said you did not wish to marry without love. I decided that I knew what was best for you because I was worrying about your future and, when what seemed like the perfect man for you dropped at our feet…' He grimaced. 'I had never suspected myself of being a matchmaker.'

Her hand was still in his. *No one can see,* she told herself. 'Many people matchmake,' she said, returning the pressure of his fingers to take the sting out of her words. 'Everyone feels it acceptable to have an opinion about an unmarried woman's future.'

'I suppose it is because the position of women by themselves is so precarious. Insufficient money to maintain respectable standards, or a loss of reputation, and the downward slide is rapid.' He shifted to sit shoulder to shoulder with her and their clasped hands rested on her thigh.

Thea let herself lean very slightly into him and enjoyed the tingle that the pressure of his solid body sent fizzing through her.

'If women had a better standard of education and were trusted to manage their own affairs, then it would not be such a problem,' he added, startling her. Then she recalled Giles's revelation that had become lost in the shock of discovering that he had guessed her feelings for Rhys.

'Why have you said nothing about your work in Parliament?' she demanded. 'Giles told me that you are a valuable supporter of all the progressive legislation, that you are instrumental in persuading, or silencing, the doubters and those that try and obstruct change. Tell me, *Hermes*, why you let me think you indifferent to the suffering of others so that I misjudged you?'

'I did not want to turn your tête-à-tête with Giles into a general conversation. I was matchmaking, remember?'

'I wish you had told me. I should have known that you would have supported such causes.' She glanced sideways and saw that she was making him uncomfortable with her praise. *Good!* 'And tell me, while I am chiding you, why did you say you did not expect a wife who shared your interests? You would not expect her to want to live in your pocket, you said. Was that more flummery?'

'No, it was the truth. I told you what I wanted—a good, domestic wife. I do not want shared passions of any kind— in the bedchamber or in beliefs.'

'Oh, Rhys.' He made her want to weep. 'That is so sad. Think what you will be missing.'

'Drama? Tantrums? Jealousy? Constant demands on my time and attention? Arguments about politics over breakfast?'

'And what is so wrong with that? Not the tantrums and jealousy, of course. If you love someone and they share your beliefs and enthusiasms, surely it would be wonderful.' *You and me in harmony, working together for important goals, passionate together in bed at night...*

'I told you, I have no intention of marrying for love.'

'You will be an unfaithful husband, then? You will keep a mistress?' If only he could see what he was depriving himself of, how much richer his life would be if he could only believe that he could love and that it would be returned. If he could believe that a woman might be faithful to him.

'Certainly not. I did not say I would marry a woman I

found unattractive. I will be swearing to be faithful, and I will hold to that vow.'

Thea fixed her eyes on the vineyards they were passing through and fought to keep her temper. She believed Rhys when he said he would be faithful to his wife, which meant that he was intending to squander all that passion within himself on a tepid relationship with a woman who would never know what it was to be truly loved. As he would not. His courage was invincible, it seemed, except in this one thing: he would not risk his heart again, even if that meant settling for the safely mediocre.

'I can hear your thoughts, Thea.' He sounded amused, but she did not turn to see if he was smiling. 'You are a true romantic.' She hunched a shoulder in a pettish refusal to engage with banter and, as if in response, he opened his hand, pressing until her own palm lay flat, his still on top, long fingers threaded through hers. She became aware of a subtle pressure as the pads of his fingers pressed lightly in a rhythm she could not quite catch. It was as if a big cat, claws sheathed, was gently kneading her thigh.

Does he know he is doing that? It made it rather hard to breathe, that rhythm. Thea began to count in her head. *One, two, in, out. One, two.*

'I am surprised, you being the romantic you are, that you would contemplate becoming my lover,' Rhys said. 'Is that not a betrayal of your true love?'

Breathe. 'I know a lost cause when I see it,' Thea said, her voice steady. The pressure on her leg had become a series of short, stroking movements, moving the fine lawn of her chemise back and forth over the bare skin beneath, the silk of her petticoat sliding against the thin fabric of her gown. The friction made a soft whispering sound, almost too faint to hear.

'You meet him, then? Or was that just a figure of speech?'

'I see him occasionally,' Thea admitted incautiously. 'We do not mix socially.' The pressure of Rhys's fingers was making it hard to think. She pulled her hand away and realised too soon that doing so left his big hand firmly on her thigh. He began a slow caress down as far as her knee, and then up, her skirts riding with the movement. 'Rhys!'

'Do you not like it? Am I tickling you?'

'No. I am not ticklish.'

'You are, unless my memory is very far at fault.' Rhys's chuckle brought her round to glare at him. 'Relax, Thea, I am not going to tickle your ribs in a chaise in broad daylight.' Somehow his hand had curved to cup the top of her leg and his fingertips were caressing the inner surface. The chemise had ridden up and there was only fine lawn and thin silk between his hand and her skin.

Her breath was coming short now. She turned her head on the squabs so she was looking out of the window again, the perfect picture of a well-bred lady interested only in the passing scene.

'Rhys.' She should move. She should slap his hand away. This was broad daylight on a public highway, for goodness' sake! His hand felt wonderful. Sure, confident, skilled in administering this focused sensual torture.

'I am thinking how I would like to caress you when we are naked in bed again,' Rhys said. She shot him a startled glance, but he was turned towards the window on his side. To anyone looking in they would appear detached, conversing lightly on matters of no importance.

'I will start with your toes, I think.' He sounded thoughtful. Her toes curled in the tight little nankeen boots she wore. 'Then I will kiss all the way up to the back of your knees. I wonder if you are ticklish there. Are you, Thea?'

'I do not know,' she managed to gasp. His fingers were brushing high to the junction of her thighs now. She pressed them together and somehow that only made the heat and the throbbing worse.

'We must find out.' That wicked chuckle again. 'Then I will lick and kiss and nibble my way along here.' One finger traced a wandering path from her knee up the quivering length of her thigh to the point of the delicious discomfort. 'To the delta of Venus.'

'Delta?'

Rhys placed both thumbs tip to tip, then joined his forefingers into a triangle. 'The Greek letter delta, that mound covered in curls that hides the honeyed secrets of a woman's desire.' Thea bit down on a moan. 'Then I will part those soft white thighs and kiss—'

'Kiss?' It was more of a squeak than a word. 'Rhys, if you do not stop this minute I am going to… I do not know, but I should not be doing whatever it is in a chaise!'

He lifted his hand and caught hers. 'You are right, of course. I do not think I can stand it, either—see what you have done to me.' He laid her unresisting hand against the falls of his breeches, then groaned as she reflexively tightened her grip on the blatant erection that pressed itself into her fingers.

Thea snatched her hand away, face burning, insides quivering with mingled desire and terror. 'Is this *normal*?'

'Perfectly. What we are feeling is simply desire, what any man and woman who are sexually attracted feel. Normal, healthy and decidedly uncomfortable under the circumstances.'

'Well, there is nothing to be done about it here.' Thea retreated into her corner and crossed her legs. It did nothing to subdue the desire to throw herself on Rhys's chest and kiss him senseless.

'There is, if you were a little less innocent. Don't look at me like that, I promise to behave. And I also promise,' he added grimly, 'to find a way to be with you tonight if I have to feed that maid of yours a sleeping draught to do it.'

'As long as she does not have to sleep in my dressing room, or on a truckle bed in my bedchamber, then I will tell her I do not want to be disturbed until morning and lock the door,' Thea said firmly. 'And you must come to me.'

'But of course,' Rhys agreed. 'A gentleman can do nothing else.'

Chapter Fourteen

Polly put down the hairbrush and began to tidy the small disorder on the dressing table.

Now, how to convince her not to come into my room to-night without sounding suspicious...?

'Will you be requiring me again this evening, my lady?'

Thea looked in the mirror and saw the maid was positively blushing. 'I do not think so. I was going to read for a while before I went to bed, but I doubt I will stay up long.' The clock outside on the landing of the top floor of the inn struck ten o'clock. 'Why, Polly? Are you tired, too?'

'No, my lady. I thought... That is, Mr Hodge suggested... There's a fair down by the waterside. I'd like to go and see it.'

'With Hodge.'

'Yes, my lady.'

Goodness, Rhys had been right after all. My maid and his valet. 'Are you and Hodge courting, Polly?'

'I think so, my lady. Do you mind? I mean, I don't know what you think about followers.'

'Hodge is not so much following as travelling with us, isn't he?' Polly giggled at the feeble joke. 'I have no objection, although it really is a matter for Lord Palgrave, as he employs you both. Here, take this in case there is anything to tempt you.' She handed the girl the loose change that lay on the dressing table. 'Have a good time and be back by midnight. I will lock my door as there are other guests on the floor below us, so do not disturb me when you return, will you?'

'Oh, thank you, my lady! I won't disturb you, I promise.' Polly folded away the last items of clothing, turned down the bed and positively skipped out of the room.

Everything had conspired to smooth her path this evening. Their rooms were spread over the topmost floor of the inn, with no other guests on that level. They were spacious and well appointed, but there were no dressing rooms, so both Hodge and Polly had their own bedchambers at the far end of the corridor, while Rhys's was separated from her room by what Polly told her was the large linen store. Giles was on her other side.

Thea had pleaded tiredness after dinner so she could retreat and not have to sit making general conversation while Rhys looked at her, his lids heavy over those hot blue eyes. It had been bad enough over dinner, but she was quite certain she could not remain calm with nothing to distract her.

When would he come? She studied her reflection in the glass, her confidence diminishing by the second. What on earth was it that Rhys found so desirable about her? Perhaps she should snuff out some of the candles....

Their rooms were quiet and faced the back of the inn,

not the yard or the busy street. The silence was broken by a dull thump from outside as though something had fallen. Thea caught her night robe tight around her and went to ease open the shutters onto the balcony. Was that a faint curse from somewhere outside?

The moon was half-full, the sky clear and, as she glanced up, she caught her breath at the blaze of stars. Then a gleam of white to her left caught her eye. 'Rhys!' He was standing on his own balcony's parapet and by his foot was a black hole where a stone should have been.

'Damn thing fell off,' he whispered.

'Go back, then, it isn't safe,' she hissed back. 'Come in through the door, for goodness' sake!'

'Less chance of being seen this way.' He shifted his balance and jumped the four feet to the intervening balustrade and then down to the balcony itself.

Thea removed her hands from her mouth where she had clamped them to hold in the scream and peered at the stonework. 'This looks in very bad repair.'

'Stand back.' Rhys climbed onto the edge, and the stone beneath his feet rocked.

Thea fought the instinct to try to reach for him and retreated to the far side. Rhys jumped, the stone teetered but stayed put and he landed and jumped down with perfect grace.

'You idiotic man,' she scolded.

'I thought it would be a romantic gesture.' He held the shutter for her, then followed her into the room. 'Is the door shut? No?' He strode across and locked it.

'Romantic? You don't have a romantic bone in your body.' Thea plumped down on the dressing-table stool and tried to recover her breath. 'I thought you would fall off—and a mangled lover at the foot of the wall is not at all romantic.'

He grinned, unrepentant, and began to brush dust and lichen off his evening breeches, which were all he appeared to be wearing apart from his shirt, open necked. 'I should have put riding breeches on,' he observed. 'Lord knows what Hodge is going to make of these.'

'He has gone to the fair and taken Polly. Did you realise?'

'It was my idea.' Rhys looked smug. 'I suggested he might like the evening off and he jumped at the chance. He even managed to keep a straight face while remarking that Polly might welcome the outing.' He strolled towards her with what seemed dangerously like a prowl. 'Why are we bickering about the way I arrived here and discussing our servants' love lives, Thea?'

'Because I am frightened,' she admitted. Where had that come from? She slid round to the far side of the stool.

'The other night you were lying naked in my arms.' To her intense relief Rhys leaned against the bedpost. 'I do not think that fear was uppermost amongst your emotions then.'

'You are not mellow with red wine and I am not angry now,' Thea explained, as much to herself as to him.

Rhys smiled, lazy, dangerous and yet somehow reassuring. 'We do not have to do anything.'

Thea flickered a glance at the arousal that his thin evening breeches were doing nothing to disguise. 'You are hardly going to be pleased about that.'

'Thea.' His voice was suddenly rough. It was not anger, but surely it could not be emotion? 'We are friends. Old friends. I have never made love to an unwilling woman and I am not going to start with you. This is about what you want. If you do me the honour of lying with me, I will do my best to make you happy and I know it will give me great pleasure. But if *your* happiness requires me to go out of the door now, then that is what will happen—with no ill feeling.'

'Not back along the balconies?' Something bubbled inside her, something close to happiness tinged with the traces of that fear. But now it only gave the happiness a sparkling, dangerous edge.

'If my lady commands.' He had seen the change in her eyes; she did not have to tell him.

'I think the door, later,' she conceded. 'I buffed my toe-nails.' Rhys's eyes crinkled into a smile. 'I do not know why, because I really did not understand what you were talking about in the carriage.'

'Then let me show you. Stay just where you are.' He straightened and dragged off his shirt, then his breeches.

Oh, but he was magnificent. She remembered the lanky boy swimming in the lake in his drawers and just had time to wonder where all that elegant muscle had come from before he was kneeling at her bare feet.

'And very pretty toes they are, too.' He lifted her right foot and the flounces of her night robe fell back, pulling the nightgown with it to bare her leg to the knee. When he sucked her toes into his mouth and did outrageous things with his hot, wet tongue, she did not giggle or shriek, only reached wildly for the edge of the dressing table and held on. And then he did as he had promised, and his tongue trailed up her calf to circle her knee before he switched legs, and her other foot was left tingling.

'I have never been so shocked in my life,' Thea panted. She had to say something, do something…

'In which case,' Rhys said as he got to his feet and

scooped her up in his arms, 'you haven't been trying hard enough. Now for those deliciously ticklish bits.' He laid her on the bed, her garments bunched into a mere froth of inadequate coverage at the top of her thighs, and bent her right leg.

Those broad shoulders pushed her legs apart so she could do nothing but sprawl shamelessly as he explored the delicate skin behind her knee. It wasn't ticklish; it was bliss. Wicked, wicked bliss. None of the books she had studied so surreptitiously had said anything about knees!

And then, before she could recover herself enough to understand what he was doing, his mouth was buried in the curls at the junction of her thighs and his tongue had slipped into the secret folds. All she could do was fist her hands into the bedcover and try to stop herself lifting up to wantonly press herself against his sinful, clever mouth.

One moment she was consciously fighting for control, the next something took her, took charge of her body, her mind, her soul and swept over her with an irresistible force. She heard a scream and felt Rhys move, there was a moment, or perhaps an hour—an entire night?—of dizzying pleasure and then she was wrapped in Rhys's arms, his body hot and hard and strangely gentle as he held her.

'Oh,' she said. 'Oh.' There were probably words, but she had no idea what they were or what language she needed to say them in.

'Thea,' Rhys said, his voice strangely husky, and then his weight was on her and she felt him nudging between her thighs, and she opened to him and tried to breathe as he pushed into her. So slow, not like Anthony's painful, impatient thrust. Gentle, smooth, inexorable. He was very large and it was not exactly...comfortable. She shifted instinctively, tilted her pelvis and heard him groan against her hair and, strangely, that gave her confidence.

There was discomfort. Her brain told her it was pain as he stretched and filled her, yet her body told her it was not. Her body welcomed it, sang with delight, arched against him, tightened so that the pain should have become worse, but instead became simply pleasure, shimmering through her muscles and veins, driving her thoughts into abject submission as they tried to tell her this had been an unpleasant experience before.

But that was not Rhys. She caught at the vanishing thought and sought for his mouth. *There. Kiss me. At last. Oh, kiss me. I love you....*

His body arched over her, muscled, hard, tense to breaking point, every sinew, it seemed, straining. Thrust and withdrawal, thrust, in a rhythm of spiralling tension and pleasure. Their skin was slicked with the heat of effort and the warmth of the night and her nostrils were filled with his masculine scent and what she hazily realised was the musk of their lovemaking.

She needed to be closer to him somehow, anyhow. Thea curled her legs around Rhys's hips and he cried her name and held still for a second like a hawk poised to plunge. The strange tightening, spinning sensation swept through her again as he thrust and his mouth found hers. Thea was distantly aware of him leaving her and cried out in protest. And yet, as she lost herself utterly, she felt Rhys holding her, surrounding her, kissing her. *I love you.*

Rhys stirred and drifted up to consciousness. He had been here before, his arms around these soft curves, his nostrils teased with the scent of rose and this warm, sleeping woman. But this time they were not on a makeshift bed on a ship and this time he did not have to conceal the all-too-evident fact that his body was ready and eager to make love to her. Rhys smiled into the darkness and nuzzled the soft skin below Thea's ear.

She mumbled something and wriggled more firmly into his embrace, but she was clearly still asleep. Faintly the sound of the church clock striking four drifted through the latticed shutters. There was a perceptible lightening at the window.

Time to go. He would have to wake her so she could lock the door behind him. The temptation to slide into her, wake her that way, was considerable. And inconsiderate, Rhys realised. He had no right to assume Thea would want to make love again. Her curiosity had been satisfied and, very likely, that flare of desire for him had been quenched. For him it was going to take some time to get the need for her under control if Thea decided that enough was enough.

Could they go back to the way they had been before? No, because that had been founded on his lamentably slow realisation that his childhood friend was a woman now. So what next? Rhys indulged himself by running her hair through the fingers of his left hand, the one that was free and not under Thea's ribs, fingers curved around her breast.

They could continue with this and it would become an *affaire*, or they could stop now, and find a way of coexisting until they reached Venice. Was that possible? Rhys had never been friends with a mistress and had never had to live in close proximity with one after the relationship had ended.

But he could not compare this to those past liaisons. Those had been, at heart, a business matter. True, he had done his utmost to give pleasure as well as gold, but it had still been a transaction. And this? Honest mutual desire, as simple and as fiendishly complicated as that. Because he had taken the innocence of a respectable lady, never mind that she had not been a virgin. To all intents and purposes Thea had never made love before, and she could have gone to a husband's bed with a very good chance of him never realising that someone else had been before him.

Now, not. Although, knowing Thea, he thought she would carefully explain to the man that she was not an innocent before matters progressed as far as a proposal. And then the proposal would not be made unless the suitor was head over heels in love with her and, given that she was hardly going to find herself courted by some idealistic nineteen-year-old, that was not likely to be the case. Grown men had more sense than to fall in love.

He should, he knew perfectly well, offer her marriage. And he could imagine, with a searing clarity that brought him thoroughly awake, what Thea would say to that. He had shaken her faith in him quite far enough by thinking she would accept a *suitable* marriage to Giles Benton. She wanted to marry for love, and she expected him to understand and support that.

It was a relief, of course. Thea was far from the placid, domesticated, undemanding lady he needed to marry. House, home and children would not be enough for her. She would demand to be involved—when she was not doing something outrageous like reading unsuitable books or climbing trees. That would be fine while they agreed. But when they did not? When that enquiring mind of hers decided she was not happy with one of his opinions or decisions? Would she then be wishing she was not tied by vows and friendship?

But the biggest barrier of all was that she expected to be

loved, and he could never feign that besotted state—she would see through him with one sharp glance from those clear hazel eyes. He did not know how to make that unquestioning surrender any longer, and Rhys found he could not bear the thought of hurting her.

'Wake up, Thea,' he murmured into her ear.

She stirred and then, without saying anything, wriggled round in his arms and kissed him, finding his mouth, it seemed, by blind instinct.

Rhys fought the urge to follow where that kiss was leading. He lifted his head. 'Sweetheart, I have to go.'

'Not yet.'

Her hand slipped down between their bodies and Rhys groaned. Four warm fingers and an erotically enterprising thumb closed around his erection. 'Thea, if I don't go out of the door now it will be the balconies later.'

That worked. Thea rolled away. 'You are not risking breaking your neck again.' She slid out of bed, groped her way across to the shutters and opened them, letting in the faint grey light of dawn to bathe her unashamed nakedness. 'Brrr. It is cold out here.'

'Then get back into bed.' Rhys winced as his feet hit chilly boards, but he pulled on his breeches and found his shirt as briskly as he could, trying not to look at the pale dawn ghost that was Thea as she flitted about the room setting things to rights. 'Or put on your robe and slippers.'

To his secret disappointment she pulled her nightgown over her head. 'I'll get back into bed when you have gone,' she promised. When he padded over to join her by the door she put her head on one side and laughed, clapped her hand over her mouth to stifle the sound and stood there, eyes twinkling at him.

'What?' He knew he sounded grumpy with the sheer ef-fort of not throwing her back onto the bed and having his way with her.

'You look like a tomcat going home after a very wild night on the tiles,' Thea said, and reached up to stroke his hair into some kind of order.

'Well, and so I am.'

'At least you did not yowl at the moon.'

'Oh, I did,' Rhys said with a grin and bent to brush his lips over hers. 'Inside I was making enough noise to have every boot in the neighbourhood thrown at me.' He eased the door open and checked the corridor, then slid outside and shut the door before she could reply and make him laugh even more than he was tempted to do now. Tomcat, indeed!

He reached his room without so much as seeing a sleepy-eyed boot boy. What would be heaven, of course, would be a wife for duty and Thea for fun. And passion. And some-thing else he could not quite put his finger on. Friendship, he supposed.

Rhys threw off his much-abused clothing and got be-tween his own chilly sheets. The bed needed to look slept in, so somehow he was going to have to try to sleep.

Chapter Fifteen

Thea shook out the bedding to remove any betraying jet-black hairs, remade the bed then got in to toss and turn it into a convincing state. That took ten minutes in all. After a further two hours tossing and turning she sat up and ran her hands through her tangled hair in exasperation.

What idiocy had made her think that one night in Rhys's arms would be enough, that she could keep the memory like a pressed flower in an album to be taken out and sighed over in pleasant reminiscence? All she had achieved was to make her long for him more, with the added torment of now knowing exactly what she would be missing every night for the rest of her life.

And he will be married to his dull, respectable wife and it will be positively sinful of me to feel jealous of her. Why did I assure him one night would be enough and that I would not ask for more?

It was all very well and good being undemanding and honourable and doing everything to make him not feel he was under any kind of obligation but… No, she had been right. The only thing worse than not having Rhys in her bed would be him being there, but knowing it was out of pity.

There was a faint scratching at the door. 'My lady? Are you awake?'

Thea opened the door to find Polly beaming with good humour. 'Would you like your breakfast in your room, my lady?' She came in and flung the shutters open. 'What a glorious morning it is! We don't get sunshine like this in London, that's for sure.'

'Breakfast here would be excellent, thank you, Polly.' And would have the advantage of giving her some time before she had to face Rhys under Giles's perceptive eye. Possibly she could manage not to blush like a peony when she was dressed.

'Not that it's much like a proper breakfast. The food's all right over here—better than I thought it'd be—but there's nothing to set a body up for the day in those mimsy little pastries, now is there?'

After countless breakfasts with her father demolishing bloody beefsteaks and fried eggs, Thea was grateful for chocolate and croissants and some fresh fruit. 'It suits me very well,' she said. 'I'll have my washing water first, though.'

'You've had a restless night,' Polly observed, flapping the bed into some sort of order as she passed it. 'And you've put your foot right through the bottom of this sheet, my lady.'

'Oh, dear. I must make sure it is added to the accounting.' She escaped behind the screen to hide her scarlet cheeks. That must have been Rhys.

'Did you have a pleasant evening at the fair?' she asked when, washed, dressed and feeling rather more composed, she sat down at the little table on the balcony. It was a miracle that Rhys hadn't managed to demolish that on his way to her room.

'It was lovely, my lady. I bought ever such a pretty lace trim for my Sunday best and a handkerchief and some soap. And there were swings and jugglers and a fortune teller.'

'And did you have your fortune told?'

'John... Mr Hodge, I should say, teased me until I did. But he had to come in with me or I wouldn't have been able to understand a word!'

'Sit down and tell me what your fortune is to be,' Thea urged.

'Ooh, my lady, thank you. Well, I'm to meet a dark man with grey eyes who is good with his hands and much travelled and we'll fall in love and live happily ever after and have three children. What do you think of that, my lady?'

'That possibly it was being translated by a dark man with grey eyes?' Thea teased.

'Could be, my lady.' Polly's pink cheeks dimpled into a smile. 'Not that I mind him taking an interest, mind you.'

'You will be careful, won't you, Polly?' *And who am I to lecture?* 'I'm sure if anything should... Well, you know what I mean. I am certain his lordship would insist on Hodge marrying you, but it isn't the way you'd want to start married life, is it?'

'Don't you worry, my lady,' Polly said. 'I don't believe in letting a man take liberties. A girl loses all her mystery if she does that, my sister Bethan says. You give them what they wants and then they don't want it anymore, she says. And she landed herself an attorney's clerk! A little kiss is all John Hodge is getting until I've got a ring on my finger.'

'Very wise,' Thea said as her stomach took an unpleasant

swoop downwards. Is that what would happen now? Perhaps she had only been a novelty for Rhys, and the attraction he had felt for her would evaporate now there was no mystery about the woman she had grown up to be. Perhaps, in the cold light of day, he would think less of her, believe her wanton. No, surely Rhys would not be that hypocritical.

'Is your sister's a happy marriage?' she asked, and stirred another spoonful of sugar into her chocolate for courage.

Polly shrugged. 'There's money enough and he's kind to her and the kiddies are healthy. I'd not be surprised if he doesn't stray now and again, if you take my meaning.'

'So it wasn't a love match?'

'No. Our Bethan's got her head on the right way round. She set out to catch the best man she could, provided she liked him well enough.'

Love matches would be different, Thea told herself. If a man loved a woman he would not think worse of her the next day if she slept with him. *But Rhys does not love me, not that way.* All the warm, happy, sensual glow that had been with her since Rhys's departure ebbed away, leaving her apprehensive and shaken.

What did I think, deep down, was going to happen? she asked herself. *That Rhys was going to wake after a night in my arms and realise he loved me passionately?* She hoped that was not the case. At least expressing desire frankly was the sort of thing an independent adult woman might do, but to daydream about fairy-tale endings was uncomfortably like her youthful yearnings.

'Shall I lay out your green walking dress, my lady?' She had been so deep in her troubled thoughts that Polly had already found her clean linen and was standing waiting to help her with her stays.

'Yes, please.' Another day in the chaise with either Giles and his uncomfortably perceptive gaze for company, or the agony of being with Rhys, on public display and unable to touch him, let alone ask how he felt about her now. 'No, put that back, Polly. I have an idea.'

'Are you riding today, Denham?' Benton pushed back his chair from the breakfast table and stood up.

'Hmm?' Rhys yanked his thoughts back from their review of last night's delights. 'Riding? Yes, I thought I would.' Thea might need a while to feel comfortable alone with him, and he could well do without the strain of sitting next to her in the chaise, unable to do any of the things that he would find himself aching for.

'In that case, I think I'll see if the landlord can hire me a horse.' Benton went out and Rhys drained his coffee while he tried to make up his mind how to approach Thea. She might well be regretting what had happened last night, in which case he had to make her feel confident that he would not press her for any further intimacy and that no one would ever know what had transpired between them.

On the other hand, she might want to continue their liaison, but would probably be far too shy to say so—especially after she had assured him that she expected nothing more from him than one night.

And what did he want? Well, that was easy—what he *wanted* was to continue as her lover. Her untutored, sensual, generous response to lovemaking had delighted and shaken him. To explore with her all the other delights that bed sport held would be intensely pleasurable.

But. But he had been careful last night. Every time they made love, however carefully, there was some risk of pregnancy and of discovery. And how could he be certain she would tell him the truth about what she wanted? If he made it clear he wished to continue as her lover, she might very well feel obligated to agree, and, being Thea, would put a very good face on it. Would he be able to tell if her agreement was genuine?

Rhys stared into the muddy dregs at the bottom of his cup. They seemed to have a lot in common with his thought processes. This was why he wanted a placid, emotionless marriage. No anxiety about hurting another person, no fear of them hurting you.

What he ought to do now was clear—never mind what he wanted. He should not make love to Thea again. In fact, he should pretend it had not happened. Then she would not feel pressured. And if the worst did happen, then surely he could rely on her to tell him that she was with child?

That thoroughly straightforward conclusion was curiously unsatisfying. *Do your duty,* Rhys told himself. Even that thought did not produce the immediate sense of purpose and contentment it normally did. For a ridiculous, self-indulgent moment he imagined life with Thea, then gave himself a brisk shake. This was the sort of emotional muddle he was intending to avoid. He pushed back the chair and went to pay the reckoning, the warm afterglow of sexual satisfaction ebbing with unpleasant finality.

The stable yard seemed full of horses. The post boys were supervising the four being hitched to the chaise, Tom Felling was arguing about the shoes on one of the animals the ostlers were trying to harness to the carriage and Benton was mounted, holding the reins of two other horses.

'They tell me the lady has ordered this one.' He gestured

towards a neat grey bearing a side saddle. 'And then they ran off before I could tell them they had made a mistake.'

'No mistake.' Thea walked past Rhys to take the reins. 'Will you give me a boost?' Her smile was just the same as it always was, her gaze meeting his with perfect frankness.

Last night might not have happened, Rhys thought with a flash of what he recognised as hurt pride. *Damn it!* Then he saw the shadows under her eyes and the way her smile wavered as he stared at her, and he made himself smile.

'Yes, of course. That is a charming habit.' He cupped his hands for her booted foot and tossed her up. The mare sidled, but Thea had the reins competently in hand.

'It is French,' she said with a rueful twist of the lips. 'Their gowns are fabulous and their fashions always ahead of ours, but their tailoring is not as good as London tailoring. This is meant for parading in a park, not for the hunting field, I fear.' She gave the exaggeratedly long skirt a dismissive twitch. Yes, now that he was looking for it he could see the constraint behind the facade.

'Even so, the effect for the spectator is most pleasing.' Rhys mounted, one eye on the grey. He would have much preferred to try the animal out himself before he let Thea near it. And was this wise, in any case? After all, she had been as near a virgin as made no difference, and perhaps she'd be more comfortable in the chaise.

'Are you sure you should be riding this morning?' he said, low voiced, as he brought his own bay alongside her. 'Should you perhaps be resting?'

Thea gave a snort of laughter. 'What a poor honey you must think me if you do not believe I can manage a strange horse, Rhys. You taught me to ride, remember?'

'Astride, when you were six,' he protested.

She lowered her voice, 'Or perhaps your male pride is dented because I am not prostrate with, er...emotion?'

'Thea!' Well, that answered that! Whatever she was feeling this morning, it was not shyness or an excess of sensibility. Even so, she was somehow not quite herself.

'I am tired of being shut in the chaise.' Her voice rose and Rhys saw she controlled it with a conscious effort. 'The weather is beautiful, the scenery is so new and different and the air smells delightful. I want to enjoy it.' She nudged the grey into a walk and the three of them rode out of the yard side by side.

'Where are we?' she asked. 'I never thought to ask last night.' From her calm expression and downcast lashes no one would have guessed that the reason had probably been nothing to do with tiredness and everything to do with nervously anticipating an amorous encounter.

'Just north of Montélimar.' Rhys relaxed, the grey was well behaved and Thea was obviously more than competent in the saddle, even if her attention was not fully on the horse. 'I was aiming for Orange tonight and that is only thirty-five, forty miles. Do you want to see anything in Montélimar?' he asked Benton, who shook his head. 'Then we will buy some of the famous nougat for Thea on our way through.'

'It isn't me who has the sweet tooth,' she retorted. 'It was always you who stole the fudge if Cook did not hide it well enough.'

'I am prepared to admit I would like to try nougat,' Benton interjected. 'Shall we canter?'

Thea urged the grey on and left them in a cloud of dust. Rhys let Benton chase after her and held his horse back to a more controlled pace. What had he expected this morning? That Thea would send him some unmistakable signal that she wanted to continue as his lover? Or an equally clear signal that she did not? He had not thought how tricky this would be, or how difficult it must be for her to make either inclination clear.

He must take the bull by the horns and broach the subject, making certain he gave no indication of his own wish. To put her under any sort of pressure ran counter to every instinct he possessed as a gentleman. And his instincts were usually to be trusted, he thought, recalling how reluctant he had been to bring her with him on this journey. If he had not, if he had been sober enough to find a sensible solution to her problems, then in a year or two they would doubtless have met again, both of them married to highly suitable spouses. And then his blood would not be running hot with desire for a woman who was better fit for marriage to some scholar or explorer or eccentric reformer. *And then I might get some sleep at night,* Rhys thought and urged his mount into a gallop.

'I am blissfully sticky and far too full,' Thea remarked, and sucked her fingers in a manner she knew full well was unacceptable in any lady over the age of six. Across the table in the private parlour Rhys gave a slight shudder. It must have been too hoydenish even for his tolerance. Giles, armed with a thick guidebook, had gone out to scout around the sites.

The atmosphere was strained, or perhaps it was simply her own shyness. What did one say the day after the first time one lay with a man? Or did one say nothing until you were in bed again? If that ever happened. She watched Rhys out of the corner of her eye as he sat checking the route map spread out before him and the notebook he had weighted open under the pewter sugar basin. His mouth was closed in an uncompromising line and he had not looked her straight in the eye since they had arrived, dusty and a trifle saddle sore, at the best inn in the centre of Orange.

Thea sat up straight and gave her fingers one last wipe with her handkerchief. She was a grown-up woman who had taken a lover; it was simply a matter of having a frank, adult conversation about who was sleeping where tonight. 'Um...' *Oh, for goodness' sake! That was hardly a sophisticated opening.*

Rhys glanced up, then must have seen something in her face that made him put down his pencil and give her his undivided attention. 'Yes?'

And that was hardly an encouraging response. 'Last night—'

'Thea, you do not need to be in any way concerned that I will take last night as a *carte blanche* to impose on you again.'

'You did not impose,' she protested. 'I asked you.'

'I know, but I mean, in future.' He looked about as eager as a man discussing an invitation to a three-hour poetry reading. 'You were curious and we had behaved in a manner calculated to inflame anyone's passions. I hope that at least it has removed any dread of the act that Meldreth's actions gave you.'

'Of course,' Thea agreed, finding the syllables stuttering on her tongue. 'Certainly it has.' The subtext to his words was clear enough to read. He was her friend so he had not wanted to snub her when she asked, he was concerned that she had been left with a horror of intercourse after Anthony's clumsy wooing and he had been sufficiently aroused by the situation to find it no actual hardship. If Rhys had wanted to make love with her again he would have kissed her the moment they were alone, would have told her—even if it had been a lie—that she had been wonderful last night, would have acted, in other words, like a lover.

'Thank you,' Thea said and rose to her feet. 'I am truly grateful for the care you took of me. No, please don't get up. I must go and ring for a bath or I will ache all over to-morrow!' That was really a very convincing little laugh, she congratulated herself as she left the room. It was strange how tired she felt, but that was due to spending the day in the saddle, no doubt. And she felt queasy. But that was an incautious indulgence in nougat.

Bother the dust, it seemed to have got everywhere, even into her eyes. Thea stopped outside her own bedchamber door and groped for a handkerchief to catch the solitary tear as it began to trickle down her face.

Stop it, she told herself. *You had one night of complete bliss, you slept in his arms, you will remember it always. Now have some pride or he will guess you are within a hair's breadth of going on your knees and begging him to make love to you again.*

Thea scrubbed at her face, forced a cheerful expression onto her face and pushed open the door. 'I absolutely must have a bath, Polly, or I will be as stiff as a board in the morning.'

Chapter Sixteen

At least Giles had not noticed anything amiss, Thea thought as she shaded her eyes against the bright morning sunlight and listened to him expounding on the history of the Arc de Triomphe. Rhys appeared to be genuinely engrossed. *And why should he not be?* she chided herself. *He is an intelligent and cultured man, and to view sites such as this is one of the reasons a gentleman embarks on the Grand Tour.*

'It was built to commemorate the conquest of the Gauls by Julius Caesar,' Giles explained. 'The detail shows his superiority in both land and sea warfare, as you can see from the anchors and ropes here and the prisoners on the other side of the arch.'

Thea told herself to stop moping and take an interest. 'Through here?' She walked into the shade of the massive central arch.

'They are in a state of nature,' Giles called after her. 'You may not wish—'

Having seen Rhys in such a state she was hardly likely to be outraged. 'I am certain the cultural and historical significance outweighs any scruples of that kind,' Thea said, and wondered if she had caught the fleeting glimpse of a smile on Rhys's lips.

She studied the battered carvings with a purely intellectual interest, she assured herself, although it was hard not to reflect how much more beautiful Rhys's body was than anything the sculptor had depicted.

When she strolled back to the other side both he and Giles had pocket sketchbooks in their hands. 'May I see?' *Rhys sketching?* 'But these are very good! I had no idea you could draw.'

'I took it up at Oxford. There was a group of us who were interested. It made a focus for walking holidays. I am competent, that is all. Benton has a much surer touch.'

Giles handed her his book readily. He had obviously studied more than Rhys and the standard was more than amateur, but somehow it seemed academic and lacking in the life that Rhys's rapid sketches held.

'You have a real talent,' she praised.

'Thank you.' Giles smiled diffidently. 'You should join us. We could acquire some watercolours and we could all work together.'

'Me?' Thea laughed. 'I cannot draw, let alone paint in watercolour.'

'You are too modest! I thought all young ladies learned as a matter of course.'

'Thea turned her drawing master grey,' Rhys remarked. 'Our godmother always engaged one for the summer when we stayed with her. He would have a gaggle of intense young ladies around him like a duck with ducklings—and Thea would be out in the middle of the lake in the rowing boat or up a tree or persuading the grooms to let her try out every horse in the stables.'

'You sound disapproving. You always encouraged me at the time.'

'I was no more sensible than you were,' Rhys said with something of a snap. 'Or should I say that boys have no concept of the attributes a young lady needs to acquire to fit herself for her future role in life.'

That was clear enough, Thea thought as she handed his sketchbook back to Giles with a smile that seemed to be frozen on her lips. *I was fun to play with when I was a tomboy—now I am a hoyden, unfit for a respectable marriage.*

'I have saved the best until last,' Giles remarked as he slid the book into the pocket in his coat-tails. 'We have seen the cathedral and the arch, now it is time for the Roman theatre. We must walk back through the old town, but it is not far.'

He offered his arm to Thea, who listened with only half an ear to his explanation that the hill in front of them was the old castle of the princes of Orange. Behind her she was conscious of Rhys's footsteps on the cobbled pathway and imagined his eyes on her back. Imagined his thoughts and, worse, his regrets.

Even so, the sight of the theatre stopped her in her tracks and knocked any other thoughts from her head. Battered red sandstone towered up like a cliff face, pigeons wheeling across its facade from the niches and cracks that studded it.

Giles was talking about the emperor Augustus and ten thousand spectators and something about acoustics, but she was still gawking at it and hardly listened as he led them inside.

'If you climb the steps to the seats at the back, we can

try the sound,' he said with enthusiasm, urging Thea and Rhys forward across the semicircular area. 'Be careful, the stone is very worn.'

'We had better do what our tutor tells us,' Rhys remarked, low voiced. 'Give me your hand—these are very uneven.'

In the heat, neither of them was wearing gloves. *More hoydenish behaviour on my part,* Thea thought bitterly as Rhys's grip tightened and her heart began to pound. The steps between the tiers of stone seats were broken in many places, so they had to climb from seat to seat. After the first few, with Thea grabbing desperately at her skirts to stop them riding up with the height she had to lift her leg, Rhys simply dropped her hand and boosted her from one to the other.

His hands were sure and firm around her waist and he was so close her senses reeled with the scent of hot man. If she closed her eyes, she could imagine herself back in his arms, imagine the musk of their lovemaking.

'I should have insisted we stop so you could have a glass of lemonade before embarking on this,' Rhys remarked. 'And I ought to have warned you to put on sturdier shoes.'

His words were so alien to the remembered sound of his voice, the gasped words of passion, the groan deep in his throat when he thrust deep into her, that Thea opened her eyes, lost for a moment. Below her on the dusty theatre floor was the small figure of Giles, pacing to and fro. The stone tiers of seats fell away like a crumbling mountain slope and above her the swifts dived and screamed in the hot blue sky.

'Steady!' Rhys caught her by the arm as she swayed. 'I thought you were fine with heights.'

'I am.' She shook off his restraining arm. 'I was dizzy for a second, that is all.' She had been remembering passion and intimacy and desire. Rhys had been thinking about lemonade and practicalities.

'We had better sit down, in that case. I will signal to Benton that we are ready for him to begin.'

'What is he going to do? He will have to shout if we are to hear him here.'

'Listen,' Rhys said. 'I have heard of this.'

And then Giles spoke. He was not shouting, or even speaking loudly, she realised, entranced. His voice reached her as clearly as though he was standing just in front of her and speaking conversationally. 'What is he saying?' It was Latin and she could read that a little, but she had never heard it spoken.

'It is from Caesar's *Gallic Wars*,' Rhys said. 'Trust Benton not to spout poetry.'

'The triumphal arch put him in mind of it, I suppose. How intimate it sounds.' How would she feel if it was Rhys down there speaking verse, something romantic? This place was magical—surely he felt it?

Rhys got to his feet and walked off around the arc of the seats, head tilted as he listened. 'Interesting effect. I don't understand the science. I must read up on it.'

Obviously he did *not* feel the romance. Thea slid to the edge of her perch and dropped the few inches to the next seat, sat and repeated the process. It would do her walking dress no good at all, but it was better than having Rhys's hands on her, so practical and impersonal. Touching her, being close to her, did not affect him at all, it seemed. Thank goodness she had said nothing to lead him to think she wanted to resume their intimacy.

'That was fascinating,' Thea said enthusiastically when she reached Giles, who came up the bottom steps to help her. She turned and looked up to where Rhys was silhou-etted against the sky. 'Are you coming down?' she said, half doubting her words would reach him.

He waved, but then sat down and held up his sketchbook. 'We will see you at luncheon?'

Rhys made a gesture that seemed to encompass *perhaps* and *don't wait for me* and *goodbye*.

'What about you?' Thea asked Giles. Really, with the bright smiles and the air of unconcern she was managing to summon, she was missing a promising career on the stage. 'I would like to go and look around the shops this afternoon, but I can take Polly with me. You will want to explore and sketch, I am sure.'

'If you are sure?' Giles offered her his arm and they turned and left Rhys on his lonely eyrie.

'Oh, yes. I saw some delightful printed fabrics and there are lavender oils and soaps.... I will be in terrible trouble with Rhys for buying more things, I have no doubt, but the temptation is too great.' Her laughter would reach him up there, she was certain. He would know she was quite un-concerned.

Thea came down to breakfast the next day to find the two men making somewhat stilted conversation over wide cups of milky coffee. She paused, unseen just before the doorway, and listened.

'But you obviously want to push on to Avignon now and I want to spend some more time sketching here.' That was Giles.

Rhys made a sound that might have been agreement.

'How long do you intend to stay in Avignon?' Giles asked.

'A few days. I want to buy wine to be shipped home, see

the sights, visit the dealers for artwork. Then on to Aix and down to Toulon to take ship around the coast to Genoa. What are your plans?'

He sounded a trifle cool, Thea thought. Had he and Giles somehow fallen out?

'I will spend a few more days here and then go directly to Arles. I intend on making my way to Marseilles and after that I will take ship along the coast to Viareggio and then inland—Lucca, Florence, Rome.'

'You are leaving us?' Thea entered the room and both men rose with a scrape of chair legs on the terracotta tiles. To be alone with Rhys would be blissful, and yet Giles's company had kept her anchored in the real world, a bulwark against losing herself utterly to hopeless dreams.

'I think I must. It has been delightful to journey with you and I am deeply in your debt for rescuing me at the roadside, but we all have our own route to travel now, do we not?'

Was she imagining he put some emphasis on the last, innocuous question? Warning or encouragement, she could not tell. 'We will miss you,' Thea said warmly.

'We will, indeed,' Rhys added, and to her relief he sounded regretful and not as though he was anxious to see the back of Giles.

Polly packed away the lengths of charming printed cloth in rose and gold, green and blue, and found corners for soaps and oils and Rhys had nothing to criticise when the vehicles were loaded and they rode away from the inn.

It had been hard to say goodbye to Giles, although they promised to write. 'Keep faith,' he murmured as he kissed her cheek. 'Hold on to that love.'

Thea turned and waved one last time, and then urged

her horse up to keep pace with Rhys. He was quiet, and she wondered at it. Did he dislike her kissing Giles? Or perhaps he regretted the other man's departure and had valued a buffer between himself and her.

But she could not read his mood and he had very little to say to her at all, beyond perfectly amiable commonplace remarks. 'Are you sure that wide-brimmed hat is sufficient shade from the sun?' he asked as they emerged from the cover of the town walls. 'The sun is getting very hot now and you will complain if your nose becomes pink!'

'Quite sure. And I have taken a leaf out of your book and found a linen jacket to replace the woollen one with my riding habit.' Rhys looked casual, relaxed and altogether edible, Thea thought. His hair was overlong now, for Hodge appeared to have no influence with the scissors. His skin was tanning golden in the sun, unlike poor Giles, who had turned pink and freckled, and he had changed leather breeches and his wool coat for heavy cotton and linen.

There should be a law against men with muscled forearms like that taking off their coats and rolling their sleeves up.

'Very sensible,' he commented on her jacket. 'We have no need to hurry today at all. Avignon is a very short journey, so we can linger over luncheon in the shade or explore anything along the way that takes our interest.'

Thea smiled and agreed and assured herself that this calm friendliness was what was prudent, was what she wanted—and was what she had told Rhys she expected. It was beyond foolish to feel as though she had been spurned, that her heart was breaking, that she was a hundred times unhappier than she had been before, when Rhys was simply a dream she had resigned herself to losing.

* * *

An hour later the sun was bouncing off white limestone, the road was dusty and the air was heavy with the scent of thyme, lavender and a dozen herbs Thea could put no name to. The buzz of the cicadas had gone from strange to irritating to simply part of the atmosphere and everyone had lapsed into a state of relaxation that would have scandalised polite London society.

Rhys had shed his coat and neckcloth and was letting his horse walk a zigzag pattern from one patch of shade to the next. Hodge and Polly had abandoned the inside of the coach and were perched up on the box with Tom, staring round as they fanned themselves with their hats and passed a flask of what Thea hoped was lemonade from one to another. Rhys had sent the chaise with the post boys, impatient with the strange dawdling of the English, on ahead to advise the landlord of their arrival in time for dinner.

Beside them the Rhone wove its slow way in intricate braids separated by sandbanks and islands, some wooded with scrubby trees, others bare. 'Phew.' Thea took off her hat and fanned her flushed face with it. 'That water looks tempting.'

Rhys had turned off the road and was splashing along the shoreline. 'I was thinking that.' He sounded himself again, relaxed and cheerful. 'We need a sheltered branch where there is no current—the main channel is not safe.'

'We are going swimming?' Thea urged her mare down to join Rhys. The horse went down on its haunches as it slid over the low bank of rounded river pebbles, sending driftwood shooting in all directions. 'Wonderful! All we need is one of these side channels where there are some bushes for changing.' Thea craned her neck. 'Look, that's perfect, just ahead. The water is flowing enough to prevent it stagnating, but there are no swirls and currents. You men can go behind those low willows and Polly and I can use these rocks.'

'Men, my lady?' Tom pushed his hat back on his head and scratched his ear. 'I don't rightly hold with getting wet all over. Soaks in, if you ask me. Ain't healthy.'

'Very well, you may water the horses, then sit under a tree in the shade and relax while the rest of us swim.'

'What, like at the seaside, my lady?' Polly sounded shocked, but she looked at the water with longing. 'We haven't got any bathing machines.'

'We don't need them.' Thea kicked her foot free of the stirrup and slid down. 'We go in wearing our shifts and the men—' she stifled a giggle '—the men will wear undergarments.'

Rhys was already out of the saddle. He tossed his reins to the coachman and sat on a boulder to pull off his boots. 'I'll try it first and make certain it is safe.'

He was rolling down his second stocking before Thea realised that Polly was tugging her arm. 'My lady! His lordship is taking his clothes off!'

'Goodness, yes, so he is. Behind the bushes with us, Polly.' She did not even try to pretend to herself that in her mind she was back all those years ago when the children had splashed and tumbled in and out of the lake without a care in their innocent heads except for what would be said about their sodden clothes when they got home for dinner. She had been watching Rhys with a very adult yearning and it would *not* do.

'Quite safe!' he called. 'Sandy bottom, gentle flow. Come

on, Hodge. We'll swim down a bit and leave the ladies some privacy.'

'Ladies,' Polly said with a giggle. 'Fancy his lordship calling me a lady.'

'We're all the same under our clothes,' Thea said, helping Polly with her buttons. *All cats are grey in the dark and one woman between the sheets is much as another, no doubt.* She had tried not to think where Rhys had got his bedroom skills from and now she gave herself a brisk mental shake. 'Just leave your chemise on. They'll dry quickly enough on the bushes afterwards.'

She peeped around the bushes. Two dark wet heads bobbed at the other end of the channel, both tactfully facing downstream. Tom was already asleep, propped under a spreading willow. 'Come on, Polly. Can you swim?'

'No, my lady, but I'll just bob about, like.' They tiptoed into the water. 'It's cold!'

'Better once you are right in.' Thea took a run and ducked under. 'Lovely,' she called as Polly bravely followed suit. Then they were both splashing and laughing and the men turned cautious heads to make certain they were safely immersed.

Don't look, don't imagine. Once they would have been diving, catching each other by the ankle, playing and teasing. But not now. Thea turned onto her back and floated, feeling the sun warm on her front while the water beneath was chilled and refreshing. She closed her eyes, paddled vaguely with her hands to keep station and let her mind go blank.

'Beware, here comes Ophelia,' a voice said by her ear and she sat up with a start, forgot where she was and promptly sank. It was deep here, her feet did not find bottom, but she opened her eyes in the brown gloom and swam confidently upwards. Legs, pale, with paler cotton drawers plastered to them by the current, loomed into sight. They trod water and then there was a convulsion as the man upended and dived down. *Rhys.*

He saw her, reached out, but she made a little gesture of reassurance and broke the surface, spluttering. 'The current is faster than I thought,' she called to the other two, who were gazing tactfully in the other direction.

'Rhys?' She looked around. No sign of him. Thea splashed round in a circle, treading water. *Cramp? A snag of dead branches? Clinging weed?* She was about to dive under when hands took her around the waist, tossed her upwards and she fell back with a great splash and a shriek.

'You wretch,' she spluttered, dragging wet hair out of her face.

'Pax,' Rhys called. He had taken refuge behind Hodge.

'Coward!'

'I know where I am safe.' He was grinning like the boy she remembered from so long ago and her heart contracted with love for him and with nostalgia for a time when all was innocent and uncomplicated.

She realised, with a jolt, that she was happy. Whatever had passed between them, however much she might love him in vain, she and Rhys were back on their old terms of friendship. 'I have a long memory,' Thea threatened, trying hard not to laugh as she swam back to Polly as decorously as she could manage.

'Snails in my slippers?' Rhys called after her.

Thea rolled onto her back and assumed her best society expression and voice. 'You may have reverted to thirteen years of age, Rhys Denham, but I have put no snails in slippers since I was eight.' That reduced even Hodge to hoots of laughter and Rhys... It was clear Rhys attached no importance to their night together.

Chapter Seventeen

It had been almost time for the evening meal when they finally arrived in one of Avignon's smarter hostelries, close by the Porte du Rhone. They'd still been rather damp about the underwear and decidedly relaxed.

'The proprietor obviously thinks the circus has come to town,' Thea remarked as they met in the hallway an hour later. 'Either that or he will expect all English visitors to arrive removing water weed from their hair.'

'The place is like a morgue,' Rhys complained. He had been looking forward to dinner, to enjoying good food and wine while watching Thea laughing. She seemed to have recovered her poise after their reckless interlude, and it was good to have her so comfortable with his company again. He only wished he could put it behind him so easily, but desire was not to be suppressed.

'I was told it was clean and comfortable,' he grumbled now, focusing on that and not on the memory of her slim waist as he had caught her in the water, as near naked in her clinging shift as made no difference. There had been a moment as their eyes had met, the second before she hit the water, when he had imagined he'd seen a yearning as intense as his. *Wishful thinking.*

'It *is* perfectly clean and well appointed,' Thea pointed out.

Rhys felt a perverse desire to disagree. 'I suppose it is a superior establishment, but I do not fancy eating my dinner in a private dining room that looks as though it was decorated for one of the gloomier popes.'

'I was forgetting that the popes were here for some of the Middle Ages.' Thea tucked her hand into his elbow and he had to consciously keep himself from squeezing it against his ribs. 'Were they gloomy?'

'Probably not. There's a very splendid papal palace and acres of vineyards—I would wager they had rather a good time.'

'I wonder what the music is.' Thea went out to the front terrace and Rhys followed her.

'There is a festival, *madame.*' The proprietor came through the doors as she spoke. 'One trusts the noise will not disturb you.'

'It sounds delightful. Will there be food down there?'

The man looked down his nose. 'Rustic fare, *madame.* The eating places of the townspeople, vendors with stalls. Wine sellers.' He made a very Gallic flicking motion of dismissal with his fingertips.

'Sounds excellent,' Rhys said. 'We will eat out. Hodge!'

'My lord?' The valet emerged from the shadows.

'Tell Polly and Tom we're going down to the fair and you can all have the evening off. All right?' He raised an eyebrow at Thea.

'That sounds wonderful. I would like to try the local food.' She adjusted her shawl over her shoulders, took his arm again and made for the steps.

They strolled amidst the old stone buildings, gilded by the setting sun, then wove their way through narrow alleyways and across tiny squares, headed for the music and then followed the smell of roasting meat. The Place du Palais had three great fires that had obviously been nursed since early morning—a whole ox, two sheep and three pigs were turning on spits with waiters hurrying to and fro between them and the tables grouped around to form impromptu eating places.

Other stallholders shouted their wares from boards laden with pies, breads, salads, sweetmeats and fruit. Down the middle of the long open space, dodging the cursing waiters and tripping each other up, a group of men were laying boards over the cobbles.

'A dance floor. What fun.'

'You want to dance?' Rhys asked with a sinking heart. He danced out of duty, because it was expected of a gentleman, and he always felt a fool promenading about, despite being assured by any number of young ladies—with much fluttering of lashes—that he was an excellent dancer.

'I love to dance,' Thea said firmly.

They strolled around the *place* amidst the ladies in their local traditional costume, skirts wide with frothing white petticoats, lace in their headdresses and at cuff and throat, the men with coloured waistcoats and wide sashes. One side was dominated by the Palais des Papes, more a fortress than a religious building, Rhys thought.

'This one,' Thea decided and stopped by a group of tables, each topped with a spotless chequered cloth, some red and white, some blue and white. 'See how busy this is, which should mean it is good. It is not too near the fires and there is a table here with a good view of the dance floor.'

Rhys pulled out chairs, settled Thea at the table and clicked his fingers for the waiter. 'Bring us a good selection of what you would recommend. And as for wine, a Châteauneuf-du-Pape.'

The waiter suggested adding some of the local *crémant*. 'As sparkling as the *demoiselle*'s eyes, *monsieur*,' he said, and hurried off.

'I cannot wait,' Thea said. 'Good food, wine, music, dancing. Bliss. You do dance these days, don't you, Rhys?'

'Not if I can help it, no,' he responded. His mood had soured again with the waiter's mildly flirtatious comment about Thea's eyes. He wanted to be at that little table over there, half-hidden by a drapery of creepers, not here, on display. He wanted to feed her titbits of food, to watch her eyes sparkle with the wine, to hold her hand under the table and steal kisses. And then they would dance, but not in this square under the stars, but in his bed, which was wide and plump with snowy sheets and a goosefeather mattress and the dance would be the ancient pavane of loving…

'Oh. Of course, I expect you do not care for it anymore.'

Her face fell as if he had snubbed her and he supposed he had. How not to hurt her? It was like picking his way across a scatter of broken glass, barefoot with his eyes closed.

'I never did.' Rhys found it impossible to keep the edge out of his voice. 'Serena cared for it, so I danced, that is all.' Now he really had cast a damper over the proceedings. Thea bit her lip, upset, he supposed, that he should mention that name. 'I have little talent for it,' Rhys added, striving for a lighter tone.

The musicians started to group together, fiddle players, drummers, various woodwind players and one with a strange device that they guessed was a hurdy-gurdy. Couples were coming onto the dance floor, girls giggling and pretending reluctance, young men in their best suits, swaggering and showing off, older couples, stocky and more sombrely clad, but moving together with the ease of long acquaintance.

'*Madame?*' A pleasant-faced, stocky young man stopped at the table and bowed. 'You would care to dance? If *monsieur* permits?'

Thea jumped to her feet, took the stranger's hand and left without a glance back at Rhys. He heard her laugh as they took their places in the lines of men and women and say something to the pretty girl on her right. Then the fiddlers stuck a chord and they were off, weaving and spinning, promenading, a human plait.

She turned wrongly, bumped into two other women, righted herself and they laughed good-naturedly, turning her back into the measure. Now the women were waving neckerchiefs over their heads. Thea tugged the lace fichu from her shoulders and used that. She looked beautiful, Rhys thought. Graceful, happy, full of life and enthusiasm, her face transformed with a flush of colour, a wide smile.

When the dance ended, her partner brought her back, bowed and went to the next table in search of another girl. Thea sat down, fanning herself. 'That was such fun!'

Before she could sit down another man approached, bowed. '*Madame? S'il vous plaît?*' He was tall and dark and even Rhys could appreciate that he had looks that would set any woman's heart aflutter.

Thea darted a glance at Rhys. Not asking permission,

that was certain, and yet there had been something in her eyes…. Yearning? For what?

He was still puzzling when she turned to the Frenchman. '*Merci, monsieur.* You do not mind, do you, Rhys?' Without waiting for an answer she took his arm and they went back to the dance floor.

'Mind?' Rhys snarled under his breath. *I'll tear his head off if he so much as puts a finger wrong with her.* He glowered at the colourful scene. The dancers were turning, then the women spun beneath their partners' upheld arms. Thea was smiling up at her Frenchman, chatting despite the speed of the steps.

Rhys splashed out more wine and slid farther down in his chair, the glass cupped in both hands, shoulders hunched. He was perilously close to sulking, he told himself. It was bad enough to do something so juvenile, but worse when he wasn't at all sure what he was sulking about.

Thea returned at last, with a small group of eager young men, all pressing her for a dance. And this time she did not so much as glance in Rhys's direction.

He dumped the glass on the table, levered himself out of the chair and strode over to meet her. 'This dance is mine.'

Thea did not take kindly to being ordered about, he knew that of old, but he was determined to win this. He was not going to watch her laughing up into another man's face, happy and carefree. She was damn well going to suffer trodden toes with him.

'I would love to!' Her smile took his breath and Rhys struggled for some poise as she turned to her followers with a pretty apology in French. 'Thank you,' she murmured as she slid her hand into his. It felt small and delicate. Puzzled, Rhys glanced down at her. This was Thea, with confident, strong, long-fingered hands—what was the matter with him? Her immaculate coiffure was coming loose and tendrils of hair curled and fluttered on her brow, which was slightly damp from her exertions.

Desire burned through him like flames licking along his veins, and yet all he wanted was to hold her and keep that smile on her lips, that sparkle in those hazel eyes. The band struck up a lilting air and couples turned into each other's embrace.

'A waltz,' Thea said. 'How dashing. I do not believe the patronesses of Almack's have presented you as an eligible partner, my lord.'

'I am willing to risk the scandal if you are,' Rhys offered, and gathered her firmly into his arms, all sweet curves overlying a lithe strength that only emphasised her femininity. His bad mood vanished like smoke.

Thea looked up, her face serious. 'We have already risked it. And yet…we dance.' There was no regret in her voice, nor teasing, either. Her eyes were soft and held the smile her lips did not. Rhys moved without conscious thought into the opening steps of the dance, feeling that he had been punched in the gut and had no air in his lungs. Could she mean what he thought she meant?

'I would very much like to be that scandalous again,' he said when he had found his voice. 'But I can well understand if you do not. Forgive me for—'

'Yes,' she said.

'Yes?'

'If you truly want to.' He must have looked incredulous, for she shook her head and smiled, despite the blush that was turning her cheeks rosy. 'I said I had no expectations beyond that one night, and I would hate it if you felt obliged by gentlemanly scruples to return to my bed.'

'Gentlemanly scruples should keep me from it,' Rhys said wryly, knowing that nothing on earth was going to do that now. This was madness, but madness with a term to it. How long before they reached Venice and a return to sanity? Two weeks, perhaps. He wanted to invent diversions, convince himself that reaching Venice should involve going via Rome, Naples, Sicily. But he could not. It was not fair to Thea; it was not fair to himself.

'It will not change anything, will it?' she asked now. 'Our friendship, I mean. I felt I had lost you, these past years.'

'You had,' Rhys confessed. 'I think I had lost myself, too. I should have realised that I did not need to cut off the whole of my past simply to leave behind one part of it. Now we will not lose each other again, whatever befalls us. We will write, often, I hope.'

Thea quirked an eyebrow. 'Until your marriage. I doubt your wife would look kindly on a correspondence with an unmarried female.'

His wife. That theoretical, nebulous lady. Rhys knew he had lost sight even of her outline these past few days. All that remained of her was an arid list of requirements. Arid, but safe. Sensible. He'd think of her again once he had left Venice. 'Yes, of course. But you may be back in London by then. We will meet.'

Thea across a dance floor in the arms of another man. Thea married, perhaps. Thea in another man's bed. Or unmarried, available, but not to him because he had married some near stranger with good bloodlines and a placid temperament.

'The music has stopped.'

'And you may stop laughing at me, you provoking chit.' Around them couples were smiling. Some ladies even appeared to be regarding them with a sentimental sigh. 'For goodness' sake, they look as though I've gone down on one knee in the middle of the dance floor, just because I kept turning for a few bars!'

'About a minute, actually. The French are romantics,' Thea said with an abrupt return to her prosaic tone. 'Come and have your supper. It will get cold.'

Of course Rhys cared for her, Thea thought as she picked up a spoon and delved into the first of the interesting platters before them. And he loved her as a friend and, miraculously, he desired her as a woman. But he did not want *her*, not as a wife, not as a lover for ever. *We will write*, he had said. And when he was married no doubt she would be invited to dinner and to parties at his town house or to stay at the Norfolk estate.

It had been foolish to mention his marriage. What had she expected? That he would drop to one knee, as he had joked just now, and declare that he had been blind, that he had loved her all along and they must marry at once? He was treating her precisely as she had asked. She would be delivered to Godmama, much educated in the sensual arts and with her heart in tatters, for now she knew the adult man as a friend, and a lover and a companion, all day and every day. She would know him as well, if not better, than a wife.

Rhys reached towards the plate of cheese-and-herb pastries. 'Oh, no, you don't, that's the last one.' Thea pounced on the remaining flaky morsel. It melted on her tongue, an instant's pleasure. That was what she must do, live for the instant. Then, when Rhys had left, she would rebuild her life with all the courage she had. *As if he had died.*

They finished the food with sighs of mutual pleasure, then fell silent. Or possibly Rhys was simply distracted by the subtle assaults he was launching on her composure. His arm lay warm across the back of her chair and his thigh touched hers beneath the cover of the cheerful tablecloth. Both limbs were an incitement to lean into their strength; both promised a leashed power that made her shiver with anticipation. From the slight curve of Rhys's lips she knew he could feel that tremor.

'Shall we go?' Rhys stood and Thea looked up at him, tall, dark, broad-shouldered, somehow unmistakably English against the golden stone, lit now by flickering torches. Desire quivered through her as he took her hand and then trapped it hard against his side as she came to her feet. *I will become addicted to him,* Thea thought with a sudden plunge into despair. *I will be like a laudanum user, only half-alive without his touch. If I was strong, I would tell him no. This should end here. But I will not.*

They turned at the mouth of a dark alleyway to look back at the festive scene. 'There are Polly and Hodge, dancing.' Rhys pointed at the two figures, Polly, lively and laughing, and Hodge, upright and respectable as ever, even in the midst of a country dance, a great grin on his face.

'At least they are happy.' She spoke her thought aloud and Rhys looked down at her.

'And you are not? Ah, Thea…' He stepped back into the darkness and pulled her into his arms. 'Tell me what you want.'

Chapter Eighteen

'Tell me what you want.'

This was the moment to be strong and sensible. The moment to tell him it was a mistake, that they should resist this attraction and to leave him quite clear that her actions were simply driven by sexual desire.

But if to love was to be weak, then so be it. She would have to find her strength soon enough, because she would not wallow in despair and loss. After Rhys she would rebuild her life, but she had perhaps two weeks to give him everything but the words.

'I want to be with you. I want to make love with you again. I want to spend the night in your arms.' It felt sinful and wonderful to be like this in the open air, in a dark alley in a foreign city pressed against the aroused body of her lover.

'That seems clear enough.' Rhys's voice rumbled in her ear as she pressed her cheek to his shirtfront. He turned and she was trapped against the wall. 'I tried this in a Paris

alleyway and got threatened with a hatpin for my pains.'
There was laughter in his voice and a husky anticipation
of passion. 'I wanted to kiss you then. What will happen if
I kiss you here?'

'Try.' Thea put her arms around his neck and ran her
fingers into his hair, closed them tight and pulled his head
down.

It must have hurt, but he simply growled, deep in his
throat. 'You want to play rough games, do you?'

She was not certain what he meant, but it sounded...ex-
citing. 'Yes,' she managed to get out before Rhys's mouth
crushed down on hers. He lifted her, his hands spanning her
waist, and raised his leg so she was riding his thigh, her feet
off the ground, her back to the wall, her full weight bearing down on the point where her body ground against his.

Rhys slid one hand between them to cup her breast, his
fingers teasing at the nipple through the fine fabrics until
somehow he freed it from the constriction of her stays.

Thea moaned against his mouth as his tongue plunged
in, filling her with the taste of him. His fingers rolled and
pinched the hard peak past the point of discomfort into a
thrilling, shocking dazzle of excitement that flashed like
lightning to her core. It was uncomfortable, exciting, wild.
The wall was unyielding, his body as hot and as hard as
the stone. She tried to move, to rub against the hard muscle
of his thigh to reach for the pleasure that seemed just out
of reach. She felt full, swollen, wet down there. 'I need...'
she panted.

'Tell me.'

'I need to move.'

'No. I am in control here.' He left her nipple, slid his
hand down, bunched up her skirts and pushed his fingers

between his own leg and the swollen folds that ached for him. 'Is that what you want?'

'Yes. Rhys…please.'

Then he touched her, one long, sliding stroke perfectly placed, and she shattered, sobbing, limp in his arms.

'Can you stand?'

Thea found herself with both feet on the ground, Rhys still holding her pressed between his body and the wall. 'I think so.'

'Good. I cannot see our host approving of me sweeping you through the front door and up the stairs in my arms.' He eased away and took her arm.

'A pity, it would be so romantic.' She sighed with pure contentment, all her dark worries fled. 'The darkness and the starlight. These ancient buildings, the warm air and the scents. The music…'

'Venice will be more so. Gondolas and beautiful palazzos reflected in the canals.'

Venice would be wonderful, and it would be the end. Once she was safe with Godmama, Rhys would leave. There would be no romance in Venice, only safety. Safety from a drab half-life, safety from the pain of being with Rhys. 'I am resolved to enjoy every moment as I live it,' Thea said, pushing the thoughts away. 'Tonight, teach me to make love to you, Rhys. Show me how to give you pleasure.'

'You already do.' His voice was husky.

'You are being careful with me, I know. Show me, Rhys.' She sensed both his arousal and his reluctance to what? Shock her? 'It excites me to think of touching you. I want to drive you wild.'

'Continue talking like that and you will have succeeded. Talking is even more powerful than thinking, sometimes.'

'We're here.' Thea made herself walk sedately up the steps to the front door. *'Bonsoir, monsieur.'* She nodded to the proprietor. 'I'll retire, I think, my lord,' she added to Rhys, 'and leave you to your brandy.'

'Goodnight, Lady Althea.' She heard him talking to the Frenchman, discussing Cognac. When she reached the landing she picked up her skirts and ran to her chamber. There was something she had bought in Orange, just for Rhys, never thinking he would see it.

She had bathed before they went out, so now she threw off her clothes and sponged herself all over with the tepid water on the nightstand, dabbed rosewater behind her ears, between her breasts and behind her knees. The nightgown she had bought slid over her curves like the water of the Rhone had done that afternoon, silky, fluid, semitransparent, honey coloured. Her hands went to the pins holding her hair up and then left them. Rhys liked to take it down; she had learned that already.

What else might he like? She was going to find out and the waiting was killing her. Thea paced back and forth, the new silken gown swishing around her ankles. Would he like it? The *vendeuse* had assured her it would bring any lover to his knees.

The sharp intake of breath behind her was all the warning she had that Rhys was in the room. He closed the door and leaned back against it. 'Is this my birthday?' He fumbled behind him with none of his usual coordination and managed to turn the key in the lock. 'You no longer believe you are plain, do you, Thea?'

'I am not beautiful. Rhys, you do not have to flatter me—it is more than enough that you desire me.'

He pushed away from the door and began to walk towards

her, shedding clothes as he came. Neckcloth, coat and waist-coat fell to the floor. 'No, you aren't beautiful.' He heeled off his shoes. 'You are extraordinary.' He dragged his shirt over his head and dropped it. 'You leave me speechless,' he said as he unfastened his breeches and kicked those and his stockings out of the way.

Thea swallowed at the sight of all that male magnificence right in front of her. 'Your body is communicating quite adequately without words,' she managed. His erection stirred as if it had a life of its own. 'But you had best find the words to tell me what to do.'

'Explore. You have me at your mercy, do what you will.' His eyes were half-shut, his hands fisted at his sides, his chest with its light pelt of dark hair rising and falling with his breathing. 'Men are very visual animals—we are aroused by what we see. And our minds are aroused by what we hear,' he added, his gaze fixed on her lips. 'And what we imagine.'

So much control and so much banked heat. What would happen if she forced him to even exert even greater control? Thea padded forward and threaded her fingers into the hair on his chest. Rhys lifted his hands. 'No, don't touch, leave them by your side. I am exploring.'

To her surprise he obeyed, even when she raked her nails lightly over his nipples and he growled, deep in his throat. A big cat, provoked, she thought, hardly daring to breathe.

She slid her hands down, over the rippling, corded muscles of his stomach, across to his flanks, down his thighs, ignoring the reflexive thrust of his hips that demanded she touch him where he most wanted. 'Lie down on the bed. Face down,' she added and was rewarded by the flare of curiosity in his eyes.

Still in the silken nightgown Thea climbed onto the bed and straddled his thighs. She leaned forward and palmed his buttocks, intrigued by how hard the muscle became as it tightened under her hands. She slid them up, her thumbs following the groove of his spine, stroked them over the scars and healing bruises from the accident. 'Where do you get all this muscle from?' she asked, bending low so her nipples touched his back through the silk.

'Riding, sparring, fencing, swimming.'

'I am taking off the nightgown,' Thea murmured. She stroked it down his back and over his buttocks, and his hands fisted in the thick white cotton of the bedspread. 'Now I am taking out my hairpins and letting down my hair.' She knelt up and bent to sweep it across his shoulders, up and down until he shivered beneath her, muscles bunching with his effort to stay in control.

'What are you doing now?' Rhys rasped when she sat back to recover her breath.

What would drive him wild? Dare she? Thea murmured, 'Touching my breasts.'

Rhys rolled faster than she could react. Thea found herself pinned beneath him, staring up into dark blue eyes burning in a face stark with desire. 'You are more provoking than the most skilled courtesan could ever be. It is all instinct and honesty with you, isn't it? No wiles, just natural, sensual skill.'

'Skill?' she faltered. 'But I don't know what I am doing.'

'You are driving me wild, that is what you are doing.' He caught her wrists and held them one-handed above her head so he could nuzzle her breasts, use teeth and lips and tongue.

'I was…exploring,' Thea gasped, writhing against his hold on her wrists, 'and you stopped me. Next time I will tie your hands to the bed head with my stockings and then I can do what I like.' Rhys went very still. 'Would you dislike that?'

'I have never wanted to lose that much control,' he said slowly and ran his tongue over his bottom lip. 'But perhaps…'

'It excites you.' Thea arched up against the rigid evidence of just how much.

'*You* excite me.' He dipped his head to brush his cheek, rough with the evening regrowth of his beard, over her sensitive nipples. 'You could probably suggest making love in a bath of cold custard and it would be arousing, you witch.'

'I don't think—' Thea broke off, panting, and curled her legs around his hips. 'I don't think they make custard in France.'

'*Crème anglaise.*' Rhys gasped and eased into her on one long stroke, hot and hard and overwhelming.

'Whipped cream,' she murmured against his mouth as she rose to meet him. 'Chocolate sauce…'

'Thea.' Rhys dropped his forehead to hers and held himself still. She could feel his heart hammering. 'If you mention one more sweet, slithery foodstuff or item of underwear or thing to tie me to, then I am going to lose control completely.'

'Warm strawberry jam, corset strings, bed posts,' she whispered as she twisted to curl her tongue into his ear. 'Oh… Rhys!'

An hour later Thea snuggled up against him, sleepy, satiated, warm. Rhys *had* lost control and had been hard, urgent, almost desperate, which was very satisfying. And then, of course, he had to make up for it by making slow, tender, exquisitely careful love to her. It seemed incredible that she could excite him so, could satisfy him. Could even, she thought with a sleepy smile, shock him a little. What would it be like to have that big, beautiful body helpless while she investigated what pleased him?

'I can feel you smiling.'

'I was thinking that if I tied you up I would never dare untie you.'

'I will teach you knots so I can free myself and you can have a head start. Now go to sleep before I give in to the temptation to kiss you all over—and you know where that would lead.'

Three days later the landlord was standing on the steps of the Porte du Rhone, surveying their cavalcade of chaise, coach and two riding horses with the smug air of a man who had just received a substantial payment.

Thea felt subdued, but Rhys seemed even more so. *How strange—we've been so happy here. Perhaps it is simply sadness to be leaving that makes us both so serious.* Rhys said nothing, simply tossed her up into the saddle and mounted himself, but when they had left the city and taken the road south-west towards Aix, she challenged him, 'Why the frown, Rhys?'

'That was an idyll—now we are back to reality.'

And very scratchy and real it felt, too. But what was the matter with Rhys? She was the one who was in love, the one who was fighting the entire time to keep her fears for the future under control. Strangely, they seemed to get worse the farther away from England she travelled.

'If you are going to be so bad-tempered, I could wish Giles back!'

'Regretting you did not accept his offer of marriage?'

'For goodness' sake, Rhys. Of course not. But he is a friend.'

'Rather more, I think.'

'He is a clergyman, even though he does not minister. I found him easy to confide in.'

'What? You confessed all to him, did you? Did he give you penances for your sin of sleeping with me?' He looked like thunder. Sounded like it.

'No! Certainly not. I was able to talk to him about something else that was on my mind, that is all.'

Rhys's saturnine expression deepened. 'Your mysterious love? Is it on your conscience that you make love with me while you have those feelings for another man?'

Thea knew she was blushing; she could feel the heat mount up her throat to her cheeks. What could she say? *You and he are the same man?* 'You are jealous, that is all,' she shot back. If she feigned temper, that would explain her flushed face. The mare she was riding skittered sideways, unnerved by whatever she could feel along the reins.

'Watch your horse,' Rhys snapped. 'Of course I am not jealous. What need have I of jealousy?'

'And what does that mean, pray? That no one would bother with me or that you are such a superior specimen of manhood that you cannot conceive of a female straying from your side? Oh…' She realised what she had said as soon as it escaped her lips. Rhys's face was expressionless, his eyes fixed on the road ahead. Only his horse's sudden toss of the head betrayed that his hands had tightened on the reins.

'I am sorry. I did not think. Serena…' Her voice trailed away as she lost herself in a morass of words, none of which would call back the ones she had spoken.

Rhys dug his heels in and set off down the road at a canter. 'Come,' he tossed back over his shoulder. After half a mile he reined in and waited for her. The following carriages were out of sight. 'Listen to me,' he said without preamble. 'I trust you, Thea. You do not lie, you do not dissemble and you do not flirt. Other men most certainly would want to take my place, but you would not encourage them. That certainty does not mean that I enjoy the thought that you share secrets with another man, however innocently. I am possessive and you will have to accept that.'

'I did not mean to—'

'To allude to Serena. I understand that. When she ran off with Paul I felt betrayed and used. What I did not feel, I realised once I had sobered up, was heartbroken. I did not love Serena. I am not jealous of Paul and I do not think he *took* her from me. I think she was always his and they used the fact I was dazzled by her for their own ends. Is that clear?'

'You did not love her?' Thea realised she was staring blankly at him. 'You never loved her?'

'I thought I did. I was young, idealistic and in lust. If I had been a little wiser in the ways of women, I would have tumbled her in the summerhouse and then, no doubt, the truth would have come out with a slapped face from her and a punch on the nose from Paul. Serena was never going to put herself in a position where she might betray her lover with more than a few sweet words and batted eyelashes in my direction.'

'You think they were lovers?' Thea felt as though the ground had trembled. Rhys had never been truly in love with Serena? 'What happened to them?' No one had spoken of the pair since that day, not in public and not to her. But Rhys would know, surely?

'I have no idea.' He looked out indifferently over the rolling countryside, dotted with olive trees, rising to the blue hills beyond. 'I told you, I did not care.'

'If you had loved her, you would have cared,' Thea murmured, thinking aloud.

'Exactly.' Rhys's sharp ears had picked up her words. 'That is what convinced me I did not. Now, have I shocked you, you little romantic? I know you think I have been nobly bearing a broken heart and an undimmed image of my golden-haired love all these years.'

'But you *do* believe in love.' Desperate to convince him, Thea leaned out of the saddle and put her hand on his arm. 'The very fact you recognised that you did not feel it for Serena proves it. Rhys, don't you see how much happier you would be if you married a woman you loved, rather than settled for a loveless marriage of convenience?'

'Love led Serena and Paul to betray those who loved and trusted them. They could, for all they knew, have broken me. That is an emotion that is selfish, weakening, dangerously sentimental.'

'Sentimental?'

'Serena no doubt told herself that she was making sacrifices for love, that love is too grand a thing to allow considerations of trust and honour and decency to stand in its way.'

'You cannot blame love for that, only the character of the person who loves....' But he had spurred the horse on, leaving her mouthing her beliefs to the hot, scented air. *Oh, Rhys. You let me dream and now you are going to break my heart.*

Chapter Nineteen

Thea cantered after Rhys, but made no attempt to ride through his dust cloud to catch him. Twice she saw him rein in, turn and stand in his stirrups as if to reassure himself that she was still there, then he cantered on.

She had made him *feel*, she realised. For a contained and self-controlled man such as Rhys, that was probably an unforgivable sin. Now she understood why he wanted a marriage with no emotions attached and why the rumours were that he was rake, a man not to be trusted to give anything more of himself than what a mistress might expect. And he had been avoiding the marriageable girls, the ones he would have to choose from sooner or later if he continued in his determination to marry with his head and not his heart.

There will be two of you unhappy, Thea thought when at last she saw his bay gelding tied up in the shade outside a wayside inn. *Why not marry me? At least you can trust me. At least you desire me. At least we are friends.*

She slowed the mare to a walk while she digested that

thought. *Marriage? Don't be a fool. What are you going to do? Propose to him and ruin your friendship for ever?* As she came closer, Rhys got up from a bench under the vine-covered pergola that stretched along the front of the building. He had been slumped, long legs stretched out, hat discarded beside him.

He strolled across to take her reins, the blue eyes half-closed against the sun, that sinful mouth relaxed into a smile of welcome. Thea was not fooled. He helped her down and, as her body slid down the length of his she looked up, trying to read his eyes. They were implacable, closed, private. Friend or no friend, lover or not, she would get no closer. She had dragged secrets from him, feelings that he had never wanted to speak of, and now he was on his guard. Rhys would no more marry a woman who laid open old wounds, as she had done, than he would forgive Serena for her betrayal.

'Wine or lemonade?'

She saw there was a table under the arbour. Pitchers, glasses and dishes of olives were already set on it. 'Lemonade, please.'

'Have we just had our first lovers' tiff?' Rhys enquired as he handed her the glass of cloudy white liquid,

'Rather more than a tiff, I think,' Thea said coolly. She was not sure she was ready to forgive him, although what his crime was, she was not certain. Making him love her? Breaking her heart? He was not responsible for either. Never having loved Serena? There was still a shameful glow of pleasure deep inside at that knowledge. For being so pig-headed over his own happiness? Yes, that was probably it.

'I do not enjoy having the scabs torn off old wounds,' Rhys said. He lifted the wine pitcher, then put it down again and poured himself some lemonade. 'I prefer to let them heal in peace and quiet. Of course, if you want to tell me all about your lost love, then I will let you probe my wounds all you wish.'

'Thank you, no.' Thea put down her glass and ran a finger down the moisture on the outside, chasing droplets until they pooled at the base, staining the table with a dark patch. 'I will put away my scalpel. Truce?'

'Truce.' He lifted her wet fingers and kissed them. 'Here come the carriages.'

They rode slowly through the starkly beautiful countryside all day, amongst fields of lavender and groves of olives, past stone farm buildings that seemed carved from the rock itself, where barking dogs on long chains made their horses shy. The sky was cloudless and eagles soared, their mewing cries plaintive in the hot air.

Aix-en-Provence was, to Thea's eye, more elegant, more formal and more modern than Avignon. It was a university town, Rhys explained as they strolled along the fashionable Cours Mirabelle under spreading plane trees with the splash of fountains all around them.

Thea wore the best of the half-dress gowns she had bought in Paris with a lace scarf from Lyon thrown over her hair. The town felt so elegant that dressing up for it seemed only right, and Rhys, resplendent in black breeches, dark blue swallowtail coat and gleaming white linen, had obviously felt the same.

'Where are we going?'

'To a café called Les Deux Garçons. It was opened just before the Revolution and apparently has managed to survive as the place to see and be seen. I thought we would eat at the hotel, but that you might like some refreshment now.'

He was more formal somehow, as though the wicked lover had become a respectable escort. Thea put aside naughty thoughts of silk stockings and bed heads; one glance at Rhys told her that he was going to want to be in total control of events that night.

He was relaxed, charming and—what was it he had called himself? Possessive, that was it, Thea decided. She was flattered that he appeared to find it necessary to guard her quite so carefully, as though the sight of her might cause a stampede of amorous French admirers. A passing gentleman had only to meet her eye, doff his hat and then glance at her companion to hurry on.

'Is there some signal between men that I cannot read?' she asked him, a silver spoon loaded with a luscious confection of cream, fruit and fragile pastry halfway to her lips. 'You have just routed those young gentlemen with one look.'

'Students.' He caught her eye and smiled. 'I told you, I am possessive.'

'But how do you do it?' Thea persisted. Rhys looked at her, all the amusement gone from his face as he lifted one eyebrow fractionally. Thea's pulse leapt. 'Goodness! I can almost hear the clash of antlers.'

'You compare me with a rutting stag, do you?'

'Mmm.' Thea licked the cream from the spoon very slowly, her eyes locked with Rhys's. 'Are we very far from the hotel? We walked around in a circle, I think.'

'Ready for dinner already, despite that confection?' He glanced at her lips. 'You have a tiny smear of cream, just there.' He brushed it with his finger and then licked the tip.

'No, I don't want dinner. I want you.'

The blue fire flared in his eyes. 'I keep thinking you cannot arouse me any more than you do, Thea, and then I find I am wrong.' He gestured for the waiter. 'But how do you intend to distract your maid from the fact that there is a man in your bed?'

'By having the foresight to tell her that I would not need her until I finally retired for the night and suggesting that she and Hodge go and explore the town and have their evening meal out.' Thea gathered her shawl and reticule and stood up. 'I gave her the money to pay for it. She was delighted.'

'And you are smug.' Rhys dropped a kiss on the end of her nose. 'Excellent.'

Nothing was said, and yet the pace of the journey had slowed. Thea knew that Rhys had intended, that night in Avignon, to be in Venice within the fortnight. Now it had taken them a week to reach Toulon, three days to find a boat that he was prepared to accept, then another week around the coast to Genoa. Rhys had found something to explore at every cove, every village, every little port.

'It is as if time has stood still.' Thea leaned on the ship's rail and watched the scattered lights twinkling like stars along the darkening coastline. Out in the bay the sea was studded with bobbing lights: the fishing boats were at work. 'Where are we?'

'Italian coast somewhere,' Rhys said vaguely. He dipped his head and nuzzled beneath her ear. 'Genoa tomorrow, impatient one.'

'I am not impatient.' She shifted to give him better access. 'Not to arrive, anyway.' This was like a honeymoon, a romantic, sensual, idyllic journey, first through beautiful countryside, now on a placid, gentle sea, every day sunlit with the coast slipping past, every bay and headland a new kingdom to explore.

Thea had given up caring that Polly and Hodge knew that she and Rhys were lovers, just as she closed her mind to the fact that the maid and valet were, too, despite Polly's stated resolve not to give him more than a kiss. They were all adults—besides, she was certain the two would marry just as soon as they arrived somewhere with an Anglican clergyman.

Her mind, distracted by Rhys's mouth on her skin, drifted back to where that chain of thoughts had begun. Honeymoons ended in a married life together—this one would end in separation. A phrase came to her. Was it a song or a poem?

'Rhys, where does the line, "Journeys end in lovers' meeting", come from?'

'What made you think of that? It's Shakespeare. The clown sings it in *Twelfth Night*.' He hummed a few notes. 'We performed it at Eton. Let me see if I can recall it.' When he sang his voice was a rich, clear tenor. Thea realised she hadn't heard him sing since he had been a youth.

"Trip no further, pretty sweeting,
Journeys end in lovers' meeting—
Every wise man's son doth know.
What is love? 'Tis not hereafter;
Present mirth hath present laughter;
What's to come is still unsure:
In delay there lies no plenty,—
Then come kiss me, Sweet-and-twenty,
Youth's a stuff will not endure."

'Then come kiss me,' he repeated. 'Kiss me, sweeting.'

What is love? The words echoed in her head as she went into his arms. *'Tis not hereafter.* It would last, this loving, only until Venice. That was why Rhys was dragging out the journey, because he was already anticipating its end. She might daydream—his mind was quite clear.

'There it is—Venice. Magical,' Rhys murmured. A heat haze hung over the lagoon, blurring sea and sky, water and mud bank. In the distance, the mirage of the city shimmered, floating.

The small boat that they had taken from the coast skimmed over the water, the men bent to the oars, their efforts scarcely seeming to move them over the vast liquid expanse.

The carriages had been left on the mainland, with Tom to guard them. He was happily ensconced in an inn run by a buxom widow and appeared to be making considerable headway with her, despite not having a word of Italian.

Rhys spread a map of Venice open on his knee and glanced from it to the vista in front of them while the skipper of the boat traced the route with his stubby brown finger.

Godmama had taken a palazzo on one of the canals off the Grand Canal. It sounded impossibly romantic to Thea, who sat, her fingers entwined with Rhys's, and watched the fairy-tale city that marked the end of her fairy-tale journey come slowly closer.

It was all a dream, she thought now. She had a fever, or perhaps had simply not woken up, because this could not be real, could not be the end. Last night Rhys had made love to her with the tenderness of a man parting from his lover for ever. She imagined that a man going out to die in a duel at dawn or setting out on a voyage to the distant Arctic, expecting never to return, might make love like that, as though he was creating a memory almost too fragile to hold. Then, without a word, he had left her and gone back to his own room, something he had not done since Aix, and she had finally allowed herself to weep, silently, into her pillow.

Now the water traffic got busier, the buildings began to loom out of the haze, exotic, like the work of a confectioner spinning architecture out of sugar. Rhys pointed out the Doge's Palace, the massive church of San Giorgio Maggiore, the pillars marking the waterfront of St Mark's Square, but all she could do was stare, unable to focus on one thing out of the shifting scene.

'Santa Maria della Salute,' the boatman said, and they skimmed into a wide canal. Thea unlaced her fingers from Rhys's and stiffened her spine. They had arrived. She was awake, this was real.

'This is the Grand Canal.' Rhys shifted the map on his knee to align it. 'We are almost there.'

Every building lining the canal looked like a palace to Thea. Their walls rose straight from the green water. Gondolas were moored in front of landing stages, small boats laden with everything from barrels to a vast load of hay criss-crossed their path. 'It sounds so different,' she said. 'No carriages, no horses, just people and the lapping of the water.'

'It smells different, too,' Rhys remarked. 'Of the sea and old stone.'

The boat made a sweeping turn into a smaller canal. Walls rose on either side, above them were balconies, now and again stone landing stages jutted into the water, all with their striped mooring poles. *'Ecco, Ca' Riccardo,'* the boatman announced, and brought their vessel alongside a wide platform. In the wall were double-ironwork gates with a courtyard behind them. The boat with Polly and Hodge and more of the luggage came in behind them as Thea schooled her face to show nothing but pleasure. Of course, she wanted to see Godmama again and of course she wanted to be in Venice. Pride kept her from showing any of the other feelings that left her mind dazed with unhappiness and her stomach tense with expected pain.

Hodge pulled the heavy iron ring that hung by the grill. Faintly they heard a bell, then several pairs of feet on stone steps. The grill was thrown open by two liveried footmen, and an imposing, gaunt figure stood in the opening. 'Lady Althea, Lord Palgrave. Welcome to Venice.' He bowed.

'Edgerton!' Rhys ignored the man's bow and shook him vigorously by the hand. 'Good to see you after so many years. I had no idea you had travelled with Lady Hughson. My letter from Paris to say we were on our way has arrived, judging by your lack of surprise.'

It would take more than the unexpected arrival of a few travellers on his damp threshold to surprise Godmama's secretary, Thea thought with a smile.

'Indeed, yes, Lord Palgrave. Allow me to bring you inside.'

They followed him across the courtyard, which Thea supposed served to keep the living rooms well clear of the water in times of flood, up a wide flight of steps and in through imposing wooden doors. It was a palace, she thought, staring around her at the painted, arched ceiling, the high walls, the expanse of inlaid marble floor. Empty, cool, very quiet.

'The salon,' Edgerton said, throwing open yet another set of double doors and ushering them into a lofty chamber with pillared walls, gilded carving and high arched windows, swagged with yard upon yard of crimson brocade. 'I will send for refreshments, but first, I regret, there is a slight problem.'

'A problem you cannot deal with, Edgerton?' As Thea sat down on one of the long sofas, Rhys went to the window and gazed out. 'You surprise me.'

'You are kind enough to say so, my lord. However, this is not a situation I am able to remedy. Your letter arrived and, as her ladyship's secretary, I naturally opened it. Unfortunately, she had left the week before.'

'Left?' Thea stared at him. Of all the things that could go wrong with her plan, it had never occurred to her for a moment that she would not find Godmama here. 'Surely not to go back to England, not if you are still here?'

'Lady Hughson is at present travelling on board the private yacht of Prince Frederico d'Averna.'

'A prince?' Thea said, visions of the Prince Regent swirling through her head.

'Of a very minor principality,' Edgerton said with a faint smile. 'A most amiable gentleman, with a most handsome yacht.'

'It could be an eighty-four-gun ship of the line, for all I care,' Rhys said, stalking away from the window. 'When is she due back?'

'I regret to say that I have no information on that. It could be another month. Or longer. His Royal Highness had the intention of showing her ladyship the island of Sicily, but if the weather remains clement they may well continue around the coast to the Bay of Naples.'

'On board a yacht with a prince,' Thea said faintly. 'That sounds so unlike Godmama.'

'Indeed, Lady Althea.' Edgerton's voice was so dry it would have been used for toast.

'You do not approve of him?'

'I believe he is who he says he is—the introductions were beyond reproach. The vessel is lavishly equipped and appears perfectly seaworthy and well crewed. I have been unable to find anything to the prince's detriment, despite exhaustive enquiries.'

'On whose behalf?' Rhys asked.

'Mine, my lord. I would not countenance Lady Hughson placing herself in such a position with anyone who was not of the utmost respectability.'

'You intrigue me,' Rhys remarked. 'What would you have done if you had found something to his detriment and Lady Hughson did not agree with you?'

'I would have contrived to have the prince removed from her ladyship's orbit,' the secretary said. 'This is Venice after all.'

Thea decided she did not want to know whether the secretary meant murder, kidnapping or, more probably, a nighttime visit from a group of gentlemen with strong persuasive powers.

'How very Gothic of you,' Rhys drawled.

Thea smiled, then realised she was on the verge of bursting out into relieved laughter. No Godmama meant that their idyll was not at an end. She was sorry that Godmama was not there, of course; she loved her and wanted to see her again, but it sounded as though she was having a wonderful adventure of her own.

Then she caught the edge in Rhys's voice and turned to look at him. Whatever he was feeling was not inspiring him to laughter. 'This is a pretty coil,' he said, his mouth a hard line. 'Now what the devil am I going to do with you?'

Chapter Twenty

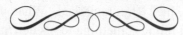

Thea stared back at him. *'Do with me?* Why, nothing, my lord!'

Now what the blazes is she annoyed about? Rhys suppressed an exasperated sigh. It was he who was responsible for her, he who would have to sort out this mess.

'I can remain here until Godmama returns, can I not, Mr Edgerton?'

'Certainly, Lady Althea. There is a most respectable widow living nearby who has become quite a friend of her ladyship's. I am sure she would be delighted to move here and chaperon you if I were to explain the situation.'

'What situation?' Rhys demanded. One word out of Edgerton that implied that he knew Rhys was anything other than Thea's courier and he would be retrieving his teeth from his gullet.

'That her escort has had to leave Lady Althea here without a female companion,' the secretary rejoined smoothly.

'There is no need for the *contessa* to know that Lady Althea has not travelled with an older woman at her side.'

Rhys felt the flare of temper subside. He knew perfectly well what the matter with him was. Since he had left Thea's bed last night, his conscience, subjected to a thorough dose of reality with the prospect of the end of their journey, was giving him hell.

'That would seem to be the best solution. Thank you, Edgerton.' He raked his hand through his hair and tried to think like a responsible friend and not a frustrated lover. 'I had best remove myself and find some other lodgings. What would you suggest?'

'Oh, no,' Thea protested before the secretary could speak. 'That is unfair. Why not stay here? Your obliging *contessa* does not need to know when we arrived, does she, Mr Edgerton?'

'No, indeed, Lady Althea. And it is normal for ladies to go around the city masked, so you may see the sights *incognita* until Lord Palgrave leaves Venice. And, as you say, her ladyship would wish you both to stay here.'

'You see, Rhys! You would be so much more comfortable here, and I know Godmama would expect it.' To Edgerton Thea's face would reveal nothing more than a concern that her travelling companion was not inconvenienced, but Rhys read a plea and a promise that she put into careful words a moment later. 'I am sure there is a room for you where you will be…undisturbed.'

That was a promise not to come to his chamber at night. Thea was a woman of her word: their liaison had been for the duration of the journey and she was not expecting him to put any greater strain on his conscience by making love to her in their godmother's home. After all, last night she had done nothing to keep him at her side, had said nothing when he had left her bed.

The problem was, it was not his uneasy conscience that was giving him most pain, despite it reminding him constantly that he should never have slept with Thea, that having done so, he should never have continued and, having continued, he should do what society would consider the only right thing: marry her. The real problem was that the thought of parting from her was agony, yet it was obvious that, as good as her word, she did not want this liaison to last. And he...he did not know what he wanted.

But he was a man, not a boy to throw a tantrum over the loss of something precious. Thea had just made it clear that she expected their liaison to end but that she still wanted his company. He owed it to her to give her what she wanted.

Rhys looked reluctant to stay. Perhaps she needed to speak to him alone and assure him she had no intention of making demands on him. Absently Thea rubbed the small of her back, where a dull ache was worsening. It would be good to retire to bed and not be travelling, just at the moment. She supposed she ought to be relieved that her courses had begun that morning, but, somehow, she felt nothing of the kind. Perhaps, deep down, she simply had not been worrying because she trusted Rhys so much.

'I am rather tired,' she said. 'Perhaps you could show me to my room and send my woman to me, Mr Edgerton. I will rest until dinner.'

Rhys came to her side as she followed the secretary out. 'You look a trifle pale. Are you unwell?'

'Goodness, no. I suppose it is journey's end—I will be

much better for a few hours with my feet up and nothing rocking, jolting or shying under me!'

'We need to talk, Thea.'

'No.' She stopped and gave them a little space as Mr Edgerton walked on ahead. 'There is nothing to talk about, not in the way I think you mean, Rhys. Nothing to warrant that serious face, at least.' She smiled up at him, loving the way he worried about her. 'And we cannot talk now, in any case. I will see you at dinner.'

Polly was waiting for her in what proved to be not just a bedchamber, but a suite of rooms. 'There's the bedroom and a dressing room and a room for me and a sitting room, my lady,' she reported. 'Lovely, it is. But you come and take your gown off, and those stays, and lie down and rest. This is no time of the month to be travelling, that's for sure.' She fussed around and then, as she helped Thea into her wrapper, remarked, 'At least it means there's nothing to worry about, if you know what I mean.'

'I never thought there was.' Rhys had been very careful, Thea knew, although she supposed nothing was foolproof. Then something in Polly's tone made her look at the maid's face as she moved about the room tidying up. 'Polly... Do *you* have something to worry about? Come and talk to me.'

'Might have.' The maid put down the gown she had been shaking out and sat on the end of the bed. 'Not sure. But John will marry me anyway. He's asked me.' She fiddled with the tassel on the edge of the bed hangings.

'Before you told him there might be a baby on the way?'

'Oh, yes, my lady. I'd have married him whether I thought he was doing it out of love or duty, but I'm glad he asked before he knew. We women don't have much choice, do we?'

'No, not unless we do not mind a scandal,' Thea said, thinking of Serena. 'Has Hodge said anything to Lord Palgrave yet, do you know? After all, he employs you both. I am delighted for you, but he might think differently.' She would have something to say to Rhys if he did.

'He'll ask him today. There's sure to be an Anglican clergyman in Venice, John says, with all the English visitors.'

'Excellent,' Thea murmured, snuggling down. 'I am sure it will all work out happily.' Which was more than could be said for her entanglement with Rhys.

Thea insisted that Mr Edgerton join them for dinner. He was a professional man, after all, not a servant. The meal was excellent, with a wide range of seafood, and, with her backache subdued to a dull twinge, she was feeling considerably more cheerful.

Rhys, she suspected, was not. Despite conversing with apparent ease on a wide range of subjects, he was drinking more wine than he normally did and was picking at a superb dish of clams in cream sauce as though it was gruel.

Men always complained that women were complicated creatures, Thea mused as she speared the last prawn on her plate. In fact, she was certain that men were far more troublesome with their infuriating reticence about their true feelings.

'If you would like to go out this evening, I will put one of our gondolas at your disposal with a reliable man who speaks some English. And I will find you masks, of course,' Mr Edgerton said.

'For both of us?' Rhys queried.

'It is usual for gentlemen who wish to be discreet. It raises no curiosity, as it might in England.'

'Then I will take you up on the offer of both boat and mask. Thea?'

'I will come, too,' Thea said, reflecting that a mask would probably suit Rhys if he was in one of his enigmatic moods. He looked as though he was about to speak, but she put her hand on his wrist. 'I am feeling quite rested now.' Under her light touch she felt him tense, then he slid his hand away. No doubt she was being a trifle indiscreet in front of the secretary, but still, the subtle rejection stung. Before they had become lovers he would have accepted that passing touch without question, as from a friend. Now she was beginning to wonder what she was to him.

'I will tell the boatman to take you for a tour of the main landmarks to start with,' Edgerton said as the footman brought in a dish of sweetmeats. Thea was itching to ask him about Godmama and the prince, but she knew perfectly well that he was far too discreet.

She popped a marchpane-stuffed date into her mouth, resisted the temptation to demolish the whole plateful and stood up. 'I will go and find my cloak and change into some more suitable shoes—I noticed the gondolas that we passed all had some water in the bottom. I'll meet you on the landing stage, Rhys.'

It would be good to have a few moments to think about what she was going to say to him, Thea thought as she hurried along the corridor. She should reassure him that there was no chance that she was with child, which was embarrassing, although considering how intimate they had been, that seemed irrational. And then she must assure him that she expected nothing from him now other than his continuing friendship, which was going to be...tricky. It would be all too easy to protest too much, she suspected, trying out suitable phrases in her head as she went down the stairs to the entrance courtyard.

It was deserted, filled only with the sound of water lapping outside and the scent of jasmine from a tub by the ancient wellhead. The surface of the canal, lit by torchères on the landing stage, was reflected back on the vaulted roof of the internal colonnade, a shifting pattern of ripples that was almost hypnotic.

These past weeks have been very special, but it is as well we have... You know how much I... Rhys, we have always been such good friends, I hope we can continue...

There was the sound of voices from the canal, the slapping of the water became louder and a series of bumps heralded the arrival of a gondola at the landing stage. Thea drew back into the shadows under the stairs. Without a mask she felt vulnerable, and there was no telling who the visitors might be.

There was a low-voiced argument going on and she thought it was in English, but she could not make out any words. A man and a woman, by the sound of it. Through the grill she could make out figures, both cloaked. One of them tugged on the bell pull and almost immediately there was the sound of feet running down the stairs above her head. One of the footmen opened the gate.

'*Madonna* is not at home,' he said in heavily accented English before the visitors could speak.

'Damn it, she must receive us!' English, educated and strangely familiar.

There was a scuffle and the footman was forced back a pace. The visitors stepped through the grill and into the pool of light cast by one of the torchères as someone else came down the stairs.

'Now look here, Edgerton, just go upstairs and tell our godmother that we are here, will you? This nonsense about her not being at home—'

But I know that voice....

'Is the truth. Lady Hughson is not in Venice at the moment and is unlikely to return for some weeks.'

'In that case, we'll stay. Don't tell me you haven't room in this barn of a place.'

'Mr Weston, Lady Serena, I have no instructions to receive or accommodate you.'

Thea sat down on the edge of the well, heedless of moss and ferns, and held on to the iron bucket winch for support as the torch-lit scene shifted and blurred in front of her. Paul Weston, Rhys's once best friend, and Serena, his fiancée who had jilted him at the altar.

She was hardly aware of a soft tread on the stairs, of the brush of a cloak as a tall figure passed her, until another man loomed up in silhouette beside the secretary. *Rhys.* Serena gave a little scream and clutched at Paul. Thea got to her feet, knowing even as she moved it was too late.

Rhys stepped forward, flicked one edge of his cloak over his shoulder, clenched his right fist and drove it straight into the other man's jaw. Paul reeled backwards, made a futile grab for the iron grill, slipped and fell into the canal with a splash that echoed round the courtyard. Serena shrieked and fainted into Edgerton's arms, the footman stood with his mouth open, gaping, and Rhys turned on his heel and stalked back towards the stairs.

As a boy Paul Weston had never learned to swim. Thea knew that. So did Rhys. She only hoped he had forgotten that in the heat of the moment and had not intended murder. The gondola that had delivered the couple had gone, she realised as she slid to a halt on the landing stage. In the water Paul was floundering, sinking. She yanked a boat-hook from the wall and held it out to him. He grabbed for it, missed and sank.

'Rhys Denham!' she shouted without turning. 'Come back here or I am going to have to go in and get him myself!'

For a moment she thought Rhys had not heard her, or did not believe her, or simply did not care. Then he was at her side, shedding coat and cloak, kicking off his shoes. He hit the dark water in a shallow dive and surfaced with his arms full of struggling man.

'Keep still, you fool, or I'll hit you again.' He hauled Paul to the edge of the landing stage as Thea pushed the footman forward to help.

'Give her to me,' she told Edgerton, who was still clutching Serena. 'It is a faint at worst, play-acting at best. Help Rhys.' She pulled the other woman into her arms. Serena gave a faint moan. 'Stop that. Go and sit on the steps or I'll drop you,' Thea warned.

Serena shot her a look of deep reproach and staggered to the steps. 'Althea? Oh, how could you be so unfeeling?'

'Very easily,' Thea snapped. Paul was out of the water, gasping in a puddle like a landed fish. Rhys levered himself out with a strength that she spared a fleeting moment to admire, and sat in his own small lake, coughing.

'Go and get blankets and brandy.' She tugged at the footman's arm. 'Tell the kitchen to heat hot water for baths. Hurry.'

When she knelt beside Rhys he shook himself like a dog and spat into the canal. 'Sorry, but that is the filthiest thing

I have ever tasted. If we don't come down with dysentery, I'll be amazed.'

Servants began to run downstairs, flapping blankets, supporting the men and Serena up to the main floor. In the end they all found themselves in the main salon. Rhys and Paul dripped on the marble floor and tossed back brandy, Serena lay on a sofa, moaning, and was comprehensively ignored and Thea and Edgerton were left to organise baths, dry clothes and a room for Paul and Serena.

'I do not like to have them under this roof,' Edgerton said when they found themselves outside the salon for a moment. 'Lady Hughson has no idea they are here and they have sponged enough on her goodwill and purse, in my opinion.'

'She has been supporting them? For how long?' Thea gestured a maid with armfuls of linens into a bedchamber as far as possible from Rhys's.

'Since virtually the time they eloped. If it was not for her, they would be in debtors' prison, I have no doubt,' Edgerton said, the set of his mouth showing clearly what he thought of the matter.

'I find it hard to believe,' Thea murmured. 'They betrayed Rhys….'

'Does it seem to you that Lady Hughson added to that betrayal by helping them afterwards? She told me that if Lord Palgrave loved Lady Serena he would not want her destitute, whatever happened and, besides, she had sworn to care for all her godchildren. In a way, I think she felt guilty that she had not realised what was going on and that she had not been a better influence on Lady Serena.'

'I doubt anything, short of a miracle, would have changed Serena.' She stopped a hurrying maid. 'Are the baths ready? *Il bagno?*'

'*Si, madonna.*'

Thea mentally rolled up her sleeves and went back into the salon. 'Gentlemen, your baths are ready. Rhys, I have told the footman to take some clothes from your room for Paul. Mr Edgerton's would be too small. Serena, I suggest you go and lie down.' For a moment she wondered if her cavalier disposal of Rhys's wardrobe to the other man would be the final straw, but he put down his brandy glass and stalked out with a nod of acknowledgement in her direction.

'I will order refreshments for an hour's time,' Edgerton said. 'I doubt anyone wants to go out tonight.'

Chapter Twenty-One

Thea surveyed the salon and wondered if social situations ever got much trickier. Mr Edgerton had tactfully removed himself, leaving one earl; two earls' daughters, one of whom had jilted the said earl and the other who had been his mistress; and a gentleman who had wronged the earl, created a scandal and whom the earl had just punched on the jaw. *Fortunately, this is not an English drawing room,* she thought, suppressing an hysterical giggle, or someone would start discussing the weather or worrying about the seating plan for dinner.

As it was, she had the tea urn by her side and an array of tea cups before her, and that was English and unreal enough, under the circumstances.

'A cup of tea, Serena?'

'How could you?' the other woman said with a shudder from the corner of the sofa where she was draped like a tragic Muse.

'Very easily. I am positively parched after all that excitement.' Thea poured herself a cup. 'I could order you coffee, if you prefer?'

'You were always so prosaic.' Serena turned her gaze from a moody examination of the darkening bruise on Paul's jaw and stared at Thea through narrowed eyes. 'But you've changed. What have you done?'

'Grown up?' Thea suggested sweetly. 'I am several years younger than you, don't forget, Serena.' It was unworthy, but she could not resist the barb. Serena's hair was still as blonde, her big eyes still as blue, but there were faint lines at the corners and more pronounced ones from her nose to the corner of her lips. She must have spent too much time with an expression of dissatisfaction.

'Rhys? Paul? Tea?' Neither man had spoken to the other since Rhys had hauled Paul out of the canal.

'Thank you, no.' Rhys went to the decanters, poured two brandies and offered one silently to the other man. After a moment's hesitation, Paul took it. 'You will not stay here beyond tonight,' Rhys said, resuming his place before the empty hearth. 'In Godmama's absence Mr Edgerton controls this household, and he does not welcome you here.'

'Can you not forgive me?' Serena demanded. 'I know I broke your heart—'

'No,' Rhys said, his voice flat. 'You broke your parents' hearts, you dealt my self-esteem a severe and probably very healthy blow and you caused great embarrassment and distress to a number of people. But if you have spent these past years imagining me pining away for love of you, Serena, you are much mistaken. I was infatuated and dazzled, yes. In love, no.'

She gaped at him. Thea, in a muddle of confused emotions, knew she was probably gaping, too. Somehow she had never quite believed that he had not loved Serena, but there was no mistaking the stark truth of what he was saying now.

'Then why the hell did you damn near drown me?' Paul Weston demanded.

Rhys looked him up and down. 'For betraying my trust, for lying to a friend, for distressing all our families. How is that for a start? There was no need for any of that drama. If you had been man enough to tell me that you loved Serena—and if she had not enjoyed being courted by two men quite so much—then I would have helped you, somehow.'

'But we didn't want to hurt you,' Serena wailed.

Thea wanted to leave, to get away from Rhys's brutal frankness on one side and Serena's dramatics on the other, but this was too much. *'Hurt him?'* she demanded. 'You mean you didn't want to face up to what you had done. You had no concerns about hurting *anyone*, just as long as you were not around to bear the consequences. Paul was weak and deceitful and a bad friend, but you were selfish and heedless. Did you not realise that if Rhys had come after you he could have killed Paul? He is a better shot and better swordsman.'

'What stopped you?' Paul was white-faced, the bruise still red and stark. With his blond hair and dark eyes Thea had always thought him the more conventionally good-looking, but now, comparing the two as grown men, she saw the weakness in his face and the signs of self-indulgence around his waistline and jowls.

'Thea stopped me.' Rhys did not look at her as he spoke.

'I have had more than enough of this.' Thea got to her feet. 'It was bad enough at the time without raking over the cold ashes of it now. I do not feel well and I am going to my bed.' It was true enough. Her stomach was cramping, her back was aching and all she wanted was to lie down.

Thea looked white and drawn and as though she was in pain. Rhys wondered whether he should go after her or whether it was best to leave her to Polly. She'd probably had more than enough of his company today.

'Of course! How silly of me never to have suspected it,' Serena said, her eyes bright and full of delighted speculation. 'Thea was in love with you all along, the secretive little cat! She stopped you coming after me because she wanted you for herself. And she is in love with you still—I could see it in her face. The maid said you aren't married, but you've been travelling together. Lord, who is the one making a scandal now?'

Even as he controlled his expression Rhys knew he could not stop the blood draining from his face. He could feel the cold, tight sensation over his cheekbones.

'Don't be ridiculous, she was sixteen, Serena. Hardly a *femme fatale* plotting to ensnare a man. Thea is my friend and always has been, although I realise that friendship between a man and a woman is a difficult concept for you to grasp. I have escorted her here to Godmama because she had left home after a falling-out with her father—that is the scandal if you are so avid for one.'

'And she was as plain a child as you could come across, and a tomboy to boot, Serena,' Paul chipped in, almost earning himself another thump on the jaw.

'Well, she isn't plain now,' Serena snapped. 'She's not a beauty, but she's got style.'

'What does it matter to you whether she's an Incomparable or bracket faced?' Rhys demanded, desperate to get

Serena's, and his own thoughts, off the subject. 'Now, where are you two living?'

'Oh, horrible lodgings,' Serena began. 'So damp and—'

'They aren't that bad,' Paul put in. 'Just rather simple. And the rent's due,' he added.

'What have you been living on?' *Other than Godmama?*

'My father pays my allowance on condition we don't go back to England. I play cards a bit. I've acted as courier for English tourists now and again.' Paul shrugged and glanced down at Serena. 'We get by, don't we, my love?'

Her lush, lovely mouth trembled and Rhys was reminded, painfully, of how much he had once desired her. He expected her to make some complaint, but she looked up at Paul and held out her hand to him. 'Yes, we get by.' She shot a resentful glance at Rhys. 'It is called love.'

She really does *love him,* he thought. *They have been together for six years and it cannot have been easy and yet somehow they are still together.* Paul had acted like a dishonourable idiot, but he was not unintelligent. He would have come to his senses soon enough if he had simply been infatuated as Rhys had been. Was Thea right? Was love a real, lasting emotion that could form the basis of a happy marriage under even these circumstances?

'You'd better go to your room,' Rhys said abruptly. He followed them out and went, without a word, to his own room, unlocked his writing case and drew out a *rouleau* of guineas. He was probably an idiot, but forgiveness was supposed to be a virtue, wasn't it?

Before he could change his mind he went back to their room, knocked and when Paul opened the door thrust the money into his hand. 'Call it a wedding present.'

He felt better for doing it, he realised when he got back to his room, his fingers sore from Paul's heartfelt handshake on top of the effects of that knuckle-grazing punch. It was like drawing a line under the whole damn mess.

But Thea... Could Serena possibly be right? Could Thea have been in love with him ever since she was sixteen? Hodge stood patiently and Rhys gave himself a mental shake, pulled the pin out of his neckcloth and began to undress.

His own voice seemed to echo in his head from weeks ago, as the chaise had rattled towards Dover. *Did he break your heart?*

And Thea had smiled and said, *Not deliberately. He had no idea of my feelings, you see, and besides, he was in love with someone else.*

Surely not. His fingers slowed on his waistcoat buttons. Thea was not a good actress, but she had wanted to be his lover. Would she have given herself to him if she loved another man? But then she had appeared quite calm about the end of the *affaire*, so...

'My lord.'

'Hmm? Sorry, Hodge, I was woolgathering. You're no doubt anxious to be off to your bed.'

To his amazement the valet blushed. 'Er, my lord. I wanted to ask whether you'd have any objections to me and Polly Jones getting married. Here, if we can find a clergyman. It wouldn't stop us working, my lord.'

'I can't pretend I hadn't noticed you two were courting, but this is a bit sudden, isn't it?'

'Think it might be as well,' Hodge said obscurely. 'Polly's a decent girl.'

'And you'd not want anyone to draw conclusions from a seven-month pregnancy?'

'Quite, my lord.'

'Then you have my blessing, and when we get back to London I'll see about finding the two of you some rooms.'

Hodge beamed. 'Thank you, my lord. I wouldn't want you to think I'm only marrying her because there's a babe on the way. I love her and that's a fact.'

By the time Hodge had stopped being grateful and Rhys was in a banyan and sprawled in a deep armchair by the bed, there was no escaping the poisoned dart Serena had planted so skilfully under his skin. His confidence that such a state as love did not exist was being severely shaken today, and somehow he had never been able to dismiss the reality of the feelings Thea had so painfully confessed.

And if he was the one she loved, then what was he going to do about it? She wanted a love match and he did not think he could manage to deceive her for long; she knew him too well. He liked her, admired her and desired her, but he could not live with emotion, with opening himself up to trust a single person with the essence of himself.

When he had admitted to her that he had never loved Serena, her concern, her need to understand and to question him had felt like a surgeon probing a wound. For a moment he had wondered if that would help, wondered if he could pass through the pain and be healed. And then he had known that was just a sentimental dream.

Perhaps he was wrong. After all, a sixteen-year-old girl would never be able to hide her feelings as well as Thea would have had to do.

'Coxcomb,' he told himself aloud. But he couldn't just leave it, and besides, she was unwell.

He scratched lightly on her door, expecting either no response or for Polly to open it, but Thea called, 'Come in!'

She looked pale and pinched as she sat up in bed against a pile of pillows. There was a glass by the bedside with cloudy liquid in it.

'I came to see how you were. May I come in?' She smiled and his pulse did that odd little stutter it so often seemed to do when he saw her unexpectedly, or when she smiled.

'I am fine,' she said. 'Have they gone to their room?'

'Yes. Never mind about them.' Rhys sat on the side of the bed and took her hand in his, feeling for the pulse. It seemed steady enough and her skin was cool. 'I am concerned about you, Thea. These lagoons and marsh fever...'

The colour came up under her skin and she looked down at their joined hands. 'My courses have begun, that is all. My stomach cramps, my back aches, I feel like a wrung-out dishcloth—and you may congratulate yourself on the efficacy of your precautions.'

'Ah. Oh...excellent. Not that you are feeling unwell, I mean.' Probably all men were reduced to wittering idiots by the reality of the female system. His mistresses had always managed the matter by simply informing him when it was inconvenient to call.

How to ask that other question? He suspected the answer was not going to be as straightforward to obtain. 'Thea, who was it you have been in love with all this time?' *Well done, Denham, that was subtle and tactful.*

Thea shook off his light grip and sat more upright. 'Why on earth are you asking me that now?'

'It is just that Serena was hinting.' He shrugged. 'It doesn't matter.' *That's right, belittle it. Now is a good time to remove foot from mouth.*

'What has she been saying?' Thea demanded. 'You should know better than to listen to her. She manages to tie you in knots every time, doesn't she? You have hurt her feelings and I have witnessed it. Serena may have the intelligence of a peahen, but she has an instinct for making trouble.' Thea folded her arms tightly across her chest, as if to hold herself together. She looked thoroughly upset and he felt a complete swine.

An idea struck him. 'Is it Paul? Is that why you were so upset when she ran off with him? He was always the good-looking one in our circle.'

'Paul?' She laughed unsteadily. 'You clot! Of course it isn't him. And I was upset because of what they had done to you. How would you have felt if our positions had been reversed and a man, a friend of yours, had left me at the altar?'

'I'd have killed him,' Rhys said without having to think.

'Well, there you are. Ladies don't have the luxury of being able to rush off and create mayhem, so we just have to make do with being quietly upset for our friends. Mind you,' she added, 'if I could have got my hands on Serena just then, I think I might have pulled her hair out.'

They sat in silence for a while. Rhys relaxed, leaned back against the bedpost as Thea fidgeted with the laces at the neck of her nightgown. Then she raised her head and looked him straight in the eye. 'What was she hinting?' When he shook his head she said, 'Tell me or I'll ask her myself.'

'That it was me.' He waited, braced for tears, an armful of woman, anger…

'You must think me a very good actress,' Thea said flatly. 'Do you think I could hide that, living with you for weeks? That I could accept the end of our *affaire* so easily?' She swallowed. 'I am sorry, you must find this hideously embarrassing.'

'No, it is my fault. I should have taken no notice of Serena. You are right, she is a troublemaker and, as you say, how could someone as honest as you keep feelings like that hidden?'

'I cannot imagine.' That was more like it; the tart edge was back on her tongue. 'But I think you had better leave Venice, very soon. I will be fine here with Mr Edgerton and his respectable widow, and if you go there will be less for Serena to gossip about. I would hate it if somehow your prospects of making the match you desire are spoiled by her. She still has friends she writes to in England, no doubt.'

'Leave?' *Leave you?* he almost said.

'I am sorry, because it must be one of the most spectacular of all the cities you were planning to visit, but you can always come back once Godmama is here and I have gone.'

'You are, as ever, sensible.' He supposed Thea was right—if he was anywhere in Venice it could cause problems for both of them.

'You believe now that leaving home was sensible? That becoming your lover was prudent?'

Trick questions, Rhys thought. *There are no correct answers.* 'If those were the right things for you, then yes.'

He stood up. 'I'll leave in the morning, just as soon as I am certain those two have gone back to their lodgings.'

'Where to?'

'Rome, I thought,' Rhys said, plucking a city out of the air. He bent to drop a kiss on the end of her nose. 'Goodnight, Thea.'

When he glanced back from the door she was quite composed. She must have seen something in his face for she shook her head at him, smiled and blew him a kiss.

Chapter Twenty-Two

No one would have guessed that she had spent the night wide awake, Thea reassured herself with a quick glance in the overmantel mirror as they sat around the breakfast table. She had finally dropped off to sleep as the bells were chiming five o'clock.

Paul and Serena were subdued but civil and left, to Mr Edgerton's ill-concealed relief, after the meal. Paul and Rhys, she noticed, shook hands. To her shock, there was a boat at the landing stage for Rhys, his bags already in it.

'I got up early and Edgerton arranged everything,' he explained. 'I thought the sooner the better.'

'Yes, of course. But what about Hodge and Polly?' she asked, halfway down the steps to the courtyard. How could Rhys just leave like this, as though he could hardly bear to stay another minute? Had she failed to convince him? Was he certain she was inconveniently and tiresomely in love with him?

'I am leaving Hodge with you. They have two months' wages in hand. Edgerton will help him arrange the wedding.'

'But…'

'I'll find myself an Italian valet for a while, or do without. I'm not that much of a dandy.' He stopped at the foot of the steps and grinned up at her. 'Now, am I?'

'No, but…'

'And when Godmama returns she'll find you a maid and Hodge and Polly can catch me up, wherever I've got to.'

He looked cheerful, alert, ready to move on. Thea swallowed the words that almost escaped her and said, 'Don't forget to write and tell me all about Rome, will you?' She came down until she was standing on the first step, almost eye to eye with him.

'Of course not. Goodbye, Thea. Take care and give my love to Godmama. May I have a farewell kiss?'

All she had to do was lean a little closer. Thea put her hand on the strong, steady shoulder and tipped her face, her eyes wide open. Rhys bent, then hesitated, a breath above her mouth. 'Thea.' Then he kissed her, a light brush of the closed lips, brotherly, friendly. She fought to stop her fingers closing, gripping through the broadcloth and linen to the man beneath.

In a heartbeat something changed. He lifted his hand from the rail and pulled her to him, off balance on the edge of the step so that she had to catch at him with both hands. The pressure of his mouth increased, the familiar, intimate demand of his tongue pushed between her lips and she opened to him, forgot prudence and disguise, sank into his embrace and the heat and the passion of the kiss.

When he released her she stumbled and he steadied her, but he did not speak. His eyes were dark and wide as though he had sustained a shock. Then he turned on his heel and strode to the boat, stepped in and sat with his broad back to her as the boatman cast off the lines and the oarsmen picked up the stroke. She ran to the edge of the landing stage and watched as they reached the Grand Canal and turned, out of sight. Rhys never looked round. Not once.

'Lady Althea, are you certain this is prudent?' Mr Edgerton was as close to agitated as she had ever seen him.

'No,' she admitted. It seemed she had done nothing that was prudent since she'd stood outside Papa's study door and heard how he and Anthony had betrayed her. Leaving home had not been prudent, going to Rhys had not been prudent. Becoming his lover had been thoroughly imprudent.

Being imprudent was dangerous, and sometimes the results hurt. But pain showed you were alive. After Rhys had left she had donned cloak and mask and gone with Polly and Hodge to the Anglican minister to arrange their wedding and then to visit shops.

'Don't you want to see the sights, my lady?' Polly had asked. 'Lovely, isn't it? But strange.' She'd still been bubbling with excitement over the wedding, which had been arranged for two days' time.

'We have shopping to do for your bride clothes,' Thea had said. 'And I want to go to a map shop. We will have time to explore later.'

Now, with Polly safely Mrs Hodge, a sailing boat chartered and crewed under Edgerton's eagle eye, Thea was ready to set out on yet another thoroughly imprudent enterprise. 'I can see Venice when I return with Lady Hughson, but I find I have grown accustomed to travel. I would like to explore the coast of Italy, and so I shall.'

Her money would hold out, for she had never managed to persuade Rhys to let her pay for more than her clothes shopping. Mr Edgerton had reluctantly admitted to knowing a completely reliable captain and crew and introduced her to Signor Vincenzo, who was a courier with an excellent reputation. 'I will come back with Godmama or, if I do not find her, I will turn around when I reach Sicily and return,' she promised the secretary.

Mr Edgerton assisted her into the boat that would take them out into the lagoon and the waiting ship. 'After working for Lady Hughson all these years I suppose I should not be surprised at what her godchildren do,' he said with a sigh. *'Bon voyage!'*

Thea did not turn her head as she was rowed towards the Grand Canal. Rhys had not and neither would she. She had no wish to see the place where he had kissed and left her without a backwards glance.

The rowers negotiated their way into the crowded Grand Canal. This was the start of the rest of her life. She had lost her virginity and gained her independence. She was mistress of her own destiny now.

Venice was beautiful; the light sparkled off the water and lit the exotic curves of windows that seemed transported from some Eastern palace. Soft pink brick and white stone, stained by water and weed, riches and decay, palaces, churches, prisons. She would come back here and explore, and then where? Constantinople? Greece?

Without thinking she pointed out an exquisite little palazzo. 'Rhys, look… I mean, Polly, do see that charming little building.'

The small cold knot inside her tightened into pain. So lonely without him. She knew she would miss him in her bed, but she had not realised how much she had talked with him, how they had shared new wonders, amusements, moments of beauty.

Perhaps he would meet Giles in Rome. She hoped so; she wanted him to have a companion, resilient and independent as he was. Someone to share with.

'Pull into the landing at St Mark's Square,' she called to the boatman. 'I want a stationer's shop.'

Signor Vincenzo was instantly alert. 'But yes, *madonna*, there is a charming one under the arcade.'

He helped her out and guided her to the shop. 'I want a journal,' she explained. 'A thick one. Several, in fact.' She would record everything, her thoughts, all her experiences as though she was telling them to Rhys.

They were beautiful, the covers made with the marbled papers that Venice's book binders were famous for, feathered with patterns made by floating oils on water, stroking it into swirls and then laying on the paper. She added pencils, coloured inks, new pens. *Live for the moment and record it all for the dark days.* Because there would be dark days when she was not feeling so strong, when the memories were too much and it was no comfort at all to know that she had chosen to preserve those recollections.

The coast was every bit as lovely as she had hoped and the towns strung along it as fascinating. Tiny fishing harbours with Venetian forts towering above them, busy little ports, cities filled with treasures that left her breathless— she felt she might never recover from Ravenna—slipped past in sunlight and under blue skies as though the weather was conspiring with her.

They anchored each night as darkness fell, and as the

nights passed she became familiar with the moon and stars
as she never had in cloudy England or on the voyage from
Toulon when she had eyes only for Rhys. Was it a cliché
that every lover stood and stared at the moon and thought of
their beloved looking up at the same sky? Through Signor
Vincenzo she talked to the helmsman and learned the names
of the stars and wrote them in her journal. *If you were here,*
you would draw the constellations, she wrote to the man
who would never read her words. *Orion, the Great Bear...*

Ancona, Pescara, round the spur on the heel of Italy to
Bari. Two weeks after they had left Venice, dawdling on
light winds, watching dolphins and stopping to buy fish
straight from the nets as they were hauled ashore, they
rounded the heel and reached the lagoons of Taranto. It
was hot here and Thea and Polly wore light muslins and
wide-brimmed hats as they strolled through the streets to
stare at the forbidding bulk of the Governor's Palace and
to buy in the market: dates from Africa, melons, oranges,
strange fruits she had no names for. There were palm trees
amongst the crumbling grey stones and a great fortress and
yet another harbourmaster who assured them that *il prin-*
cipe's yacht, the *Aquila*, had moored here.

'But yes, *madonna*, they sail a week ago after being here
four days. They go to Crotone, the captain says.' He gestured out across the wide bay to the south-west. 'They do
not hurry. Is romantic, no? A honeymoon on the sea.'

'Honeymoon? No, you are quite mistaken, *signor*, merely
two friends on a voyage of pleasure.' Thea realised she was
gossiping with a complete stranger and moderated her tone.
'Thank you, we will be sailing immediately.'

There was no hiding her surprise from Polly. 'Surely

Godmama cannot have got married without Mr Edgerton knowing? He is her confidential secretary.'

'They don't have to be married, do they, my lady? But she's quite old, isn't she, Lady Hughson?'

'Old? Not above forty-five,' Thea said after a moment's thought. 'When I was a child she seemed ancient and age-less, of course, but she was widowed very young. It was a true love match and a terrible tragedy that he died.'

'A long time to mourn,' Polly said as they reached the quayside. 'Especially if she has a second chance now.'

Did it really take that long to heal? Thea leaned on the ship's rail and watched the low coastline vanish into heat haze as they struck out across the wide bay. She had thought herself cured of her love for Rhys when she had agreed to Anthony's courtship. Now she realised that she'd had a for-tunate escape. Even if he had been an honestly sincere man, she would never have been happy with him because her heart would never have been free. From the corner of her eyes she could see Hodge and Polly sitting quietly together, his arm around her, her head on his shoulder. At least her actions had brought two people together.

Three more days and Thea was woken by Polly bounc-ing into her cabin. 'Oh, my lady! Come and see—it's a vol-cano, a real one with smoke and everything!'

'Mount Etna,' Thea said, rubbing her eyes as Polly bun-dled her into her wrapper. 'It won't go away.'

'But come and see!' Polly danced out of the cabin, more excited by the mountain than she had been by Venetian ca-nals, dolphins or African traders.

Thea had to agree that it was a staggering sight when she joined Polly and Hodge on deck. Against the pink morning

sky the plume of smoke trailed sideways in long stream-
ers from the top of the conical mountain. At its foot lay
Taormina and a string of small towns and villages. 'I would
not want to live there,' she said with a shiver. 'There was a
city called Pompeii that was buried when another volcano,
Vesuvius, erupted in Roman times. They say Napoleon had
scholars digging it up.'

'Brrr.' Polly gave an exaggerated shiver. 'We're not stopping here, are we?'

'The harbourmaster at Crotone said he thought the *Aquila* was making for Syracuse, farther along the coast, so we
will go straight there.' Thea was beginning to have qualms
about descending unexpectedly on Godmama. What if she
really was on a romantic escape with a lover? At least with
her own ship she could be independent and not intrude. She
would have to play it by ear—if they ever caught up with
the prince's yacht.

'Dolphins,' Signor Vincenzo called from the stern. He
had learned that Thea had an inexhaustible passion for the
creatures, however many they saw and, in the absence of
much else to do, he had become dolphin lookout.

Thea joined him. 'We are being followed.' Well behind
them another ship of a similar size was on the same tack.

'He has been there since dawn,' the Italian said. 'Heading for Syracuse, too, I hope.'

'You hope?'

'Black sails, fast lines. Perhaps he is a pirate. With the
end of the fighting there are no French or British warships
to keep them in check.'

'That is perhaps more excitement than I wanted.' Thea
shaded her eyes to watch the sinister ship in the distance.

'Will you tell the captain that I wish to make straight for Syracuse with good speed?'

And here we are, safely in Syracuse harbour, Thea wrote in her journal that evening. The night air was cool and she had gone to her cabin after dinner, leaving Hodge and Polly the privacy of the deck to stroll, hand in hand.

We have found the Aquila *and the harbourmaster at Taranto was right: Godmama is in love. We saw the yacht at once: sleek and white with brown sails and a huge figure-head of an eagle in gold. I did not want to intrude so I borrowed the captain's telescope and there they were on deck, arm in arm, so intent, with eyes only for each other. Just talking, but I could feel the closeness even across the water.*

I will send a note over tomorrow morning to warn her, then Godmama can make certain I see only what she wants me to see. I hope he is a good man. I pray he makes her happy, for she deserves joy for herself after all she has done for others.

The black 'pirate' ship came into harbour before we sat down to dinner, so it is a harmless voyager after all. You would laugh at me if you knew I was quaking in my shoes at the thought of pirates, Rhys. Or perhaps the fluttering in my stomach was caused by foolishly romantic ideas of a corsair: I have definitely been reading too many novels from the Minerva Press!

I am sure the reality is far more sordid. Besides, what use is a dashing pirate villain if you are not there to rescue me? I can imagine you, knife between your teeth as you swing on board to do battle....

The cabin door creaked open and Thea pulled a sheet

of loose paper over the page. This journal was her private letter to Rhys.

'Polly?' She looked up to find the narrow doorway filled, not with a woman's slender figure, but the bulk of a broad-shouldered man silhouetted against the bulkhead light behind. The pen dropped from her fingers, leaving a splatter of ink across the paper. Hodge would not open her cabin door without knocking and no other man would approach her here.

Thea got to her feet, sending the chair thudding to the deck behind her as she reached for the paper knife. Were her lurid imaginings real after all?

The man ducked his head and came into the cabin and she found her wits and her courage. 'Get out or I will scream!'

Chapter Twenty-Three

'I would rather you kissed me.' Rhys closed the door and leaned back against it. The candle flames on her desk flickered and steadied as the air stilled.

He was wearing a white shirt, open at the neck, form-fitting black breeches, soft black boots and nothing else.

'I was thinking about corsairs,' Thea said and he caught her meaning and laughed as he pushed his over-long hair off his face.

'I am sorry. I should have swung on board at the head of a gang of ruthless pirates, I suppose.'

'Just you is enough.' Enough to remove the air from the cabin and the sense from her head. Enough to leave her so weak she had to grip the edge of the desk to stay on her feet. 'Is the black schooner yours?'

'Yes. Is that what put corsairs into your head? It was the fastest thing I could find at Venice.' He studied her face, but made no move to approach her. 'Why are we discussing corsairs and ships?'

'Because I am in shock and I have no idea why you are here.' It was the truth. 'I thought you had gone to Rome.'

'Yes. Dreadful journey. I felt...wrong. Didn't know why, thought I was coming down with marsh fever perhaps. First thing I did was to go to the British Consulate to sign the book and the third person I saw there was Benton. He took one look at me and said, "You left her, then, you bloody idiot?" No greeting, just a flat statement. I hit him.' He rubbed the knuckles of his clenched right fist into the palm of his left and winced.

'Poor Giles! Was he hurt? And in the Consulate of all places.' Thea groped for the chair, set it upright and sat down before her legs gave out.

'No, he wasn't hurt and I bribed the porter not to make a fuss. Benton took me back to his lodgings—he's having a fine old time in some library or other—poured a large brandy down me and observed that I might be a fool, but at least I had a respectable right hook.'

'What...what did he say about me?' Surely Giles would not have betrayed her?

'Beyond enquiring punctiliously about your health, nothing. Nor did he explain himself. We went out to eat, got roaring drunk. I woke up the next morning rolled in a blanket on the floor of his parlour with a head like a steam hammer, but a very clear understanding of why I felt so bad. I left for Venice just as soon as we'd downed a pot of coffee.'

'Why did you go back?' It took her two attempts to get the words out of her dry mouth.

'For you.'

'We...agreed that it was not a good idea to continue our affair. We agreed there might be scandal and that would affect your chances of making the marriage that you want.

We had *always* agreed that you would leave me in Venice.'
It was not easy to sit there and not go to him. All that kept
her in the seat was the knowledge that to be with him again
and then face another parting would break what was left of
her heart. 'This is not sensible, Rhys.'

'I love you.'

*No. No, he does not believe in love. He does not mean
it. Does not want it.* 'No.' Apparently she had been wrong.
All it took to break her heart was to hear Rhys say those
three words.

'Yes. And I think you love me.'

'No! I told you…'

'You never denied it. I should not allow myself to forget how very good you are with words when you need to
be, Thea.'

'So you believe I love you and your gentlemanly conscience has driven you back to Venice and then right along
the coast of Italy in search of me to do the decent thing, has
it?' She pushed herself upright and flung away to stare out
of the porthole into the darkness.

'No, the realisation that I cannot live without you has
done that.' From his voice, he had not moved from his position flat against the door. It was as though he would not
use his touch, his body, his lips—only his words.

Somehow that was the most convincing thing that he
could have done. Faint hope began to flutter deep inside
her. 'You do not believe in love.'

'I was wrong. I did not understand how being with you
made me feel. At first I thought it was a mixture of friendship and lust. Then we made love and I understood that I
desired you, that I felt more fulfilled in your arms than I

had with any other lover. But I talked myself into believing it was our friendship that made it special.'

Thea kept her gaze on the porthole. She could see Rhys reflected in it, just part of his hand and arm where he had rested his palm on the bulkhead. His hand was shaking. Tears she could not understand and did not know how to stop began to run down her face.

'It was not friendship,' Rhys said, his voice as steady as his hand was not. 'It was our love.' He must have heard her sob, despite her effort to choke it back. 'I know how much love means to you, Thea. I would never tell you I loved you if it were not the truth, even if you begged me on bended knee. I would not lie to you—'

And then his voice did crack and he moved, caught her by the shoulders, pulled her round. 'My love, say something, for God's sake. I never meant to make you cry, Thea.'

'I think it is happiness overflowing. I love you, Rhys. I have loved you since I realised why I was so jealous of Serena. That she was beautiful and I was ordinary did not matter, but she had you, and that did.' Her face was buried in his shirt front now, her wet cheeks dried by the soft, warm fabric, her senses full of the feel and scent of him. 'I thought I had managed to suppress it. After all, I cannot fly, however much I might want to—yearnings can be accepted and controlled.

'I thought it was safe to come to you, to travel with you. I thought, fool that I am, when I sensed that you desired me, that it was safe to be your lover, that you would never know.' His hands were warm and steady now, one around her waist, the other gentle on her hair. 'It was almost more than I could bear to hide my feelings and to know it must end.'

'Will you marry me?' His voice was muffled in her hair.

Thea pushed a little so she could look up into Rhys's face. He looked very serious, but there was joy and something more, deep in those blue eyes. 'I am not at all the sort of wife you wanted. I will get involved in causes and argue with you about politics. I will probably say the wrong things to important people and I will not stand for being left in the country with the children.'

'You will, will you? That sounds remarkably like a *yes*, Thea.' Rhys dropped his head so his forehead rested on hers. 'I was an idiot. I wanted to shut all the messy, difficult, painful, emotional stuff out. We will argue sometimes and it will hurt. It won't be calm and safe, Thea.'

'I can promise to be difficult and messy. And probably painful.' Thea reached up and took a handful of hair and tugged. 'Very painful if you don't kiss me.'

'Is there a lock on this door?'

'A wedge.' Thea ducked down and pushed it into place as Rhys hopped on one foot, dragging at the other boot. They fell on the bunk together, both of them laughing and jostling as they pulled at each other's clothes.

When they were naked Rhys looked down at her and shook his head. 'Why didn't I realise?'

'You had to outgrow an adolescent yearning for blue-eyed blondes of a coming disposition and I had to grow up,' Thea suggested as he bent to her breasts, her eyes drifted shut and all desire to tease and laugh fled.

He was not gentle or respectful or careful. This was a claiming and a masculine shout of triumph and Thea revelled in the strength of his body as he bent her this way and that, as mouth and hands explored her as if they had not been lovers for weeks.

She gave back with a fierceness that matched his own, leaving the marks of her nails and her teeth on his back and shoulders as he ravaged her body. He was determined to reduce her to quivering submission; she was desperate for his possession. When he would only tease her with the pressure of his erection against her she wrapped her legs around his hips and clung, arching up to capture him.

'Witch,' he groaned in surrender, and thrust hard and deep. She was ready for him, more than ready, but she saw his set face and the hard lines of the tendons in his throat as he plunged and withdrew, mercilessly possessing her; he wanted to make this last for ever, yet he wanted to reach that peak of fulfilment. She wanted it, too. As he lodged deep inside her she gripped, held, refused to yield.

'Stay with me,' she gasped and for the first time in their lovemaking he lost control, shuddered and hung above her as the heat of his climax flooded inside her and she screamed and reached for him even as she shattered and fell, knowing only that he was with her, totally. And for ever.

The wedding, in the chapel of Prince Frederico's residence in Syracuse, took place a month later, the day after Agnes, Lady Hughson, became *la Principessa d'Averna*. The ceremony was performed by the British consul's chaplain, ably assisted by Reverend Giles Benton in borrowed vestments. It was attended by a small but select party of guests, including the bride's father, the Earl of Wellingstone, who appeared faintly stunned that his difficult daughter had made such an excellent match and was off his hands at last, and, to the delight of the gossips, Mr Paul Weston and Lady Serena Weston.

The wedding breakfast lasted well into the evening, but

finally Rhys took his wife by the hand and led her, without ceremony, out into the great square in front of the cathedral and down the slope to the ancient spring by the harbour. 'See?' He pointed at the strange plant growing in the clear water with trout weaving through its stems. 'Real Egyptian papyrus. No one knows how it comes to be here. Shall we take it as an omen and visit Egypt on our honeymoon?'

'I don't mind where we go, as long as it has a bed and you.' Thea took the corsage of flowers that was pinned to her shoulder and tossed it to a group of little girls who were staring open-mouthed at her wedding finery.

'We will set sail at dawn and head east, then see where the winds take the *Aquila*. After all, the prince said we can use it for as long as we want.' He looked down at her as she smiled at the children, wondering why he had ever thought her ordinary or could have taken her for granted. 'Come, we have a wedding night before us.'

He swept her into his arms when they reached the yacht and carried her up the gangplank to the applause of the crew, then into the sumptuous master cabin. He was alone with his bride, at last.

'Oh, look, a proper big bed!' Thea gasped as Rhys lowered her onto it.

'I know.' He began to unbutton the gown of pale gold silk. 'We may never want to go home.'

He made love to her slowly, carefully, as though it was the first time. Her flesh softened for him as he caressed her, her body opened to him as he entered her and his strength overwhelmed her as she clung to him. More than words, the certainty of his claiming convinced her of his love.

The tension grew and spiralled and Thea opened her eyes

to find Rhys watching her, his face stark with the effort to control his building climax. 'I love you,' she gasped and he smiled and kissed her so she took his shout of triumph into her and she fell free into a swirl of light and dark and, finally, peace.

She woke to find dawn light flooding through the portholes and the ship in motion. Rhys was propped up on one elbow, looking down at her.

'What is it?' Thea scrubbed at her eyes. 'Is my hair in a tangle?'

'I was just making up for years of not looking at you properly,' her husband murmured. 'Just this past hour I have found three new freckles and discovered that there is a tiny mole behind your left ear.' He bent to kiss it. 'How long is it going to take for me to discover everything about you?'

'Seventy years?' Thea hazarded as Rhys threw back the bedclothes and began, with a growl, to explore.

'At the very least, my love.'

* * * * *

FORBIDDEN JEWEL OF INDIA

Chapter One

The palace of Kalatwah, Rajasthan, India—
March 1788

Patterns of sunlight and shade fell through the pierced stone panels on to the white marble floor, soothing to the eye after miles of dusty roads. Major Nicholas Herriard rolled his shoulders to loosen them as he walked. The physical stresses of the long journey began to fade. A bath, a massage, a change of clothes and he would feel human again.

Running feet, the faint, sharp scratch of claws on marble. The hilt of the knife in his boot came to hand with the familiarity of long practice as he twisted to face the side passage, crouched to meet an attack.

A mongoose shot out of the opening, skidded to a halt and chittered at him, every hair on its body fluffed up with aggravation, its tail stuck out behind like a bottle-brush.

'Idiot animal,' Nick said in Hindi as the patter of running feet became louder and a girl followed the mongoose, her wide crimson skirts swirling around her as she caught her balance and stopped. Not a girl, a woman, unveiled and unescorted. The part of his brain that was still dealing with an attack analysed the sound of her footsteps: she had changed direction twice just before she emerged, which meant this was one of the off-set entrances to the *zanana*.

She should not be here, outside the women's quarters. *He* should not be here, staring at her with all the blood in his brain heading south, his body poised for violence and a weapon in his hand.

'You may put away your dagger,' she said and it took him a moment to adjust and realise she was speaking in lightly accented English. 'Tavi and I are unarmed. Except for teeth,' she added, showing hers, white and regular between lips that curved into a smile of faint mockery. It masked, he was certain, shock. The mongoose twined between her bare, hennaed feet, still grumbling to itself. It wore a gem-studded collar.

Nick got a grip on himself, pushed the knife back into its sheath as he straightened and brought his hands together. '*Namaste*.'

'*Namaste.*' Over her own joined hands dark grey eyes studied him. The shock seemed to have turned to suspicion edged with hostility and she was making no effort to disguise either emotion.

Grey eyes? And skin like golden honey and hair that showed streaks of mahogany and deep brown as it fell down her back in a thick plait. His quarry, it seemed, had found him.

She did not appear disconcerted to be alone, unveiled, with a strange man, but stood there and contemplated him. Her full red skirts, weighted with heavy silver embroidery, hung just above her ankles, giving a glimpse of close-fitting trousers. Her tight *choli* revealed not only delightful curves and elegantly rounded arms decked in silver bangles, but also an unsettling band of smooth golden midriff.

'I should go. Excuse me for disturbing you,' Nick said in English and wondered if he was perhaps the more unsettled of the two of them.

'You have not,' she replied with crushing simplicity in the same language. She turned and walked through the opening she had appeared from. '*Mere pichhe aye,* Tavi,' she called as the skirts of her *lehenga* whisked out of sight. The mongoose followed obediently, the faint click of its claws fading along with her light footsteps.

'Hell,' Nick said to the empty passageway. 'That is quite definitely her father's daughter.' Suddenly a simple duty had become something else entirely. He squared his shoulders and strode off in the direction that led to his rooms. A man did not become a major with the British East India Company by being disconcerted by acid-tongued young women, however beautiful. He needed to clean himself up and seek an audience with the raja, her uncle. And after that, all he had to do was to transport Miss Anusha Laurens safely halfway across India, back to her father.

'Paravi! Quickly!'

'Speak Hindi,' Paravi reproved as Anusha entered her room in a flurry of skirts and trailing scarf.

'*Maf kijiye,*' Anusha apologised. 'I have just this moment been speaking to an Englishman and my head is still translating.'

'*Angrezi?* How can you be speaking to any man, let alone an *angrezi?*' Paravi, plump and indolent and her uncle's third wife, raised one exquisitely plucked eyebrow, but she pushed aside the chessboard she had been studying and sat upright.

'He was in the corridor when I chased Tavi just now. Very big with hair of pale gilt and in the red uniform of the Company's soldiers. An officer, I think—he had much gold on his coat. Come and see him.'

'Why so curious? Is he so handsome, this big *angrezi*?'

'I do not know what he is,' Anusha confessed. 'I have not seen one so close since I left my father's house.' But she was curious. And there was something else, a tug of yearning, deep inside, at the memory of another male voice speaking English, of another big man, scooping her up in his arms, laughing with her, playing with her. The man who had rejected her and her mother, she reminded herself as the memory turned sour.

'He is different from the men I am used to, so I can-not decide if he is handsome or not. His hair is so pale and tied back tightly and his eyes are green and he is tall.' She waved her hands to illustrate. 'He is big all over—broad shoulders, long legs.'

'Is he very white? I have never seen an *angrezi* before except from a long way away.' Paravi was becoming in-terested.

'His face and his hands are golden.' *Like my father's were.* 'But the skin of all the Europeans goes brown in the sun, you know. Perhaps the rest of him is white.'

Imagining *all* of the big Englishman produced a not-un-pleasurable shiver which he did not merit. But any novelty was welcome in the restricted world of the *zanana,* even if this novelty brought with him unsettling reminders of the world outside the fort. The faint sensual tingle was lost in a wave of something close to apprehension. This man made her uneasy.

'Where has he gone now?' Paravi uncoiled herself from the heap of cushions she had been occupying. The mongoose immediately dived into the warm spot she had created and curled up. 'I would like to look on a man who makes all those expressions chase across your face.'

'To the visitors' wing—where else should he go?' Anusha tried not to snap. It was not flattering to be told her face betrayed her. 'He was very dusty from the road, he will not be seeking audience with my uncle like that.' She gave herself a little shake to chase away the foolish fancies. 'Come with me to the Sunset Terrace.'

Anusha led the way through the familiar maze of passages, rooms and galleries that filled the western wing of the palace.

'Your *dupatta*,' her friend hissed as they left the women's quarters to cross the wide terrace where the raja would sometimes sit to watch the sun sink over his kingdom. 'There are no grilles here.'

Anusha clicked her tongue in irritation, but unwound the neglected length of cerise gauze from her neck and draped it so it covered her face to the chin. She leaned on the inner balustrade of the terrace and looked down into the courtyard below. 'There he is,' she whispered.

Below, on the edge of a garden threaded with rills of water in the Persian manner, the big *angrezi* was talking to a slender Indian she did not recognise. His body servant, no doubt. The man gestured towards a door.

'He is telling him where the bath house is,' Paravi whispered from behind her own *dupatta* of golden gauze.

'There is your chance to see whether Englishmen are white all over.'

'That is ridiculous. And immodest.' She heard Paravi laugh softly and bristled. 'Besides, I am not in the slightest bit interested.' Just burningly, and inexplicably, curious. The two men had vanished into the guest rooms overlooking the garden. 'But I suppose I had better see whether the water has been heated and someone is in attendance.'

Paravi leaned one rounded hip against the parapet and glanced up as a flock of green parakeets screeched overhead. 'This man must be important, do you not think? He is from the East India Company and they are all-powerful in the whole land now, my lord says. Far more important than the Emperor in Delhi, even if they do put the Emperor's head on their coins. I wonder if he is to be the Resident here. My lord said nothing about that last night.'

Anusha rested her elbows on the parapet and noted that her friend seemed to be in favour with her husband. 'Why would we need a Resident? We do not do so very much trade with them.' The intriguingly pale head appeared below as the man re-emerged from the door to the guest rooms. 'I suppose we might be in a useful position for their expansion—that is what *Mata* used to say. Strategic.' Her mother had much to say on most subjects, being both well read and greatly indulged by her brother the raja.

'Your father is still a friend to my lord, even though he never comes here. They exchange letters. He is a great man in the Company: perhaps he thinks we are more important these days and deserving of a Resident.'

'It must be a matter of great importance for him to bestir himself to think of us,' Anusha said. Her father had not visited the state of Kalatwah since the day, twelve years ago, when he had sent his twelve-year-old daughter and her mother back, displaced from his home and his heart by the arrival of his English wife.

He sent money, but that was all. Her uncle added it to her dowry chest when she refused to spend it. He told her that she was foolish, that her father had no choice but to send her and her mother home and that Sir George was an honourable man and a good ally of Kalatwah. But that was the talk of men, of politics, not of the love that broke her mother's heart, even while she agreed with her brother that there had been no other option.

Her father wrote to her uncle, she knew that, for he would tell her there were messages. There had been a note a year ago when her mother had died. She had not read it any more than she had read the others. The moment she saw her father's name she had thrown it on the brazier and watched it burn to ash.

From the flash of dark eyes behind the veil Paravi was sending her sympathetic glances, which is not what she wanted. No one had any right to be sorry for her. Was she not, at twenty-two, the pampered niece of the Raja of Kalatwah? Was she not indulged with the right to turn down every approach that had been made for her hand in marriage? Was she not supplied lavishly with clothes and jewels and servants and all the luxury she wished for? Did she not possess everything that she could possibly want?

Except knowing where I belong, the nagging little voice in her head said, the voice that, for some reason, always spoke English. *Except knowing who I am and why I am and what I am going to do with the rest of my life. Except for freedom.*

'The *angrezi* is going to the bath.' Paravi drew back a pace from the parapet even as she craned to see. 'That is a fine robe. His hair is long now it is loose,' she added. 'What a colour! It is like that stallion my lord sent to the Maharaja of Altaphur as a gift when the monsoon ended, the horse they called the Gilded One.'

'He has probably got as high an opinion of himself as that animal had,' Anusha said. 'But at least he bathes. Do you know, many of them do not? They think it unhealthy! My father said that they do not have *champo* in Europe— they powder their hair instead. And just wash their hands and faces. They think hot water is bad for them.'

'Ugh! Go and see and tell me about him.' Paravi gave her a little push. 'I am curious, but my lord would not be pleased if he thought I was looking upon an *angrezi* without his clothes.'

He would also have much to say if his niece was discovered doing just that, Anusha reflected as she ran down the narrow stairway and along the passage. She was not at all sure why she wanted to get closer to this stranger. It was not any desire to attract his attention, despite the shiver which was, of course, simply a normal female reaction to a man in his prime—far from it. She did not want those green eyes studying her—they seemed to see too much. There had been a flash of recognition in them when they had met. Recognition and something far more basic and male.

She left her sandals in the doorway and peeped around the corner of the bathhouse. The Englishman was already naked and face down on a linen sheet draped over the marble slab, his body gleaming with water. He rested his forehead on his linked hands as one of the girls, Maya, worked the mixture of *basun* powder, lime juice and egg yolks into his hair. Savita was bent over his feet, oiling and massaging. Between head and heels there was a great deal of man to be seen in an interesting shading of colours.

Anusha walked in with a warning nod to the two girls to stay silent and keep working. His neck was the colour that his face and hands, both hidden by his wet hair, had been. His shoulders, back and arms were a paler gold. His legs were lighter still and the skin behind his knees was almost white, a pinkish shade. The line where his belt must habitually lie was very clear, for his buttocks were as pale as the backs of his knees.

His legs and arms were dusted with brown hair, she noticed. It was wiry and much darker than his flaxen head. Was his chest like that, too? She had heard that some Englishmen were so hairy that their backs were covered with a pelt of it. They must be like bears. She wrinkled her nose in disgust at the thought, then found she was standing right next to the slab. How did his skin feel?

Anusha reached for the jar of oil, poured a little into her palms and placed them flat, one on each shoulder blade. Under her hands she felt his muscles tighten, the skin twitch with the contact of the cool liquid. Then he relaxed again and she brought her hands sliding down slowly until they rested at his waist.

The pale skin felt just like any other skin, she decided. The muscles though, those were…shocking. Not that she had any basis for comparison, of course. She had never touched a man's naked flesh in her life.

Maya began to rinse his hair, pouring water from a brass ewer and catching it in a bowl. Savita had moved up to his calves and was kneading the long muscles. Anusha found she was stuck, unwilling, for some mysterious reason, to lift her hands, too disconcerted by the feel of a man's body to venture any further.

Then he spoke, the vibration of his deep voice reaching her through her palms. 'Am I to hope that you will *all* be joining me in my room after this?'

Nick felt the stir in the air, the faint pad of bare feet on the marble. Another girl—he was being treated as an honoured guest, which boded well for his mission. The strong, skilled fingers massaging his scalp made him want to purr, the muscles of his feet and ankles were relaxing into something approaching bliss. The new arrival brought with her a faint suggestion of jasmine to mingle with the sandalwood of the oil and the lime in the *champo*. He had smelt that earlier, somewhere.

Hands, coated with oil that had not been allowed to warm, settled on his back and hesitated. In comparison to the other two, this attendant was either unskilled or nervous. Then his brain placed the scent as the hands slid downwards to his waist and stopped again.

'Am I to hope that you will *all* be joining me in my room after this?' Nick said, in English. As he expected the sure hands at his head and on his calves did not pause in their smooth rhythm, but the fingers at his waist tightened into claws. 'All three of you at once should be most pleasurable,' he added with deliberate provocation, his voice sultry with suggestion as he teased her. 'I shall ask for the bed chains to be fixed to the ceiling hooks to make a swing.'

There was a sharp indrawn breath and the claws tightened in a fleeting pain before she lifted her hands away. 'How interesting that even the bathhouse attendants here speak good English,' he added. It was only sporting to let her know he had realised she was there and had spoken deliberately.

The faintest hiss of indrawn breath, the silken whisper of her clothing, the brush of air on his skin and she was gone.

Nick found he was breathing hard and made himself relax. If he was feeling aroused it was because he was stark naked while his body was massaged by highly skilled hands. George's daughter had nothing to do with it. The little witch had doubtless thought it would be amusing to play a trick on him—she would not make the same mistake again. He made his mind blank and gave himself up to the sensations surrounding him.

'Well?' Paravi clapped her hands for the maids. 'We will drink pomegranate juice while you tell me all about him.' She cocked her head on one side and her nose ring swung with the movement, its tiny gold discs jingling.

'He is a pig.' Anusha plumped down on the pile of cushions opposite and disentangled her scarf with an impatient tug. 'He knew it was me, even though he had his eyes closed, and he deliberately provoked me with indecent suggestions. The man must have eyes in the back of his head, or he uses witchcraft.'

'So he had his back to you?' Paravi appeared to find this disappointing.

'He was lying face down on the slab being massaged and having his hair washed.'

'So how did he know it was you?'

'I have no idea. But he spoke in English to trap me.' Paravi clicked her tongue. Anusha took a deep breath and attempted to report dispassionately. 'He is not *white,* but the parts of him that have not been in the sun are pinkish. Like the muzzle of a grey cow is. Only paler.'

'So.' Paravi stretched. 'He uses witchcraft, he is the colour of a cow's nose and he is not a fool. Is he a good lover, I wonder?'

'He is too big,' Anusha said with the absolute confidence of a woman who had studied all the texts on the subject and had looked at a very wide range of detailed pictures while she was at it.

A wife was expected to have considerable theoretical knowledge of how to please her husband and *Mata* had made sure that her education in that area had not been neglected. Anusha sometimes wondered if knowing so much was not responsible for her reluctance to agree to any of the marriages that had been proposed for her.

If one had the luxury of choice it did make you look at the man concerned very carefully while you considered the matter. And then you tried to imagine doing those things with him and…and, so far, those mental pictures had been quite enough to make her reject every one of the suitors offered to her.

'Too big?' Paravi was still dwelling on her description of the scene in the bathhouse. Her eyes were wide with an amused surprise that Anusha was not certain she quite understood.

'How could someone so large be supple and sensual?' she added in explanation, with what she felt was crushing logic. 'He would be a lump. A log of wood.' He had certainly felt like teak under her hands. A contrary memory flickered through her mind of him twisting, fast as a snake, the knife in his hand. But that had simply been trained violence, not the subtle magic of the sensual arts.

'A lump,' her uncle's wife echoed, her lips curling into a wicked smile. 'I must see this human log more closely.' She gestured to the maid. 'Find out at what hour my lord holds audience with the *angrezi* and in which *diwan*.' Paravi turned to Anusha, suddenly every inch a rani. 'You will join me in my gallery.'

Chapter Two

Nick changed, choosing his clothing with some care—the message from the raja had stipulated no uniform. When the escort came he walked, relaxed, between the four heavily armed members of the royal bodyguard. He had not expected to be received with anything but warmth, but it was good to have that confirmed. If Kirat Jaswan had decided his interests lay elsewhere than with the East India Company now that his sister was dead, then Nick's mission would have become both dangerous and exceedingly difficult.

He supposed, if diplomacy failed, it was possible to remove an unwilling, intelligent and able-bodied princess from a heavily fortified palace in the middle of her uncle's kingdom and get her back across hundreds of miles to Delhi with an angry raja's troops at his heels, but he would prefer not to have to try. Or to start a small war in the process.

As it was, he felt good. He was clean, he was relaxed by

the bath and the massage and the amusement of teasing the infuriating female he had to escort out of here.

Now, with her mother dead, and her father's own wife gone, there was no one to hurt by George removing his daughter from the raja's court and turning her into an English lady. And there were a number of very good political reasons for bringing her to Calcutta into the bargain.

Nick strode into the *Diwan-i-Khas*, the Hall of Private Audience. In his peripheral vision he was aware of marble pillars, the men in the robes and the ornate *safa* turbans of the elite on either side, of guards, their weapons drawn in ceremonial salute.

He kept his eyes on the slight figure in a gold embroidered *chauga* seated amidst piled cushions on the silver-embossed throne on the dais before him. As he reached two sword-lengths from the steps he made the first obeisance, aware of the flutter of silks, the drift of perfume, from behind the stone grillework of the gallery. The ladies of the court were there, watching and listening. Those in favour would have access to the raja, would give him their opinion of his guest. Was Miss Laurens there? He was certain that curiosity would have brought her.

'Your Highness,' he said in English. 'Major Nicholas Herriard, at your service. I bring salutations from the Governor of the Calcutta Presidency with most grateful thanks for the honour of my reception.'

The white-clad *munshi* looked up from his writing desk at the raja's feet and spoke in rapid Hindi. Raja Kirat Jaswan replied in the same language while Nick kept his face studiously blank.

'His Highness, Lord of Kalatwah, Defender of the Sacred Places, Prince of the Emerald Lake, Favoured of the Lord

Shiva…' Nick stood frozen in place while the *munshi* reeled off the titles in English. '…commands you to approach.'

He stepped forwards and met the shrewd dark brown eyes that were regarding him from beneath the jewelled and plumed brocade of the turban. Overhead the ropes of the *punkah* fan creaked faintly.

The raja spoke. 'It gives me pleasure to welcome the friend of my friend, Laurens,' the secretary translated. 'You left him in good health?'

'I did, your Highness, although low in spirits from the death of his wife. And…another loss. He sends letters and gifts by my hand as does the Governor.'

The secretary translated. 'I was sorry to hear of his wife and that his heart is still in grief, as mine is for the death of my sister last year. I know he will have shared my feelings. There is much to discuss.' He waved a hand at the *munshi*. 'We have no need of a translator, I think,' the raja added in perfect English. 'You will join me and we will relax, Major Herriard.'

It was a command, a great favour and exactly what Nick was hoping for. 'My lord, you do me honour.'

The rani's position in the women's gallery around the audience hall was the very best position for observing and listening. Anusha had settled comfortably against the piled pillows next to Paravi as maids placed low tables covered in little dishes around them.

'We should hear well,' said the rani as they waited for the raja to arrive. The acoustics had been carefully designed in all the rooms: in some to baffle sound, in others to enable eavesdropping with ease. Here, in circumstances where the raja would consult with his favourite after a meeting, a conversation in a normal tone would reach easily to the pierced screens.

'Savita tells me that your log of wood is as supple as a young sapling,' Paravi added mischievously. 'Such muscles...'

Anusha dropped the almonds she had just picked up. Rummaging in the cushions to retrieve them at least gave her the chance to compose her face and suppress her unruly imagination. 'Truly? You amaze me.'

'I wonder if he has read all the classical texts,' Paravi continued. 'He would be so strong, and most vigorous.'

Anusha took an incautious mouthful of nuts and coughed. *Vigorous*...

'And he has very large...feet.'

There was no answer to that, especially as she was not sure what Paravi meant and suspected she was being teased. Anusha feigned interest in the arrival below of the male courtiers as they poured in to fill up the hall in a noisy, jostling, colourful mass. As the servants went from niche to niche, lighting the *ghee* lamps, the mirror fragments and gems in the walls and ceilings began to reflect back the light in scintillating patterns like constellations in the darker sky of shadows.

Faintly, there was the sound of the musicians tuning their instruments in the courtyard. It was beautiful and familiar and yet Anusha felt an ache of something she was beginning to recognise as loneliness.

How was it possible to feel lonely when she was never alone? To feel she was not part of this world when it had been her life for ten years, when she was surrounded by her mother's family?

Her uncle walked through the crowd and took his place, gestured for the courtiers to be seated, then beckoned.

A tall figure in a *sherwani* of gold-and-green brocade over green *pajama* trousers walked through the seated men to the steps of the throne. For a moment Anusha could not place him until the pale gold of his hair, falling on his shoulders, caught the light. He bowed his head, his cupped right hand lifting to his heart in the graceful gesture of obeisance. As he straightened she saw the green fire of an emerald in his earlobe.

'Look,' she whispered to Paravi. 'Just look at him!' In the costume of the court the major should have looked more ordinary, but he did not. The brocade and the silks, the severe lines of the long coat and the glitter of gems, made the pale hair and the broad shoulders and the golden skin seem more exotic, more strange.

'I am doing so!'

The raja motioned impatiently to the servants and they lifted the cushions from the foot of the dais and arranged them on the right side of the throne where the *munshi*'s desk had stood. 'You will join me,' Kirat Jaswan said.

'My lord. You do me honour.' The Hindi was accurate, perfectly accented. The big Englishman sank down and crossed his legs beneath him with the ease of an Indian. The raja dropped his hand to his shoulder and leaned over to speak.

'I cannot hear,' Paravi complained. 'But here is the food, they cannot both whisper and eat.'

Indeed, as a succession of small dishes were presented to the raja, and he offered them in turn to the *angrezi*, the two men straightened up and most of what they said could be heard. But, to Anusha's frustration, it was all the most innocuous conversation.

She ate absently, her eyes on the fair hair beneath, the glimpses of the Englishman's profile as he turned his head to answer her uncle. His voice held the easy rhythms of a man who had not only been taught Hindi well, but who used it, day in, day out. What had he said his name was? Herriard? A strange name—she tried it out silently.

Then the food was finally cleared away, the scented water and cloths presented for the washing of hands and the great silver *hookah* was brought, with an extra mouthpiece for the guest. Both men appeared to relax as the music began.

'They are discussing something of importance now,' Paravi said. 'See how they use the mouthpieces to shield their lips so that no one can read them.'

'Why should they be so concerned? It is only the court around us.'

'There are spies,' the rani said after a swift glance. She lifted her hand with apparent casualness to shield her own mouth. 'The Maharaja of Altaphur will have men in the court and agents here amongst the servants.'

'Altaphur is an enemy?' Surprised, Anusha twisted to face her. 'But my uncle considered his request to wed me and sent him a fine horse when I refused. He said nothing then about any enmity.'

'It is safer to pretend to be friends with the tiger who lives at the bottom of one's garden than to let him see you know about his teeth. My lord would not have allowed the match even if you had agreed, but he made it seem the refusal was a woman's whim, not a ruler's snub.'

'But why is he an enemy?'

'This is a small but rich state—there is much to covet

here. And, as you said earlier, we are in a position that interests the East India Company so they will make concessions to whoever rules, perhaps.' Paravi spoke as though she was just working this out, but Anusha sensed a deeper knowledge behind the words. She caught an edge of fear in the other woman's voice. Much had been hidden from her, she realised. Even her friend had been wearing a mask. No one had trusted her with the truth. Or perhaps they just thought her not important enough: the niece with the English blood in her veins.

'There will be war?' The state had been at peace for almost seventy years. But the court poets and musicians told the stories of past battles and of terrible defeats as well as glorious victories, of the men riding out, dressed in their ochre funerary robes, knowing they were going to their deaths, and the women filing down to the great burning pyres to commit *jauhar,* ritual suicide, rather than fall into the hands of the conqueror. Anusha shuddered. She would choose to ride out to die in battle, not go to the pyre.

'No, of course not,' the rani said with a confidence that Anusha did not believe. 'The Company will protect us if we are their allies.'

'Yes.' It was best to agree. Anusha looked down at the golden head, bent listening. Then the Englishman looked up to meet the raja's eyes and she caught the intensity in his face as he spoke with sudden passion, his hand slashing out in a gesture she could not interpret.

The court was moving back to clear space for a *nautch.* The dancers entered amidst the music of the bells on the silver chains around their ankles. Then they began to move, perfectly together, their wide, vivid skirts swinging out like exploding fireworks. But the two men did not spare them a glance and Anusha felt a cold finger of apprehension trail down her spine.

She went to her bedchamber unsettled and restless, her mind churning with her anxieties over the threat from across the border and the humiliation of the bathhouse.

'Anusha.' Paravi came in, her face serious.

'What is it?' Anusha dropped the book she was thumbing through and pushed back the loose hair that spilled over her shoulders.

'My lord wishes to speak with you privately, without his councillors. Come to my chamber.'

Anusha realised that there were no maids present—neither her own, nor any with the rani. She stood up from the low couch, slid her feet into sandals and followed Paravi while her mind whirled with speculation.

Her uncle was unattended, his face starkly under-lit by the little lamps flickering on a low table by his side. Anusha made her reverence and waited, wondering why Paravi had pulled her veil over her face.

'Major Herriard here has come from your father,' Kirat Jaswan said without preamble. 'He is concerned for you.'

Her father? Her pulse jolted with something close to fear. What could he want with her? Then the raja's wording struck her. 'Here?'

The big man stepped out of the shadows and bowed, unsmiling. He was still in Indian dress. The lamplight caught the gleam of the emeralds in his ear lobes, the silver embroidery and buttons of his coat. He looked both exotic and utterly comfortable, as at home in this guise as he seemed in the scarlet uniform.

'I thought you were from the Company,' Anusha challenged him in Hindi. 'Not my father's servant.'

The raja hissed a word of reproof, but the Englishman answered her in the same language, his green eyes meeting hers with a bold, assessing stare. No man should look at an unveiled woman not of his family like that. 'I come from both. The Company is concerned about the intentions of the Maharaja of Altaphur towards this state. And so is your father.'

'I understand why they should be concerned about a threat to Kalatwah. But why is my father thinking about me after all these years?' Her uncle did not reprove her for not veiling herself. It was as though he was suddenly treating her as an Englishwoman, she thought with a shiver of alarm. The rani had slipped back into the shadows.

'Your father has never ceased to concern himself with your welfare,' the man Herriard said. He sounded irritated with her and when she shook her head in instinctive denial he frowned. 'He saw the offer of marriage from Altaphur as a threat, a way of pressuring the Company through you.'

Her father knew about that? Kept such a close watch over her? It took her a moment for the meaning to force its way through resentment and the unsettling atmosphere of conspiracy. 'I would have been a hostage?'

'Exactly.'

'How dreadful, that I might inconvenience the Company and my father in that way.'

'Anusha!' The raja slapped his palm down on the table.

'Miss Laurens—'

'Do not call me that.' Her knees were shaking, but no one could see beneath the long skirts of her robe.

'It is your name.' Presumably the man spoke to his troops

in this manner. She was not one of his troops. Anusha's chin went up—that stopped it trembling as well.

'Your father and I agree it would be better for you to return to his house,' her uncle said. His quiet voice with its expectation of instant obedience cut across their hostility.

'Go back to Calcutta? Go back to my father after he threw us out? He does not want me, only to stop me interfering with his political schemes. I hate him. And I cannot leave you and Kalatwah when there is danger, my lord. I will not run away—never!' In her mind the crackle of flames and the clash of steel mingled with the sound of a big man's belly-laugh and her mother's stifled sobs.

'Such drama,' Herriard drawled, blowing the swirling images away like a draught of cold air. She itched to slap his well-defined jaw. 'Ten years ago your father was in an impossible position and did the only honourable thing open to him to ensure the well-being of yourself and your mother.'

'Honour! Pah!'

Herriard went very still. 'You never, in my hearing, defame the honour of Sir George Laurens, do you understand?'

'Or?' Her neck muscles were so tense it was painful.

'Or you will find it a matter for regret. If you will not leave because your father commands it, then do it for his Highness, your uncle. Or are your grudges so deep that you would hamper the defence of his state, the safety of the family, to indulge them?'

Grudges? He can calmly dismiss feelings about the betrayal of love, the rejection of a family, as a grudge? The marble floor seemed to quiver like sand beneath her feet. Anusha choked back the furious retort and looked at her uncle. 'Do you want me to go, my lord?'

'It is best,' Kirat Jaswan said. He was everything to her:

ruler, uncle, surrogate father. She owed him her total obedience. 'You…complicate matters, Anusha. I would have you safe where you belong.'

So I do not belong here? No matter how she had been feeling these past months, this was too sudden, too abrupt. Her uncle had cast her out too, as her father had. Now she truly was adrift with nowhere to call home. To protest, would be futile, and beneath her. She was a Rajput princess by training, even if her blood was mixed. 'I do not belong with my father. I never did, he made that clear as crystal. But because you, my lord and uncle, ask it, I shall go.'

And she would not weep, not in front of that arrogant *angrezi* who had got what he came for, it seemed: her surrender. She was of a princely house and she had her pride and she would do what her ruler commanded and not show fear. If he had commanded her to ride into battle to her death with his troops she would have done. Somehow that felt less frightening than this. 'When must I go?'

The Englishman Herriard answered. It was as though her uncle had already washed his hands of her and had given her over to the other man. 'You leave as soon as the vehicles and animals can be gathered and the journey provisioned. It is a long way and will take us many weeks.'

'I remember,' Anusha said. Weeks of blank discomfort and misery, clinging to her mother who was too proud to weep. Sent away because the big, loving, bear of a man who had hugged her and spoiled her, who had been the centre of her world and her mother's universe, had cast them out. Because love, it seemed, was not for ever. Expediency conquered love. It was a lesson that had been well learned.

Then what Herriard had said penetrated. 'Us? *You* will take me?'

'Of course. I am your escort, Miss Laurens.'

'I am so *very* sorry,' she said, baring her teeth in a false smile. She would make every league a misery for him, if she could, the insensitive brute. 'You obviously do not wish for this duty.'

'I would walk the entire way in my bare feet if Sir George asked it,' Major Herriard said. The cold green eyes looked back at her without liking or anger, as hard as the emeralds in his ears. 'He is as a father to me and what he wants, Miss Laurens, I will ensure that he gets.'

A father? Just who was this man whose devotion went so far beyond a soldier's obedience? 'Fine words,' Anusha said as she turned to leave. 'I do hope you will not have cause to eat them.'

Chapter Three

'If that man sends one more message about what I must and must not take I will scream.' Anusha stood in the midst of harried, scurrying maids and searched for a word to describe Nicholas Herriard. With a phrase quivering on her tongue she caught Paravi's amused gaze and compromised. *'Budmash.'*

'Major Herriard is not a villain or a knave,' the rani said, her tone of reproof in conflict with the curve of her lips. 'And he will hear you—he is only on the other side of the *jali*. It is a long journey. He is right to make certain you will have everything you need, yet not too much.'

'What is he doing there?' Anusha demanded, raising her voice. If the wretched man was listening behind the pierced screen wall then he deserved to hear her opinion. The men who ruled her life had left her two choices: she could weep and give up or she could lose her temper. Her pride would not allow the first, so the major must bear the brunt of the other. 'This is the women's *mahal*.'

'There is a eunuch with him and curtains have been hung around the room,' Paravi hissed. 'He is checking everything as it is packed.'

'Hah! My uncle says I may have twenty elephants, forty camels, forty bullock carts, horses...'

'And I say it is too much,' said a deep voice from behind the far wall of pierced stone. Anusha jumped and stubbed her toe on a studded chest. 'Anyone would think you are going to marry the Emperor, Miss Laurens. And besides, your father will want you to wear Western clothes and jewels in Calcutta.'

'*Mata* told me about those clothes.' Anusha marched across a stack of carpets until she was next to the *jali.* A large shadow on the silk hangings was all she could see of him through the screen. 'Corsets! Stockings! Garters! She said they were instruments of torture.'

There was a snort from the other side. 'They are not things a lady mentions in the presence of a man,' Herriard said, laughter quivering in his voice.

'Then go away. I do not require your presence here. I do not require your presence at all, anywhere, gloating because you are getting your way. If you listen from hiding like a spy, then you must endure whatever I say.' There was a faint moan from the rani behind her. 'Go away, Major Herriard. Twenty elephants are no slower than ten.'

'Twenty elephants eat twice as much as ten,' he retorted. 'We leave the day after tomorrow. Anything that is not ready, or will not go on half the transport you have listed, will be left behind. And whilst I feel the greatest satisfaction in following your father's wishes, I am not gloating.'

Anusha opened her mouth to retort, but the sound of footsteps leaving the other room silenced her. It was intolerable to be prevented from arguing because the man had the ill manners to remove himself.

'Find me a dagger,' she said, narrowing her eyes at the nearest maid, who was apparently rooted to the spot. 'That at least I will take—I can imagine a nice broad target for it.' And she would take all her jewels because when she was in Calcutta and Major Herriard was no longer her jailer she would need them to pay for her escape from her prison. From her father's house.

Her dagger was in her hand and she would use it because the wretched *angrezi* was shouting at her and shaking her and drums were beating the alarm and there was danger all around.

'Ah! *Ra*—' Anusha's shriek of *rape* was choked in her throat as a large hand clamped over her mouth. She had been asleep, dreaming, but now—

'Quiet,' Nicholas Herriard hissed in her ear. 'We must leave, at once, in secret. When I take my hand away you will whisper or I'll clip you on the jaw and carry you out. Do you understand?'

Furious, frightened—*do not let him see that*—Anusha nodded and he removed his hand. 'Where are my maids?' He jerked his head towards the corner and she opened her mouth to scream as she saw the two crumpled bodies lit by the flickering light of one *ghee* lamp. The hand came back, none too gently. The skin bore the calluses of a rider and chafed her lips. He tasted of leather.

'Drugged,' he murmured in her ear, pressing his palm tight over her mouth to foil her attempt to bite. 'There are spies, I cannot risk it. Listen.' He freed her mouth again.

Now she was awake she realised that the drums that had

been echoing through her dream were real, their sound vibrating through the palace. She had never heard them like this, at night, so urgent. 'An attack?'

'The Maharaja of Altaphur has moved fast. There are war elephants and cavalry not four hours distant.'

'He discovered you are here? That you had come for me?' Anusha sat up, dragged the covers around her as Herriard sank back on his heels beside the low bed. He was wearing Indian dress again, but now it was plain riding gear with boots and a tight, dark turban to cover the betraying shimmer of pale hair.

'He was already mobilising his troops—he must have been to get so close so fast. Then his spies told him that someone from the Company was here, perhaps that I intended to take you away, perhaps that I was negotiating. My guess is that he decided on a pre-emptive strike to seize the state before your uncle made an alliance with the Company.'

'My uncle will not surrender to him!' The floor was cold under her bare feet as she scrambled out of bed, the night air chill through the thin cotton of her shift.

'No, he will stand firm. The raja has already despatched riders to his allies in Agra and Gwalior and to Delhi. The Company will send troops as soon as it receives the news and then I suspect Altaphur will back down without further fighting. Your uncle only has to withstand a siege for a matter of weeks.'

Was he attempting to soothe her with easy lies? Anusha tried to read his face in the gloom and control her churning stomach. 'You will stay here and fight?' Why one more soldier would make any difference, she did not know, but somehow the thought of this man at her uncle's right shoulder made her feel better. He was arrogant, aggravating and foreign, but she had no doubt that Major Herriard was a warrior.

'No. You and I are leaving. Now.'

'I am not going to leave my uncle and run away! What do you take me for? A coward?' His eyes flickered over her and she was suddenly aware of how thin her garment was, of how her nipples had peaked in the cool air. Anusha swept the bedcovers around her like a robe and glared at him as he got to his feet. 'Lecher!'

'I rather hoped I could take you for a sensible woman,' he said with a sigh. He added something under his breath in English and she pounced on it.

'What is this? A *tutty-hooded female*?'

'Totty-headed. Foolish,' he translated. 'No, clawing my eyes out is not going to help.' He caught her wrists with contemptuous ease. 'Listen to me. Do you think it will help your uncle to have to worry about you on top of everything else? And if the worst happens, what are you going to do? Lead the women to the pyres or become a hostage?'

Anusha drew in a deep breath. *He is right, may all the demons take him.* She knew where her duty lay and she was not a child to refuse out of spite. She would go, not because this man told her to, but because her raja willed it. And because this was no longer her home. 'No, if my uncle tells me to go, then I will go. How?'

'You can ride a horse?'

'Of course I can ride a horse! I am a Rajput.'

'Then dress for riding—hard riding. Dress as a man and wear tough cloth and good boots, wrap your hair in a turban. Bring a roll of blankets, the nights are cold outside, but only pack what you must have. Can you do that? I will meet you in the court below. *Jaldi*.'

'I may be *totty-headed*, Major Herriard, but I am not a fool. And, yes, I understand the need to hurry.'

'Can you dress without help?' He paused on the threshold, a broad shadow against the pale marble.

Beyond words, Anusha threw a sandal at him and its ivory toe-post broke against the door jamb. He melted away into the darkness, leaving her shivering, the drumbeats vibrating through her very bones. For a moment she stood there, forcing herself to think clearly of what she must do, then she ran to the two maids. Under her groping fingers the blood beat strongly below their jawbones. Spies or not, they were alive.

She lifted the nightlight and took it round the room, touching it to the wicks of the lamps in every niche until there was enough light to see by. The mirrored fragments in the walls reflected her image in a myriad of jagged shards as she pulled out the last of the trunks, the one containing clothes for use on the journey. She dressed in plain trousers, tight in the calf, wide at the thigh, then layers above, topped by a long, dark brown split-sided coat. Her soft riding boots were there and she pulled them on, slid a dagger into the top of the right one and another, a tiny curved knife, into her belt.

It was quick to twist her hair into a tight plait to pile on the crown of her head and she wrapped and tied a turban out of dark brown cloth, fumbling as she did so. Sometimes she secured her hair like this when riding, but her maids had always tied it.

Money. How much money did Herriard have? Anusha pulled the long cloth free, rummaged in the trunk again and found the jewels she had intended to wear as they arrived in Calcutta, chosen to emphasise her status and her independence. She stuffed the finest into a bag, coiled her hair around it and rewrapped the turban.

Two blankets rolled around a change of linen, toilet articles, a bag containing hairpins and comb, tinder box. What else? She rubbed her temples—the drums stopped her thinking properly, invaded her head. Soon someone would come to check on her, fuss over her, shepherd her to the inner fastness of the palace where she really wanted to be. Where it was her duty not to go.

Anusha found her little box of medicines, added that, rolled up the blankets, tied them with leather straps and caught up the bundle in her arms. The walls were honeycombed with passages and stairs and she took one of the narrowest and least-used ways down, tiptoeing as she reached the doorway.

But Herriard had seen her. He stepped away from the wall, his eyes glinting in the reflected torchlight, and reached for the bundle.

'I can manage. No, not that way, I must say goodbye to my uncle, to the Lady Paravi—'

'And risk being seen? They know what we are doing and they have other things to think about just now. Come *on*.' He pushed her in front of him through the door, back into the palace. He seemed to know the way as well as she, pulled her into alcoves as servants ran past, knew when to stop and slide into the shadows to avoid a distracted sentry, his attention on someone shouting on the battlements.

A slender figure stepped out right in front of them and she stopped so abruptly that Herriard ran into her and gripped both her arms above the elbow to steady himself. His body was hard and immovable against her back and his voice was a soft rumble. Suddenly she was glad of his size. When he released her it was as though a bulwark had been removed.

'Ajit, are the horses ready?'

'Yes, *sahib*,' the man said and she recognised the major's servant. He must have run up the steep road from the base court for he was panting. 'Pavan and Rajat and a good mare for the lady. The lower gate is still open for soldiers taking up positions outside the walls, but we must hurry or we will be noticed.'

They ran, skidding on the black stones worn smooth by the passage of elephants and horses and men over hundreds of years, hugged the walls that loomed over them, slowed at every one of the gates where the road changed direction, all the better to confuse attackers if they got within the outer defences.

One more gate, Anusha thought, as she bounced painfully off a ring set in the wall. There was a cry ahead, a thud and Herriard stopped, bent over Ajit's sprawled figure.

'Collarbone, *sahib*,' the man gasped. 'Broken. I am sorry.' He sat up and she saw his right shoulder sloped down at an unnatural angle. In the torchlight his face was grey.

'You must stay.' Herriard helped him to his feet and propped him up against the wall. 'Go back up and see the court physician. He is to be trusted. Tell him to let his Highness know we are safe away.'

'*Sahib*, take my bundle, too—there are weapons.'

'I will. You take care, Ajit, my friend, I will see you in Calcutta.'

Herriard picked up the fallen bundle, took Anusha's arm and dragged her on. 'How good a rider are you?' he demanded as they slowed for the final gate before the lower court. He stopped, watchful, the shadows of the vicious spikes set at the height of an elephant's forehead lying in bars across his face.

'Excellent. Of course.' She looked up at the rows of hand-prints at the side of the gate, left by the women who had gone through it to become *sati* on their husbands' funeral pyres. She shuddered and the Englishman felt it and fol-lowed her gaze.

'Another good reason for not marrying a maharaja twice your age,' he observed as he took her elbow and steered her into the courtyard.

'Do not touch me!'

He ignored her until they were past the bustle of the el-ephant lines and into the straw-strewn stables, virtually empty now the cavalry had ridden out. Then he stopped, jerking her against him. He would say it was so he could keep his voice low, but she knew it was a show of domi-nance.

'Listen to me, Miss Laurens. Hard as it may be for you to believe, your beauty does not inflame me with lust and, even if it did, I am not fool enough to waste time dallying with you when a small war is about to break out around our heads.'

He released her and began to strap the blanket rolls be-hind the saddles of the three horses that still stood in the stalls: a handsome, raking grey, a smaller, well-muscled black and a bay with the brand of her uncle's stud. 'Take this.' He thrust the bay's reins into her hand. 'When I need to touch you, I will touch you, and when I do you had better be prepared to obey me because it will be an emergency. I promised your father I would get you back to him, but I did not promise him not to tan your backside in the process.'

'You…*swine*,' Anusha hissed.

Herriard shrugged. 'If I am, then I am the swine who is going to keep you alive. And, while we are on the subject of touching, I should point out that you are the one who sneaked into the bathhouse and touched me when I was naked. Your hands were cold and your technique could do with some work.' He led out the other two horses and tied the black's reins on its neck—the blanket rolls were strapped to its back. 'Here, I'll give you a leg up.'

'I do not need your help.' Anusha jammed her foot in the stirrup and swung into the saddle. 'And I only wanted to see—' She shut her mouth in confusion at where her temper had led her.

'See what?' He was up on the grey now. In the torchlight his lean features showed nothing but amused curiosity.

'What colour you were,' Anusha snapped.

'And your curiosity was satisfied?' Herriard clicked his tongue and the grey and the black moved out into the yard. Anusha dug in her heels and sent her horse after them.

'Yes. Where you are not touched by the sun you are pink. Not white at all.' She would not be shamed or embarrassed by him.

'I suspect that after many days with you I will be turning white on a regular basis,' he said. 'Now, be quiet and cover yourself.' He pulled the tail of his turban round and tucked it in to veil the lower part of his face. Seething, Anusha followed his example and the three horses passed out of the main gate and down the road towards the town without challenge.

She twisted in the saddle for a last look at the great walls towering above her, the fort that contained a palace, the palace that had been her home. Now she was simply a fugitive, neither Anusha, the raja's pampered niece, nor Miss Laurens, the rejected daughter of an Englishman. The thought was frightening and strangely liberating. She did not have to think about where she was going or how she would get there—for days she would be floating on the stream of fate.

At the pressure of her heels the bay drew alongside Herriard's big grey. 'Where do we go?' she asked in English. She had best practise it, she supposed.

'Allahabad to start with. Speak Hindi.'

'So we do not attract attention?' Anusha tucked the end of the cloth more snugly into the turban as he nodded. 'You do that without a word spoken. You are too big and too pale.' She would die rather than admit that she found the sheer size of him comforting.

'With my hair covered I can be taken for a Pathan,' Herriard said.

'They are tall and light-skinned and they have grey eyes, some of the men from the north, I have seen them,' she agreed. 'But your eyes are green.'

The town was seething like a disturbed ant heap with the news of the maharaja's approaching army. The bay snorted and sidled at the press of bullock carts, the running figures and the trains of camels. Herriard reached for her rein, then withdrew his hand when she hissed at him. She had her mount back under control within seconds.

'I am flattered that you noticed my eyes.' He skirted round a cow that lay in the middle of the road chewing the cud as it ignored all around it with complete indifference.

'You should not be. Of course I noticed—you are different. Strange,' she added to make certain he did not think it a compliment. 'It is a long time since I saw someone like you.'

He did not answer her, but guided his horse around a spitting, grumbling knot of camels and out over the rickety bridge that spanned the river. So, he was either not easy to goad or he simply dismissed her as unimportant. The moon was up, noticeable now they were away from the torches and the fires, and the *angrezi* stood in his stirrups to survey the road in front of them.

'We can take that track there.' Anusha pointed. 'It cuts through the fields and it will be deserted now. We will make better time and no one will see us.'

'And we will leave the tracks of three horses plain on soil that is trodden only by bare feet and oxen. Here, on the road, we will be less easy to track.'

At least he explains, Anusha conceded, then the implication hit home. 'We will be followed?'

'Of course. Once it is realised that you are no longer in the palace the maharaja's spies will pass the word out. I am counting on half a day's start, that is all.'

Anusha's stomach tightened. Suddenly the Englishman's frankness was no longer so welcome. 'It is more dangerous out here than in the fort. Why did we not stay there until help came?'

He shot her a glance, the silvery light catching his eyes, making them unreal, like the greenish pearl of the inside of a shell. 'Because your uncle could not be certain that he could protect you within the palace. Your father makes you a very tempting prize for a man who wishes for nothing but his own power and to keep the Company at bay.'

'I was in danger *within* the palace?'

'I think so. I removed you easily enough, did I not?'

'Yes.' She took a deep breath. Treachery, spies, danger, lies. And she had thought her life had been so tranquil, so... boring. *I could have been kidnapped at any time.*

'Frightened?'

'Of what?' she demanded. 'There is much to choose from.'

That surprised a laugh from him. 'Of the pursuers, of the journey, of where you are going. Of me.'

'No,' Anusha lied. She was afraid of all of those things, but she was not going to admit it. His faint snort of derision showed what he thought of that.

'You appear to be competent, so I imagine you will evade pursuit,' she said. It seemed important to convince him of her courage, her ability to undertake this journey. 'I look forward to being able to look around me, to see things openly and not through the screens of a travelling palanquin. I will deal with my destination when I get there. And as for you, Major Herriard, you are a—' She searched for the equivalent in Hindi and resorted to English. '*Gentleman*, are you not, if you are an officer? And my mother said that *English gentlemen* must behave honourably to ladies.'

'That is the theory,' he agreed, his voice dry. And then he laughed and spurred his horse into a canter, leaving her to follow, her body tight with apprehension.

Chapter Four

'Why are we stopping?' Anusha demanded. The horses had dropped into a trot and then a walk as Major Herriard turned off the road. Beneath their hooves the ground was stony and uneven. 'This is a terrible surface, we cannot canter on this.'

'Are you going to question every decision I make?' he asked without turning his head.

'Yes.' Now she did not have to concentrate on keeping her aching body in the saddle the desire to slide off and simply go to sleep was overwhelming. Perhaps when she woke it would all have been a bad dream.

'The moon will be down very soon and then it will be hard to see where we are going. There are trees over there, cover. We will make a temporary camp and sleep until sunrise. I turned off here because the ground will not show tracks.'

'Very well,' Anusha agreed.

'That is very gracious of you, Miss Laurens, but your

approval is not required, merely your obedience.' Herriard was a dark shape now as he sat motionless on the horse and studied the small group of trees and thorn bushes in what was left of the moonlight. He spoke absently, as though she was peripheral to his interest.

'Major Herriard!'

'Call me Nick. Stay here. Your voice has probably scared off anything dangerous lurking in there, but I will check first.'

Nick. What sort of name was that? She translated to take her mind off the fact that she was suddenly alone and things were rustling in the bushes. Quite large things. Was *nick* not something to do with a small cut? Well, that hardly suited him—the man had the subtlety and brutal force of a sabre slash.

'There is a small shrine in there, a stone platform we can sleep on and some firewood. We can light a fire and it will be shielded by the walls,' he said as he rode back to her side. 'There are water jars for the horses, which is good fortune.'

'You would plunder a shrine?' Anusha demanded, more out of antagonism than outrage as she guided her horse after him. Taking water was hardly plunder.

'We will do no damage. We can leave an offering if you wish.' He swung down as he spoke and came to hold up a hand to her.

'I can manage. And what is a Christian doing leaving an offering at a Hindu shrine?' Her feet hit the ground rather harder than she had been expecting and her knees buckled. Nick's hand under her elbow was infuriatingly necessary. 'I said I can manage.'

He ignored her and held on until she had her balance. It felt very strange to be touched by a man, a virtual stranger.

It felt safe and dangerous all at the same time. 'It would cause no offence, I imagine. And after twelve years in this country I am not at all sure what I am. A pragmatist, perhaps. What are you?'

It was a good question. She supposed she had better decide before she reached Calcutta. Her mother had converted to Christianity after she had lived with Sir George for five years. For ten years Anusha had gone with her to church. And in Kalatwah she had lived as a Hindu. 'What am I? I do not know. Does it matter, so long as one lives a good life?'

'A sound philosophy. At least that is something we do not have to fight over.' He did not unsaddle the horses but loosened the girths and then dumped their kit on the stone platform.

'We do not have to fight at all, provided you treat me with respect,' Anusha retorted. *And stop watching me like a hawk.* She found a twiggy branch and began to sweep an area clear of the leaf litter that might harbour insects or a small snake.

'I will treat you with the respect that you earn, Miss Laurens.' Herriard... *Nick*...hefted an urn over to the stone trough by the horses and poured out water. 'You are a woman and your father's daughter, which means I do not deal with you as I would a man. After that—' he shrugged '—it is up to you.'

'I do not wish to go to my father. I hate my father.'

'You may wish what you will and you may think what you wish, but you will not abuse Sir George in my hearing. And you will obey me. Stay there.' In the semi-darkness she could not read his face, but Anusha heard the anger. Again he showed that fierce, puzzling, loyalty to her father. He turned and walked away.

'Wait! Where are you going?' Surely he was not going to punish her by leaving her here in the dark?

Nick vanished into the scrub and she heard what sounded like boots kicking at the low branches. When he walked back he was doing something to the front of his trousers and she blushed in the gloom. 'There is a nice thick bush there,' he said, gesturing. 'With no snakes.'

'Thank you.' With as much dignity as she could muster Anusha stalked down the three steps to the ground and over to the bush. The mundane implications of being alone like this with a man were beginning to dawn on her. There might be vast areas with hardly a bush. How was she supposed to manage then? The wretch seemed to have no shyness, no modesty about mentioning these things at all. Never, in the ten years until she had chased Tavi and found herself in that corridor with Nick, had she been all alone with a man, even her uncle or one of the eunuchs.

When she emerged his attention was, mercifully, on lighting a small fire in an angle of the wall. The flames made a pool of light on the platform, but would be hidden from anyone approaching from the direction they had come. A bed of blankets had been made up close to the fire.

In the shadows she could see the stumpy pillar of the Shiva *lingam* and the firelight glinted for a moment on something that trickled down its side. 'People have been here recently.' She went and looked at the pool of fresh oil on the head of the ancient stone phallus, the spray of flowering shrub that had been laid on the curve of the stylised female organ that it rose from.

'I have,' Herriard said as she joined her hands together in a brief reverence. It seemed that, whatever his beliefs, he knew how to show respect to the gods, if not to her. More in charity with him, she turned back and he gestured to food laid out on a large leaf beside the blankets. 'Here. Eat and drink and then rest. Do not take anything off, not even your boots.'

'I have no intention of removing anything!'

'Then you are going to have a very uncomfortable few weeks, Miss Laurens. Oh, sit down, I am far too weary to ravish you tonight!'

That was a jest. She hoped. Warily Anusha sank down on to the blankets. 'Eat and keep your strength up. Now we can only rest for a short while. Tomorrow night I hope we may take longer.'

'Where are you going to sleep?' She took a piece of *naan*, folded it around what looked like goat's cheese and ate, surprised at how hungry she was.

'I will not sleep. I will keep watch.'

'You cannot do that every night,' she pointed out.

'No,' Nick agreed. 'I will rest when it is safer and where you can keep watch.' He tore off a piece of the flat bread and ate it. She caught a glimpse of strong white teeth.

'Me?'

'Look around you, Miss Laurens. Who else is there? Sooner or later I must sleep. Or are you not capable of acting as a look-out?'

'Of course. I am capable of anything. I am a—'

'Rajput, I know. You are also your father's daughter, which should mean that there is a brain in there somewhere, despite all evidence to the contrary.'

Anusha choked on a mouthful of water from the flask. 'How dare you! You are used to this sort of thing, I am not. I have been dragged from my bed, forced to ride through the night with a man—I have never been alone with a man for ten years—I am worried about Kalatwah…'

'True,' Nick conceded. It was not much of an apology. 'I will do my best to preserve your privacy and your modesty, but you must behave as much like a man as you can, for your own safety. Do you understand that?'

'As you guessed, I do have a brain,' she retorted. 'Now I am going to sleep.'

'Namaste,' he said, so politely that he must be mocking her.

'Namaste,' she returned as she rolled herself into the blankets. She would just close her eyes, rest her aching body. But she would not sleep—she did not trust him.

Anusha woke, suddenly and completely alert, with that thought still in her mind. She had been foolish to fear, it seemed. Her rest had been undisturbed, her blankets were still tight around her. Herriard was moving about, attending to the horses.

From the light it was just past dawn and she must have slept for at least two hours. And he had slept not at all. Anusha watched from beneath half-closed lids as he checked the horses, led them to a patch of longer grass where they might snatch a few mouthfuls. Lack of sleep seemed to have simply made him more alert, the lines of his face tauter.

He was not at all like the men she had lived among for so many years, Anusha decided. Most of the Indian men were slender, lithe. There was an English word and she searched for it. Yes, *sleek*, that was it. Nick Herriard was not sleek, he was too big, too overtly physical. The high cheekbones, the big nose, the strong chin—all asserted power and will.

Anusha remembered the feel of his muscles under her hands and shivered, just as he turned and found her watching him.

She thought that colour came up under the golden tan, then he gestured towards the fire. 'There is water heating if you want to wash. I will go and scout the road.'

Anusha waited until he had walked out of sight, his musket in one hand, then disentangled herself from the blankets. She used the convenient bush, then washed as best she could. He came back, whistling tactfully, as she was rolling up the blankets.

'All right?' He did not wait for her answer, but squatted by the fire and began to make tea, throwing leaves into the boiling water from a pouch that lay amongst the food he had set out. It was the same as last night and the bread would be dry. And she supposed from the brisk manner with which he was preparing it that she should have done this while he was away. She had never been without servants before, either.

'Eat,' Nick said, pushing the food towards her and pouring tea into a horn beaker. 'There is no one in sight, we should get on.'

'When will we be able to get more food?' Anusha chewed on the dry bread and wondered if the cheese had been this pungent the night before.

'When we come across someone who can sell us some.'

'The next big village is—'

'We are not going through villages, big or small. Do you want to leave flags to mark our route?'

'But surely they will give up? We could be anywhere by now.'

Nick washed the stale *naan* down with tea that was too hot and contemplated the haughty, exquisite face of the young woman opposite him. It was a reasonable question and she was sorely in need of reassurance and comfort, despite the mask she was putting on.

But what Anusha was going to get was a bracing dose of reality and he was going to allow his irritation with this entire situation to ride him. It was the only way he was going to be able to ignore the tension in his groin and the heat that seemed to wash through him whenever he looked at her. Or when she looked at him. He was still recovering from the impact of those grey eyes studying him as he dealt with the horses. It was odd that she should affect him so—Miss Lauren's spiky personality was hardly alluring.

'How many armed men do you think it would need to take me?' he asked. When she just shook her head, he answered himself. 'Eight, ten perhaps. I have three muskets, but we have lost our other marksman and besides, muskets take time to load. I am good, Miss Laurens, and lucky— I would not be alive today if I was not—but I am just one man. And the maharaja's spies will have told him that. It will be a blow to his pride that you have escaped him, so he can easily spare a dozen riders to come after us. And they'll know we'll be heading east, that is the logical direction to go in.'

He expected fear, possibly tears. Instead she looked at him down the straight little nose that she had definitely not inherited from her father and said, 'Then teach me to load a musket and go somewhere that is not logical.'

So, he had not been wrong—she had her father's intelligence after all and her late mother had the reputation for both learning and political cunning. He could have his hands full with her. Even as he thought it he winced at his choice of words—he wanted very much to have his hands full of Anusha Laurens.

'All right, I'll teach you to load, that makes sense.' At least, it would if she could manage it. He had short India Pattern muskets with him, not the British army Land Pattern version, but even so she would be wrestling with a weapon almost forty inches long. 'And I can aim directly at the Jumna River to find a boat and not head further southeast to Allahabad. But I must do it by the sun and stars—there were no detailed maps of this area and any deviation will add time.'

'I do not wish to be with you, Major Herriard, but I would like even less to be with that man. Take however long is necessary.'

'Then we will go more to the east than the road to Allahabad,' Nick said, getting to his feet and recalculating. The map that he had studied before he had set out was fixed in his memory, but it was sketchy to put it mildly.

'The muskets?' she demanded, rising from the dusty stone with the trained grace of a court lady.

The wish that he could see her dance came into his head, irrelevant and unwelcome. A well-bred lady would only dance with her female friends, or for her husband. To do otherwise was to lower herself to the level of a courtesan. Nick found himself pursuing the thought and frowned at her, earning a frigid stare in response. She was not used to being alone with men, and it was a long time since he had been alone with a respectable young woman for any length of time. How the devil was he supposed to treat her? What did he talk to her about?

'Muskets?' Anusha repeated, impatience etched in every line of her figure. She was slender, small—the top of her head came up to his ear. He would have to stoop to kiss her… Nick caught himself, appalled, and slammed the door on his thoughts, remembering another slender woman in his arms, of how fragile she had been, how clumsy she had made him feel. But Miranda had been frail as well as fragile—this girl had steel at her core.

'When we stop to rest at noon.' He was equally impatient now. The more distance they had between themselves and the fort, the happier he would be. He strapped the blanket rolls on the bay horse and led Rajat, Ajit's black gelding, forwards for her. In a crisis he could let the bay go and leave her with a horse as highly trained as his own Pavan.

'Why this one?'

Must she question everything? But he almost welcomed the irritation, it distracted him from fantasies and memories. 'He knows what to do. His name is Rajat; let him have his head.'

Anusha shrugged and mounted. Nick tied the end of the bay's long leading rein around his pommel and led them away from the shrine, not back to the track but out across the undulating grasslands, following the line he had mentally drawn on the map in his head.

'This is deserted,' Anusha observed after half a league.

'Yes. Except for the tigers.'

'We will starve or be eaten. You are supposed to be looking after me.' She did not sound petulant, merely critical of an inefficient servant.

Nick breathed in hard through his nose and controlled his temper. 'We have plenty of water. The streams are still running. The horses will sense tigers.' *I hope.* 'Food we can do without for a day or two if necessary. I am, as I promised your father and your uncle, keeping you safe. I never made any promises about comfort.'

She was silent. Then, 'Why do you dislike me, Major Herriard?'

Pavan pecked, unused to a jerk on his rein. 'What? I do not know you. And I am not used to young ladies.'

There was a snort and he glanced across at her. The little witch was grinning. 'That is not what I heard.'

'Respectable young ladies,' he said repressively.

'No?' She was still laughing, he could hear it, although she was managing to keep her face straight. 'Is your wife not respectable?'

'I do not have a wife.' *Not any longer.* Nick gritted his teeth and concentrated on scanning the undulating plain before them, plotting a route away from the stands of trees that might harbour a striped death.

'But why do you not have a wife? You are very old not to have a wife.'

'I am twenty-nine,' he snapped. 'I had a wife. Miranda. She died.'

'I am sorry.' She sounded it; the mocking edge had gone from her voice. 'How many children do you have? Will you marry again soon?'

'I have no children and, no, I have no intention of marrying again.' He tried to remind himself that this intense curiosity about family was simply the normal Indian polite interest in a stranger. He was inured to it, surely, by now?

'Oh, so you were very much in love with her, like Shah Jehan and Mumtaz Mahal. How sad.' When she was not being imperious or snappy her voice was lovely, soft and melodious with something deeply female in it that went straight to the base of his spine.

'No, I was not—' Nick snapped off the sentence. 'I married too young. I thought it was expected of me as a career officer. I married a girl I thought was suitable, a sweet little dab of a thing with no more strength to cope with India than a new-born lamb.'

'What was she doing here, then?' Anusha brought her horse alongside.

'She was newly arrived in India as part of the Fishing Fleet.' She murmured a query and he explained. 'The shiploads of young ladies that come out from England. They are supposed to be visiting relatives, but actually they are on the catch for a husband.

'I should have taken one look at Miranda Knight and realised that the country would ruin her health within the year. And it did. If I had not married her she would have gone back to England, wed a stout country squire and be the mother of a happy family by now.'

'She must have loved you to marry you and risk staying here,' Anusha suggested.

'Do not turn this into a love story. She wanted a *suitable* husband and what did I know about marriage and how to make a wife happy with my background?'

'What background?'

He glanced at Anusha, saw her read his mood in his face and close her lips tightly. After a moment she said, 'I beg your pardon,' in careful English. 'I forgot that the Europeans do not like personal questions.'

He was going to be alone with her for days, weeks probably. It was foolish to make a mystery out of himself. Best to get the questions over and done with now. 'My parents made a suitable, loveless match. It turned very rapidly into boredom on my father's part, then anger when my mother persisted in wanting...more. I am not certain I would know what a happy marriage looks like.'

How simple it sounded put like that. All those years of distress and unhappiness, not just for his mother but for the little boy in the middle, aching for the love that both parents were too busy tearing each other apart to give. He was not a little boy now, and he knew better than to expect love. Or to need it.

'Oh.' She rode in silence for a while. Then, 'So you have many mistresses now? Until you marry again?'

'Anusha, you should not be discussing such things.' She regarded him quizzically. Of course, she was used to an entirely different model of marriage and sexual relationships. 'There is no reason for me to marry again. I do not live like a holy man—a _sadhu_. But neither do I have more than one mistress at a time, and none at the moment.'

'And did you have a mistress while you were married? No, do not say _Anusha_ like that. I want to understand.'

'No, I did not. Some men do. I do not think it right.' And his resolve had been sorely tried after a few weeks of Miranda's vapours. However careful he was, however gentle, she had decided that sex was crude, unpleasant and for one purpose only. Her relief at becoming pregnant and having a good reason to bar him from her bed had been all too obvious. The familiar guilt came back like an aching bruise: he should have had the self-control to stay out of her bed until she had grown acclimatised to India, talked to her. Not got her with child.

Women before and since had assured him they found bliss in his arms. It seemed he was an acceptable lover and a failure as a husband.

'I am sorry if I should not have asked these things. Thank

you for explaining,' Anusha said in English, sounding not at all contrite.

'Don't mention it,' he replied in the same language. She was demanding, both emotionally at some level he was not used to, as well as practically. And she was distracting him, taking him away from the present and into the past, and that was dangerous.

The hairs were prickling on the back of his neck—he had learned to listen to his instincts. Nick wheeled Pavan. The grass was still long and lush although the ground was dry. The light wind was already blurring the marks of their passage so it would be hard to see how many horses had just passed.

Anusha had turned with him. 'There is no one behind us,' she said. 'Is there?'

The prickling unease was still under his skin. Nick stood in his stirrups and shaded his eyes. There, in the distance, was a small puff of dust kicked up by a group of riders coming at the gallop. 'There is. See?'

Chapter Five

'There is no cover, not for three horses.' Anusha was proud of how calm she sounded. She could not see the pursuers, but if Nick said they were coming, then she believed him. She loosened the little dagger in her sash.

'Follow me, exactly,' he said and turned to ride over a hard-pan of dry baked mud where the rains had once made a large pool. At the middle he swung down from the grey, took the bundles from the back of the bay horse and flung them over Pavan's saddle. 'Stay here.' He swung up on the bay and left the hard ground. As soon as he was on the softer earth he kicked it into a gallop, then lashed it across the flanks, swung down and rolled clear as it careered off into the distance.

'Take Pavan.' He tossed her the reins when he got back to her. 'Walk slowly towards that bush.'

Puzzled, but obedient, her heart thudding uncomfortably high in her throat, Anusha did as she was told. Behind her Nick walked backwards, sweeping a branch over their tracks. She realised as she reached the bush that it was on a very slight swell in the ground, but even so, it was too thin and too low to hide a donkey behind, let alone two horses.

'Are you going to shoot the horses?' She slid to the ground as he backed behind the thorn bush next to her.

'No need.' He removed both saddles, then whistled, two clear notes, and the horses folded their legs, sank to the ground and rolled on to their sides, necks stretched out. 'Get down.'

Anusha lay behind the swell of Pavan's belly as Nick spread the dun-coloured blankets over both animals, then propped the two muskets up on Rajat's flank and began to check over his hand guns. He laid everything out in order—ammunition, guns, sabre—loosened the knife in his boot and then glanced across at her. 'Army horses, both of them,' he explained, then glanced down at her hand. 'What the devil have you got there?'

'A knife, of course.' She would keep the one in her boot hidden until it was absolutely necessary and she had to kill someone. Or herself. A dark excitement was surging through her, as strong as the fear. She wanted to hurt the people who were attacking Kalatwah, her family, her kingdom. For the first time she understood what had taken those warriors out to fight to certain death, understood the spirit of the women who had gone to the flames rather than face slavery and shame.

'You are not going to need it.'

'But there will be a fight, a battle.' She could hear them coming now, the faint drum of hoofbeats. The maharaja's men had picked up their tracks.

'Not unless I have made a mistake.' Nick was rubbing handfuls of dust over the musket barrels to mask their shine.

'They should ride past, find the bay, conclude it was a ruse to send them off the road.'

'But we must kill them!'

'Bloodthirsty little wild cat,' Nick said, low-voiced. She sensed amusement in him. He had a strange sense of humour if he found this funny. 'If they do not come back, then the maharaja knows they have found us and will send more men. If they go back without seeing us, he will conclude we have gone another way.'

'Oh. Strategy.'

'Tactics, to be exact. Now, be quiet.'

There were eight riders. They passed at the gallop, vanished. Anusha released her pent-up breath and slid a little closer to Nick.

Time stretched on. Her left leg was becoming numb. *'They have gone.'*

'Wait.'

As Nick spoke she heard them returning more slowly, scanning the ground as they came, the bay on a leading rein. They rode past, then the only sound was the buzz of insects, the rumbling of Rajat's stomach under her ear, the mew of a hawk high overhead.

'Stay here.' Nick began to ease away. 'You can let go of my coat.'

'Oh!' Anusha's fingers cramped as she released her death-grip. 'I didn't realise I was holding it.' But Nick was already moving, a musket in each hand, pistol in his sash, keeping low over the ground as he dodged from bush to bush.

It was like trying to see a ghost—if she took her eyes from him he would vanish. She blinked and he was gone into the long grass. Even behind the bulk of the horses she felt incredibly exposed, utterly alone. She had not realised what a large emotional space he filled. An infuriating, man-shaped, protective space.

What would she do if she heard shooting? Anusha studied the weapons he had left behind. One musket, one pistol, the bag that contained the ammunition, his sabre. Now was not the time to learn how to reload, but she could take it all to him. She worked out the best way to carry the weapons, wondering if the horses would obey her and get to their feet.

A hand closed around her ankle.

Anusha twisted, her knife in her hand, her other lashing out, fingers bent, nails raking down.

Nick laughed and rolled to one side, releasing her foot. It was the laugh that made her temper snap, that and the long-held tension. Anusha dropped the knife and launched herself at him, intent on hurting his male pride, if nothing else.

The next moment she was flat on her back with her hands pinned above her head and the weight of one very large man on top of her. And he was still laughing. 'Wild cat. I was right.'

'You—' Words, and breath, failed her. 'Get off me.'

For a long unfathomable moment he stared down into her eyes and his own seemed to darken. Nick stopped laughing. For an instant she thought he had stopped breathing.

'It is not seemly,' she managed to say as her mind tried to assimilate all the new sensations of a hard male body pressed against her own softness. She liked them. All of them.

'No, it is not.' Nick rolled off her and got to his feet in one fluid movement. *He is as supple as a young sapling,* Paravi had said. Heat washed through her. 'I am sorry, I could not resist it. You were quivering like a hound wanting to be let off the leash.'

'I was listening for shots,' Anusha said with as much dignity as she could muster, flat on her back and filled with what she was horribly afraid was sexual desire. 'Have they gone?'

'They have, no doubt thinking that only a fool would head into the wilds with only two horses and a princess.'

He meant to mock her when he called her *princess,* she knew that. 'And *are* you a fool?'

Nick reached down a hand and hauled her to her feet. 'No, but I am going to do it anyway.' He pulled the blankets off the horses and brought them to their feet with a whistle, shaking like dogs to get rid of the dust. 'We will ride on a league or so and when we are out of earshot I will bring down some game for dinner. Then the muskets will be empty. We will rest a while, drink and I will show you how to load.' He picked up one of the guns and looked from it to her with a grin. 'Although I think you will have to stand on a rock to do it, Miss Laurens.'

'Do not call me that.' It was intolerable that he should treat her so casually and yet address her with *angrezi* formality by the name she rejected.

'Anusha, then?'

'Anusha,' she agreed warily. 'Nick.'

They remounted and rode on in a silence that seemed somehow more companionable than it had yet done.

After two leagues Nick halted and left her with the horses while he took the guns and padded off into the scrub. 'Drink,' he said, 'and get into the shade.'

'Yes, Major,' she muttered, but did as she was told, not that there was much shade to be had.

Anusha heard four gunshots and when he returned Nick

had a sand grouse and a hare dangling from his hand. That was good shooting with a musket, she knew.

He hunkered down in the small patch of shade beside her and reached for the canteen of water. It spilled from the sides of his mouth and she watched it run through the stubble on his cheeks, saw his Adam's apple bob as he swallowed.

'You are a soldier, so this is taking you from the army,' she said when he put down the water and ran the back of his hand across his mouth. 'Why did they not send a diplomat for me?'

'Because there was always the chance that something like this might happen. And I am a diplomat, of sorts. I move between the army and the princely courts as the Company requires.' It explained why his Hindi was so good.

'But this is not for the Company, this is for my father.'

'His interests and those of the Company coincide when it comes to removing you from this situation,' Nick said drily. 'But he is so senior that if he wished me to go on his personal business there would be no objection.'

Sir George is like a father to me, he had said with the force of deeply held feeling. At the time the words had been a puzzle. Now, watching the relaxed, broad-shouldered figure, a startling idea struck her, and with it a stab of something that was disconcertingly like jealousy.

'Are you my father's son?' she demanded.

'No!' Nick frowned at her. 'Whatever made you think that?'

'You look like him, you said he was a father to you.' Now she felt a fool. But a suspicious fool, even so.

'I do *not* look like him. I am the same height, the same build. But my eyes are green, his are grey—like yours. His nose is hooked, mine is straighter, my hair is lighter.'

Why was that a relief? If he was her half-brother, then she would have nothing to fear from him as a man, or from her own unruly desires. 'But if you feel so much for him, then I suppose your real father is dead.'

'No, he is in England. I have not seen him for twelve years, when he sent me out to join the Company as a writer at the age of seventeen.'

'A clerk? That is very humble for a gentleman.' Her mind kept worrying at that flash of relief. Surely she would not be jealous if Nick was her brother? That was very petty, for she did not love her father, after all. He could have fathered half-siblings all over Calcutta for all she cared—he would treat them and their mothers as badly as he had her, she was sure. She did not want to think about him—he did not want her and she did not want him. She should forget him, but the pain would not let her, like an old wound around her heart, forever nagging and weakening.

'A writer's post is the first rung on the ladder,' Nick said. He seemed to be looking inwards, not at her, and whatever foolish emotions were plain on her face. 'With luck and hard work—and provided one stays alive—it is very difficult for a writer not to become wealthy.'

'So you must have been pleased at the opportunity.'

He was frowning, as though the memory was not a pleasant one. 'Pleased? No, I was appalled. So I refused. I had no ambition to be a writer, no desire to go into trade, no wish to leave England. It did not help that I had no idea what I *did* want to do.

'So then he beat me, cut my allowance and, when that did not work, had me forcibly delivered to the ship. Halfway out I contracted some kind of fever and I would have died if it were not for Mary—Lady Laurens. She deposited me, like a half-dead rat, on her husband's front porch and he took me in.'

Anusha stiffened at the name. Lady Laurens, her father's wife, the woman he had married before he came to India and who had refused to come with him. And then, fifteen years after they had parted, she decided it was her duty to be with her husband. Instead of ordering her to stay away as any wronged husband should have done, her father had allowed his wife to come out to India, had dismissed Sarasa, Anusha's mother, and sent them back to her brother.

The disobedient, wilful wife, the one who had not borne him any children, was rewarded and the faithful mistress and companion, the mother of his daughter, discarded.

The memories of that day were still vivid. Despite the tears and the preparations she had not believed her mother when she said they must go. And then the ship from England arrived early and they were still in the house and there was Lady Laurens and all her baggage in the front yard and Sir George's other family at the back. Sarasa had shut herself into the women's quarters and ordered her servants to load their baggage animals immediately. She would not wait to be ordered out of her own home by this interloper.

But Anusha, not understanding, had run out to look for her father and wriggled through the bearers and the carts and the chaos. She had slipped up the steps on to the veranda and heard her father's voice inside and a strange woman, speaking English, and she knew her mother was right: his wife who was a stranger to him had come and he did not want them any more.

She had turned around, swallowing the tears and the awful hurt, and bumped into a stretcher that had been laid out across chairs in the shade. On it there was a still figure.

Now she stared at Nick. 'But I saw you! I saw you lying on the veranda. You were skinny and white and I thought you were dead. You were white and your hair was like straw.'

'I thought I was dead, too,' Nick said with a twist of his mouth that might have been dark humour or might have been remembered pain. 'Between them George and Mary saved my life and my future.'

'You were a boy, so more interesting than a mere girl, no doubt, even if you were not their blood,' Anusha said, then bit her lip as she heard her own betraying bitterness. For her pride's sake he must not think she cared.

'You think I was a substitute for you?' Nick got up and began to tie the legs of the game securely together. 'No. I was a distraction at first, I think, something for them to worry about together as they rediscovered each other. And then, when I confounded all the doctors and did not die, George grew to like me and to take an interest in my career. But you have always come first in his heart.'

He tightened the knots and hooked the limp bodies over the pommel of his horse, not seeming to hear her snort of derision. Did he think her a fool to believe that? If she had any value to her father, he would not have sent her away. He only wanted her now because she had become a political pawn in some violent game of chess.

'For Mary, I was almost a son, that is true. She had lost a child at birth and then was unable to have any more.'

'Is that why my father left her for all those years in England? Why did he not get another wife if she could not give him sons?'

'Because that is not legal in England. You must get a divorce and that is a ghastly process.'

'Then why did he not bring her to India?' Anusha demanded, determined to get to the bottom of this.

'They became…estranged after the child's death. The doctors said there would be no more children. She would not come to India with him, so he provided for her financially and left her in England.' Nick swung up into the saddle and waited while she stood where she was, frowning up at him. 'They corresponded and somehow things healed with the years. Then she received a letter from his secretary when Sir George was very ill with fever and decided it was her duty to be with him.'

'My mother nursed him when he was ill,' Anusha flared. 'He was better before the letter could have reached her. That woman had no need to come and because she did, he sent us away.'

'She was his legal wife,' Nick said with what sounded like strained patience. 'Things are different in English society, the laws are different. If you want to know any more, you must ask him—I have no right to discuss it.'

Anusha mounted Rajat and sent him after Pavan with an impatience that made the black break into a canter. She reined him back, fuming. 'So you are not his son, you are his obedient servant?'

'Indeed,' Nick said, so placidly she could have slapped him. He was humouring her. She wanted to fight, to argue, to shout at him and she did not understand why. Her fight was with her father—if she did not manage to escape before he had her in his clutches again. She fell in behind the grey and glared at Nick's back. His very upright back.

He was good to look at, she admitted. His broad shoulders tapered to a narrow waist cinched by a dark blue sash; the skirts of his coat fell over the saddle, but she had seen his naked body and knew his buttocks were firm and shapely, his thighs long-muscled. He rode as though he and his horse were one, easy in the saddle and yet as focused as an archer before he loosed the bowstring.

'Stop sulking,' he said without looking back.

'I am not sulking,' Anusha retorted, startled to realise that she was not. *I am looking at your body and thinking that I desire you, that I would like to put into practice all those things that the texts show a woman and a man can do together...* Aghast, she blinked, as though that would turn him into a short fat clerk or a skinny youth or... No, Nick Herriard was still just as he had been when she closed her eyes and so was the hot, tight feeling low in her belly. She had to do something.

'Ma ub gayi hu,' she said and dug her heels into Rajat's flanks.

'Bored? You are *bored?*' she heard Nick say as she passed him. 'Hell, woman, what do you get up to in Kalatwah every day if you find this boring?'

'I find *you* boring,' she tossed back and slapped the reins on her mount's neck. For a moment she thought he would let her go, then the hoofbeats behind her speeded up, began to gain. Anusha glanced back over her shoulder—Nick had taken up the challenge and was racing.

'Little witch,' Nick muttered under his breath. He was tempted to let her go, gallop off her sulks and bad temper. If she had been a youth, he would have done just that, but, he thought with resignation, she was George's daughter and they were in tiger country and so—

'Chalo chale, Pavan!' The big grey needed no urging. He gathered his hocks under him and surged after his stable-

mate. Damn it, but the girl could ride, she had not exaggerated. *I am Rajput, indeed,* he thought as he let her keep the lead for the moment. *She's going to be a handful to turn into a little English lady.*

He eased the reins and Pavan responded, up to the black's flank now, then his nose was level with the girth. Anusha looked across and grinned and kicked for more speed.

Nick looked at the strong, slim legs gripping the horse, remembered the feel of her hands, cool and hesitant on his bare skin, and shuddered as the wave of desire went through him. *No.*

His hands must have jerked. Pavan pecked, recovered and, with a triumphant little crow of laughter, Anusha urged Rajat ahead again. Then there was a sinuous movement in the dust before them, the black horse swerved violently and jumped clear over the lethal creature beneath its hooves.

Anusha was thrown sideways, landed out of the saddle, high on Rajat's neck, then fell, tumbling in the sand towards the king cobra that had reared up, hood spread, furious and lethal.

Chapter Six

Nick swung out of the saddle as Pavan reared to avoid the other horse. He rolled as he landed, his hand drawing the dagger from his boot even as he came to his feet. The reptile swayed, hissing, its hood spread wide, its head darting from side to side, undecided whether to strike at the nearer danger—Anusha sprawled motionless—or himself, moving, but further away.

'Lie still!' He waved his hand and the glittering eyes followed the movement, the coils shifting to balance the swaying, deadly head. Anusha was either unconscious or frozen in obedience, he could not tell. Nick edged further to the side, still gesturing with his hand, drawing the creature's attention from her body.

Then Anusha moaned and stirred, her fingers clenching into the sand. She must have been stunned, he realized, as the snake swayed back, raising itself to strike the closer figure. There was no time for subtlety or calculation. Nick launched himself into the narrow space between her body and the cobra, his left arm coming up to take the strike, his right swinging round to plunge the knife into the body below the hood as its fangs fastened on his wrist.

As it bit he slammed his left fist down on to the ground, taking the snake with it, pulled out the knife, struck again and ducked back instinctively as another knife flashed down past his shoulder to slash into the thick, writhing body. Nick wrenched his arm free from the fangs and fell back, pulling Anusha with him away from the creature's thrashing death throes.

'It bit you.' She twisted in his arms, tore at his sleeve. 'A tourniquet, hurry. Then we must cut the wound, squeeze—'

'It did not bite me.' Nick tried to get a grip on her, steady her so he could check her for injuries, but she pulled free and caught at his clothing, as intent on his wounds as he was on hers.

'Do not be a fool, of course it bit you. We have minutes at most. Less, if it caught a vein.' There was a thready note of panic beneath her sharp orders. Nick ripped back the sleeve so she could see his arm and the leather wrist band he wore to support an old injury when he was riding for long distances. 'Oh.' She touched the two deep indentations in the leather with a shaking finger. 'Did it go right through?'

Had it? With a sick twist in his gut Nick unlaced the strap. The skin beneath was marked by the pressure of the bite and she caught at it, stretched it smooth with both hands to check for punctures, then snatched up the leather and held it to the light.

'*Oh,*' she said again and swayed where she huddled in the dust. 'But it might have missed the strap. It might have killed you.'

'And you might have broken your foolish little neck,'

he snapped, his fear for her mixing with his body's reaction to the struggle with the cobra, that sickening realisation that it might have left its venom in his body. He hated snakes, would sooner face a tiger than a big king cobra, and his stomach was churning now. What if he had hesitated, had let that fear master him? Anusha would be dying in his arms now.

Stop it, he snarled inwardly. Imagining death slowed you down, got you killed. *You did not hesitate, you are both alive.*

The snake had ceased to twitch. Anusha was the only target for his feelings. 'What the devil were you playing at? Are you hurt? Have you broken anything?'

'No, I am not hurt. Why are you angry? I helped you, I had my knife—' Her turban had come off, her hair lay in a coil as thick as the great snake across her heaving breast and her face was paler than he had yet seen it. She still clasped his left forearm with both hands, then released it with a sob and burrowed into his lap as he sat on the crushed grass.

Instinctively his arms closed, cuddling her close. Against his body he could feel her, rounded and slender and trembling, and he smoothed his hand down her back, the fine hairs escaping from her plait catching on the roughed skin of his palms. Could she feel his heart pound, his pulse race? Was it the aftermath of the encounter with the snake or something far more dangerous, a response equally as primitive?

Lust burned through his veins, the desire to possess, to celebrate being alive, to bury the memory of that second when the flat black eyes had locked with his and he looked at his death. And he wanted her, wanted this woman who was an innocent and who must stay that way.

Anger was the only way to deal with it, anger at himself, anger at the woman in his embrace. 'What the hell are you doing with a knife? You are not safe out with a weapon.'

Anusha recoiled against the cage of his arms, the pressure of her squirming backside on his groin only inflaming both desire and temper even more. 'Of course I have a knife! You saw it when the maharaja's men came. And I can use it.' She was shaking still, but with shocked anger, not with fear now. 'They will not take me alive. I—'

'If they take you alive, someone can rescue you. If you are dead, you are dead and a lot of use that will be, except to start a war,' Nick snarled as he opened his arms and she fell with an undignified thump from his lap to the ground.

He got to his feet and pulled the knives from the limp body of the cobra. Hers was an expensive, deadly little gem with a damascene blade and a jeweled-ivory handle. He wiped it and stuck it in his boot next to his own. 'If you have lamed Rajat…'

'You cannot beat me. I am a princess,' she flashed at him, scrambling to her feet. Apparently his exasperation was all too clear on his face and she had remembered his empty threat to tan her backside.

'Then behave like one,' Nick said and bent to check the black's legs.

'Is he all right?' Anusha asked after a minute's crackling silence.

'Yes,' Nick conceded and made himself look at her. The turban was back in place, but she was still ashen and her lips were compressed tightly as though to hold back a sob or to stop herself shouting at him.

'You were afraid,' she said, a statement not a question. 'That is why you are angry with me.'

'Only a fool is not afraid of a king cobra,' he said flatly. If a man had accused him of fear, he would have struck him.

'I was not… I did not mean—' She broke off and shook her head, impatient with both of them. 'You did not hesitate for one second. *That* is what I meant. You were right to be afraid and yet you risked your life and killed it. My father sent a brave man for me.'

The wide grey eyes fixed on him and Nick felt the colour rise over his cheekbones as he fought the need to look away from the painful honesty in her gaze. If he walked across and took her in his arms, she would yield to him, he realised. Not out of wantonness or admiration for his actions, but because something had happened just now that stripped feelings bare and left only what was elemental and basic. Anusha was too brave and too honest to hide those feelings. And too innocent to know what they were, he told himself.

'Are you certain you are not hurt?' he asked as though nothing had been said since she asked him about the horse. Anusha nodded, her expression once more veiled and wary, that moment of burning clarity gone. She turned and he watched her closely as she walked across to take Rajat's reins and stroke his sweaty neck. She moved stiffly, but that was all.

'You…' she began, her face against the horse's shoulder. Then she pushed herself upright and turned to face Nick. 'You saved my life and I thank you for it.' The raw emotion was gone, and, as her chin came up and she looked at him, she was every inch a princess for all the dust and her travel-stained clothing.

Her courage doused the fierceness of his anger and the heat in his blood, but Nick could not find it in himself to be gracious. 'That is my job,' he said, his voice cool. 'To deliver you back alive and in one piece to your father.'

'You will not let me thank you?' She took the step that brought her toe to toe with him. 'They kiss to say *thank you*, the English, do you not?' With Pavan solid at his back he could not retreat. Anusha put her hands on his shoulders and stood on tiptoe, her body pressed against his. For an endless moment her mouth touched his, warm and soft.

Her lips parted slightly, an invitation he knew she did not understand. Time stood still while he fought the temptation to snatch her to him, plunder that beautiful mouth, lose himself in an innocence that wanted him. *Him*.

Instinct told him not to hurt her pride or give her a challenge. Hands at his side, he returned the pressure of her mouth, then raised his head. 'Unmarried young ladies of good family do not kiss men, I fear,' he said with a smile to take any sting from the words. His body tightened painfully, but he thought he had kept the desire from his face.

'No?' Her eyes were wide and very dark and the colour was up under the fine skin of her cheeks and temples. 'Then I will not do it again.'

'Good.' She was destined for marriage, this girl, not a dalliance. While he was briefing Nick for this mission Sir George had confided that he intended to make a good match for his daughter with an eligible Englishman. And he, Nick Herriard, soldier, adventurer, failure as a husband, was most definitely *not* eligible, even if he would ever be rash enough to give up his heart for another pounding.

He kept his voice light and amused as he turned to his horse. 'All I can say is that I have the deepest sympathy for the poor man who has to turn you into a young lady.'

'I am a young lady already.' Anusha pushed her foot into

the stirrup and mounted, although not after a moment or two of undignified hopping about. She was more shaken than she let on. Behind that sharp tongue and fierce courage there was a vulnerability that made him want to protect her from whatever threatened—the maharaja, snakes... Men like himself.

Nick swung into the saddle. 'You are not an *English* young lady and that is what he will want you to be.'

'Hah! Corsets,' Anusha muttered.

'And curtsies and learning to dance and to converse with men at parties.' Nick had his temper under control again. He seemed positively amused, describing such indecent things as dancing with men, talking to them.

It was very dangerous to mix the sexes like that. She was discovering it only too vividly herself and this was just one man. Anusha gave herself a little shake. It was incredible how danger and a shock made one feel. For a moment back there every inhibition had vanished, leaving only a primitive urge to lie with this man, to roll naked in the dust with him. She could only hope he had not realised.

How did Englishwomen cope with this constant nearness to the opposite sex? But perhaps they were not really alone with them as she was with Nick, perhaps there were rules and older married women to stop things becoming... elemental.

But English women were allowed to fall in love, so Mama had told her. Even in Altaphur, for a lady of the court, one with influence, there was the possibility of choice. *Is that why I kept turning down those marriage offers? Did I think it would happen for me as it did for her?*

Apparently her mother had taken one look at her father and then acted in the most scandalous manner to make sure she met him. Anusha could not understand it. Her own first sight of an *angrezi* as an adult woman most certainly did not provoke any desire to place her entire future in his hands, whatever alarmingly lustful feelings he provoked. And her mother had done that foolish thing—she had fallen in love and thought George Laurens had too. Obviously he had not. Or he had fallen out of love, which proved how fickle men were. How cruel.

She urged Rajat up alongside the big grey so she did not have to look at Nick riding in front of her. That had been what had led to all this in the first place.

'I do not want to be an English lady,' Anusha stated.

'What do you want, then?' he asked, still tolerant. Anusha shot him a sideways glance, but his face was unsmiling.

'To travel.' It had never occurred to her before, but now, experiencing the freedom and the dangerous excitements of being free, it was as though she could see the entire world unrolling before her.

'Rich unmarried European ladies of rank travel alone, often in disguise, I have read of them. A Lady Montague, I think, and others. I will go to Europe and North Africa and the lands of the Middle Sea.' Moving on, not settling, meant she would never have to decide who she was, would never have to face not belonging anywhere.

'Eccentric spinsters,' Nick said with distaste. 'Rich ones with a bee in their bonnet. They end up sick and old, dying in some ramshackle castle, miles from family and friends, preyed upon by unscrupulous dragomen and fortune hunters.'

'Spinsters? That is an English word I do not know. Do ladies spin, then? And why would they have bees in their hats?' Bonnets she did understand. Mama had told her about ludicrous *angrezi* hats. And piles of false hair even when one had perfectly good hair of one's own and corsets to pinch you in and push you out and padding.

'Unmarried women who are on the shelf—beyond marriageable age—are called spinsters. And having a bee in your bonnet is to have a foolish obsession with something.'

'Hah! Well, I am not on a ledge, it is only that I do not choose to surrender myself to some man. And I have no bees in my hair. But when I have my money—'

'What money?' Nick enquired and this time when she glanced across at him she saw he was smiling, a quizzical smile that made her want to hit him.

'My father is a rich man, is he not? So I am rich. I am his only child.'

'He will make you an allowance, of course. When you marry a man he approves of, then he will settle money on you for your children.'

He was telling the truth. She had learned to believe what Nick said in that calm way he used when he was explaining things. So, she would have money, although there would be more when she married. And she had her jewels. There were not many, but they were very fine. And perhaps her father would feel guilty about the way he had treated her and her mother and she could persuade him to give her more money, more gems, enough to run away with.

It had been foolish to give Nick some hint of her plans, even if he mocked them and did not believe she could do it. 'Is it acceptable for a lady to be alone with a man as I am with you?' she asked after a few moments, the continuation of her earlier thoughts presenting a possible escape. Surely not, not when there was the possibility of a kiss like the one they had just shared. He had hardly touched her and yet her heart was still beating too fast as she thought of it

'It is not. It is scandalous, but there is no need for anyone to know how you reached Calcutta,' Nick said. There was something in his voice, or perhaps the sudden tension in the long body, that warned her that she was on dangerous ground, but she did not understand why.

'Yes, but if they *did* know,' Anusha pressed, 'will they not think I am no longer a virgin and refuse to receive me?'

'Are you suggesting that it would be assumed that I would have ravished you?' Nick enquired, his tone so even that for a moment she missed the fury beneath it.

That was a way out of having to be turned into an English lady. 'Well, there might be suspicions...' Carelessly she had let the thought colour her voice and he picked up on it at once.

'And you would blacken my name, impugn my honour so that you could wriggle out of whatever plans your father has for you?'

There was no mistaking it now—he might as well have hit her over the head with a brass cooking pot to express his anger. 'I am sorry,' she stammered. 'It would be thought so very bad of you, then?'

'It would bar me from decent society and jeopardise my position in the army, besides causing me deep personal shame,' Nick said tightly. He was staring straight ahead between Pavan's ears but the colour slashed across his cheekbones like a warning flag. He was looking, sounding, very angry, almost as if she had pricked his conscience. Which was absurd because he was behaving just as he ought.

'Then I would never say anything about it,' Anusha hastened to assure him. This *angrezi* honour was a very

different thing. Any Indian nobleman who had such an opportunity would snatch at it without hesitation, use her as a
bargaining counter to secure concessions and riches from
her uncle in return for marrying her once she had been compromised and shamed. They would think Nick a fool. He,
it seemed, would consider them wicked and unprincipled.
'Only…someone must know we are together.'

'There will be a handful of people who will know that
this journey did not take place with a full escort from your
uncle. They will be left under the impression that I had my
groom with me and you had a palace eunuch and a maid
with you.' He appeared to be relaxing again a little.

'Then perhaps it would be better if we pretend that I am
your brother,' she suggested. 'I am dressed like a youth. If
we practise that, then we can enter Calcutta unobtrusively.'
And it would make life much more comfortable. Nick made
a sound that was halfway between a laugh and a snort. 'You
do not think you can think of me that way?' True, she could
not imagine him as a brother, either. 'Your sister, then?'

'I have no sister, so I do not know how to behave to one,
but I can assure you, I find it hard to think of you in that
role.' This time it was definitely a laugh, but one with an
edge to it.

'No sisters? Brothers?'

'I am an only child, unless my father has remarried, although I doubt he would find anyone who would have him.'

'So your mother is dead?'

'Yes.' From the set of his jaw he did not appear to want
her sympathy on that. She could understand it—when people sympathised with her about *Mata* she was hard pressed
not to cry, even now.

'But then your father sent his only child away. Did he not

desire to keep his heir by his side?' Nick had said his father had bullied and beaten him to make him come to India and had then forced him on to the ship.

'There was little to be heir to,' Nick said. 'My father is a second son so it was up to him to make his own way in the world. He could have gone into the army or the navy, the church or have made the small estate he inherited from an uncle into a larger one. He chose to marry a woman for her money and then to spend it on drink and gaming. She made the mistake of falling in love with him and spent the rest of her life breaking her heart over him.'

'His father must have been angry,' she ventured. It must have been dreadful growing up in such a household. It had been bad enough for *Mata*, but at least the break was final and she did not have to live with a man who abused her.

'My grandfather disowned him.'

Nick said it lightly as though it were no great matter, but Anusha sensed that it was, that it was like a black cloud somewhere in Nick's consciousness. 'Then why did your father not want to keep you with him? I would have thought—'

'I was no use to him and I criticised him,' Nick said. 'When my mother died I—' He broke off as though he realised he was betraying more of his secrets than he had intended. 'We quarrelled badly. I seem to have been a reproach to him whenever he looked at me. I took after my mother in looks, a little, and I was probably a sanctimonious brat.'

She still felt the pain of her father's rejection twelve years ago very deeply—how must it feel to have a father who spurned you, a grandfather who had cast his son, and therefore his grandson, away?

'Your grandfather is still alive? Is he an important man?'

'I suspect he will live for ever. He is sixty-eight now and, reports say, as tough as a whip. As for importance, he is a marquis. Like a maharaja, I suppose. A duke would be a very senior maharaja. A marquis comes next. Then an earl is a third-ranking nobleman—a raja.'

'So you are a milord?' *Mata* had tried to explain the English nobles to her, but it was very complicated and strange.

'No. I do not have a title. My father is styled the Honourable Francis Herriard. His elder brother uses my grandfather's second title, Viscount Clere—he is called Lord Clere. My grandfather is the Marquis of Eldonstone.' He glanced across at her and the expression on her face seemed to lift his mood, for he grinned at her. 'Confused?'

'Completely. Why are you not a prince?'

'Because only the sons of the king are princes and they are usually dukes as well.'

'But—' She broke off as Nick reined in and sniffed the air.

'I smell smoke.'

People, danger? Her dagger, the one in her boot that Nick had not found, was still there when she reached down and trailed her fingers unobtrusively over it, bracing herself for whatever was going to be thrown at them this time.

Chapter Seven

Nick inhaled deeply. 'There is a village ahead. I can smell cow dung burning.'

'Will it be safe?'

Please let him say it will be, pleaded the tired, frightened part of her mind, the part she was trying so hard to ignore. The thought of the company of other women, of being able to wash, to sleep on a bed, even if was only a crude *charpoy* with ropes threaded on a wooden frame, made her ache with longing. And this was only the second day.

Anusha stiffened her spine. She had boasted that she was *Rajput* and she would not show weakness even if Nick said this was not safe and they must spend the night in the open again with no food.

He sent her a flickering look. Reassurance or assessment? 'Let us hope so. This has been an eventful day and, speaking for myself, I have had about enough of it. We are a long way from any source of news here, they cannot have heard about us,' he added.

They saw the goats first, then the white humped cattle. Small boys, sticks in hand, leapt up from where they crouched guarding the animals and dogs came skirmishing out, barking.

'*Are!*' Nick called. 'Where is your home?'

They crowded round, skinny in their skimpy loin cloths, all dark eyes and eager tongues, chattering in excitement and vying to point out their village to this man on horseback who towered above them. He was surely a raja, Anusha heard them say, a great warrior with his firearms.

'Do many men on horseback come this way?' she asked, leaning down to speak to the tallest lad.

'*Nahi.* Not for many months, not since the tax collectors came before the rains.'

Nick caught her eye and nodded approval of the question. Their pursuers had not visited here—they were safe for a night at least.

'We are travellers,' he said. 'Will you take us to your headman?'

The boys broke into a run, streaming ahead of them, the dogs yapping. The village appeared behind a low bluff of land: a dozen or so round huts of mud brick, their roofs thatched with thin branches and straw, the whole surrounded by a mud-brick wall, mended here and there with bundles of thorn.

Women were gathered round a well and they turned, pulling their veils across their faces with one hand as they balanced the big copper water vessels on their heads with the other. Their clothes were vivid crimson and orange and sharp, acid green. The men clustered in the gateway, the boys falling silent as the headman walked forwards to deal with this unexpected visitation.

He was bent, thin-shouldered, but had once been tall. His drooping white moustaches fell below his chin and his turban was huge, a construction of twisted white-cloth ropes coiled together.

Nick swung out of the saddle, dropped the reins and put his hands together. '*Namaste.*' Anusha followed his example, waiting behind him as the greeting was returned.

'We come from the west,' Nick said in his clear, idiomatic Hindi. 'We travel to the Jumna to sail down to meet the Mother Ganga and we seek shelter for the night.'

There were murmurings and much gesticulating at the mention of the sacred River Ganges. The villagers would feel they had gained merit by helping pilgrims.

'Welcome.' The headman's rheumy eyes studied Nick and then turned to her as she stepped to his side, pulling the tail of her turban across her nose and mouth—she had no wish to offend.

'This lady is under my protection. I take her to her father,' Nick said.

They were too polite to stare or to speculate. The group parted, ushering them into the compound, and the headman called to the women, 'Wife! Daughters! Make our guests welcome.'

Anusha expected to be hurried off out of sight, but the headman was speaking to Nick as he led him towards the largest hut.

'You will drink opium?' Nick turned to her.

It was a traditional welcome in the villages, she knew that, although she had never been offered it. 'You use opium?' she asked.

'Smoke it, do you mean?' He looked at her and grimaced as though at an unpleasant memory. 'I have done. I think

in my time I must have tried everything that this land offers that is supposed to lead to forgetfulness. But, no, I do
not smoke it now—the dreams it gives lead nowhere. Like
this it is harmless. The most it will do is ease your tiredness and your bruises a little.'

They sat down cross-legged on a straw mat opposite the
headman, flanked by two men who looked enough like him
to be his sons. With the studied care of a ritual he placed a
dark-brown substance into a small cloth funnel on a stand,
then poured in water. As it drained through into a boat-
shaped wooden vessel below, one of the others poured it
into the cloth funnel on the other side of the stand. It took
some time, the careful pouring and collection, re-pouring...
Anusha began to feel light-headed. Perhaps that was part of
it, part of the process to relax the weary guest.

Finally the old man seemed satisfied. He poured a little
of the liquid over the little metal Shiva *lingam* in the centre
of the stand, then cupped his right hand, filled it and extended it to Nick. Nick bent forwards and sucked the liquid
directly from the side of the wrinkled palm.

The man gestured to him and Nick held out his own right
hand, cupped to receive a trickle of the liquid, then turned
to her. 'Drink.'

Anusha bent forwards as he had done and touched her
mouth to the side of his palm below his little finger. Under
her lips the flesh was warm, yielding; the touch seemed
sensual and intimate. A gesture of trust.

'Suck,' he murmured, so she did, swallowing the bitter
liquid, his hand tipping so that her lips moved against his
palm. Her tongue came out, just the tip to catch the final
drop, and she looked up and saw his eyes, dark and fixed

on her face. Slowly, she leaned back, her gaze still locked with his.

The headman coughed. Nick turned, bowed his head. '*Dhanyvad.*' Anusha bowed too, echoing the thanks. 'Go now,' he murmured. 'The women are here for you.'

Anusha woke, disorientated and stiff, on a thin mattress of quilted cotton. Ropes creaked under her as she shifted and her nostrils were filled with the smells of cooking, of cattle, of dried-dung fires.

They were in a village, she recalled as she sat up and looked around her, squinting into the shadowy boundaries of the round hut.

'You are awake?' The soft voice behind sounded wary. Anusha twisted around and smiled at the elderly woman standing just inside the door. She must seem strange and shocking to her, a woman in youth's clothing.

'Yes. I slept well.' The woman came further in and, from the quantity of bangles and the size of her nose ring, Anusha realised she must be one of the headman's wives. 'Thank you for your hospitality, you are very kind.'

The woman made a gesture with her hands—hospitality to travellers was expected. 'Where are your woman's clothes?' she asked.

'I have none. I had to leave them behind.'

'This man, this *angrezi* who speaks like us, he is your lover?' The woman sat down on the end of the *charpoy*, wariness replaced by lively curiosity.

'No! I mean, he is my escort. My bodyguard to take me to my father. There is a man who would marry me by force and I...my father does not want him to wed me.' It hurt her

pride to use her father as an excuse, but it was an explanation that would make sense to the other woman.

'Ah. My name is Vahini. What is yours?'

Anusha thought of lying. But what was the point? 'Anusha. And he is Herriard *sahib.*'

There was whispering outside. 'Come, then. Our visitor
is awake,' Vahini called and the hut was filled with a dozen
women of all ages, all staring. 'This is Anusha and she has
no women's clothes and she flees from a bad man to her
father.' There was much sympathetic muttering.

'I could not carry clothes, I had to run away very quickly,'
Anusha explained.

That provoked tutting and shaking of heads. Then one
of the younger women stood up. 'She is of my size. It is not
right that she is with a man and has to dress as a youth.'

'I cannot ride as a woman,' Anusha protested as the
speaker left the hut.

'But when you are not travelling, then he should look on
you as a woman,' one of the others said. 'If he looks at all.
It is only fitting. Padma will have something.'

When Padma returned, her arms were full of cloth. 'You
must wear this tonight,' she said, shaking out a deep-blue
kurta, lehenga and red trousers. There were sandals as well,
and a gauzy red veil and a long blue scarf.

Anusha looked at their faces. They were poor. These were
probably Padma's best clothes out of very few, perhaps they
were her wedding clothes. She had no gift to reciprocate
with, only gem stones, and they were of no use to villagers
miles from anywhere and who would probably be cheated
if they tried to sell them.

'That is very kind and these are beautiful,' she said as she
ran her hand over the intricate metallic embroidery around

the hems. 'When I reach my father's house I will have them returned to you with a gift from my heart in thanks.'

'Then we will bring water and you may wash,' Vahini announced, her words sending some of the younger women scurrying out. 'And you can tell us all about yourself. How many years do you have?'

Washing and changing was obviously going to be a public performance. Anusha put a brave face on it—to be clean she was prepared to answer any number of questions.

The women gathered together around the cooking hearths, the firelight flickering across their faces, gleaming off nose rings, bangles and the flash of a smile. Behind, in one of the huts, a child whimpered in its sleep and someone got up to go to it. Others moved back and forth, bringing water, chopping vegetables, carrying food to the men who sat before the headman's hut.

She felt soothed and yet also emotional. The way these women lived was so distant from her own mother's privileged, cultured life, but they had gathered her to them like a long-lost daughter. It had been like talking to *Mata* again. They had asked about her suitors, told her about marriage settlements for the younger women, laughed about their husbands, teased her gently about Nick.

Paravi was a good friend and yet she could not talk to her as she had to her mother. And of course, these women, kind and motherly as they were, were not the same. *Mata* had died a year ago of a sudden fever. One day she had been there, strong, intelligent, passionate. The next, gone. In the last few hours before she had sunk into unconsciousness, she had held Anusha's hand, her speech rambling and faint.

'Love, Anusha,' she had muttered. 'It is life. It is the only thing. Even if it breaks your heart. Love...'

Sometimes love sounded wonderful, worth pain, worth loss. And sometimes it seemed too dangerous, too much of a risk. *Oh,* Mata, *I wish you were here to talk to.*

Anusha found her vision was blurred, blinked to clear it and realised she was looking at Nick, sitting cross-legged on a mat beside the headman at the centre of the male group. They were all smoking thin black cheroots that she suspected had come from his saddlebags and discussing something with much animation, but also careful attention so that each gave his opinion.

Nick said something, straight-faced, and there was a gale of laughter, echoed by the boys who were hiding behind the hut, watching their elders. Someone called out to them and they ran off.

At last the food was laid out, the cheroots stubbed into the dust and the men began to eat. Only then did the women gather round their own fire and begin their meal. Careful of her borrowed clothes, Anusha sat where she could watch Nick from beneath the hem of her veil as she lifted it to eat. He was so at ease, so relaxed, that it was hard to remember that he was one of the Company, a foreign soldier and the ally of the father who had rejected her.

'He is a fine man, that one,' someone said, low-voiced, and the women moved their heads in the sinuous shake of agreement that the *angrezi* never seemed to master. Except Nick—he could do it, she realised. 'He moves like one of us,' the woman added as if reading her mind. 'He is a warrior.'

'Yes,' Anusha agreed. 'He is a brave and skilful fighter.' And a wise one, she thought, recalling the way he had eluded the maharaja's troops.

'Perhaps your father would give you to him,' another voice suggested. 'He would make you fine sons.'

'No!'

Nick looked up, unerringly at her, even though she was veiled and he could not know what she was wearing. Shaken, Anusha dropped the hem of her veil, her breath suddenly tight in her chest.

A warrior, brave and skilful. A handsome man, despite his unfamiliar looks and those uncanny green eyes. A kind man, for all his imperious orders. A man who showed respect equally to a raja and a humble villager. It felt like the bars of a lock sliding into place, each with a click in her brain. You learned early to pick locks in the *zanana* to find treasures and secrets. Was Nick Herriard a treasure, one that she wanted to hold, to possess?

'He does not want a wife,' she replied. *It cannot be him.* Which was a good thing, for however much she might desire that man—and the ache low in her belly and the tingling that went through her when he touched her told her that she *did* desire him—she feared him also.

He would deliver her to her father and then he would watch her like her father's hunting hound, alert for any attempt to escape, for she had been foolish enough to let him glimpse her hopes and dreams. If she was foolish enough to fall in love with him, then she would make herself as vulnerable as her mother had done, for this man was so like her father: strong, independent, arrogant in his self-confidence. If he wanted something, he would go after it, if he no longer wanted it, then no sentiment would stop him rejecting it.

But even if he did desire her his duty to her father would keep him from acting on it. *It cannot be him,* she repeated to herself and shivered a little at the loneliness that crept upon her. She would be trapped in the alien world of the *angrezi,* amongst people who knew that her mother had not been married to her father and who would despise her for it, amongst people who expected her to wear those horrible clothes and follow their alien ways and she would never be free. Never belong.

The food was eaten, the dishes cleared. Anusha tried to help and was pressed back into her place, a guest. It would never have occurred to her to so much as hand a plate to a maid in the palace. Now she saw the thin, work-worn hands of the women who shared their food with her and felt ashamed to be waited on. 'Please, let me do something.'

The woman nearest her smiled and went into her hut, came out with the fretful baby in her arms and offered it to Anusha. She cradled it cautiously and clucked her tongue at it. The small face wrinkled up, prepared to wail, then the child thought better of it and stared instead. Anusha stared back, then stroked its cheek with one finger. It wriggled its hand free of the wrappings and curled minute fingers around hers.

She began to croon to it, rocking it back and forth, soothed by the warm weight in her arms. All too soon its mother returned, smiling, and took her sleeping baby back to lay it in the hut and a pang went through her. Freedom and no husband meant no children, no baby of her own to cradle, no tiny hand curling trustfully into hers. Heat pricked at the back of her eyes and Anusha took a deep, shuddering breath. Where had that come from, that fierce desire for a child? Honesty gave her the answer—it had come with her awareness of Nick, her desire for him. Their children would be tall, golden-skinned, pale-eyed, brown-haired.

They would be hostages to fortune, she reminded herself. Just as she had been.

The rhythm of drumbeats had her starting up, tense and ready to run, before she realised that it was the patter of hand drums from amidst the circle of men. Anusha relaxed back and the drumbeats settled into a pattern, a *tala* of sixteen beats. The other men began to clap on the correct beats: one, five, thirteen with a wave of the hand on the empty beat, nine.

The women shifted round in their places to watch, clapping too, and one of the men got up and began to dance, his bare feet slapping on the hard earth, his body twisting and swaying. Another man stood, then two more and the drumming became stronger as another musician joined in. Anusha realised it was Nick, his hands moving over the taut skins of the *tabla* as though he had known this music from birth.

'Come,' Vahini said. The women rose and began to dance too, out of sight of the men, their skirts whirling out into multi-coloured bells as they spun round. Anusha did not need a second invitation. Her lingering aches and pains, the tinge of melancholy over the baby, the unsettling desire for Nick—all vanished in the familiar intoxication of dance.

She looked up as she joined crossed hands with the woman opposite her, whirling round in the centre of the circle of clapping dancers. She leaned back and the stars spun above her in the deep-blue velvet of the heavens and the smoke curled up and somewhere, out beyond the village, a jackal howled, infinitely lonely.

The beat of the drums became her pulse—the pulse of desire and the need to dance for Nick, a thing she must not do, a thing only fit for a courtesan or a nautch-girl.

* * *

The laughter of the women was clear over the drumbeats. One of them was singing, a song without words, to mark the *raga*, the melody, of the music. Nick glanced across, careful not to stare or cause offence, but they were hidden behind the huts, only their shadows, thrown by the firelight, danced against the walls.

Anusha was dancing with them—he heard her laugh and take up a snatch of the song. How he knew it was her voice he could not have said. He had never heard her sing, or, he realised with a shock, laugh out loud. But she was there, happy for a short while. She had never known poverty or simplicity like this before and yet she was at home here. Would she ever laugh like that after George had her turned into an English lady?

He almost missed a beat and caught himself, focused on the taut skin under his fingertips. She was an unmarried woman and her place was with her father, and then her husband. The Indian world she had known for twelve years was no longer safe for her.

Then why was there this nagging uncertainty at the back of his mind? He lost track and threw up a hand in apology as the dancer shot him a reproachful look. He was feeling sorry for the girl, that was all. She would settle soon enough with a husband and babies. Someone began to sing, a love song, yearning and sensual. Nick let his hands follow the new, subtle, rhythm running beneath the *tala*. The beat echoed his pulse, the pulse became a need, an uncomfortably insistent physical demand.

Damn the woman. She was doing nothing overt to tease him sexually—she was too inexperienced for that, whatever her theoretical knowledge, and yet he could feel her as though she sat next to him running those long cool fingers down his back, down his legs— With a cry from the singer the dance ended. Nick fought for control, thankful for the *tabla* in his lap, hiding his embarrassing state of arousal.

'*Aye!*' the man sitting next to him exclaimed. 'You will dance now?'

'No.' Nick shook his head. 'No, I cannot dance.' What he wanted now was his bed, a flask of *raki* and oblivion, but he was not going to get it, he knew. It would be poor return for the villagers' hospitality if he left now.

'Sing, then,' the man urged.

None of the songs he knew in Hindi were fit to be sung within women's hearing—they were camp songs, marching songs. 'Very well,' he said. 'I will sing in English for you.'

That provoked a buzz of interest. Nick tapped out the tune on the little drum then,

Our 'prentice Tom may now refuse
To wipe his scoundrel master's shoes,
For now he's free to sing and play
Over the hills and far away...

Chapter Eight

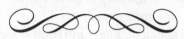

The queen commands and we'll obey,
Over the hills and far away.
We all shall lead more happy lives
By getting rid of brats and wives
That scold and bawl both night and day
—over the hills and far away.

At dawn the words of the song still ran around Anusha's head as she dressed in her riding gear and folded the borrowed clothes carefully into her pack.

So that was what Nick thought of wives and children, was it? She should have guessed, instead of feeling sorry for him that his wife was dead. Probably he had been grateful for the freedom, if he would but admit it.

As she came out of the hut he was whistling the same tune. Anusha marched over to the horses and dumped her pack at his feet. 'Is that what the *angrezi* call music?'

'Yes.' He had washed his hair and it was still wet, clinging to his head in the sunlight as it dried patchily into fairness again. 'What is the matter with you this morning? Did you get out of the wrong side of the bed or have you been drinking *raki* with your new friends all night and have a hangover?'

He was talking incomprehensible rubbish. What difference did it make what side of the bed she got out of? And what would she be hanging over?

'Neither. And that is not proper music.'

'It is soldiers' music.' Nick strapped the pack onto the saddle. 'Have you eaten?'

'I have.' She turned her back on him and frowned at the huts, the villagers going about their morning business. 'This is a poor village.'

'I am sorry I could not find you a better one, Princess.'

'I do not mean that!' Anusha swung round and stumbled over her own feet. Nick steadied her with a hand on each arm and raised an eyebrow in a particularly infuriating manner. 'I mean that we have taken food they can ill afford.'

He nodded. 'But we cannot refuse hospitality and I cannot give them the money I need to get you home.'

Home? Hardly, she thought. But there were aspects of it she could exploit. 'I will have my father send them a cow in calf.'

'A what? How the devil do you expect Sir George to transport a pregnant cow halfway across Rajasthan?'

She shrugged and his big hands slid up and down her arms, trailing shivers in their wake. 'Your wonderful East India Company can do anything. No doubt someone will work it out if the important Sir George Laurens commands it.'

His long fingers tightened, banding her upper arms.

'What has put the vinegar on your tongue this morning, Anusha? I had hoped that female company, food, a good night's sleep would put you in a better mood.'

'Nothing is wrong with my mood. You had best look to your hair—it is dry and the wind is tangling it.' As she spoke it blew across his face and he let go with one hand to swipe at it. 'Oh, leave it to me.' A strand had tangled in his eyelashes which were thick, and far too long, in her opinion. They hid his feelings all too well when he chose to lower them. 'Stand still.'

Nick did as she asked, uncharacteristically obliging, while she reached up and brushed the hair from his face, caught the final strands between finger and thumb, then pushed it back to the sides of his face with her palms. 'Where is the cord to tie it?'

'In my pocket.' He rummaged while she stood there and tried not to think about the strong bones of jaw and cheek, the way his hair felt like raw silk, the faint prickle of stubble on cheeks that had doubtless been shaved hurriedly in cold water. They were standing very close, her face tipped up to his so she could see what she was doing. If she slid her hands into his hair, took half a step closer and he bent his head...

'Got it. You can let go now.' There were traces of colour over his cheekbones when she lifted her hands and stepped back. Warmth from her skin—or was her closeness responsible for it? Surely not—Nick had managed to control any amorous instincts she might provoke with unflattering ease so far.

'Say your goodbyes, we are going now.' He turned on his heel with the precision of a soldier and strode off to the headman's hut. Anusha glared after him, then caught

Vahini's sympathetic gaze. The other woman rolled her eyes and lifted her hands, palms up. The gesture needed no words. *Men!*

By the time she had made her farewells Nick was mounted, his hair hidden beneath a turban again. 'Come on, we did not get up at dawn in order to linger here until the sun was hot.'

That was something she recalled from her days living in her father's house—the European obsession with punctuality and time. There was one clock in the palace in Kalatwah, and a man who carefully wound it, but no one looked at it for the time, only enjoyed the wonderful whirling works and the chimes. What did a minute, or thirty, matter? The sun was guide enough to the routines of the day.

The boys ran with them for half a mile, the dogs barking at their heels, jaunty tails curled over their backs. When their followers fell back Nick raised a hand in salute and kicked Pavan into a canter. Anusha looked back, but they had been swallowed up by the rolling landscape and she and Nick were alone again.

'You never showed me how to load a musket,' Anusha said when Nick brought down some hares for their supper the next day.

'No more I did. We got distracted talking of my coming to India, if I recall.'

And about my father rejecting Mata *and me and that woman he called his wife coming to take our place.* Anusha schooled her face to show none of her thoughts. 'That is so. You will show me now?'

'Very well.' He tied the hares to the saddle bow and rested all three muskets against a tree. 'I will do this one, you follow what I am doing with one of the others. You take a cartridge, like so.' She fished one out of the pouch. 'And bite the end off.' Anusha grimaced at the bitter taste of the black powder. 'No, don't swallow it, spit if you have to. Tip a little into the pan, like this. Lower the hammer—don't bang it down!—then tip the rest down the barrel with the bullet and the wad and pull out the ramrod.'

He waited patiently while she struggled to pull out the long rod, her hands ending up over her head before she found she could stand on a rock for the extra height. 'And ram down the charge. Take out the ramrod—unless you have run out of bullets and want to spear the enemy—put it back. There, you have loaded a musket.'

'It was very slow,' she grumbled.

'Indeed, we would have been overrun by the enemy or eaten by the tiger by now. Try again.'

'I need more practice,' Anusha lamented when the second musket took almost as long as the first. 'You do it so fast.'

'I was drilled in it until I could load in the heat of battle or in total darkness. Even on an elephant.' Nick took the weapon back from her and ran his hand down over the barrel, down the polished stock, like a lover caressing a woman. 'Like all things, it needs practice.' He glanced up. 'Now what have I said to put you to the blush?'

Practice. 'Nothing!' Of course making love needed practice as well, not just the theory gained from looking at books and listening to the married women. She would be hopelessly clumsy at first—her foolish daydreams about Nick catching her in his arms and being enraptured by her sensual skills were just that, foolish. And, of course, if he did try such a thing, common sense would take over and she would push him away, slap his face, remind him of who he was and who she was. 'Nothing at all.'

And she did not want him to make love to her anyway, not really. He might be beautiful to look at, but he was her father's man and he had no sympathy for her at all. Perhaps Nick was jealous of her. She pondered the idea as he slid the muskets back into their sheaths on the saddles. He had been like a son to her father all these years and now a real child of Sir George would be in his home.

'Do you enjoy fighting?'

'Yes,' he said without hesitation.

'Killing?'

'Not for itself, no. If the enemy would all surrender or run away, I would be very happy, but if they want to kill me, then…' He shrugged. 'I find satisfaction in the politics of war, the use of strength to gain power and then build on it. But I enjoy doing that by talking and dealing just as much as by fighting.'

'You would have been a very poor clerk,' she observed as they moved off again.

'Indeed I would. Sir George saw that, too—you both know me better than my own father did.'

'Perhaps he did not realise when you were so young that you would want to be a warrior.'

'Perhaps. I certainly did not.' They fell silent as the horses began to pick their way down a slope towards what must be a stream, its water hidden by thick foliage and trees.

'Where are we?'

'About seventy-five miles west of Sikhandra. If we keep going in this direction, we will find the Jumna River just above or below that town, then we can take a boat down to the confluence with the Ganges and then down to Calcutta.'

Nick spoke absently, his head moving as he scrutinised the land ahead and then the increasingly soft ground beneath their horses' hooves.

'What are you looking for?'

'Tiger.'

'Oh.' It came out as a squeak and Anusha turned it into a cough. She had seen many tiger hunts, but only with scores of armed men, beaters, elephants and stout stockades for the watchers. Out here she felt as though slitted amber eyes were already fixed on her unprotected back.

'I am comforting myself with the thought that a tiger is likely to be at least as scared of us as we are of it,' Nick remarked.

'*You* are scared?' That was no help at all. She did not want Nick to be capable of being scared of anything. He had admitted to being frightened of the cobra, she recalled. But he had killed it anyway, without hesitation. Soldiers must be afraid a lot of the time and have to learn to ignore it. She wished she could.

'Oh, yes,' he said with a cheerfulness that had her glaring at his back as her stomach swooped. They were in tall grass now, over the heads of the horses. 'There could be anything in here—rhino, buffalo, tiger, leopard. Keep talking nice and loudly.'

Her mouth felt as dry as dust. Anusha groped for something to say as Pavan plunged down the stream bank and up the other side. 'Look.' Nick pointed down at the mud. 'Tiger spoor.' The paw prints looked enormous.

'I wish I was on an elephant,' Anusha confessed as they rode up the other side.

'That,' Nick agreed drily, 'makes two of us. The grass is getting shorter though.'

'What do we do if one attacks us?' She tried to speak as lightly as he did.

'I kill it with great skill and bravery while you ride in the opposite direction as fast as you can.'

That was comforting. 'Have you killed many tigers?'

'This would be the first.'

Oh. 'Are you not supposed to be reassuring me by telling me there is no danger and you have it all under control?' she enquired, despising herself for the fact that her hand shook on the reins.

'If you were an empty-headed chit, I would, yes. As it is, you'd see right through that and, if you are on edge, then that's two of us watching like hawks. There,' he added as they came out of the tall grass on to the higher, drier ground, 'We can see for miles now.'

Anusha let out her breath in one *whoosh* of relief. 'Is an empty-headed chit like a totty-headed female?'

'More or less.' He was grinning, the wretch. 'I said you appeared to have your father's brains.'

'I have my mother's. She was an educated and intelligent woman!'

'Remind me to start you on the subject the next time we are in heavy cover,' Nick said, digging his heels into his horse's flanks. 'If you had made that much noise back there, every tiger for forty miles would have headed for the hills.'

'Oh! You…you…*man*!' But he was already almost out of earshot. Anusha gathered the reins and sent her mount after his. Insolent, scheming, manipulative man. He had deliberately played on her nerves back there. He should be cosseting her, soothing her fears, treating her like a lady. Seething, she rode on.

* * *

They had spent another night in the open on an island in a small river, another day untroubled by tigers or pursuing troops, then a night in an abandoned herder's hut. Anusha stretched as she rose at dawn, wanting warm water and hot food and a pile of soft cushions.

Nick was boiling water for the usual strong tea that she was learning to tolerate, if not like. He had been restless the night before and had left her to sleep alone in the hut. She heard him padding around outside every time she woke and there were faint blue shadows like thumbprints beneath his eyes.

'Did you not sleep last night?' she asked. She squatted down beside him and studied his face. 'You look tired.' She did not want to think of him having any vulnerabilities, it made him too real.

'I dozed.' Nick shifted and stood up as she lifted a hand to touch the lines of strain at the corner of his eye. He had become more taciturn over the past twenty-four hours, she realised. Anusha searched her memory for anything she had done to anger him, but could find nothing. Perhaps he was simply bored with her company, tired of this journey. He stopped kicking at the fire and glanced at her, frowning. 'We should be near the Jumna by now.'

'That is good, isn't it?' Anusha ventured.

'Yes,' he agreed. 'Of course. Never mind my mood, I am just…distracted.'

I am just bloody randy, Nick thought with deliberate crudity in an attempt to shock himself into focus. But it was more than that—he didn't want to have *a* woman, any woman. He wanted this one, and for more than a tumble. He wanted to make love to her, slowly. He wanted to uncover those long limbs, that honey-coloured skin, unbind the thick plait the colour of toffee and teak. He wanted to lose himself inside her slender, strong body. *That innocent body*, he reminded himself as he had throughout the long, restless night pacing around the hut while Anusha slept inside.

The urge to seduce her warred with the instinct to protect her. He had felt it with Miranda, although his wife, whom he failed, had simply expected it, whereas Anusha alternately spurned his offers of help or pretended to berate him for scaring her with tigers.

For some reason, while he had found it easy enough to lie beside her in the open, the enclosed hut felt dangerously intimate and, once the thought had got hold of his imagination, his body had done the rest to ensure a sleepless night. No amount of reminding himself what a wilful, haughty, unpredictable—and completely untouchable—female she was helped in the slightest.

And, worst of all, perhaps, in the small hours, came the suspicion that the ache he was feeling was not just desire, but loneliness. He wanted to reach out to something within her that she was not prepared to let him touch.

The landscape was every shade of grey and violet in the pre-dawn light. As they rode, it gradually brightened and the colours intensified until the river valley was plain before them. There were the craggy hills behind, still purple in the shadow of sunrise, the lush green fringing the watercourse, the short-cropped grass and scrub where village flocks had eaten their fill. In the distance, downriver, there was a haze of smoke marking a town or a big village.

A buffalo cart loaded with sugar cane creaked across the rough track ahead. '*Namaste!*' Nick called to the driver. 'What place is that, brother?' He pointed downriver. 'Is it a big town? Can we find a boat there?'

'It is Kalpi, brother, and only one or two *kos* away,' the man said and pondered the other questions. 'Yes, it is big, for they make sugar there and there is much trade. Assuredly you will find many boats.'

Nick waved his thanks and turned Pavan to take the track downstream. 'Almost there, then. Have you been on a river before?'

'No, only the lake. Is it pleasurable?'

'It can be,' Nick said with some caution. Goodness knows what they would find to hire or buy. Something with separate sleeping accommodation for Anusha, that was certain. He wasn't spending more than a week cooped up at night with this woman, her big, questioning grey eyes and soft, inquisitive hands and his own aching loins. Not if he could help it.

They were closer to the river now and it spread across perhaps half a league, its numerous channels braiding into loops and sandbanks. They would have the current to help them down, but he'd need someone who knew the river over a good distance, not simply a local boatman—

What is that? In front. Movement jerked him from a mental list of things to be done and back, with a jolt, to the present. Three men came out of the trees to the right, two on foot, one on a horse. Nick twisted in the saddle: two more men on foot behind them. The river cut sharply into the bank to their left, to the right the land rose to a heavily forested bluff. They had ridden right into an ambush.

'Dacoits.' He drew his sabre. 'Stay behind me and don't stop, whatever happens. I'm going to ride them down.'

One of the men on foot knelt, lifted something to his shoulder.

'And keep low—they have guns!' He sent Anusha a rapid glance, saw the dagger in her hand and then kicked Pavan straight at the man with the musket. It would spoil his aim, he would get up and run—

The blow, the pain, came before the sound of the shot. Nick reeled in the saddle, grabbed for the pommel, his left shoulder on fire. He hung on grimly, locked his fingers and raised the sabre. Pavan, trained to battle, rode right into the gunman, lethal hooves slashing, then turned, answering the pressure of Nick's knees, to charge the horseman. A sweep of the sabre and the man was screaming, clutching his face where blood streamed down, before spurring for the forest.

There did not seem to be any sound. As if time had slowed, Nick hauled on Pavan's reins and the excited horse spun again. Anusha had ridden Rajat straight at the third man and the black was rearing, lashing out. Behind them the remaining dacoits were running for cover.

Rajat's front hooves hit the ground and the terrified man scrambled to his feet and dived into the brush. Anusha turned, her face white, the dagger clenched in her raised fist. There was blood on it. He saw her lips move, but he could not hear what she was saying. The pain in his shoulder was monstrous, a beast dragging at nerve and muscle with savage claws.

'Go!' he managed to shout. 'Ride for the town!' But she paid no heed. Perhaps he had made no sound, Nick thought as the forest tilted. Something was wrong, the ground shouldn't be...

Chapter Nine

We have done it! With a cry of triumph on her lips Anusha twisted in the saddle, brandishing her knife. Five dacoits and she had helped Nick rout them!

Then she saw him fall across Pavan's neck, the dark blue of his coat stained black over his heart, and her own heart seemed to stutter and stop. *'No!'* She spurred Rajat forward. 'Nick!'

The gelding reached its stable mate before Nick toppled to the ground and the horses seemed to know what to do, perhaps trained for this, she thought distractedly as she reached for the limp body that Rajat's shoulder was supporting. With a heave, and strength she did not know she possessed, she got Nick back in the saddle and breathed again when he moved under her hands.

'Thank you, Lord Krishna,' she gasped as she steadied him. 'He lives.' She gave him a little shake. 'Nick, can you hold on? I dare not dismount, they might come back.'

'Yes.' He dragged his eyes open with a visible effort. 'Stop the bleeding...'

Anusha tore open her saddle bag and pulled out a linen shirt, worn for two days, but the best thing she had within reach. The horses stood like rocks while she fumbled Nick's coat open. There seemed to be blood everywhere, but when she put her hand on his back it was dry. 'The bullet's still in there,' she said as she stuffed the linen under his shirt. 'Can you hold that?'

He grunted, so she turned Rajat, Pavan wheeling with him as though understanding the need to keep Nick within her reach. But he managed to stay upright in the saddle, one hand on the reins, the other pressed to his shoulder. He was doing it by sheer will-power, as far as she could see—his face was white under the tan, his eyes unfocused.

Anusha smelled the town before they reached it. The thick, cloyingly sweet smell of boiling sugar filled the air and they began to pass small sugar-mills along the side of the road with pairs of oxen yoked to a beam that turned the crushing wheels while men pushed in the canes.

'These look honest people. We must stop.'

'No.' She leaned from the saddle to catch the muttered words. 'The town...there'll be a Company agent.'

That was true. Anusha fought the instinct to get help, any help, as quickly as possible and rode on. A qualified doctor and someone of influence, that was what they needed. She began to call to people as they passed and the road became busier, lined with market stalls, an encampment of gypsy tinsmiths, more sugar-mills. They all pointed onwards.

Assuredly there was an *angrezi*, at least six of them, came the replies. Where? At the big house or at the sugar-boiling place or perhaps at the riverside. Who could tell what the *angrezi* would do?

There was no one, *no one* in this bustling, stinking chaos, she thought in despair and then, suddenly in front of her, there was figure wearing a broad straw hat, head and shoulders above the crowd.

Anusha urged Rajat forward, shouting in English, abandoning Nick to catch the man before he vanished into some side street. 'Sahib! Sir! Help, please, for an officer of the Company who is hurt!'

The man started, frowned at her and pushed forwards, the bearers at his back hurrying with him. 'An officer? Where, boy?'

'There!' She pointed and the men ran and caught Nick as he slid, completely unconscious, into their arms.

'The bullet will have to come out, of course. As soon as possible.' The cadaverously thin doctor stood looking down at Nick, hands on hips as though sizing up a choice cut of meat on the butcher's block. His patient was laid out, stripped to the waist, on the agent's best spare bed on to which he was bleeding sluggishly.

'Not yet.' Nick opened his eyes and Anusha sat down with a thump on the nearest chair, ignored by the entire household. She had thought he was dying, dead, if it had not been for that steady soak of blood, yet he could speak. She scrubbed the back of her hand across her eyes and tried not to sniff.

'And why not, might I ask?' Doctor Smythe was already reaching for his instrument case.

'Because it is going to take some digging. I don't think I

am going to be at my best when you've finished and there are things I need to organise first.'

'There is nothing you need to organise!' Anusha exploded from the corner and pushed to the bedside to glare down at Nick. 'Nothing except getting better, you stupid, stubborn man,' she added.

The doctor and the agent both turned on her. 'Now look here, boy, your master may give you licence to speak your mind,' Mr Rowley, the agent, snapped, 'but insolence I will not have—'

'Gentlemen, allow me to present you to Miss Anusha Laurens, daughter of Sir George Laurens of Calcutta and niece to his Highness the Raja of Kalatwah.' Nick's voice was slurred, but he sounded amused. 'One does not have to give Miss Laurens licence to speak her mind, she does it anyway.'

'Ma'am.' They both bowed, both looked utterly scandalised.

'Major Herriard is taking me to my father,' Anusha said quickly, scrabbling for her English. Better to explain and hope Nick would stay quiet and rest. 'It was necessary to not be found...to evade...the Maharaja of Altaphur who wishes to marry me, which is why I am as a boy, disguised. We were ambushed by dacoits outside the town.'

'Outrageous!' It was not clear whether that was directed at the dacoits, the maharaja or her travelling, dressed as a boy, with a man. Probably all three. 'Well, you are quite safe here, Miss Laurens. You will doubtless wish to change into your proper clothes and make yourself comfortable while the doctor deals with Major Herriard. My wife will organise that.'

'I have no proper clothes and I do not leave Major Herriard.' She did wish Englishmen were not all so large. Anusha set her feet apart and squared her shoulders—he was going to have to carry her out of there.

'Rowley, I need a pinnace, something that will get us downriver safely to Calcutta.' Nick cut through the argument raging over his body. Anusha shut her mouth and listened. 'And I need it crewing, equipping and provisioning. And I need our horses taken down by reliable grooms. If you can give me a round reckoning for that, I can pay for it now and remit any shortfall when I arrive.'

'Plenty of time to worry about organising that, let alone paying for it.' The doctor was laying out an appalling array of instruments on a strip of linen. Anusha swallowed before her heaving stomach got the better of her. 'You won't be fit to travel for a week or so after this. It will—'

'We go as soon as a boat can be made ready,' Nick interrupted him, propping himself up on his right elbow. 'The day after tomorrow at the latest. Altaphur has many agents and he will have sent word out faster than we could travel. If we had arrived in the town quietly I would not be so concerned—as it is, we might as well have sent trumpeters to announce ourselves.'

'Lie down,' Anusha snapped in Hindi. 'You are as white as a sheet. You are very aggravating, but I do not want you to die.' There was a hideous lump in her throat and she was terrified she was about to cry.

'In that case I will do my best not to,' Nick replied in the same language, then switched back to English. 'Rowley, will you organise the boat and the horses?' To her relief he lay down flat again.

'Certainly. You won't be up and about as soon as you

think, but I'll sort it out right away, if that will keep you quiet. Now, come along, Miss Laurens.'

'No.' She was not going to leave him, not alone with that doctor who looked like a skeleton and his instruments of torture.

'But I don't want you,' Nick said. His hands were spread flat on the sheet as though he was fighting the need to fist them.

Mr Rowley took her arm and drew her aside. 'This isn't going to be pleasant, Miss Laurens,' he murmured. 'If he wants to scream or pass out or throw up, he won't while you're here. And if you faint it will simply distract the doctor. So think about the major and not about yourself. Yes?'

Anusha stared at him. 'You mean it would be…' She searched for the English word '…selfish, to stay?' He nodded. 'Very well.' She marched up to the doctor, opened her mouth, then snapped it closed. None of the things she wanted to say—*Don't hurt him, don't kill him*—would be any use. But princesses did not plead, they gave orders.

'Do it properly,' she said, fixing the doctor with her haughtiest stare. 'If he lives, my uncle the Raja of Kalatwah will reward you. If he dies—' She left it hanging, turned on her heel and walked out of the room without a backwards glance.

'You have no English clothes of any kind?' Mrs Rowley sounded appalled.

'No. And I do not wish to borrow any, thank you, ma'am.' That, Anusha believed, was the right way to address a married lady, but she was not sure. She no longer felt like a haughty princess, but an unsatisfactory child who had disappointed this woman in her strange tight bodice and big bell skirts. She was obviously the mistress of the house although she wore hardly any jewellery.

It was very strange—there were no women's quarters here at all. Mrs Rowley had led her to her own bedchamber, but that was right next to Mr Rowley's room, and in the corridor outside both male and female servants came and went. There was no bathhouse either, just a tub, but she had been grateful for the cool water and the soap and the big towels and had tried to concentrate on getting very clean and not thinking about what was happening to Nick.

'You are betrothed to Major Herriard, I presume.'

Anusha wrestled with the English. Mrs Rowley did not seem to have any Hindi beside very basic phrases for giving orders to her servants 'Betrothed?'

'You are going to marry him?'

'Oh, no. He was supposed to be escorting my caravan back to my father.' It seemed wise to add, 'Who has sent Major Herriard for me.'

'But there is no caravan!'

'No, ma'am. Because of the maharaja's attack. But no one knows of the lack, except you and Mr Rowley and the doctor, of course, so it cannot matter, for I know you will not speak of it.'

'Not matter! Of course it matters—you have been *ruined*, my dear.' She looked rather scandalously pleased at this pronouncement, as though she normally expected the worst and was gratified when it happened.

Ruined? Anusha worked that out. 'Oh, no.' She smiled at the other woman in what she hoped was a reassuring manner. 'I am still a virgin.'

Mrs Rowley pursed her lips. Perhaps there was another word she should have used. 'I should hope so! But that, my

dear, is neither here nor there. You must marry the man—
your father will insist upon it.'

Neither here nor there. Anusha liked the phrase. 'And
that is neither here nor there also. I will not have him.'

'Not have him? My dear, Major Herriard is…and you
are…'

'Yes? I am the granddaughter of a raja. So, if I wanted
him, it would be quite all right.' *And I do want him, but not
as a husband. I do not want any man as a husband and he
does not want me.*

The other woman's lips had vanished into a thin line. *If
she says I could not marry Nick because my parents were
not married, or because I am half-Indian, then she will be
very sorry for her insolence.*

Something must have shown on her face, for Mrs Rowley gave a petulant shrug. 'That can all wait until you reach
Calcutta. Do not fear: I will let no one know you are here.'

'The spies of the Maharaja of Altaphur will know already, I have no doubt.' But the house and its grounds had
a high wall around them and there were sentry boxes at
each corner, she had been relieved to see. They would be
safe enough in here.

'I meant any of the English society here.'

Mrs Rowley believed that what a gaggle of gossiping
traders' wives thought of her was any cause for concern?
Anusha almost said as much, then recalled that she was
speaking to the wife of a trader and held her tongue. She
needed this woman—or, rather, Nick did.

'Surely the surgeon will have finished by now?' The
house was uncannily quiet. Had something gone horribly
wrong and they were afraid to tell her? 'I will go and see
what is happening.'

The older woman looked horrified, but then, that seemed to be her usual expression. Nick's bedchamber door was standing slightly ajar so she applied her ear to the gap.

'If you were not so stubborn and would simply pass out, Major, you would make life much easier for both of us.' The doctor sounded as though he was speaking through gritted teeth. Anusha sympathised with him.

There was a grunt of pain, then the rattle of something metallic dropping into a bowl. 'There, that's out, all in one piece. Now I will dress the wound and bleed you.'

'Over my dead body.' Nick sounded a trifle breathless, but very much alive. Anusha sagged against the doorframe.

'It *will* be your dead body if you develop a fever.'

'No.'

'No,' Anusha echoed and marched into the room. The doctor was bandaging Nick's shoulder, there was a heap of bloodstained rags on the floor, bowls of unpleasantly red water, and the instruments looked even worse now they had been used. Nick was white around the mouth, but he rolled his eyes at her and one corner of his mouth twitched into a smile.

'If he does not want to be bled, then he will not be,' she added. 'Thank you, Dr Smythe. What do we owe you for your services?'

'I will send you my accounting when the patient no longer requires those services, Miss Laurens. I have every expectation of being recalled to his bedside before the day is out to find him in a dangerously febrile state.' He twitched the sheet into place and bowed. 'Good day to you.'

'He looks as though he has sat on a poker, foolish man,' Anusha remarked in English as the door closed.

Nick snorted, then winced. 'Do not make me laugh, I beg you. Where did you get that vulgar expression?'

'I heard Papa... I once heard my father use it.' *Papa.* When was the last time she had even thought of her father like that? 'That is not important—what do you need?'

'Nothing except something to drink. Tomorrow I will give you a list of things that we will need and things to be done so you can check what Rowley is doing—I don't trust him to get on with enough urgency. This is a damnable nuisance, but I'll fall flat on my face if I try to do anything much for twenty-four hours—I don't need a sawbones to tell me that.'

'Does it hurt?' He shot her a look that spoke volumes. 'I am sorry, of course it does. Would opium help?'

'No.' He spoke with some feeling. 'I need my wits about me, not scattered in dreams. Are *you* all right, Anusha? You fought like a Rajput warrior—both against the dacoits and the doctor.'

She beamed at him and he blinked. 'Thank you! I enjoyed it, except when you were hurt.' But she did not want to think about the sheer terror of that, the seemingly endless search for help. 'They have given me a room and water to wash in and food and that woman with the face like a purse with the strings pulled tight has been insolent, but I think she means well and does not understand. She wanted me to put on clothes like hers and was offended when I refused.'

'I told you not to make me laugh,' Nick said with a gasp.

'Oh, I am sorry. I complain about that woman and all the while you are hurt and in pain.' He made no answer, but his eyes closed slowly, as though they were too heavy to keep open. His breathing deepened and she realised he was asleep, or perhaps in a faint, tried beyond endurance by the doctor's probing and finally able to let go.

Repentant, she fell on her knees beside the bed. 'I wish I could do something. Are you warm enough?' *Foolish question*, she told herself. *He cannot hear me*.

Nick was flat on his back under a single sheet pulled up to his armpits, his arms outside. Above the sheet the bandaging was stark white on his left shoulder, and down to his chest. The other shoulder was bare. Anusha laid her palm on the right side. 'You feel all right,' she murmured. 'Warm, but no fever.' His eyes moved beneath the shielding lids and he tensed under her hand. 'Now I have hurt you! I am so clumsy.'

He muttered something.

'What did you say?' She leaned closer to catch the words he had hissed between clenched teeth. Her plait slid over her shoulder on to his chest and she could feel his breath on her lips. 'Tell me what you need, Nick.'

'This,' he murmured, eyes still closed. His right hand slid up to her shoulder, all that was needed to tip her down, breast to breast. Their lips met. For a heartbeat neither of them moved, then his palm was cupping the back of her head and his lips parted.

He is kissing me. This was not like that careful touch of the lips after he had killed the snake. Nick hardly stirred, only his lips against hers spoke, not with words but with sensation, warm and firm and tasting of the spirits they must have given him to dull the pain.

She expected to be alarmed and found she was not, only excited and shy. None of the texts she had read spoke of kissing and, when she had imagined it, she thought the man would be on top. But Nick was controlling things perfectly well, Anusha thought hazily. Who would have thought that one hand and a pair of lips could tie her to the spot, unable to move, hardly able to breathe?

And why did this touch, this exchange of breath, of heat, make her whole body tingle? Her breasts, tight under her man's coat and shirt, ached as though they had suddenly become larger. There was a restless tingle down the inside of her thighs and an insistent pulse low down.

Anusha spread her hand on the naked skin of Nick's shoulder and leaned closer into the kiss. She wanted to see him, she realised, look at him while he made love to her mouth. As her eyes opened so did his, deep and green. Slowly, they focused.

There was not much room for him to recoil, but his convulsive movement was as violent a rejection as a slap. Anusha jumped back and fell on her bottom with a thump. 'Ouch! Nick, what—?'

'Get out. Just get out of here, Anusha.'

She scrabbled to her feet, stumbled, her legs uncertain and her vision blurred with anger and humiliation. 'With pleasure,' she spat at him. 'I only kissed you because I was sorry for you—not because I wanted to.'

Chapter Ten

Blood loss, shock, a potent slug of spirits and virtually no sleep the night before were as good as a blow to the head for knocking the sense out of a man, Nick thought muzzily as he fought his way back to consciousness. It was morning to judge by the light and the lack of noise, so he had slept the night through.

He knew where he was and how he had got there. That was a relief. The last time he'd been wounded it had taken a day to get his memory back clearly and this time he could not afford the luxury of lying about, not with a boat to organise and Anusha—

Anusha. He sat up with a jerk and swore as the pain knifed through his shoulder and his head swam with dizziness. Anusha. Hell, had he kissed her or had he dreamt it? It had seemed all too real, both the delicious feel of her body, soft and curved, the cool of her hand on his bare skin, the untutored sensuality of her lips on his. The taste of her. And the words she had flung at him as she had backed out of the room: those where exactly what he would have expected her to say.

And yet he would not have kissed her, he could not have been that dazed, that unable to control his impulses, surely? No, it was a dream, he was almost certain. A delicious, arousing dream that left an ache of emptiness on waking.

Almost was not as reassuring as it might be. Nick threw back the sheet and swung his feet off the bed, hissing when his feet thumped on to the matting and jarred his shoulder.

Almost immediately the door opened and a servant peered round the edge. '*Sahib*! You are awake, but you must not get up.' He flapped his hands as though to shoo Nick back into the bed. 'The Doctor *sahib* will be angry. Go back to bed, Herriard *sahib*, and I will call him to you.'

'You will not.' The youth stared at him anxiously. 'I want water to wash, tea to drink—a lot of tea, with sugar,' Nick ordered in Hindi. 'Then I want my clothes.'

'But—' The servant shrugged and began to back out of the door. 'Rowley *memsahib* will have much to say about it.'

'Tell her I threatened to come downstairs in the sheet if you did not obey me,' Nick suggested. It was tempting to lie down to wait, but he fought the dizziness and made himself stay where he was.

When the door banged open it was neither his outraged hostess nor the servant with hot water. 'What are you doing from your bed already?' Anusha demanded. In English, he noted. Her plait swung lose over the shoulder of her coat and a shaft of desire lanced through him at the memory of that moment in his dream when she had leaned forwards and it had fallen on to his bare skin.

She looked furious, and flushed, and she was eyeing him

in a way that was new. 'Why are you so angry?' he asked, a sinking feeling in the pit of his stomach warning him that it was not simply the fact he was sitting up.

'Because you do not listen to the doctor and so you will make yourself ill and you will be here in bed being a nuisance and not taking me down to Calcutta as you should.'

'Thank you for your concern,' he said drily.

'I am not concerned about you. You do not deserve any concern.'

'Why not? You were concerned yesterday, Anusha. What has happened to change that?'

She blushed, an angry darkening of the honey-coloured skin. 'You can ask? Mrs Rowley warned me how it would be and I thought her foolish.'

'So I *did* kiss you last night?' Nick ventured, with, he realised the moment he said it, a crashing lack of tact.

'If you can call that a kiss,' Anusha snapped, reverting to Hindi. 'It was not very interesting—perhaps that is why you forgot about it.'

'I am extremely sorry. It was a mistake.' *And so was saying that.* Anusha's nostrils flared and he found himself glad she did not have her knife about her. 'I mean, I should not have kissed you—I thought I was dreaming.'

That seemed to please her rather more. 'You mean you dream of kissing me?' she enquired with a purely feminine curiosity that would have made him smile under any other circumstances.

'No.' He had to put a stop to this right here and now. 'I mean I was not myself, I was on the edge of consciousness and I am afraid that if a man finds himself pressed up against an attractive woman, in a bed, when he hasn't his wits about him, then instinct is apt to take over.'

'So you would have kissed anyone?' He nodded. 'Mrs Rowley?'

'I said *attractive*, Anusha.'

She bit her lip, but he could tell she was on the verge of laughing. With any luck he had reduced that massive mistake to an embarrassing slip in her eyes. Which just left him mentally flagellating himself for such a betrayal of trust. 'What did Mrs Rowley say about me?'

'Only that it was shocking that we were travelling together and that men could not be trusted. But I told her we had spoken of such things and that you were a gentleman and were shocked that anyone might think you would ravish me.'

Oh hell. And I got on my high horse, too. Damned hypocrite. The moment my guard was down...

'*Major Herriard*!' Mrs Rowley stood in the doorway, elbows akimbo, the servant peering past her.

His first thought was relief that they had not been speaking English. Then Nick realised that he was wearing a bandage, a roughly draped sheet and nothing else. His chest was bare, his legs were bare from mid-thigh. He did not dare glance down to make sure the sheet was covering his groin adequately. 'I was looking for my clothes and unfortunately I did not hear Miss Laurens knock.'

'*Tsk*! Miss Laurens, you must leave at once.' Eyes averted, she bustled Anusha out leaving the servant to bring in the water ewer. His expression said quite clearly in any language, *I told you so.*

'And my clothes?'

'I will get them from the *dhobi wallah*, *sahib*. He says

the blood has come out and the *darji* has mended the coat. Your breakfast is coming, *sahib*.'

It took altogether too long to wash and shave and dress. Nick ate one-handed, tried to control his fork with a hand that shook and cursed dacoits, bullets and his own physical weakness and lack of will-power.

The fact that he had been virtually delirious when he kissed her was no excuse, he told himself savagely. Damn it, George had trusted him with his daughter. The way he felt about George, the man who had given him everything a father should—even his life—practically made the chit his sister. He had told her to trust him himself. But the truth was, from the moment he first saw her, his common sense had gone south along with most of his blood.

He threw down his napkin. *I had better get a grip on my self-control again, because anything more than a fuddled kiss when I haven't the strength to lift myself off the pillows is going to end up at the altar.* He thought he could square it with his conscience not to confess last night's idiocy to George, but anything more and the old man would be reaching for a shotgun, with good cause.

The thought of another marriage made him shiver. Women wanted too much that he could not give and needed too much that it seemed he was unable to provide. He should never have married Miranda. He could not shake off the memory of his wife's death. The image haunted him of her fragile body, swollen with the child he had planted in her, racked with fever in the steaming heat of a Calcutta summer, too weak to fight.

He had no need of an heir, no title or estates to leave. What wealth he acquired he would leave to some charity or another, his body could moulder away in the English cemetery at South Park Street in Calcutta and the creepers and ferns would mask whatever inscription they put on it soon enough, with no one to shed dutiful tears over it.

'*Sahib*? Some more tea, *sahib*?'

'No, thank you.' He was growing thoroughly morbid now. Nick gave himself a mental shake. He had a career, ambition and the world was full of willing women who did not need a ring on their finger. His place in any cemetery would wait for many years, if he had anything to say to it. It must certainly wait until he got Anusha Laurens down river to Calcutta and the new life that awaited her. Moving like an old man, and hating it, Nick hauled himself to his feet and made for the door.

'That was easy. I do not know what the fuss was about.' Anusha sat cross-legged with her back to the mast of the little sailing boat and viewed the prospect of the river in front of them with satisfaction.

'Easy?' Nick grunted from the folding canvas chair beside her. 'You call finding a boat that doesn't leak, a crew that won't murder us in our beds, buying sufficient provisions, sorting out the horses and extracting you from Mrs Rowley's grasp, and me from the doctor's, all in two days, easy? It was down to my superior logistical skills and force of character.'

It took her a moment to translate that. They were speaking English most of the time now and she found it came back remarkably easily, for *Mata* had continued to speak it to her as much as she spoke Hindi. But many phrases were strange and needed working out.

'You are just tired, which makes your mood distempered, so Mrs Rowley said. Does your shoulder give you much pain?'

'A little.'

She did not know what distemper was, but it seemed unpleasant. Nick had been decidedly short-tempered since he rose from his sick bed. 'I have unpacked all our things in our cabins. There is not much room—why did you make them put in that wall? With the doors it takes up too much room.'

'So we have a cabin each.'

Ah, so we are back to that kiss. She could still taste him in her memory, that mixture of brandy and spice and man. Anusha ran her tongue tip over her lips as if she could recapture it.

Nick had said nothing about it since that morning and at first she thought he must simply have dismissed it from his mind. Now she knew he had not, it was flattering to think that he did not trust himself alone with her any more: it made her feel womanly and strangely powerful. On the other hand, if he did kiss her—and do the other things, the things she thought about every time she looked at that long, lean body and those big hands—then he would be even more short-tempered afterwards and if her father found out he would insist Nick married her.

And she did not want to marry a man who, if he wanted her at all, only wanted one thing. She tried to imagine life as Nick's wife. She would have to be whatever a European wife was. She would not be in a *zanana*, she knew that. She would have to wear those horrible clothes and learn to order a household like Mrs Rowley's and be *respectable* in the *angrezi* manner, which seemed even more restricting than the rules of the women's *mahal*.

Nick would go off on adventures, or march about the country making war, while she sat at home and had babies in a world that she did not belong to. He would not love her, even if she was unwise enough to fall in love with him. And it would hurt, every day, like tiny knife cuts.

No, she must take her life into her own hands, create herself in a new world where she would not let anyone close enough to hurt her.

'What is the matter?'

She twisted round and saw Nick was watching her, a frown bringing his eyebrows together. Anusha almost confessed something of her fears of Calcutta, the vista of loneliness that she envisaged lying before her. But, no, she must not forget he was on her father's side in this. He would see her safely delivered, even if he had to put her in a sack to do it. But she could afford to behave as he wished for now: he would get her safely to Calcutta and there she would gather the money and gems with which to escape. 'The river is interesting, but I miss Rajat.'

Nick seemed comfortable enough, his right arm hanging relaxed by his side, so close that if she leaned over, just a little, the back of his hand would brush her shoulder. It was tempting to move that tiny distance and see if his touch would wake those little thrills under her skin, the ache between her legs.

It was sexual desire, which was very interesting. Men seemed to feel it for virtually any woman who was not actually repulsive, but did women, once they were aware of it, feel it for any man? What if she had agreed to a marriage with one of her suitors for whom she felt nothing—would she have felt desire for him? All those intriguing things that men and women did together seemed embarrassing and puzzling if there was no desire. What did it mean that she felt desire for Nick?

'Why have you taken off the sling?' she demanded. A

battle would take her mind off wondering what it would be like if he made love to her.

'Because it was a nuisance.' He flexed his fingers on his knee. 'And because I do not want to appear weakened to any onlookers.'

'You think we are still in danger?'

He nodded. 'Perhaps.'

'You do not seem to wish to shield me from anxiety. Is that how you treat all English ladies? I thought they were protected and sheltered by gentlemen.'

A shadow seemed to pass over his face, but he answered her robustly enough, 'Do you want me to lie to you? Treat you as though you had no wits and no courage? I thought you boasted you were Rajput—a warrior.'

'I am. And I do not wish you to—what is the word?— hide me in the dark.'

'Keep you in the dark. Perhaps there is nothing to worry about from Altaphur's men, but even if there is not, there are still those who steal from boats.' He picked up the musket which lay on the deck at his side and propped it up more visibly against his chair. 'Have you your knife still?'

'I have one of them, you took the other.'

'I will give it back to you. Sleep with them both to hand and do not go out of your cabin at night unless you know I am there.' The banks were slipping past at speed now as the flow of the river carried them down and she realised that Nick's gaze was on them, with only fleeting glances at her when she spoke. The jungle came down to the riverside in places, in others there were sandbanks, or rocky outcrops. There was a shout from the stern as the cookboat, flat-bottomed and unwieldy on the end of its tow-rope, bumped into them.

'Fool of a son of a camel,' yelled the man at the tiller. 'Use your poles to keep off us!'

'We must moor at night and the men will sleep on the shore,' Nick said. 'They prefer to eat there in any case.'

'But that means anyone could attack us, and we waste time.'

'Look.' He pointed a little ahead where a rounded black shape rose out of the water. 'We will lose more than time if we hit one of those rocks.'

'What will we do with ourselves, on this boat for so many days?' she wondered aloud, then felt the heat rise up her neck at the thought of what they could be doing.

'You wanted to travel—now is your chance to see one of the great rivers of the world. We will be joining the Ganges soon. It will make the Jumna look like a stream, so you will have constant entertainment just watching the banks.'

And it will carry me down to a new world. Travel seemed less interesting now; she wanted, yet dreaded, her destination. 'Tell me what it is like to be an English lady,' Anusha asked.

'How would I know?'

'You were married to one,' she said tartly and saw his hand clench as though she had prodded his wounded shoulder. 'Your mother was one, you live among them when you are in Calcutta. Tell me what I must do to be one of them.'

Nick hesitated and Anusha twisted round on the deck at his feet, her hand on his knee to shake it, as though to force an answer out of him. 'You do not tell me—is it that I will never be one of them?' Not that she cared for what those unknown women thought, but if she was to live in that world, make her escape into it, she had to understand.

'You will always be different,' he said slowly. 'How can it be otherwise? The whole way you have been brought up is different.'

'And I do not look like them,' she pointed out, determined to face all the problems. 'They will be pink like you and I am brown.'

'You are golden,' Nick said. 'Like honey. And your eyes are like your father's, grey, and your hair is brown, not black. You could be European—Italian or from the south of France perhaps. But that does not matter, they will not be prejudiced against you because of your mother.' His mouth twisted into a rueful smile, 'At least, they won't once they know who your uncle is—deference to rank applies in society all over the world, I suppose.'

'But they will know my father did not marry my mother.' That would not matter at home in Kalatwah. The raja had three wives, four courtesans and numerous occasional lovers. Children were treated according to their merits in their father's eyes and how skilful their mothers were in bringing those merits to his attention. Europeans only took one wife at a time, their courtesans were hidden and not spoken of.

'That is true.' Nick seemed to be pondering the problem. At least he seemed willing to discuss this honestly with her, which was a relief. She needed to understand what her position would be. 'Your father has considerable standing and much respect. He is wealthy and of a good English family. There is no reason for you not to be accepted.'

He was silent for a while as they passed a village, the naked children splashing in the water, the women crouched at their washing, a man casting his net, thigh deep in the swirling muddy river.

'You will have teachers to show you how to dance and to perfect your English and your etiquette. Some of the married ladies will take your wardrobe in hand, I have no doubt, and fit you out with clothes and shoes, then you will attend balls and receptions and you will make friends.'

It sounds terrible.

Chapter Eleven

'What is the matter? You've curled up like a hedgehog.' Whatever that was, Nick seemed to find it amusing.

'What is a hedgehog?' Had she curled up? Anusha straightened her back and unwrapped her arms from around her raised knees. Perhaps she had. She did not like the sound of this new world with its lessons, its threats of the dreaded European clothing and its shocking behaviour. Dancing with men—her body had betrayed her agitation.

'*Sharo*,' he translated. 'I've never seen one this far to the east. It is a small animal with its back covered in spines and when it is in danger it curls up into a ball and there is nothing for its enemies but a nose full of prickles.'

'Like a porcupine—*sayal*?' They were ugly creatures. It was not danger that had her curling in on herself; she would be brave enough to escape, she was certain. No, it was the prospect of so much embarrassment first.

'They are much smaller than porcupines.' He showed

with his cupped hands. 'Rather endearing, really. They snuffle, like little pigs.'

'I do not snuffle.'

'Not when you are awake, no,' he said with a grin and stood up. 'Don't look so outraged, Princess, I did say *endearing*.'

'Do not call me that,' she muttered as Nick strolled away to speak to the steersman. If he saw how it annoyed her, he would tease her more. She was not truly a princess, even if she was the daughter of one, for her father was not of the royal blood. And she was not an English *memsahib* yet either, and she was not going to pretend to be one of those for a moment longer than it took to learn what she needed to survive in the world alone.

The lush green of the banks blurred and Anusha blinked, angry with herself for the moment of weakness, and waved with determined cheeriness at some small boys leading the family buffalo down to the river for its evening bathe.

I will watch, learn, collect up all the money and jewels I can, she told herself. *Then I will find a ship and sail to England where no one knows me and I will be whatever I want.* Only she did not know what she wanted, only to belong somewhere and to be wanted for herself. She found her eyes were fixed on Nick's broad back. *So strange, to have this ache inside and yet, somehow, to be happy.*

There was silence from the compartment next to his. Either Anusha was not asleep yet, or she had taken to heart his teasing about her snuffling in her sleep. He had become used to the odd little wiffling noises she made sometimes—dreaming, he supposed—it had been unfair to call it *snuffling*.

Nick stretched out his long legs on the roughly made

bunk and regarded with disfavour the evidence of what seemed to be a constant state of arousal. Will-power did not seem to work, neither did the illusory safety of a thin wooden barrier shut Anusha out of his imagination.

He eased his sweaty back against the pillows, uncomfortable in the heat. To call the spaces they were sleeping in *cabins* was a wild exaggeration—cupboards was more like it. There were no portholes and, with the hatch closed as it was at night, precious little ventilation.

Nick got up and rolled his shoulders experimentally. *Not too bad*, he thought. Luckily he had always healed well and he doubted anyone observing him would realise how bad the wound had been. He pulled on the *pajama* trousers and a *kurta* that was loose over his bandages, picked up his musket and a pillow and eased open the door. Then he wedged Anusha's door ajar and climbed the ladder to unbolt and push open the hatch onto the deck.

On the flat expanse of sand the small crew were gathered around a fire, talking quietly now their meal was finished. Soon they would be asleep, a man at each of the four mooring ropes, one at the foot of the gangplank, the others on the cook boat.

He laid the pillow by the open hatch, put the musket within reach, slid his dagger under the pillow and stretched out. Like this some air would filter down to Anusha and he would have the relief of several more feet between them. His wound throbbed, his groin ached, but the air, at least, was cool on his hot body. Nick willed himself to sleep.

'Teach me about etiquette.' Anusha was proud of herself for getting her tongue around the word. Her first word of French. 'What must I know?'

Nick, slumped in the canvas chair, sat up and sighed. 'I find it a dead bore at the best of times: I am not a dratted governess!'

'Please. I do not wish to seem foolish.'

'Very well. When you meet someone new you should wait to be introduced. If you are of higher rank than they are, they will be presented to you, and the other way around. If they are the same rank as you, then you defer to an older person.

'Then you curtsy. After that, if they are of higher rank and you meet them, you make a little curtsy. For everyone else, a slight bow of the head, or shaking hands.'

'Show me how to curtsy,' she demanded.

'How should I know? I can't see under ladies' skirts when they are doing it!' Anusha merely waited. She was finding that if she gazed soulfully at Nick for long enough he usually did what she wanted over trivial matters. She had not tried it in any major clash of wills yet.

'Er…put your heels together, toes apart. Now bend your knees outwards, keep your back straight and sink down.' He frowned as she obeyed. This was no effort, her thigh muscles were strong. 'That looks about right—and up again. The more important the person, the lower you curtsy.'

'That was easy. And bowing my head?'

He stood up and inclined his head. 'Good afternoon, Miss Laurens.'

She copied him. 'Good afternoon, Major Herriard. That is easy too. But shaking hands? I only do that with ladies?'

'Oh, no, anyone of rank.'

'Men? I touch hands with them?'

'Certainly. Some may then kiss your hand.' Anusha whipped both hers behind her back. 'Come, let me show you—you will be wearing gloves, of course.' Nick held out his right hand. 'Give me your right hand.'

Their fingers slid together. His big, warm hand enveloped hers as he closed the grip in a light squeeze, then released her. Surely he could *feel* her blush from its heat, let alone see it! He must be able to feel her pulse, jumping erratically, as she had felt his, strong and steady. His palms were slightly rough, with rider's calluses. Anusha hid her hands again.

'No, it is nothing, the merest pleasantry,' he assured her. 'Now, pretend we are at a reception and you have been introduced to me. Give me your hand again, palm down, like this.' She copied him, wary. Nick caught the ends of her fingers in his, bent, raised the back of her hand almost to his mouth and kissed the air a rice-grain's width above her skin, released her hand and bowed. 'Miss Laurens, you are in great beauty this evening. Now you curtsy and smile and say *You are too kind, Major Herriard.*'

'You are too bold, you mean!' She took a step back, hands gripped together. His breath had feathered the sensitive skin on the back of her hand. She had felt his lips even though they had not touched her, and her pulse was all over the place. 'That is indecent—and I am meant to endure those caresses from men I have only just met?'

'It is the custom, but you will never be alone with these men, there will always be older married women around you so there is nothing to fear. They will flirt a little, you will flirt back. It is quite acceptable.'

'Flirt? I do not know that word.' She sat down on the hatch cover, a safe distance from his chair, although quite what she was keeping safe from, she was not sure.

'Flirting is a game, a courtship game, that all the young ladies and the single men indulge in. A sort of teasing. The men say gallant things, compliment the ladies. The ladies pretend to dismiss such blatant flattery, they blush a little, shield their faces, but their eyes tell a different story. Then in turn they say things that make the men feel strong and manly and laugh a little that they are so bold, and so it goes on.'

'And that is allowed? You must teach me how to flirt.' It sounded shocking, but if that was necessary to be accepted, to fit in, then she would do it.

Nick shrugged and she caught a slight wince, hastily suppressed. He had denied having any discomfort, so she should not fuss. 'I am no good at flirting,' he said.

'Oh, but a man as gallant and brave as you cannot be afraid of talking to young ladies surely, Major Herriard.' She opened her eyes wide at him, wondering the next moment if it was a safe thing to do.

'You need no lessons, Miss Laurens.' He shook his head, one of his rare smiles making him look years younger and far less formidable. 'You are already an accomplished flirt. Look, we will be mooring in a moment. I will show you how to make dinner-table conversation while we eat.'

I would rather flirt, she thought, then caught herself. It was dangerous to play at love. Nick's heart might be armour-clad—hers, she was beginning to worry, might not be.

'That is a relief,' Nick remarked as they regained the deck after going ashore to the port officer at Allahabad to check on the situation in Kalatwah. He had received news only that morning, he had told them.

'Just got a message—it should be accurate. Altaphur's camped outside the walls, making a lot of threatening noises. The raja's sitting tight, wise man—he's not making foolish sallies outside. There are Company cavalry within a few days' march and his neighbours are gathering—none of them wants Altaphur turning on them next. My correspondent predicts that the maharaja will march away within twenty-four hours.'

Now, as the crew pushed off from the steps, Anusha stood beside him looking at the scene on the *ghat* with huge piles of marigold flowers and the garland sellers who were threading them, a barber shaving his client and a procession making its way with a shrouded corpse to the burning *ghat*, a little downstream.

'May locusts consume his crops, his wives all be barren and his guts be filled with worms,' she said in Hindi.

'Quite,' Nick replied with a grin. 'I do not blame you, but it's not exactly dinner-party conversation, Miss Laurens.'

'I know,' she sighed, reverting to English. 'I have spent three days learning how to address an earl, a bishop, the governor and their ladies. And I have learned that at the dinner table one may only talk about foolish things and that women are not expected to have a brain.'

'Unfortunately yes.'

'Even this flirting is foolish. Do the men not want to know that their wives will be skilled in bed? Do they really want ignorant wives?'

'Yes,' Nick said with some emphasis as the boat's sails were raised. The steersman took them out into the central current and they began to move downriver.

Anusha went to sit on the hatch cover that had become her favoured perch. 'How strange. We are all taught how to pleasure our husbands.'

Nick was halfway into the canvas chair and sat down with a suddenness that made him swear under his breath.

'*Please*, not *pleasure,* Anusha. *Pleasure* means to please him in, er, bed.'

'But that is what I meant.' Was the little wretch teasing him, or genuinely curious?

'And how do you—no, do not tell me, I do not want to know.'

He did not want to talk about wives and the marriage bed. He did not want to remember Miranda shrinking in distaste from his caresses, forcing herself to *do her duty*, as she put it. He tried to tell himself, as he had so many times during that short marriage, that someone had told her something to frighten her or that she was naturally cold. But the conviction remained that he simply did not know how to make a respectable woman happy. He was a rake with too much experience, with tastes and habits that had shocked Miranda to the core.

He must be concealing his thoughts well enough, he realised. Anusha was blithely answering his question. 'By reading the classical texts, of course. And studying the pictures and talking to our mothers and sisters. Why? How did you imagine we might learn?'

'I was attempting *not* to imagine,' Nick said. He could picture her, lying in silks on heaps of cushions, idly turning the pages of some illustrated text. Those long limbs would stir restlessly in the heat with her imaginings, those full lips would curve into a sensual smile as she propped her chin on her hand and...

'I am sorry to mention such a subject,' she said penitently. 'I was forgetting that it must be many days since you lay with a woman.'

'Anusha—'

She slanted a glance in his direction. 'Do English ladies not discuss sexual matters?'

'No! At least, unmarried women do not discuss them. Unmarried girls are not supposed to know anything about such things.'

'So their husbands are supposed to teach them?'

'Yes.' He tugged off his neckcloth and opened the neck of his shirt. It was hot, that was all.

'That might be rather nice if the woman is in love with the man,' she mused. 'But if not it must be a dreadful shock.'

'I couldn't say,' Nick said, trying to keep the edge from his voice. She looked at him, lips parted. Something in his face must have given her pause, for she lowered her lids and stayed mercifully quiet. *I couldn't say because my wife obviously did not love me. I thought I could make her love me, teach her to love. But then, you see, I doubt I am very lovable. Though I am skilled enough in bed if I am matched with a woman of experience...*

Stop it. He caught at his bitter, unravelling thoughts. *Hurt pride is all it is. Hurt pride and a valuable lesson.* He made his voice firm and matter of fact. 'Anusha, I beg you, when we get to Calcutta, do not say anything about illustrated texts, or pleasuring men or *bed*.'

'Very well, Nick,' she said.

Anusha turned to look out over the water and he caught a glimpse of her eyes, thoughtful and with all the teasing gone. She guessed he had been thinking about Miranda. Nick felt a sudden urge to tell her everything, share the pain and the anger and the sense of failure, to break through the self-sufficient loneliness. *Self-indulgent weakness.* He stared at the sun-dazzle on the water until he was certain the blurring in his eyes came from that alone and the impulse was beaten back where it belonged.

Anusha woke in darkness. It felt very late and the air was finally cooling. A little breeze brushed over the bed, which was strange because she always closed her door properly at night. But now she came to think about it, she was never as hot and uncomfortable as she might have expected in a closed cabin. The door, she realised, was ajar. Had someone opened it every night? Silent as the breeze, she slid out of bed and went to look. The door had been wedged open, but Nick's door was closed.

As she stood there in her shift, puzzling over it, there was a faint sound from the deck, a grunt, as though someone had stubbed a toe and was suppressing the exclamation of pain. Anusha reached for the dagger that lay on her pile of clothes and climbed the ladder to the open hatch.

The moon was full, lighting the wide sandbank where the blanket-wrapped forms of the crew surrounded the banked embers of their fire. The silver light washed across the deck and the man who sat cross-legged, his back to the mast. Nick.

Anusha froze, her eyes just above the rim of the hatch. There was a pillow and a blanket on the deck, a musket by the side. She knew him well enough now to guess what this meant—Nick was sleeping on deck so he could leave the hatch and her door open to let the cool night air below decks for her, while he slept on the hard boards to guard her.

But why was he not resting now? As her eyes adjusted to the light she saw him clearly. He was barefoot, bare-chested, wearing only light *pajama* trousers and he was unwinding the bandage from around his torso.

I had forgotten his wound, Anusha realised with a stab of guilt. *How could I have done that?* But he had seemed so unaffected by it that after the first day she had ceased to worry and then, unforgivably, had managed to disregard it. He was a man, a warrior—of course he would not mention it until he fell flat on his stubborn, proud face.

Nick finished unwinding the bandage, but he was still twisted round, doing something to the dressing on his shoulder. In the stillness she heard his hiss of pain and was up on the deck and running to his side before she could think about it.

As he got to his feet she laid her hand on his uninjured shoulder. 'Nick, your wound—I am so sorry, but you should have said it needed redressing. Let me see.' She tried to press him back down to sit on the hatch. He resisted.

'I can manage, go back to bed, Anusha.' The moonlight turned his hair to silver, his bare chest was so close she could see the individual hairs, the way the brown aureoles of his nipples had tightened in the cool air.

She pushed aside his hand and lifted the trailing bandage. 'This has stuck to the wound.'

'I had noticed,' he said wryly.

'Then it needs to be soaked off and the wound redressed. Come down and I will do it. You need to be lying down and in my cabin there are all those lamps you gave me. I cannot see clearly enough up here.'

'I can see far too clearly.' Nick sounded grim. 'What the blazes are you wearing?'

'My shift—you have seen it before when you woke me the night we left Kalatwah.' She pushed the end of the bandage back into his hand, abrupt because she was moved by his stoicism and felt guilty about her neglect of his hurt. 'Why are you up here on this hard deck and not sleeping? How can you look after me properly if you make yourself ill?'

'Do you know, I had not considered that,' Nick said. 'Go back to bed.'

'Not without you.' His eyebrows soared. 'Foolishness,' she scolded. She would not let him see how that unspoken thought affected her. 'Is that all men ever think about?' It eased her conscience to put him in the wrong. 'I want to dress your shoulder and I want to know why you are up here.'

Nick allowed her to tug him towards the hatch. 'It was too hot below to sleep. I opened the hatch, and your door, but then it needed guarding. I can manage.'

'No, you cannot or you would have changed the dressing before now.'

He picked up the musket and went down the ladder. 'I suppose I will get no peace unless I let you torture me.'

Anusha did nor dignify that with a reply. She filled a copper urn from the water barrel tied to the foot of the mast and followed him down. 'No, go to my cabin, the lights are better and I need my things.'

Chapter Twelve

The fact that the infuriating woman was right was no consolation. He should have redressed his shoulder at least three days ago, it was going to be a devil of a job doing it himself and Anusha's cabin had the broader bed and the better lamps.

It also smelled of the jasmine oil she used on her hair, the myriad of feminine potions and lotions that she seemed to have acquired in Kalpi and, most distractingly, of herself.

It would be simplest to take the line of least resistance, do what she wanted and then escape.

'Lie down,' Anusha said, wriggling past him with a jug in one hand and a basin in the other. The pressure of a rounded backside against his thigh was more than enough incentive to obey. Nick lay down, swamping the hollow her body had made in the thin mattress, his head on a firm, Anusha-scented pillow.

'Lie still.' She sat on the edge of the bed, her hip against his, snipped through the loose length of bandage with a pair of tiny scissors, then leaned close to peer at the part that had dried on to the wound. Nick closed his eyes and gritted his teeth. 'I haven't done anything to hurt you yet,' Anusha protested.

No, but that shift is virtually transparent with the lamp behind you, your right breast is squashed against my chest and I am fantasising about simply rolling over and crushing you into this mattress. 'Lying down must have jarred it,' he lied with an heroic effort of self-control. Why he was bothering to pretend when she only had to glance below his waist to see what the problem was, he did not know. He was rock hard. For all her theoretical knowledge she would be terrified.

Anusha got up and began to set things out on the shelf. 'It is a good thing I packed my medical box.'

Nick opened a cautious eye. 'Do you know what you are doing with it?'

'Of course.' She dropped a small sponge in to the basin and picked up a sinister sharp object. 'It is part of our lessons in the women's *mahal,* to know how to care for our man if he is sick or wounded.'

He realised that she was speaking Hindi again, as though what she was doing was taking her mind back to Kalatwah. *Our man.* She said it with complete unconcern. She was not flirting, it had been an unconscious slip. Nick felt his groin tighten again and locked eyes with Anusha. The thin, loose trousers were no shield for his all-too-obvious thoughts.

'Now, I'll just put these towels here and sponge the dressing free,' she said, settling beside him again.

She was good at this, he realised after a minute. She did not dab, overcautious and hurting him more as a result. She was firm but gentle, her hands moving on his body with an assurance that only served to fuel his hopeless fantasies.

'There,' she said with a final wriggle of the probe to lift the dressing free. 'That is better now.'

'Yes, thank you.' And it was—the heat and tightness around the wound were immediately relieved.

'But it needs cleaning,' she added, reaching up to the shelf.

'Oh, no—'

'Oh, yes. This might sting a little,' she said, tipping the contents of a small phial directly on to the half-healed wound.

'Blood and sand!' Nick reared up off the bed and was promptly pressed back down again.

'I am sorry.' She did not sound remotely regretful as she used a piece of soft cloth to sponge the liquid into the raw area. 'Now I will kiss it better. That is what *Mata* always used to say.'

'Does it work?' He could hear the desperation in his own voice, even if she could not. There was only so much will-power a man could exert.

'Tell me,' she suggested and bent to drop a kiss on the skin just beside the wound.

'It does not help at all,' Nick said with complete truth, unfisting his hands from the sheet before he tore it.

'A pity.' He could not see her face, but she sounded re-gretful. 'Now I will bandage it again. Can you sit up?'

Nick sat and she swayed upright with him, her fingers light on his shoulder. 'I have clean dressings and the old bandage is all right to use again if I cut off the ends.'

'Good,' he managed as she redressed the wound and began to wind the bandage around his chest and over his shoulder. Which was fine, provided he could ignore how close she had to sit or how her arms went around his rib cage and how her fingers brushed across his skin, which he had never considered particularly sensitive and was now acting like one large, throbbing erogenous zone.

'Anusha.'

'Yes?' She frowned in concentration as she tied the end securely.

'Thank you.' He could do this. He could behave like a gentleman, thank her and get out of the cabin safely. Nick produced what he hoped was a friendly, grateful smile. 'I will just go and—'

'Please, wait.' Anusha bit her lip, her lashes lowered so he could not see her eyes. *This is so difficult...* 'There is something I must say to you, something I should have said before now. When you came for me to Kalatwah, I hated you because you are the agent of my father and because I had never met a man like you.'

'You have not met many men,' Nick said. He sounded uneasy.

'No, that is true.' She glanced up and looked him directly in the eye. 'I did not trust you. I learned quickly that I was wrong when I worried about trusting you with my body. But I did not trust you with my future,' Anusha added doggedly.

'Your future? I do not understand.'

'I need to be free, to be independent, to discover who I am. That could not happen at Kalatwah, I was beginning to realise it. But it can happen in Calcutta if I can be accepted into society there—and you have begun to teach me, and you have given me confidence.' And it was true. She had not realised how frightened she had been, deep down, at what awaited her. 'Otherwise I would be shut up in my father's house and not able to go out and be free if I did not know how things were to be done.'

'But your father will find you teachers and older women to guide you,' Nick explained.

'Yes, but they will be thinking about finding me a husband.'

'And that would not be a good idea?'

'No, of course not. Why should I want a husband if I can be free? I have turned down suitor after suitor at Kalatwah because I do not want to be tied.' *And because somewhere, out in the wide world, there might be love, like* Mata *found. Only this time a love that lasts.*

'My father is a rich man, so I am rich, am I not?'

'He will give you a dowry, yes,' Nick agreed cautiously.

'So you see? I did not know how to behave and whether I would have any money, so I was planning to sell my jewels and run away from you before we got to Calcutta. But now you have been kind and explained things and looked after me so I do not need to run away.'

Nick stared at her. 'Jewels?'

'It is all right, I have them hidden.' He looked worried, but he had no need to be—she had kept them well concealed.

'Excellent,' he said, but he did not sound very relieved. 'Your father…'

'He only wants me back because of these foolish politics, because I am a nuisance to the wretched Company if I stay in Kalatwah. He does not want *me*, I do not want him.'

Nick's lips compressed, but he did not lecture her for speaking disrespectfully. It was as though he was thinking about something else entirely.

Anusha lifted a hand to his shoulder, craving the comfort of touch. Under her palm his skin was hot, smooth. He
did not try to dislodge her hand. 'Nick, it will be as *Mata*
used to say, will it not? She said English women did as they
pleased and no one forced their daughters to get married.
That is right, is it not?'

She felt the deep breath he took, as if bracing himself
for something. Then he smiled. 'Of course. You will be a
wealthy young lady with all the freedom you could wish for.'

'Yes? *I will be free. I can choose.* 'You prom—'

Nick caught her against his chest and kissed her. The suddenness was shocking, liberating. She melted against him,
her arms around his neck, her breasts so tight against his
bare skin that she could feel his nipples hardening through
the thin cotton shift she wore.

Under the demands of his mouth her lips parted without
hesitation, her tongue meeting his to explore and stroke. He
tasted of tea and spice and something dangerous and male.

His hands slid down from her shoulders, down past her
waist to the curve of her hips as she sat on the bed, and he
lifted her so she sat across his thighs. Anusha gasped against
his lips as she felt the hard ridge of his desire. *He wants me
that much. He needs me. I need him. This is meant, this is
right...*

Nick turned her to cup the weight of her breast. She had
always thought them too small, but she filled his palm as he
teased the tight bud until she was gasping into his mouth.
This was arousal, she realised, she could feel her own moist
heat, smell the heady musk of their mutual desire.

Nick lifted his head and set his hands to her waist as if to
lift her away. Anusha opened her eyes and looked into his
face. He had released something in her: a passion, a femi-

nine understanding that had not been there before. He had told her she did not have to marry. This adventure had given her the courage to be free, to make her own world. And she knew what she wanted: this strong man who shielded his own hurt as well as he shielded her. She could not have him for long, she understood that, but…

'Nick, please—lie with me.'

'*What?*' Nick recoiled. It felt as though he had slapped her. *He doesn't want me. That was just a few moments' dalliance for him.* 'Anusha, I am sorry, I should never have touched you.' She saw his struggle for the kind words, the right tone to save her pride. 'You see why ladies must be chaperoned? You cannot trust men.'

He was allowing her to pretend she had not understood what she was asking, giving her a way to salvage her pride. She would not take it. 'I can trust you. I am not saving myself for a husband, so why should I not make love to a man if I want him?'

'Because it would be dishonourable of me to take your virginity. I should not even have kissed you, or touched you like that.' His eyes had become dark, the colour she had learned to associate with pain, mental or physical.

'It would be dishonourable if I did not want it,' she countered.

'I could get you with child.' He said it as if snatching desperately at an excuse.

'No, it is the wrong time of the moon,' she said with calm practicality. 'And besides, I have the means to stop it happening.' She nodded towards the pack of medicines. She had alum in there. It worked for stopping bleeding, and sweating, but it also helped prevent conception, although she did not know how.

'Your father—'

'Am I his slave?'

'No, but I am his man.' She opened her mouth to protest, but he pushed on. 'You say you trust me—he trusts me also. Would you have me betray both of you?'

'No,' she said after a moment. 'No, I would not ask you to break your trust. *Maf kijiye.*'

'Do not be sorry, Anusha,' Nick answered her in Hindi. 'You do me much honour, but it is a gift I cannot take.'

So, he salves my pride by pretending he is sorry. My protector. She managed to smile as he took his shirt and slid from the bed. She could pretend, too. Perhaps he was right, not for the reasons the gave, but because there was something fragile and tentative between them she could not put a name to, and that intimacy, with guilt on his side and something like desperation on hers, would have shattered it.

'Tomorrow we will reach Calcutta,' Nick said. They were on the Hooghly River now, he had explained, one of the arms of the River Ganges, the one that flowed to the sea through the great river port of Calcutta.

It was not exciting any longer, this journey through muddy plains, jungle, the occasional low rise with a village or a cluster of temples. Green trees, brown river, brown mud, hot blue sky and Nick being kind and proper and pretending that she had not said those things to him in her cabin, that they had not been locked together, mouth to mouth, breast to breast and that she had not felt the heat, the reality, of his desire.

Every night she ached for him. And every night she told herself to be thankful that he had shown *angrezi* honour and resisted her.

'It will be late, I think, but we will be safe back.' Anusha could hear the relief in Nick's voice. It was no wonder—they had been together for three weeks now and he had not wanted to be alone with her any more than she had at the start of this. Nick would want to hand her over to her father and go back to his own life, his own home and, no doubt, another woman for his pleasure.

Had she betrayed that she felt more than simply desire for him? She still did not understand what it was that she felt: liking, admiration—both those, of course. But there was something wounded inside him that she wanted to soothe, to heal. It was something to do with his marriage, she was certain. He must have loved his wife desperately, whatever he said, because otherwise, why was he so alone in his spirit?

Anusha leaned on the rail as they swept by a large village with fishing boats drawn up on the muddy beach, then a bend in the river took them and they were back between low bluffs covered in vegetation. It was peaceful—the current was no stronger than usual, there were no rocks. All the warning she had was a shout and then she was tumbling across the deck, her ears full of an ominous cracking of wood as the cook-boat swept down on them, struck them hard on the stern and slammed them into a sandbank.

'The tiller has broken!' the steersman shouted.

'*Dhat tere ki!*' Nick swore. 'If they've holed the thing…'

But the damage was only to the rudder.

Half an hour later the crew stood around the slabs of splintered wood on the sand and watched Nick warily.

'Can it be mended?'

'No, *sahib*. But we can have another made at the village we passed. They had many boats, they will have carpenters.'

'Go, then,' Nick said. 'And make haste.'

'We must pole the cook-boat upriver,' the captain explained. Nick's restraint seemed to unnerve him. 'It will take all of us against the current, and then it will be dark.'

'Then hurry,' Nick said. 'Anchor this boat securely, leave us food and be back early in the morning.'

Within half an hour they had gone, leaving the pinnace moored fore and aft on a large, flat sandbank in midstream.

'There is no need to worry,' Nick said.

'I am not. No animals from the bank can reach us, the men will be back tomorrow.' It felt safe to be with Nick, even when danger threatened. Somehow, although he instinctively threw himself between her and any attack, he had given her the confidence that she could fight, too.

'All true. I will light a fire on the sandbank. Do you want to cook for a change?'

'No,' Anusha said firmly. 'I have never had to cook— there were always servants to do that. Why can you cook so well?'

'All soldiers can, although the results are not always very edible. Let us see what they have left us.'

Night fell and the jungle was dark and full of noises. Overhead the dark-blue velvet of the sky was powdered with stars and on the sandbank the fire blazed high as Nick fed it with the driftwood she had gathered while he cooked.

Anusha leaned on the rail and watched him as he sat cross-legged, the three muskets stacked as a tripod beside him. 'Go to bed,' he called without looking back over his shoulder as though he could feel her eyes on him.

If the men came back at dawn with the rudder, then this

was the last night they would spend together. Her last night as a princess of the court of Kalatwah. Tomorrow she would be *Miss Laurens*, trying to recall all Nick's lessons in vocabulary and etiquette. Over the fish that he had cooked he had dismissed her thanks with a shrug—it was his duty, he had said. Perhaps he was worried that she would try to seduce him again. She just wanted to put her arms around him and hold him tightly, two people together with aching hearts.

Nick reached out and pulled something from a bag by his side. She could not see what it was, but after a few moments a soft beat floated on the still air. He had brought the *tabla* from the village.

Her feet moved, almost of their own accord. Tonight she was still Anusha and there was one gift she could give Nick.

Chapter Thirteen

The *tala* came without conscious thought, his fingers striking the taut drum skin in the rhythm that the men in his troop had taught him on long, quiet nights in camp. He could listen for danger despite it and the intricate pattern kept him alert and awake.

But it did not stop him thinking, and another sleepless night thinking of Anusha was a penance. Perhaps he deserved it—his conscience still nagged him about the lies he had told her, the way he had deceived her about the life she was going to. But how could he tell her the truth, that her father would be expecting to arrange a marriage for her, that her life as a married English lady in Calcutta would be almost as restricted as life in the *zanana*, that her dowry would go to her husband, not to her?

That she had believed him was clear from the way she had offered herself to him. She wanted to enjoy that new freedom and she thought there would be no danger that she might have to marry.

There was something else, he had see it in her eyes, heard it in her voice. *She wants to fall in love, she wants romance like her mother did.* He had almost told her he knew, almost told her it was a cruel dream and a fantasy, but who was he to give lessons in loving? Anusha deserved to hope, perhaps even to find love with a man who deserved all that she could give.

If she realised the truth, Anusha would bolt at the first opportunity unless he locked her in her cabin, he was convinced of it. *What could I tell her? That marriages at her level in society would not be forced, but they would always be arranged? That her father would keep her closely chaperoned and give her only pin money?*

She had been on the verge of asking him to give his word. He'd had a split second to prevent her from making him choose between honour and duty.

Anusha had offered herself with a shy courage that had him impossibly hard and needy at the first touch. She tasted of tea and spices and rosewater, of sex and woman and innocence and, remembering, something shifted in Nick's chest as though his heart had jolted. It was what he had wanted almost from the first moment he had seen her, the fantasy that had haunted his nights.

He closed his eyes and let himself believe for a moment, believe that she was his and that she was not an innocent who wanted love and deserved cherishing, but an experienced, worldly-wise courtesan from whom he could part without pain on either side.

Tomorrow night, provided all went well with the rudder, he would have her back where she belonged and if she hated him for it, then that was the price to be paid. He would not be around to see those grey eyes look at him full of hurt betrayal. He would just have to live with the memory of them.

Now when he tried to remember Miranda her blue eyes were overlain with long-lashed grey ones, her pale skin that had flushed so painfully in the heat was a pale ghost behind honey-gold curves.

Alert as he was, the subtle addition to his own drumming took him by surprise. Nick froze as a figure spun into sight, swirling skirts, tight trousers, the chime of bangles, bare feet slapping down on to the hard sand with the beat of the drum.

Anusha danced into the firelight, her shadow thrown long and dramatic behind her, the blue and red of her garments picking up the colours of the flames, the silver thread sparking gold with reflected light.

She was doing something no respectable woman would do, except for her husband or her female friends, performing one of the classical court dances. Her head moved in impossible, stylised sideways movements, her hands twisted and turned, conveying the meaning of the dance to those who could read its language. Her bare feet stamped and slapped in a complex counter-rhythm to his own hands as, almost mesmerised, he let the pace of the music increase.

The tension rose with the speed until Nick breathed as though he was running, or making love with vigorous, urgent strokes. His heartbeat echoed the *tabla* and he felt himself panting with the effort, but still Anusha twisted and wove her way through the *tala* until, just as he thought they would both collapse, she looked directly at him and brought her palms together with a sharp slap.

Nick lifted his hands from the drum and she stopped, poised like a temple carving, only the rise and fall of her breast, the sheen of perspiration on her forehead, the swinging folds of her *lehenga,* betraying that she was a living woman.

His hands shook as he put down the drum and broke the spell. Anusha moved, pushed back her heavy plait, sending the bangles clattering down her arm, and smiled at him. 'That is something I have never done before,' she said. 'I do not expect I ever will dance for a man again, so it is my thanks to you. The thanks you will not take in words.'

Speechless, he watched her pass him and did not turn as he heard the sound of her footsteps change when she walked up the gangplank and on to the deck. She had taken his breath away and he wondered if he would ever get it back.

'We are here.' It was not a question. Old memories were coming back, although not of landmarks exactly, for it was dark now and all she could see were the myriad of lights both on land and on the boats that seemed to swarm over the surface of the Garden Reach, the great pool of water that was Calcutta's harbour. Anusha leaned on the rail, recollection helped by the mingling smells of the city: human and animal waste, cooking fires, spices, flowers.

'I remember this, I think—all the great ships.' And they were still there, the merchantmen, anchored under the protection of Fort William. 'My father took us up on to the battlements of the fort to see the view once.'

'We will go to the fort now,' Nick said. 'I do not want to take you through the streets without an escort, and besides, Sir George may not be at the house.'

'Is it still the same one?'

'Yes.'

Dancing for Nick had unlocked something inside her,

lifted her spirits with the release of movement, the joy of doing an outrageous thing because she chose to. *Freedom.* Now the old apprehension slithered back to fill her stomach with cold apprehension and the sour burn of old betrayal. What if she could not hide how she felt well enough for her father to do what she wanted?

'I had not thought it would be the same house, somehow.' Full of memories of *Mata* that no doubt the other woman would have tried to brush away.

'You will find it changed, perhaps,' Nick said in an echo of her thoughts as a small skiff bumped alongside to take them ashore.

Yes, it would be changed and perhaps that was not a bad thing. The present was hard enough to manage without the ghosts of the past lying in wait around every corner. Anusha climbed down into the skiff and stood with Nick to catch their meagre bundles as they were tossed down. The crew was already chattering and happy at the prospect of a night in the city with wages fattening their purses.

Anusha watched them as the skiff was poled towards the shore. They were poor, they worked hard, their lives were uncertain—was she foolish to envy them their laughter and their careless joy for one night?

'Courage.' Nick was looking at her. 'You are Rajput, re-member?'

'I do not know what I am now,' she countered. 'But I will find out.' His mouth tightened. 'What is it? Does your shoulder still pain you?'

'No.' He shook his head and smiled. Knowing him as she did, it looked a little forced. 'My conscience poking at me, I suppose.'

They were speaking English, but she lowered her voice

even so. 'Because you kissed me? Because you came to my cabin?'

'That must be it,' he agreed.

'There was no harm. You were very strong and said no.' She tucked her hand companionably into the crook of his arm and leaned against his shoulder, wanting to give comfort. 'You see? We are just friends now.'

Friends? A tremor ran through her as though he had touched her intimately instead of it being she who had offered this harmless gesture.

Her nostrils flared, absorbing the scent of the soap Nick had used and of the day's sweat. Under her hand there was the solidity of muscle and the beat of his heart under his ribs where the backs of her fingers touched. She was as aware of him as she had been when she had danced for him, aware at a far deeper level than the physical attraction that had flashed between them in her cabin, when he had kissed her. This was like that second when his gaze had found her in the village when, veiled and in shadow, he could not have known her by any rational means.

Shaken, Anusha looked up at the still profile, black against the lights of the Princip *ghat*, the nearest landing steps to the fort. There was nothing to read, only strength and a strong masculinity of line and something of tension in the way his jaw was set. 'Friends,' she prompted, needing reassurance, although against what, she was not sure.

'Remember that,' Nick said. She thought he would add something, but all he said was, 'Keep hold of me when we land, it is crowded tonight.'

There was a festival for some minor deity. Crowds were jostling on the wide, wet steps of the *ghat*, dropping chains of marigolds into the water, setting little earthenware saucers with lighted candles on the surface to bob away on the current. There was music and sweetmeat sellers and children shrieking with excitement.

Anusha let Nick swing her ashore, then stood, feet braced on the slippery granite while he paid the ferryman. 'Calcutta at last,' he said, slinging one bag over his uninjured shoulder and taking the other from her. 'Now all I have to do is get you another half-mile and my mission is accomplished.'

He sounded pleased about it and she supposed she could not blame him, Anusha thought as she clutched his sleeve and followed him towards the river gate of Fort William. With the memory of Kalatwah so fresh, she found the low walls and star-shaped fortifications unimpressive, but there was nothing slack about the response of the guards on the gate or the efficiency with which they were brought inside and a palanquin was fetched. Either Nick's name or her father's worked like a magic charm, it seemed.

Anusha climbed into the palanquin, let the curtain drop and held tight to the sides as the bearers lifted the long curved pole on to their shoulders. Then they were off. 'Nick!'

'I am here. Are you all right?' It sounded as though he was walking beside her.

'Yes. It was…just very dark and very closed. I have become used to riding and to the river. The open air.' Now she felt like a prisoner. But it would not be for long, she reassured herself. Their destination, Old Court House Street, was only behind the great government buildings and houses of the Esplanade, just north of the *maidan,* the wide expanse of grass that surrounded the fort. And she would never be a prisoner again, confined behind screens and guarded doors, forbidden to go out, veiled and hidden.

'*Nick.*' It was a whisper. She did not know what she wanted, but a hand pushed aside the curtain and curled over the edge of the window opening. Reassured, Anusha put her own over it and felt the panic subside as she was moved, blind, through the streets.

'We are here.' His hand was withdrawn, the palanquin stopped and hung, swaying, there was the sound of excited, raised voices, the clang of a gate opening. 'Call Laurens *sahib*, tell him the daughter of the house has returned.'

The palanquin was set down, the curtain drawn back. Anusha emerged blinking into a courtyard surrounded by high, white-washed walls, a wide veranda and the low bulk of the house.

'That was where I saw you laid out like the dead,' she said as Nick came to her side. It was all so familiar and yet different. The yard seemed smaller, the house larger. Trees loomed unexpectedly and all the servants who were hurrying towards her were strangers.

'Anusha! Anusha, my dear child.' The man on the veranda was her father and yet not her father. The strong voice was the same, the height and the width of shoulder, but his hair was grey now, no longer dark gold as she remembered, there were lines on his face and what was once a flat belly now had a little paunch.

Ten years. Did I expect him to look the same, not to have changed while I have grown up? She took a step forward. 'Pa—' *No, Papa and his little girl have gone now.* The hands that had lifted instinctively to him folded neatly together as she bowed her head and willed her wildly-beating pulse to calm. '*Namaste,* Father.'

He came down the steps beaming, took her by the shoulders and for one moment she thought he would lift her, swing her up for his kiss as he always had when he came home to her. But he had no need to lift her now. Her father stooped and kissed her on the brow.

'You are so beautiful, my child. Just like your mother.' She stiffened as she stood passive between his hands and he added, his voice tight with emotion, 'It was a tragedy that she should have died so young—you must miss her very much.'

'Every day,' she said, meeting the grey eyes that were so like her own. *What emotion do you feel, Father? Guilt?*

His brows, still dark although his hair had greyed, drew together at her tone. Anger, puzzlement or both? He released her and pulled Nick into a rapid embrace. 'Nicholas, my boy, thank you for bringing her back safe to me. I have been getting coded messages from Delhi, so I knew you were travelling alone. And we have been hearing news from Kalatwah—the maharaja has given up the siege and retreated. There has been no bloodshed.'

The relief was an almost physical thing and not until it hit her did she realise just how that worry had been filling the back of her mind, ever present like a large black vulture, patiently waiting for tragedy to strike.

'That is good to know,' Nick said and smiled at her. 'You can stop worrying now.'

'Worrying?' Her father turned at the top of the steps. 'There was never any need to worry, not with that fortress so impregnable and help on the way. Nick, you must have explained it to her. The danger was always from one or two men getting inside and snatching you, Anusha, and the furore that would cause.'

'He explained very clearly, but they are my family,' Anusha said with a glance at Nick. He smiled back, an ally. 'Of course I worry.'

Again, that frown. 'You must be tired, both of you. Come inside where we can talk. You'll be hungry, I have no doubt, and will want to wash and change before dinner. I have had the best room refurnished for you, Anusha. Do you remember it? The one at the back overlooking the garden. I hope you will like it.'

She heard the emotion under his question and steeled her heart against it. 'Thank you, I recall it.' Not the room he had prepared for his wife, then. That was a relief—she would have refused to sleep in it and somehow she did not have the strength this evening for active confrontation, only for resistance.

The wide hallway was swarming with servants, all male of course, except for one woman, patiently waiting at the rear, her *dupatta* pulled forwards to shield her face. 'This is Nadia, your maid. Nadia, take Miss Anusha to her room, we dine in an hour.'

'*Namaste,* Nadia,' Anusha said as the maidservant came forwards.

'Good evening, Miss Anusha,' the woman responded and Anusha realised that she was quite young. 'Laurens *sahib* says that I must speak English to you all the time. The room is this way. My English is good, yes? I have been having lessons from the maid of Lady Hoskins in how to be a proper lady's maid.' They passed a *punkah wallah* sitting with his back against the wall, endlessly moving his foot so the cord tied to his big toe pulled the wide cloth fans to and fro in the rooms on either side of the corridor.

The maid opened the door at the end of the passage and waited for her to go through. Anusha had forgotten the furniture would be like this: the high bed, draped in fine muslin netting, the chairs, upright and stiff and lower ones too, padded. There were no cushions on the matting-covered floor. She would have to sit upright on these chairs, something her mother had always refused to do.

A—what was it called?—*dressing table* covered in little boxes and bottles, hair brushes, a mirror at the back. A clothes press. The door to what must be the bathing room. It was all so plain—the only bright colours were the maid's clothing and a dark red throw across the bed.

The long windows were open, with slatted shutters secured across them to let in the breeze, but give privacy and security, for the whole house was only one storey high. Overhead the *punkah* creaked to and fro, stirring the air, and a faint hum of chatter from the hallway reached her through the grillework over the door.

'This is a nice room, I think,' Nadia said with an anxious glance at Anusha. 'The water boys will have filled the bath if it pleases you to take it now, Miss Anusha, and I will lay out your clothes.'

'I have no clothes,' Anusha said, and went to peer into the bathing room. The bath was large and already full of water.

'That must have been very difficult! But Laurens *sahib* asked Lady Hoskins and she has sent everything that you need. See.' Nadia threw open the clothes press and pulled out drawers. 'Gowns and petticoats and corsets and stockings and—'

'Enough. I will bathe and then I will put on these clothes again with clean linen beneath. Not my turban, though.' The maid opened her mouth to protest then, with one look from Anusha, shut it again.

'Yes, Miss Anusha.'

* * *

She remembered the way to the dining room as well, although everything within the familiar lay-out of the house looked different. The walls had been painted with pale, plain washes, the furniture was new, more European in style, she supposed. Certainly foreign and uncomfortable to someone used to soft cushions, billowing silks, quilted cottons.

By dint of sending Nadia on an errand Anusha had managed to retrieve the jewels from her turban and hide them in a loose panel beneath the window seat. Most of the seats had panels that could be prised out, she had discovered as a child—probably there were still her little caches of toys and treasures all over the house.

Now, her hair in its plait down her back, her severe men's clothing unrelieved by jewels, she was conscious of the sideways glances of the male servants in the hall. They must be used to unveiled women, but she supposed that her strange mixture of European and Indian looks, her male attire, must seem odd and shocking to them.

'She is tired, that is all. It has been a trying journey for me, let alone for a sheltered young woman.' Nick's voice came clear through the ventilation grille above the door of her father's study. Anusha slowed to listen.

'…reserved.' Her father's voice, a low rumble from further into the room. 'Cold.'

'It is a long time since she saw you,' Nick replied. 'And she has been in the *zanana*. You would expect some uncertainty, surely?'

He is making peace for me. What would she have done without Nick? He had spirited her away, kept her safe, restrained those powerful male instincts for her and taught her some of what she needed for this strange new life she must live before she could snatch her freedom. *My friend,* she thought as she walked on, unable to linger and eavesdrop with the servants hovering attentively.

He would stay, surely, for a few weeks before he went off on another mission? He must rest, allow his wound to heal, and she would have him to stand between her and this strange, half-familiar world. *Nick.*

Chapter Fourteen

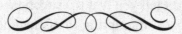

There had to be a word for Nick and the place he occupied in her heart, Anusha thought as she curled up uncomfortably on one of the big rattan chairs in the drawing room. Friend was not enough, not for the trust she felt, nor, she feared, for that tingling sense of physical attraction that she felt when he was near. She was still wrestling with words in both Hindi and English when the men came in.

'Ah, there you are, my dear. Is your room to your liking?' Her father stopped on the threshold and stared at her. 'Why are you still dressed like that? Did your maid not show you your new clothes? Never tell me they do not fit? I was sent the measurements.'

By whom? 'I am more comfortable in these tonight, Father.' Best not to start an argument now. Tomorrow she must cope with the corsets and the stockings and all the other horrors of European dress.

'Very well.' His smile was kindly, but there was a tinge

of uncertainty. *He does not know how to handle me,* Anusha thought. *He is nervous. Good!*

Her preoccupation with that little triumph distracted her and she missed what he added. '…hunting.' It seemed to be a joke, although Nick was not laughing. In fact, he looked as he had when they were in tiger country: alert and very, very wary. As it had then, that look sent a trickle of cold down her spine.

'I am sorry, Father I did not hear—'

'George, did I tell you that the situation—'

Why was Nick attempting to distract her father? The older man looked confused too. 'I only said that male attire is not suitable for husband hunting, however useful it might be for escaping across country,' he said.

'*Husband* hunting?'

'But of course. That is what we must apply ourselves to, is it not? We must find you a suitable husband.'

'I am here because Nick told me I must leave Kalatwah for the good of the state and to avoid embarrassing the East India Company.' Anusha found she was on her feet. 'I am not here to marry anyone. I do not want a husband!' She turned on Nick, whose face was blank now, although his eyes were wary. 'You told me I would not have to. You told me I would be free.'

'Nicholas?' Her father's tone was ominous. 'What is this?'

'If I had told her you intended to arrange a marriage she would have run away,' Nick said as though the words were being pried out of him at knifepoint.

'You lied to me.' She could not believe it. How could he have deceived her like his? 'I thought you were my friend,

I trusted you and you *lied* to me. What honour is there in untruths, you fine English officer and gentleman? *None.'*

'It was that or tie you up in the cabin,' he retorted. 'I knew you would run if you heard the truth.'

'You promised me!'

'No. You asked me to promise, I never gave you my word.'

'No, because you—' *You kissed me instead.* It did not take the warning jerk of his head towards her father to make her swallow the words. *That was why you made love to me, to distract me. Not because you wanted me, not because you felt anything.* 'You told me I would have money, my freedom. I will not have money—is that what you are telling me also?' she demanded.

'What nonsense have you been saying, Nicholas?' her father demanded, breaking into their exchange. 'What money?'

'Anusha believes that her dowry will belong to her, that as your daughter she will be rich and independent. She wishes to travel, not to marry.'

There was a fraught silence then, 'Be damned to that!' Sir George said. 'Of course you are going to marry, my girl. Who has put such foolishness into your head? Nicholas—what fairy tales have you been telling her?'

'What she wanted to hear. My choice was to betray your trust and risk her running away or to deceive her. What would you have me do?' Nick kept his voice calm and reasonable, but Anusha could hear the anger in it and the frustration that he was too respectful of the older man to show.

'What you did, of course.' The anger seemed to drain out of her father. His shoulders slumped. 'Anusha, you have no idea what you are talking about, no idea about European marriage. There is nothing to worry about, nothing to fear.'

Suspicious, she watched the men through narrowed eyes. 'You will not force me?'

'Of course not! Did your uncle and I not give you perfect freedom to refuse any marriage offer made to you?'

'Yes.' Anusha cut a glance at Nick's face. He was his usual impassive self again, although she could still sense his reined-in tension. But her father had been angry with him, so perhaps that was the source of it. 'And so... I can travel? I do not have to have a husband?'

'Of course you cannot travel! And of course you must have a husband, but I will not force one on you that you cannot like.'

She stared at him. 'I *must* marry, yet you will not force me? I can choose and yet I am not free? Is it my English? I know it is not perfect yet, but I cannot misunderstand so much, surely?'

Her father stared back, obviously frustrated by her lack of comprehension. 'Nicholas, you explain it to her: I'm damn... I obviously cannot.' He turned on his heel and marched out.

'Yes, please, Nick. You explain it to me,' she said sweetly. 'And I will try to believe you this time as well. Or perhaps you could kiss me again until my brain is as muddled as soup and I stop asking difficult questions.'

The betraying flags of colour were on his cheekbones again, but he took a deep breath and answered her patiently, 'There will be no kissing. Your father wants only the best for you. He will have decided upon suitable suitors for you to consider.'

'Who are these men? What are they?' The anger almost drowned the panic as she took an impetuous step forwards and took his forearm in both hands. She would shake the truth out of him if need be.

'I have no idea which poor fellow he has in mind.' Nick said with what she guessed was a misplaced attempt to mollify her with humour. 'But Sir George will want you safely married off as soon as possible. You are older than most of the single girls in Calcutta society.'

'*Married off!*' For a moment she could not work out the English idiom and she stared at him as though he had spoken Greek. 'To an *angrezi* husband he has picked out for me.'

'Of course. You are to become an English lady, that is all I know. What else would you do in Calcutta? How else would you live with him? He hardly needs a housekeeper.'

Anusha let go of his arm and took an unsteady stride away from him. 'Do? I want to do *nothing* in Calcutta except leave it! I did not ask to come here. I do not want a husband, I have turned down offer after offer.'

'I know. But this is different. We are not talking of a political marriage to a man old enough to be your father or to a princeling who could be murdered in a palace coup at any time. You will be an English lady and you may choose your husband, face to face.'

'Anyone?' she demanded, twisting to look at him over her shoulder, knowing the answer perfectly well. Choice offered by a man was nothing but a mirage. 'Any man I wish?'

'Of course not, but any eligible man your father approves. As I said, he is sure to have some in mind for you. Not just anyone, Anusha, but men of wealth and influence who will give you a good life.'

Wealth and influence. So that was why she had been summoned back, virtually kidnapped from her uncle's court.

The threat from Altaphur was real enough, but that gave her father his excuse. No doubt there was some alliance he wished to cement so he had thought of her, a pawn on his chessboard. At least it explained why he wanted her back after all this time.

Instinct had warned her that danger awaited and at least now she knew what it was: the risk of being married off to some Englishman who would treat her like her father had treated her mother. Only she would be legally tied to him, so she would be expected to stay with her husband however badly he behaved to her.

'Anusha, listen to me.' Nick caught her by the shoulders, turned her to face him. 'With the dowry Sir George will give and the influence he wields, there will be no problem in finding you a suitable husband, one you will like. A leading merchant, a promising army officer, the younger son of a noble house—that sort of gentleman.'

A promising army officer, the younger son of a noble house... She shot Nick a fulminating glance. Did he mean himself? Marriage to her would make him the son and male heir of the man he regarded as his father. It would give him more money, more standing to help him build what was obviously a promising career. Had that been what his kisses and his kindness had been about—careful first steps in seducing a bride?

If Nick married her, he would march off as soon as he had planted a child in her and go to whatever exciting and interesting things he spent his life doing and she would be left with the corsets and the babies and the *memsahibs* with their disapproving mouths, and she would never belong and never be free.

'I see.' She felt strangely calm all of a sudden. She had

been moved from the gilded, luxurious cage of the court to another cage, not so gilded, not so luxurious. And, she could see already, not so secure. 'He chooses some men, parades them in front of me, I say *no*, he finds some more… How long does this go on?'

'Until you find someone you like.' Nick watched her face with the patience she had grown accustomed to. It was the implacable patience of the hunter and, worst of all, there was pity deep in the green eyes. 'Anusha, I am sorry I had to deceive you, but you have no idea how dangerous it is out there for a gently reared lady alone—you would not have lasted a day.'

How innocent she had been, how romantic, to think that this alien warrior would be her friend or perhaps, in those half-waking dreams around dawn, more than her friend.

At the court, if she had refused a match and her uncle had insisted, she would have been shut up in her room until she submitted. Here, it seemed, there would be no physical coercion so it would be a game of cunning to escape. And she knew she was cunning—court life taught you how to be that.

'I understand.' She turned from him in case he saw the calculation in her eyes. 'And who will teach me to be an English lady that these desirable men will want to marry? Or would they marry anyone to secure my father's money and patronage?'

'They will want you for yourself, Anusha. How could they not when they come to know you?' *Yes? I know already that you will tell me any lies if it suits you.* 'And Lady Hoskins will take you under her wing. She lives three houses further along this street. She is married to Sir Joshua

Hoskins, a colleague of your father, and they have a daughter who married last year and a son of seventeen.'

An experienced matron, one who would not be easy to deceive. Best to begin now to disarm suspicion. 'I see I will have to make the best of it,' she said with a shrug. It would not do to seem too ready to accept her fate.

'Come and have dinner, then. Take your mind off your troubles by wrestling with the silverware.'

'I am certain I will have no problem.' She stalked out of the door in front of Nick. 'After all, I have had the benefit of your lessons.'

Anusha was angry with him, her nose was severely out of joint and she was, however well she was hiding it, deeply uneasy in this house, uprooted from everything she knew and understood. Nick followed on her heels into the dining room, worry and sympathy warring in his breast. On their journey, however difficult and dangerous it had been, they had been in her world and she had been the raja's niece.

Now she did not know who she was, only that she was with the father she believed had rejected her, and a man who had lied to her and lured her into coming here.

A servant held her chair for her at the foot of the table and she sat, back straight, hands folded in her lap, chin up. Nick took his own place, halfway along the board between Anusha and Sir George at the head, as servants began to bring in the dishes that made up a typical Anglo-Indian dinner.

The way the table was arranged mirrored the Indian style of setting out an array of dishes all at once, but the dishes themselves were a hotchpotch of Indian curries, chutneys and rice and English roasts, soups and vegetables. 'May I help you to anything?' Nick offered. 'A slice of lamb or chicken?'

'Thank you. Chicken.' She eyed the vegetables, then extended her right hand towards the rice and snatched it back, lips pursed in embarrassment as she found the serving spoon and used that. The servant poured wine into her glass.

Nick laid two slices of chicken on her plate. 'Might I trouble you for the vegetables?'

She managed, he saw, with ferocious concentration and by watching what he and George did like a hawk. It would never do to underestimate either Anusha's intelligence, or her ability to learn and adapt. His conscience had ceased to trouble him for lying to her—it was his duty to protect her, by any means, and he had done so—but he was very conscious that he had lost her trust. Whatever it had been between them that was so warm and so elusive had congealed into wary watchfulness on his side and hostile suspicion on hers.

'You'll like Lady Hoskins, Anusha.' George had apparently decided to deal with the confrontation in the drawing room by ignoring it. 'And her daughter Anna—Mrs Roper now—is a delightful young woman. Pass the salt, would you, Nicholas?'

It was a slight stretch. Nick suppressed the wince as the movement overextended the healing wound in his shoulder, but Anusha saw his reaction.

'Is your shoulder paining you, Major Herriard?' she asked with such sweet concern that it took him a moment to realise she had called him by rank and surname.

'Shoulder?' George looked up sharply. 'What have you done?'

'It was the dacoits, Father,' Anusha said. 'The major was

shot in the shoulder, just outside Kalpi.' She lowered her eye-lashes so they feathered her cheeks and Nick suppressed a strong desire to pick her up and dump her back in her room. She was up to something. 'And he was nursed at the house of Mr Rowley, the agent. His wife was most disapproving of me.' The grey eyes lifted and opened wide. 'Do you think I will be—what is it called?—*ruined* when she speaks of it?'

A good attempt, Anusha, Nick thought and produced a smile as false as her look of anxious enquiry was. 'No need to worry, George. I had a word with the Rowleys and the doctor. One mention of your name and they were vowing complete discretion and eternal silence.'

'So I should hope,' George said with a grunt. 'But how bad is this wound? I'll call my doctor after dinner and have you checked over.'

'Tomorrow is soon enough.' There was going to be no escaping an examination, he knew the older man well enough for that. 'It has healed well. Miss Laurens was good enough to dress it for me.'

'Was she indeed?'

'The major was incredibly brave,' Anusha remarked. 'There were the dacoits and the king cobra, and the maharaja's men and the tigers.'

'Tigers?'

'We saw one pug mark,' Nick said with a repressive stare at Anusha who was doggedly cutting chicken with the unfamiliar cutlery. 'The men sent after us were easily headed on to the wrong trail. The dacoits were…troublesome. Fortunately we had trained cavalry horses.'

'And the king cobra?' There was a smile lurking in the concern. Nick knew George had seen his youthful self swarm up trees to escape snakes and knew all too well that they brought him out in a cold sweat.

'The major was…' Anusha's voice trailed away. 'He was… He saved my life and I thought he had been bitten.' All the *faux* sweetness had gone, and so had much of the blood from her cheeks. 'Excuse me. I am suddenly very tired. I will go to my chamber.' She put down the cutlery with a little clatter, pushed back the chair before the servant had a chance to reach it and walked swiftly from the room.

'Well,' George remarked as they sat down again. 'I think a full, unexpurgated report is called for, hmm? And no false modesty, Nicholas, or I'll ask Anusha for all the details.'

Chapter Fifteen

The *punkah* had been still for over an hour. Distantly there were the noises of the city, and the house creaked as it cooled, but there were no human sounds except the watchman's sandaled feet as he had padded past a hundred heartbeats ago.

Anusha slid out of bed, miscalculated the height and gasped as her heels jarred on the floor. After a few moments, when no answering sounds reached her, she breathed again and slipped into a dark robe. Her bare feet made no sound on the matting and her door opened without a sound, thanks to the *ghee* she had used to oil the hinges earlier.

She moved along the corridor by the light of her little lamp, its flame shielded by her cupped palm, the soft sounds of her movements masked by the snores of the man sleeping across the front door. He did not stir as she turned into the passage leading to the drawing room, the one that passed her father's study.

That was where the maps would be, his strong box, news

sheets with shipping advertisements. Ammunition that she could not use now, but which she needed to locate. How easy would the strong box be to open? Anusha tried the study door, found it unlocked and went in.

It was as she remembered it from her childhood. Then she would come to this room on a Saturday to sit on Papa's— *Father's*—knee and receive a shiny silver rupee that was all hers to spend in the bazaar when her *ayah* took her there.

She sat down in his big chair now, her vision blurred as the room filled with daylight and the sound of Papa's laugh when she brought back trinkets and toys and sweetmeats to show him at the end of the day.

Weakness. Just memories of a man's indulgence to a child—now she was a woman. A daughter who was a possession and a bargaining counter, but whose value was diminished by her mixed blood and her illegitimacy.

Anusha lifted down the set of red leather ledgers and there, just as she remembered, was the heavy iron safe. It was bigger than anything she had tried to open before and it would need more than hairpins.

'An urge to visit the night bazaar and so a need for spending money?' a low voice behind her enquired. She whirled around. Nick was watching her, his back against the closed door. How had he found her? And how the devil had he got inside the room, closed the door behind him, all without her hearing him?

'I want to see if there is somewhere safe for my jewels.'

'Liar,' he said softly. 'At three in the morning?'

'I could not sleep. How did you hear me?'

'I was watching for you.'

'Where?' As her breathing steadied she began to take in details. He was wearing a robe of heavy black silk, belted at the waist and in the vee of the neckline she could see skin and a curl of hair. His feet were bare, his hair loose on his shoulders.

'In my bedchamber.'

'You are sleeping here?'

'I live here. I have a suite of rooms at the rear of the house.'

'The women's quarters,' Anusha said flatly. Where she and *Mata* had lived for twelve years.

'Yes. When you left George had part of it converted for me. I can see your window and the light shines through the shutters.'

No sooner had she and *Mata* gone than Nick had invaded their territory, filled the space they had left. 'You are spying on me.' She picked up the ledgers and thrust them back on the shelf, aligning the edges perfectly to give herself time to think.

'It seemed wise to do so. Was I right?' She had forgotten how he could move like smoke, like a tiger. He was beside her when she turned, so close that she could smell the familiar tang of his skin overlain by something new, the soap he had washed with that night, she thought, dizzy with reaction to the shock of his appearance, of his closeness.

'You cannot stay awake every night.' Somehow Anusha managed to get her tongue around the words.

'No, but I can put a watchman to sleep across your door and another to sit beneath your window. Who knows how vindictive the maharajah might be? You must be protected.'

'You do not believe he will try to snatch me here,' she said scornfully.

'No. But your father might if I suggest it.'

'And you are his spy and my jailer.'

'I am your friend, Anusha. I wish you could believe it.'
Nick moved closer. The flickering light sent shadows chasing across his face, turned his hair to gilt, made his eyes dark and mysterious. The air was thick in her lungs and it was hard to breathe.

'I—' She meant to curse him, but all that came out was a small gasp. To her horror she felt tears prick the back of her eyes. *I want to believe you. I want to trust you.*

'Anusha.' Nick gathered her to him, into the softness of silk, against the hard strength of his body. She buried her face into the fabric and felt skin against her cheek, the beat of his heart against her ear. Every fibre of her being told her that he was safety and protection and desire, every instinct told her he was danger and betrayal. *And desire.*

'It hurts, doesn't it? To be back here, to not understand. But you were a child then, you are a woman now. Talk to your father, try to reach each other. He loves you.'

The heavy silk absorbed the tears, but she still could not speak as the realisation of what these feelings meant swept through her. *I love you.* Wordless, shaking with the force of her discovery, she wound her arms around Nick's waist and held on to as much of him as she could grasp. He moved, the sensation of being supported and surrounded intensified, and she realised he had sat down on the edge of the desk and was holding her against his chest as she stood between his spread legs.

He made no move to caress her, or to touch her other than to flatten his big hands on her back, but gradually, as she relaxed, she became aware that he was aroused, hard against the softness of her lower belly as she rested against him.

I do trust him, she thought, her mind finally calm. *He did what he had to do because he loves my father and he owes*

him everything. And I want him and he will stand here all
night comforting me because he thinks that is what I need...
That is not *what I need. I love you.*

Anusha nuzzled into the overlap of the robe, the tickle of
chest hair strange and arousing over smooth skin and hard
muscle beneath.

'Anusha—' He stopped with a gasp as her questing mouth
found a nipple that contracted into a hard knot at the first
stroke of her tongue. Her fingers closed over the ends of the
sash that held his robe closed and she tugged as he shifted
to hold her away from his body. The robe fell open and she
rocked forwards against him, close against the splendour
of his nakedness.

'Anusha,' he said again and this time it was a groan. She
lifted her face to him, her lips parted in invitation, and he
bent his head and took them. She could sense the conflict
in him even as his mouth made love to hers, his tongue slipping between her teeth to stroke and plunge and plunder. He
tasted hot and male and urgent and through the thin cotton
that she wore she felt his heartbeat kick.

'No,' Nick muttered, lifting his head so the kiss was broken. But it was as though he did not have the strength of lift
right away and his breath stroked her lips and his eyes were
wide and brilliant. 'No,' he said more strongly.

Anusha clung to his neck, lifted one knee on to the desk
and then the other so she straddled him, her night robe
crumpling up to leave her exposed. Then, before he could
twist free, she lowered herself so that the heated length of
his erection was trapped along the soft intimate folds that
were hot and moist and ached for him.

'God, Anusha, *no.*' Nick bucked his hips, but that only
pressed him closer and she moved with him, rocking in a

rhythm that made her sob with need. 'Sweetheart, stop. Stop, please while I still can—'

He was struggling with himself, with her, with his fear of hurting her and his need to take her. It was a fight, a battle and one she was desperate to win...*because I love him.* Anusha stopped moving, conscience-stricken. Nick would never forgive himself if he took her virginity here, like this, she knew. It would break him, break the bond with her father, break his honour.

She fell against his chest and tried to keep still. 'I am sorry, Nick. I just... I just need you so much.' *If I tell him I love him he will leave. He does not want love.*

Silence, broken only by the sound of their panting breaths, the hiss of the lamp wick, a dog barking in the night.

'I need you, too,' Nick said, his voice harsh as though the confession had been extracted under torture.

He was a sensual, virile man and she knew he had not had a woman for weeks and here she was offering herself. Of course he *wanted* her—it did not mean anything else. Anusha tried to climb down. 'Wait.' He stood, lifting her with him, walked to the couch in the corner, sat down again and set her by his side.

His face was sheened with sweat and she could see the big artery in his neck pulsing, but his hands were steady as he wrapped himself in the robe again and tied the sash. 'You ache,' Nick stated as though he asked her if she was thirsty.

'Yes.' She wanted to touch his hair, smooth the gilt silk under her fingers, but she dare not touch, make it more difficult for him. In a moment, when her legs had stopped shaking, she would get up and go to her room and stop tormenting him.

'Come here then, sweetheart. Let me make it better.' He

lifted her on to his lap, settled her against his shoulder and kissed her, all before she could react.

She should get up… But her legs felt even weaker and his mouth was like a drug and his arms held her and she gave herself up to the kiss. Even when his hand slid up her leg, pushed back the thin cotton of her night shift, cupped her aching core, all she could do was moan into his mouth.

And then—*aah!* How could such gentleness create such violence in her body? She arched, pressing against his hand as his fingers explored, stroked, found the point… the point… Anusha stopped thinking, stopped breathing, surrendered to sensation and heat and Nick. Then his other hand cupped her breast and his fingers closed on one nipple and pinched, so lightly, and the exquisite pleasure broke over her like a wave so that she screamed and he captured the sound in his kiss.

She was vaguely aware of being lifted, of movement, of being lowered on to something soft. 'Sleep, Anusha,' Nick murmured in her ear. His hand brushed her cheek and she smiled, her body as limp as finest silk velvet, her mind utterly at peace. *I love you.* She tried to say it, but the words were lost as she drifted down into sleep.

'So you are Anusha! Welcome to Calcutta, my dear.'

'Ma'am.' Anusha dropped a curtsy. It felt very odd, her legs were still shaky after last night—the only thing that convinced her it had not all been a dream—but apparently it was correct, for Lady Hoskins smiled and nodded in approval.

'What a charming young lady, Sir George. I am sure we will get along famously, will we not, Anusha? How is your English? Do we need an interpreter and a tutor?'

'No, ma'am.' She dragged her thoughts away from memories of Nick's naked body, of his hands, his mouth… This was nothing to do with Nick, this was all about her father's plans for her and she must be constantly on the alert. But when she saw him again, would he say anything? Could he possibly have discovered that he loved her, too? *No, do not hope.*

'I recall my English from before I was sent away, and I spoke it often with my mother.' That was deliberately tactless. She noticed her father's lips draw tight and Lady Hoskins shift as though uneasy. Anusha kept her face innocently blank. She was not going to mention talking to Nick in English, she had no wish to compromise herself, not yet at any rate. Later it might be useful. *Later I might not be able to help myself.*

'Er…excellent. And your maid is satisfactory? She has turned you out very well this morning.'

'Thank you, I am very happy with her.' Anusha knew she had been difficult enough that morning to excuse outright mutiny on the part of Nadia as the maid had patiently dressed her in chemise and corset, petticoats, more petticoats to make her skirts bell out, stocking, garters and shoes that pinched her toes. And over the top of it a gown in cotton chintz with wide skirts and a tight bodice and sleeves. How anyone was expected to move in all this she had no idea— standing still and curtsying were simple by comparison.

'A new hairstyle is the first priority.' Lady Hoskins circled her. 'That weight of hair is impossible to do anything with.'

'I do not wish to have my hair cut, ma'am.' But the older woman was already gesturing to the maid. Before she could protest further, the plait was undone and shaken loose.

'It waves, it is an interesting colour, but we must have at least a foot off it. More, perhaps.'

My hair, my beautiful hair! It reached below her hips when it was loose. She'd had fantasies of letting it hang over Nick's naked body, of sweeping it back and forth until he… But that was when he had not known how keenly she desired him—he would avoid her now, she feared.

'Very well.' Whatever it took to lull her father into believing she meant to stay, meant to be a dutiful daughter. Anusha watched him from the corner of her eye. He was taking more of an interest in Lady Hoskin's attempts to turn her into an English lady than he had in anything else about his long-lost daughter, she thought resentfully.

'Excellent. Then, Sir George, with your permission, I will send for my *coiffeuse* and my maid and together we will deal with the question of hair and go through Anusha's wardrobe. I thought dinner at our house tonight? Just a small gathering of twenty to get her into the way of things.'

Anusha found that she was gazing hopefully at her father's retreating back, as though he might turn round and rescue her. But of course he did no such thing and, of course, she did not wish him to. What she wanted was to ask where Nick was, why he had not been at breakfast.

'Now, the first thing is to lace that corset properly,' Lady Hoskins said, advancing on her as the door closed. 'Your figure is far too natural.' Anusha clenched her fists and managed to smile.

'I declare it is a positive age since you came to any parties, Major Herriard. I was saying only the other day to my sister that we must quite give you up, which is such a pity, for we are always in need of handsome men in red coats.'

The elder Miss Wilkinson finished this piece of inanity with a giggle and batted her eyelashes at him over the top of her fan. It was a pretty fan and a pair of charming blue eyes and she knew it.

Nick managed a smile through gritted teeth. To think that he had spent hours sailing down the Ganges instructing Anusha in how to produce just such pointless chit-chat! At the thought of her his groin tightened and he forced his concentration back to the women in front of him—they aroused no desires at all.

'Alas, duty calls only too often, Miss Wilkinson, and drags us poor men away from the delightful company of Calcutta's ladies.'

That was apparently an acceptable response. Miss Wilkinson moved a little closer and then, to his surprise, gestured to a group of young ladies nearby. Nick found himself surrounded.

'We are all *agog* and *you* will know, Major Herriard,' Miss Annis Wilkinson breathed. 'Is it true that Sir George Laurens has his *natural daughter* staying with him and she is an Indian *princess*?' She made Anusha sound as exotic as a cage full of white tigers, but he supposed none of these girls would ever have met a member of the royal courts.

'Miss Laurens has been residing with her uncle, the Raja of Kalatwah. The state has recently been attacked by a neighbouring prince, so I escorted Miss Laurens home to her father.' There was no point in making a mystery of the basic facts.

'Escorted her?'

Nick injected every bit of *ennui* he could into his reply and managed without an outright lie. 'Court progresses are the slowest, most tedious thing imaginable. Bullock carts, palanquins, the *zanana* tents to shield the ladies...'

'Oh!' A frisson of delighted horror at the thought of the *zanana* ran through the group. 'And does she go everywhere escorted by an enormous eunuch?'

There was a stir near the door and the butler announced, 'Sir George Laurens, Miss Laurens.'

'You may see for yourself,' Nick said, turning to look. He had avoided the main part of the house all day, and sent a message to George that he had business at the fort. He was not at all sure that either he or Anusha could control their expressions or their reactions if they met just yet and he had no desire to explain to George why his daughter was slapping his face.

Last night had been exquisite, insane and appallingly dangerous. He had been unable to get the taste or the scent of Anusha out of his head all day. Somehow he had to talk to her, assure her that it would never happen again, that he would protect her innocence at whatever cost to himself, because today she must be angry, frightened and shocked.

He stared over the heads of the crowd. He could see George, talking to his host, but he could not see Anusha.

'But she looks quite ordinary,' one of the girls said, her voice flat with disappointment. 'Just like us.'

'I can't—' *Good God.* The slight figure next to Sir George *was* Anusha. Her hair was piled up into an elaborate arrangement with one glossy ringlet left to lie on her shoulder. Her waist looked minute rising from the bell of her skirts and she tossed the lace back from her sleeves as she lifted her fan in a movement that was pure coquette. Nick found his voice. 'Ordinary?'

Chapter Sixteen

Nick swallowed and got his face back under control.

'I expected she would have a sari and rings in her nose and she'd be dark skinned with black hair and big brown eyes. But she is just like us, only her skin looks as though she has been in the sun too much,' Miss Wilkinson observed. There was a murmur of agreement. 'I like that amber silk.'

Then Anusha moved, walking into the room beside her father, and Nick felt every man in the room under eighty draw a breath. She might look like a golden-skinned version of any young lady who was fashionably gowned and coiffed, but she moved like the trained dancer she was, with a feline grace that took him in the throat and then, inevitably, considerably lower. God, he wanted her. How the hell had he ever managed to stop himself last night?

'Excuse me,' he said. 'I must go and speak to Sir George and be introduced to Miss Laurens.'

'But you've met her,' Miss Wilkinson protested. 'You escorted her. You must have seen her. And you live with Sir George, do you not?'

'The *zanana,* remember? And I have my own wing of the house. *And not this woman,* he added under his breath. *I have never seen* this *woman.*

He had seen so many faces of Anusha. A haughty Indian princess in a temper; a brave, tired girl in youth's clothing fighting fear and hardship; a wrong-headed young woman with a completely unrealistic dream of freedom. Then there was the passionate half-innocent who had known all the theory and none of the realities of what happened between men and women until he had let his control slip and had shown her a little, just a glimpse of what he wanted to do with her.

But he had not met *this* woman, Miss Anusha Laurens, back where she belonged on her father's arm at an East India Company dinner party.

'Miss Laurens.' He bowed and wondered what she saw when she looked at him: the soldier in his dress uniform, controlled and disciplined—or the man from last night, half-naked, in thrall to her and to his desires?

'Major Herriard.' She curtsied, her face showing nothing but polite interest. But her eyes sparkled. Temper or desire?

'You are in great beauty tonight, An…ma'am.' He'd be stammering like a callow youth in a moment. Nick took in a breath down to his boots.

'So are you, Major.' The dark lashes swept up and down as she studied his scarlet dress uniform. 'As splendid as you were at court.' She fixed him with that candid-seeming stare that he knew could hide so much and added, 'I did not expect to see you here. Have you not returned to your regiment?'

'I am on leave, Miss Laurens.'

'I thought you must have left Calcutta when you did not join us at breakfast this morning.' She sent him a very direct look from beneath immaculately plucked brows. A reproof for avoiding her?

'I had business at the fort all day.'

Anusha glanced around, her expression perfectly pleasant, a smile on her lips as her eyes flickered from side to side. He knew her well enough now to read her. She was nervous and embarrassed in this crowd of strangers, she did not know how to act with the man who had given her her first sexual experience only the night before and it was only pride and her court training that was keeping her standing there.

He began to step back, to leave her to her father and to Lady Hoskins, but she caught at his sleeve. 'What am I supposed to do now, Nick?'

For a moment, stung by conscience, he thought she meant after his lovemaking, then she whispered, 'There are so many people I do not know. And *men*.'

He gently pried open her fingers from their grip on the gold lace. 'You take my arm.' He proffered his right arm, bent at the elbow, and murmured, 'Put your fingertips on my forearm.' She did so, then looked up at him, a spark of mischief in her eyes. For a moment the trusting Anusha was back with him. 'Now we take a turn around the room and I introduce you to people.'

'Men as well? They are all staring at me and there are so many.'

'Only ten, including me and your father. So eight strange men. And they are staring because they admire you and wish to challenge me for daring to be before them with you.'

'But you will not leave me?' Her fingers tightened on his arm.

She still trusts me, still needs me. 'No,' Nick promised, dizzy with relief. 'Not with the men, but I may have to give you up to the ladies.'

'I do not mind that,' she said. 'I am used to women.'

And she was used to the women of a princely court who would be like hunting cats amongst the pretty pigeons that were the young ladies in this room.

Anusha was quiet and serious when introduced to the gentlemen. She curtsied, managed a small smile and a few words, but her hand kept lifting instinctively as if to pull a veil over her face.

'You have no veil,' he murmured. 'Use your fan.' The trouble with that was the effect of big grey eyes, wide above the painted silk, on men whose imaginations were already overheated by rumour of her origins and whose gaze had been riveted on the graceful sway of her figure.

'I am proud of you,' he said when they found themselves alone for a moment at one end of the drawing room.

'Because I am curtsying just as you taught me? I do not think I can do the flirting, not yet. It is so *difficult* being with strange men like this.'

'You managed with me.' She looked up and met his eyes and the impulse to laugh died. Nick laid his hand over hers and thought of how her slender, soft body felt against his, of how her mouth tasted, of how she had ridden and danced and fought. *And shuddered into ecstasy in my embrace.* Of how it was his duty to protect her until she was safe here and found a man to marry. And then he could return to his next assignment and forget her.

'You are different,' Anusha said with certainty.

'Am I forgiven?' It should not matter—he had done the right thing for her protection.

'For lying to me about what my father intended?'

'And for last night,' he added.

'That does not require forgiveness. No,' she interrupted when he opened his mouth to disagree. 'It was me, too.'

'We must talk about it, but not here.'

'No, not here,' she agreed. 'And for the other thing, I have forgiven you,' she said, her face serious and a little troubled. 'I understand why you deceived me, I know your first loyalty is to my father. But I have not forgotten.'

'I see. Forgiven but not trusted.' That was just, but it hurt.

'I do not trust anyone,' she said flatly. 'Not you, not my father, not Lady Hoskins who is sorry her son is not older and who has twice mentioned her brother's *most promising* sons and her very wealthy cousin who has just lost his wife.'

'Come and meet the young ladies,' Nick said with a feeling of mild desperation. He just hoped George knew what he was doing. If he tried to force Anusha into the midst of the Calcutta Marriage Mart there was no knowing what she might be driven to. 'Ladies! May I introduce you to Miss Laurens? Miss Wilkinson, Miss Clara Wilkinson, Miss Browne, Miss Parkes.'

Anusha regarded them carefully, then inclined her head a very precise one inch. 'Good evening.'

'I'll…er…leave you to become acquainted.' Nick backed off, feeling as though he had three feet and all of them left ones. It might make him a coward, but he had no intention of being within earshot if they asked Anusha about eunuchs.

'Do you know the major very well?' the skinny blonde one asked. *Parkes, that is her name.* 'He is terribly handsome, is he not?'

'I do not know any men except my uncle, the raja, and my father,' Anusha said with a sweeping disregard for the truth. 'I find it most immodest the way one is expected to mix with men not of one's family in English society. And I find all Englishmen too big, too pale and not—' she gestured with both hands, seeking for the word '—not elegant.' *Except Nick. He moves like a tiger and his hair is moonlight on gold. My love, don't leave me here and walk away.*

'Oh.' Miss Parkes seemed somewhat crushed by this observation. 'But how will you find a good husband if you do not meet men?'

'My father will find one for me. Will your father not do the same?' These girls were the best way to find out how the English really did go about matchmaking.

'Well, yes. Papa will approve him. But how do I meet men so I can decide who I want if I do not move in society—and how can the men decide which ladies to court if we do not meet?'

'But your father will refuse any man who is not rich enough, or well born enough or who has a poor character, even if you like him. So why do you meet them all first? What if you fall for a man and he is not suitable? Much better never to meet them and to rely upon your father's judgement.' *Hypocrite,* she thought to herself. Still, it was interesting to provoke these girls into telling their true feelings.

'Yes, but...' Clara Wilkinson was frowning, '...but it will make for a much better marriage if there is mutual liking first.'

'You mean it will stop the man having mistresses? I doubt it.' The girls all went pink. Interesting—obviously one did not mention mistresses. 'At least your husbands will only have one wife apiece.' What if she married Nick and he took mistresses? It would break her heart. But he would do, of course he would. She could hardly expect him to be faithful to her. Why should he be? Not that he would marry her. The death of his wife had hurt him too much. She did not believe him when he said it had not been a love match.

'Um... That is a very elegant gown, but do you not have any jewellery?' Miss Browne asked with the desperate air of someone turning the subject.

'Oh, yes, a great deal, but it is all Indian cut and the settings are not suitable for this European gown.'

'But do you not have Lady Laurens's jewels?'

'I would not wear hers,' Anusha said flatly. 'My mother's, of course, are Indian, too.' That produced a flurry of coughs, strategic fan-waving and pink cheeks. Apparently her irregular birth was another unmentionable.

Ears attuned to the pad of bare feet on thick carpets heard the masculine tread behind her. It was not Nick. 'Ladies, I have been studying the seating plan and have come to inform you of your good fortune in your dinner partners tonight.'

Anusha turned and found herself almost toe to toe with a young man, close enough to assess the diamond stickpin in his neckcloth and smell the oil he used on his hair. He seemed to find her mouth fascinating, so she lifted her fan as a barrier between them. His eyes slid lower and she restrained the urge to kick the insolent youth on the ankle. But of course this was not insolence, this was permitted.

'Oh, Mr Peters, do tell.' Miss Wilkinson was positively simpering. 'Who is *your* lucky partner?'

'Why, you, ma'am, and *I* am the lucky one.' He bowed and

managed to take a comprehensive look at Anusha's cleavage as he did so. She folded her fan, just missing his nose.

'I am *so* sorry. Did I hit you?'

'No, not at all, ma'am. Miss Laurens, is it not? Will none of you ladies introduce me?'

'Miss Laurens, The Honourable Henry Peters,' Miss Wilkinson said with a hint of a pout. Apparently she had her eye on the gentleman himself.

An Honourable. A slight curtsy? No, he was still ogling her. Anusha gave him a cool nod. 'Mr Peters.'

'And who is escorting Miss Laurens in to dinner?' Miss Clara Wilkinson enquired.

'Let me think.' He applied the tip of one forefinger to his chin and struck a pose of mock thoughtfulness. 'You are to partner the Reverend Harris, Miss Clara.' She wrinkled her nose. 'Miss Browne has the gallant Major Herriard and Miss Laurens, I am sorry to say, has that prosy bore Langley.'

'That is Lord Langley, the son and heir of the Earl of Dunstable,' Miss Browne explained. She was apparently more than happy with her partner. 'Over there—the medium-sized gentleman with the brown hair and the blue coat. Lucky you—he is considered quite a catch.'

Along with the paunch and a double chin and a braying laugh. But he is a lord, so I am to be dangled in front of him. She tried to recall Nick's lessons. An earl was a sort of raja.

'How are dinner partners decided?' she asked.

'By rank, of course,' Miss Parkes said. 'At least, that is the start of the setting. But family members will not be put together, or husband and wife, so it is a bit muddled up. If a couple are courting, then the hostess might take pity on them and put them together. And if there are any scandals or feuds or difficulties, then she has to keep those people apart—it is all quite complicated. Have you never eaten with gentlemen before?'

'No.' Nick did not count. She tried to remember his lessons—cutlery from the outside in—and Lady Hoskins's instructions. Talk to the gentleman on her right during the first remove, then change to the left for the next one. Do not converse across the table. Put her gloves in her lap beneath her napkin. Do not let them slide off. Only sip at the wine. Pretend not to be hungry and just nibble at the food. Follow the conversational leads of the gentlemen and laugh at their jokes even when they are not amusing... *Be a little idiot with perfect deportment, in other words.*

'Dinner is served, my lady!'

The plump young lord was making his way across the room towards her, but Nick reached her first. 'Courage,' he murmured in her ear. 'You have vanquished dacoits.'

'I wish I was eating by a campfire under the stars,' Anusha murmured back. However vulnerable she was when she was near Nick Herriard, at the moment she would have given a great deal to be alone with him leagues from this crowded, alien room.

'So do I. We need to talk.'

Lord Langley introduced himself, offered his arm and guided her into the room. Anusha shot a harried glance over the table setting in front of her.

The amount of silverware flanking her dinner plate was ridiculous! What on earth did the *angrezi* need all this for? Anusha sat down with rather a thump as Lord Langley surprised her by sliding the chair in right behind her knees. She slipped off her gloves and tried to trap them under her napkin.

Everyone else was settling into their places amidst a buzz

of chatter and she glanced to her left as a tall, slim man took his place.

'Good evening. Clive Arbuthnott, at your service, ma'am.'

'Anusha Laurens.' *Was* she supposed to tell him her name? And why had he not told her his title? Now she did not know how to address him. Perhaps she was supposed to know that already. But he was on her left, so he could wait. She glanced across the table and realised that Nick was sitting opposite.

He gave her a slight nod and went back to chatting to Miss Browne, who appeared highly gratified by the attention, judging by the way she was making eyes at him. Lord Langley enquired if she did not find the weather intolerably hot for the season. For some reason this question appeared to necessitate him gazing at her mouth.

'Not at all, it seems cooler here than I imagined.' *Oh, no, that is wrong. I am supposed to agree with everything he says.* Anusha managed a vacant smile which seemed to please him.

She could hardly open her fan and shield her face behind that at the dinner table. But it seemed that the ladies found nothing amiss in the close attention the men were paying to their faces, or to the snowy slopes of bosom that were exposed by evening necklines.

The ladies were all so pale, so pink. She suspected that Lady Hoskins had chosen the deep amber of the gown she was wearing because it made her own skin seem lighter by contrast. Anusha managed a smile and told herself that she was being foolishly self-conscious. None of the gentlemen meant anything sinister by their close attention to the ladies, it was simply the custom and no one had snubbed her because of her birth or blood.

As the meal was served she managed well enough by keeping an eye on what the other ladies did and with subtle prompts from Nick who would tap his finger against the correct glass, or pause, a spoon half-lifted from the cloth, so she could observe what to use next. She sent him a fleeting smile of thanks and tried not to colour up when he smiled back.

Conversation was easy, she found. All one had to do was to listen to the gentlemen talking and occasionally agree, or make a vapid comment of one's own. They seemed quite content with that. Perhaps they did not want wives who were schooled in the classical poets, in music and in the arts, women who could converse on whatever subject they raised. It was very strange. She had thought that women of education would be valued, but it seemed only those oddly named *bluestockings* believed in female intelligence.

Nick, flanked by two admiring young ladies, appeared to be enjoying himself, Anusha thought critically. It was a fine example of flirtation in action. And none of the older matrons appeared to think anything was amiss, so the constraints on the men to behave themselves must be very great, which was a relief.

And then she thought about how Nick had shed those constraints last night, how she had so badly wanted him to lose all control, and she felt the blood colouring her cheeks. *But I love him and I do not want any of these other men— that makes all the difference.*

She ventured a question when the servants cleared the table for the second remove and she turned to her left to converse. 'I am sorry, but I do not know how to address you. Is it Mr Arbuthnott, or Lord—?'

'Sir Clive. I am a baronet.' He did not appear offended by her ignorance so she tried another question.

'And is a baronet like a knight?'

'It is an hereditary title. A knighthood is not inherited by the son.'

'So it is like a little baron?' Her father was a knight.

'It is a rank lower, yes.' Sir Clive did seem rather offended by her turn of phrase, so Anusha hastened to make amends.

'I am so ignorant about English titles, you see.' She did the eyelash-fluttering thing that these men appeared to find so attractive. It certainly worked with Sir Clive. He relaxed and settled down to explaining all about the aristocracy and, to her surprise, did it rather well. By the time she turned back to Lord Langley and dessert, she realised that she had been taking to a strange man without the slightest discomfort. Quite an attractive man, in fact.

She caught Nick's gaze as she turned—he did not look very pleased. In fact, the look he directed at Sir Clive was positively cool. *He is jealous!* The thought made her want to grin, but she caught her lower lip in her teeth just in time and managed to keep her gaze demure.

Was he remembering that night in her cabin when he had held her and had fought so hard against his own desires? Was he thinking of their kisses last night, of their naked flesh pressed intimately together, of the pleasure he had given her? He would not let that happen again, she knew. He was her father's man, and his loyalty lay there and her father wanted her for some wealthy man of influence.

Chapter Seventeen

The ladies rose at their hostess's signal, the men standing, too, and they all trooped out, maintaining an air of elegance and poise until the doors shut behind them and the entire group fell to chattering and laughing. One party, Anusha assumed, went off in search of the privy and to dab at noses made shiny by the heat of the dining room, others strolled arm in arm on the terrace, heads together and, so far as she could hear, gossiping about the men. The older matrons sat down on the rattan sofas and fanned themselves. Anusha waited to see what would happen next.

Nothing, apparently, but gossip and giggling for half an hour, by which time she was bored to distraction. Anusha strolled round the room and found a chair half-concealed behind some potted palms next to the older ladies. Their conversation had to be more interesting than that of the unmarried girls.

'...so surprised to see Major Herriard here tonight,' one

of the older matrons was saying. 'When was the last time we saw him at a formal dinner?'

'Oh, months,' one of the others remarked. 'Are you still thinking of trying to attach him for dear Deborah?'

'Would that I could, Lady Ames! He appears to have forsworn matrimony. Perhaps it was a love match with that pallid little Miranda Knight, although one would hardly think him a man of sentiment.'

'Perhaps Sir George intends him for Miss Laurens.' The comment was almost a whisper. Anusha dropped her fan and scrabbled for it on the floor, ears straining.

'One might have thought so—but I understand him to have told Dorothea Hoskins that he wanted considerable wealth for her.'

'Aiming high, under the circumstances…' Anusha's fingers curled into claws. 'She would not do for any of the titled bachelors, of course—they will be going back to England in the fullness of time and a half-Indian love-child is not going to be accepted at Court!'

'But she is a handsome young woman and very well bred in her manner. And he will dower her royally, I have no doubt. Out here her husband will have all the benefits of Sir George's influence. He will want to invest in his grandchildren.'

'Ah well, that is that, then. What Sir George wants, he usually gets.'

Considerable wealth. The waking dream of that morning, that perhaps her father would allow her to marry Nick, died. Nick was a professional soldier, not a trader, not a wealthy Company official. And besides, whatever she might dream, Nick showed not the slightest desire to marry her. Bed her, certainly. But proximity, normal male desire and the fact that she had virtually hurled herself at him would account for that.

And I do not want to marry, she thought fiercely. *If he loved me...but he does not. It is weak to love a man who does not love you—remember what happened to* Mata. *Remember the pain.*

'Anusha? Why so sad?' The men had come into the room without her noticing and Nick was standing in front of her. 'Is it about last night? Anusha, we still need to—'

'No.' She shook her head and got to her feet, her smile back in place. It was easy to smile at him, even with an aching heart, as he stood there, tall and so handsome in his uniform. 'No, I was wrong. There is nothing to speak about—it was a mistake best forgotten.' She stepped forwards bringing them toe to toe and for a moment she thought he would not give way. Then Nick bowed and stepped aside and she walked out into the room.

The whole atmosphere had changed. Anusha dragged her attention back from Nick's silent presence just behind her and made herself pay attention. It was, observed as an outsider, fascinating. The married women's eyes followed their daughters, but flickered back and forth to glance at the bachelors. She tried to work out who was an eligible suitor and who was not by the carefully schooled expressions of the mothers.

And then there were the unmarried girls, pretending indifference, clinging together in little groups, feigning not to notice the men and then blushing prettily when addressed.

The men, Anusha decided, were not serious in their attentions. They were enjoying the flirtation, but were they seeking wives in their turn? The rather older ones might

be, she supposed—they would be thinking about families
and inheritance and titles.

Her father seated himself next to their hostess and said
something to her that made her nod. They glanced at Anusha and then away, as if they had been speaking about her.

I had best do some of this flirting, she thought. *Lull Father into thinking I am being an obedient daughter. Doing
my duty.*

Several couples had gone out on to the terrace. It surprised her, but none of the older women seemed concerned,
so it must be acceptable behaviour. How well the men must
behave to be trusted so!

'Miss Laurens?' It was Sir Clive. She smiled, saw Nick
watching them and added more warmth. He must not guess
how she felt about him, she realised. 'Would you care for a
stroll around the room?'

Anusha took his arm as Nick had shown her and they
walked up and down in front of the long, open windows.

'And how do you like Calcutta, Miss Laurens?'

'I cannot say, Sir Clive. I have only just arrived. I knew
it as a child, of course.'

'The riding is very good here. The *maidan* around the
fort is excellent. I ride there every day. Do you ride, Miss
Laurens?'

'Certainly. I do not have my own horses here, of course.'

'And how do ladies ride in Indian dress?'

'Astride.'

'My goodness! That would cause a stir here, I must say.
Let us step outside—the room is growing intolerably stuffy,'
he suggested.

'Very well.' There were several couples on the torch-lit

terrace and servants standing around and the air was, indeed, more pleasant out there.

A series of loud bangs and a rainbow flash of lights were greeted by cries of delight. 'Fireworks near the fort,' someone said and there was a general rush to the balustrade.

'What a pity one cannot see better from here,' Sir Clive said. 'It seems a fine display—a wedding celebration, perhaps.' There was another explosion of colour, greeted by clapping. 'I know—let us go to the upper terrace.'

Anusha loved fireworks and the steps he led her to were marked with torches, so Lady Hoskins obviously expected her guests to use that part of the garden. There would doubtless be servants up there too.

When they arrived at the upper level the burst of lights was so spectacular that she ran to admire them and it was not until they died down that she realised that they were alone in a shadowed space, looking out on to a terrace below.

'Miss Laurens... Anusha.' He was very close. Far too close.

'We should go down, there is no one else here.'

'That is good, surely?' Sir Clive put a hand either side of her so that she was trapped against the balustrade, his forearms bracketing her hips. 'We came up here to be alone, did we not?'

'I came up here to see the fireworks, I thought other people would be here too.' She was not frightened, for surely this was only flirting going rather too far, but she was becoming annoyed and a little flustered. Anusha did not enjoy the sensation. 'Please move your arms, Sir Clive.'

'Not until I get my kiss.' He moved in closer. Now she could feel his heat, smell the sandalwood he used on his hair. His breath smelled of brandy.

'I have no wish to kiss you, Sir Clive.' He was too close in now for her to raise a knee sharply, or twist free. She began to feel rather more than flustered.

'Now don't tell me you are a little tease, Anusha.' He bent his head and kissed the side of her neck. She twisted her head away and his mouth found her cheek.

'Stop it! I am not teasing you.'

His lips moved down to her neck, down to the swell of her breast. 'Oh, but you were,' he murmured. 'Those big grey eyes, those long, long lashes, that pouting mouth.' He lifted his head and his eyes were bright, narrowed. Predatory. 'I know what they taught you in that *zanana*—how to please a man and all manner of exotic tricks to do it, too, I'll wager. Now you can show me some of them.'

'We need to speak about Anusha, George.'

Nick took the older man by the arm and steered him into a deserted retiring room.

'Now? Here?' Sir George regarded him from beneath lowered brows and Nick wondered if he still had the uncanny power to detect wrongdoing that he had possessed when Nick had been a scrubby seventeen-year-old. His conscience was giving him hell and it probably showed.

'I am worried about her. You need to talk to her about her mother, George. She'll never settle to marriage with that in the forefront of her mind because she's expecting to be rejected again, let down.'

'I never intended—'

'I know. You did the only thing in an impossible situation. But she doesn't trust you and she sees marriage as a trap at worst, a burden at best.'

'So do you, unless something has changed.' The older

man settled in an armchair, offered Nick a cheroot, then, when he shook his head, lit one for himself.

'We are not discussing my situation.' He wondered sometimes what a happy, loving marriage would be like, but that was just a daydream. He had seen his parents' marriage, seen George's troubles, experienced for himself the dull ache of a loveless union between two people without a thing in common. He should have done something—been kinder, more indulgent. Or perhaps firmer. He shook his head, exasperated at his own lack of understanding. No, marriage was not for him, not again.

'I know. And I know, too, that I put a lot of pressure on you to marry Miranda, and that was a mistake. I won't try to interfere with your love life again, believe me, Nicholas! But I want happiness for Anusha, security, respectability. I'll find the right man for her.'

'Then talk with her, convince her that you love her, that you loved her mother and never stopped. Let her see that she can trust you. Otherwise I fear she might run away.'

'She would never do that, surely?' Nick realised he understood her far better than her father. George was underestimating her fierce determination. 'But I will talk to her about her mother. I… It shook me to find her so beautiful, so grown up—so cold. I don't know what I expected when I saw her again and I haven't handled it well.' He looked up, a vulnerability in his eyes that grabbed at Nick's heart. This was his strong father-figure? George couldn't be getting old! 'Thank heavens I've got you to help me look after her.'

If she screamed it would attract a lot of attention. Anusha thought longingly of the little knife that slipped into her riding boot. 'Oh…very well.' She lifted her face and Clive bent his smirking lips to hers. Anusha opened her mouth, let his touch it, then bit hard on his lower lip.

Sir Clive jumped back, swearing, one hand clamped to his mouth, the other lifted as if to hit her. 'You little bitch!' he mumbled.

'Don't you dare touch me again!' Anusha hissed at him. 'If I had a knife—'

'If Miss Laurens had a knife she would doubtless castrate you, Arbuthnott. So be grateful that I am merely going to break your jaw.' It was Nick, smiling, green eyes glinting in the torchlight.

'The little baggage led me on. And as for you, Herriard, I'd like to see you try to lay a finger on me.'

Anusha swallowed and gripped the stonework behind her as Nick's smile changed subtly into something lethal. 'I *was* going to break your jaw. For that I am going to throw you over the balustrade.' He moved fast, caught the still-spluttering baronet off-balance in a twisting grip against his hip, and tipped him over the edge. There was a crash, a chorus of feminine shrieks and the sound of swearing.

'Oh, I say!' Nick leaned over, his voice full of exaggerated concern. 'Are you all right, Arbuthnott? I told you not to stand up there to watch the fireworks.'

'Bloody hell! I've got thorns in my ar—'

'Not in front of the ladies,' a man said below. 'Come on, Arbuthnott, let's get you out of there.'

Nick turned. 'That has punctured his dignity.'

She found it was difficult to speak. 'Thank…thank you. I thought you were going to kill him.' Tears were threatening to choke her, she realised. Where had her courage gone?

'Did you want me to kill him?' Nick asked. 'Did you expect me to call him out?'

'To duel? That is what you mean?' She swallowed hard. 'No, of course not. It was just foolishness.' *What is wrong with me? And him? He still looks so angry?*

'He called you a baggage. What the blazes were you doing up here with him anyway?' So that was what was wrong with him—he was angry with her. As though it were her fault! What hypocrites men were. 'Well?' he snapped. 'What was it? Were you looking for another man to plea-sure you, like a cat on heat?'

The injustice of it stung like a whiplash. Anusha tried to be angry, but all she felt was utterly miserable. She had been frightened, confused, she had needed him and he had come. And now he thought she had encouraged that man?

'How am I expected to know there would be no one else up here? It is all shocking and strange…all these men, being expected to flirt with them…strolling about, arm in arm down there,' she stammered. 'Do I tell one of Lady Hoskins's guests to his face that I do not trust him?'

Nick spun on his heel and stalked away to the other side of the terrace, his shoulders rigid. She sank down on a low bench and felt the tears begin to slide down her face. It was too much. *I love you and I cannot have you and now you think I am just a…just a…*

He turned as abruptly as he had left her. 'I am sorry. I apologise. You are quite right and I am not angry with you. I am angry with myself.'

'It is—' She tried to say *all right*, but her voice vanished in a sob. It was not all right, it never would be. This was the reality: she loved him, she could not have him and she would have to marry some other man who would not un-derstand her, a man she could never love.

'Hell!' He strode across the terrace and fell on his knees

beside her. 'Anusha—he hurt you?' He took her hand, but she tried to shake him off.

'No,' she managed. 'You did. I am so unhappy. I can't be brave any more, Nick. I do not want to be here, I do not understand the rules, I do not want to marry some *suitable* man and now you…you hate me. And…'

'No.' His fingers tightened on her wrist. 'I don't hate you, Anusha. It will be all right, you will become accustomed to this life and then you will meet a man you can like.'

Nick winced at the inadequacy of his own words. He was spouting platitudes and she knew it. *You hate me. God, that hurt. But not as much as she is hurting.* 'I was frightened for you and it made me angry—you must be used to that by now.'

She ignored his feeble attempt at a joke. Nick had never seen her like this, almost defeated.

'Anusha, please.' He hated this. Every instinct told him to protect her as he had tried to do ever since they left Kalatwah and all he had done was to reduce her to abject misery. How to stop her crying? He had never managed it with Miranda. 'Anusha. Oh, hell.' Nick pulled her roughly into his arms, crushing her against his jacket front, against gold braid and buttons. 'Come here and don't you dare cry.'

'I'm not.' Her voice was muffled and shaky.

'Liar.' Somehow she was locked tight against him now and his mouth was in her hair.

After a few minutes she sighed and wriggled. Nick opened his arms and she sat back, scrubbing her fingers across her eyes. 'Here.' He found a handkerchief and she blew her nose with a defiant lack of elegance that made something twist inside him. This was genuine misery, not a fit of the vapours or tears to be interesting.

'I am sorry.' She had her voice under control again, almost. 'Thank you for looking after me.'

'Better now?'

She shook her head. 'No. I do not think it will get any better. I will have to marry someone, I suppose, and try to be a proper English wife. He will not love me and he will have mistresses, I suppose.' She squared her shoulders, a little gesture that clutched even deeper at his heart. 'It is my fate, so I must not be a coward.'

'I want to help you. How can I help you, Anusha?' He would fight anything for her—tigers, rakehells, a pit full of cobras—but this blank, brave misery defeated him.

'Find me someone to marry who will not break my heart,' she said with a bitter twist of a smile.

Who? A suitable *husband would either break her until she was just another dutiful wife or goad her into rebellion and scandal. What man is going to understand her heritage, her pride, her fears as I do? As I do.* The words seemed to echo in his head. He would make a poor excuse of a husband for any of the conventional little misses dancing downstairs, but for this woman perhaps he might be better than the alternatives.

Nick sat back on his heels and tried to think with his head and not with his protective instincts. He was well born, which mattered to society, if not to her. He could afford a wife, even if he could not keep her in luxury. He would be faithful to her and that, at least, would be no hardship. And she clearly found him physically attractive enough to want his lovemaking—in that, at least, this should not be a repeat of his marriage to Miranda.

'There is one man I could think of,' he suggested, before his brain could catch up with whatever was doing the thinking for him at the moment. 'One who would do his best to look after you and understand you, give you freedom.'

She understood him immediately, he saw it in the widening of the grey eyes, still shimmering with tears. 'You?'

'You're not looking for love, I understand that,' he said. 'You needn't worry that I'd be expecting it either. And I will be away a lot, but you'll not miss me.'

'I won't?'

'And I will be faithful, so you have no need for concern about mistresses. All I ask is that you don't take any lovers,' he finished.

'I...wouldn't. Nick, you don't want to get married again, to anyone. You told me.'

'I wouldn't mind being married to you.' As he said it he realised it was true. She would be wonderful in bed, stimulating out of it. Probably reckless enough to get into any number of scrapes but, he felt deep down, honourable enough to keep her promises to him. 'I am not a rich man,' he added. 'But I can afford children if you want them. Only if you want them.'

There was an ache inside now. He could almost think it was anxiety that she might refuse. What was the matter with him? This was a practical solution to her problems that would not cost him much except some money. And George would be happy that at last she was settled, if not brilliantly. But if she said *no*, then he would try to think of something else, it was not as though his heart was involved.

'I would be such a trouble to you.'

She was wavering. The unexpected relief made him speak

roughly. 'You have been trouble since the moment I saw you, you and your damned mongoose.'

'It is Paravi's mongoose—'

'Do you never stop arguing?' He kissed her, dragging her tight against him. He wanted her, was all he could think as he plundered her mouth, felt her response, tasted the sweet, sensual tang that was uniquely Anusha. And this way he could have her and she could have what she needed.

When he let her go she did none of the things he expected. She did not smile, or slap his face or even weep. Anusha buried her face in her hands for a long moment, then lowered them and met his gaze with eyes that held the same resolution that he had seen in them when they left the palace.

'Yes,' she said, her voice steady. 'I will marry you, Nick.'

Chapter Eighteen

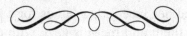

Is this wrong? The question spun round and round in her mind as Nick took her arm and led her to the steps. *But I love him and I will make him the best wife I can possibly be and he doesn't want anyone else. He will never guess I love him; he knows I desire him, he will think that is all it is.* She was still dizzy with the shock of the assault, her own misery, Nick's incredible proposal. *I am not thinking properly*, she realised as they entered the reception room again. 'There is my father.'

'Yes,' Nick agreed. 'I think we had better go home and confess.'

When they found him her father took one look at her, then glanced sharply at Nick, but said nothing except, 'Tired, are you, my dear? Then let us call the carriage.'

As the vehicle jolted over the rutted street Nick said abruptly, 'I have asked Anusha to be my wife and she has accepted me.'

'This is very sudden.' He did not sound displeased. 'I

cannot pretend that I am not delighted, of course, but are you both certain?'

Anusha could not be sure, his face was lost in the gloom of the carriage, but Nick sounded perfectly happy when he said, 'I am very certain, sir.'

'So am I, Father.' She tried to sound pleased, but not so eager that Nick might guess at her feelings.

'There will be many disappointed young men,' her father said with a chuckle as they drew up at the front steps.

'Father—'

'Anusha, I must speak with Nicholas. You are tired, child. Go to your bed, we can talk in the morning.' He dropped a kiss on her cheek and she nodded and made herself smile.

They would want to talk about money, she supposed. It would be good for Nick, if her father dowered her well. Something else she could do for him. 'Goodnight.'

'Goodnight.' Nick took her hand, just he had on the boat, and bent over it. This time he did not kiss the air above it, but her knuckles through the thin kid gloves she wore. Her fingers tightened in his, but when he released her she looked at him, a long, steady look from those grey eyes that were so like her father's, then turned on her heel and walked away, her full skirts swishing around the corner.

'She seems a trifle shaken,' George observed as he opened the door of his study.

'I found someone bothering her, dealt with him and then we talked. She is frightened of marriage, George, marriage to one of those eligible men you've got your eye on. And I realised I could see why—they won't understand her, they'll try to force her into a mould and make her lose everything that makes her unique, makes her Anusha.

'She knows I didn't want to marry, that I made a mull of things with Miranda. I expect she's afraid I'll take a string of mistresses and neglect her, whatever I promise. But she doesn't feel she belongs here and yet she knows she can't put things back as they were.' He shrugged. It was painful laying out all these reasons in cold blood, the reasons he was the solution of a problem, not the man of her dreams. 'Anusha meant it when she said she wanted to be free. She doesn't know who she is and I think she wants to find out. I can at least protect her, understand her a little—she trusts me for that.'

'Well, she's not a fool, so she should know when she's fortunate,' her father said robustly. 'She will make you a good wife, Nicholas. She's no pale little waif like poor Miranda. She's intelligent, she's strong and she doesn't appear to be shy with you. And, though I say it myself, she's a beauty. Takes after her mother.'

'The question is, can I make her a good husband? If I couldn't make a marriage work with a meek little wife who *wanted* to be married in the first place, what hope have I got with one with spirit and wits who is making the best of a bad job?' Nick enquired. *And what does a happy marriage look like, anyway? Can I make her happy?*

'I'm not trying to wriggle out of this, I just want what's best for her. I am sorry if I have disappointed you, George. Sorry if I am not the son-in-law you wanted for her.'

'Disappointed me? Hell, no! Nicholas you'd never do that. She is just too much for us to handle, that's all. I only wanted…security for her, I suppose. Safety. Just do your best to make her happy, that's all I ask.'

'Happiness I cannot promise, but I will do my level best. You have my word on it. And I will protect her with my life, that I can swear to.'

* * *

Anusha walked into her father's study as soon as she heard him moving around in there. A sleepless night fighting with her conscience had left her in no state for an Anglo-Indian breakfast.

'Anusha.' He got to his feet and came round the desk to urge her into a chair. 'You look—'

'As though I have not slept. Yes, Father, I know. It was all very…sudden.'

He almost went back to the big chair behind the desk, then came back and sat down opposite her. 'It is the best thing for you. Have you changed your mind? Don't you *want* to marry Nicholas?'

'I do not want to be a trouble to him.'

He watched her from under dark bushy brows for a minute. 'You like him, do you not?'

She nodded. *Of course I like him! Can you not see that I love him?*

'Do you desire him?'

'Father!'

'Well, do you?' He had coloured up and he was frowning, but he persisted. 'You haven't got a mother to ask you about these things. Don't pretend to me you don't know what I am talking about, not with your upbringing.'

Anusha pressed her lips together and stared up at the painting over the mantelpiece of the Garden Reach of the Hooghly River with the fort in the background. If she said anything it would all come tumbling out, how she desired him, loved him, wanted him and how selfish it was of her to tie him down in marriage. And Father would tell Nick and then he would be uncomfortable and pity her.

'I married too young,' her father remarked in a conversational tone. 'I married a very suitable bride, an intelligent, handsome woman I hardly knew.'

'I don't want to hear about—' *I do not want to hear you justifying yourself to me.*

'But I am going to tell you,' he said gently. 'And you will listen to the story of my stupidity and where it took me. I married Mary and she fell pregnant almost immediately. She lost the child after three months. We tried again. She lost another. And another. The doctors said she should not attempt to carry a child for at least a year to allow her body to recover. You understand what they were asking me?' She felt the blood hot in her cheeks, but nodded, her eyes still fixed on the painting.

'I was young and arrogant and I did not see why we should wait. It reflected on my virility that my wife was not with child, I thought, and besides, I was not cut out for self-denial. Within four months she was pregnant again and this time she brought it to term. It almost killed her because her body just could not cope. The child died and the doctors told us she could never conceive again.'

Anusha heard the pain in his voice and the self-recrimination. *It serves him right,* she thought, trying to harden her heart. Then, *Oh, poor woman. Poor things—how old had they been?*

'I had an opportunity to come out to India with the Company, to make my fortune. I assumed Mary would come, too—I did not ask, just told her. And she refused. I had almost killed her, I had ensured she could never have a child and for the first time I saw what I had done to her, not just to myself.'

'Why did you not divorce her? Or she you?'

'In English law there were no grounds for divorce in our

circumstances. A wife being barren and a husband being a selfish fool are not enough. So we separated. I made sure she wanted for nothing financially and she made her own life in England. But her sense of duty was strong. She wrote to me every month and I began to write back. Gradually it seemed we could be friends, even at that distance. Or perhaps because of it.'

'But you were living with my mother.'

'I will not pretend I lived like a monk, Anusha. But some years after I came to India I met your mother at your grandfather's court and we fell in love.'

'She deliberately sought you out, she told me.' Long hot afternoons, with her mother's voice, soft and reminiscent, telling the story of that long-ago love affair. 'It was very shocking.'

'Indeed. I was thirty-five, she was twenty. By some miracle the raja approved the relationship, because he could refuse her nothing and because he could see the Company would be a great power in the land. We were in love and we were so very happy when you were born.'

'And then you sent us away, you did not want us any more.' She tried to keep the hurt from her voice, but she knew that it showed.

'Mary thought I was ill and she had come to believe it was her duty to be with me. The letter telling me she was on her way reached me before there was anything I could do to stop her. She was my legal wife—I could reject her, risk her life again by sending her back for another three months of danger and misery at sea, or I could do what honour told me I must, and welcome her.

'I tried to discuss it with Sarasa, but she refused to even listen. I could see no way out of it except for you both to go back to Kalatwah where I knew you would be safe and treated with respect. I would not dishonour both women by keeping one as a mistress behind my wife's back.'

His voice caught and he stopped speaking. Anusha turned her head slowly, painfully, to look at him. There were tears running down his face although he made no sign that he realised.

Something turned over in her heart: his pain, as though it were hers, and the realisation that she had never tried to see anything but her own anger and betrayal. 'Then you still loved us, Papa?' Her face was wet, too, she found.

'With all my heart. Never doubt it, Anusha. With all my heart.' He reached out and she took his hand in hers.

'So it was not because, with Nick, you had a son and did not want a daughter any longer?' It was shameful to reveal her fears and jealousy, but she had to know.

'No! He was the son for Mary that she could never have. For me, it took longer, for I was still mourning you and your mother, but I grew to love him like a son. Anusha—love isn't finite. I could love both of you, and I do.'

'Oh.' She held his hand and let herself feel at last. 'Oh, Papa!' And then she was in his arms and they were both weeping and nothing else mattered except that she was home again.

'Good afternoon, Miss Laurens.'

Anusha looked up from the two miniatures her father had given her. One of her mother, the other of his wife, the woman who had saved Nick's life all those years ago. She put them down carefully and watched him as he came and stood in front of her. 'Where have you been all day, Nick?'

'I thought you and your father needed time alone together. Are you all right now? Your eyes are red.' He was still in uniform, his face cleanly shaven, his hair tied back. He looked formal and remote.

'I have been crying,' she said with dignity. 'So has Papa. He is going to send a cow in calf to that village,' she added, thinking suddenly of the way that Nick had looked up from the fireside, directly at her, and something had clicked into place in her heart. *I fell in love with him then, I just did not know it.*

Nick smiled and then, to her shock, went down on one knee.

'What are you doing?'

'This is the correct manner for making a proposal. I feel a trifle idiotic, but if you will forgive that… I hardly did it properly last night. Miss Laurens, will you do me the honour of accepting my hand in marriage?' When she did not answer him, and continued to look at his clasped hands resting on his raised knee, he added, 'I wanted to make sure you had not changed your mind.'

Does he want me to? Is he hoping that I have? Anusha looked into the face so close to hers and knew that she should say *no* and knew that she simply did not have the strength.

'I will do my best to look after you, to give you as much freedom as I can, to make you happy,' Nick said as she was silent, not trusting herself to speak.

'But you wish you did not have to.'

'Make you happy? Of course I want to do that.'

Strange how she had never noticed that thin scar across his right knuckles, how the tendons stood out when his hands were tightly clasped. Perhaps he was as nervous as she was. She knew she was blushing and saw from his face that he could read her mind, a little.

'There are more ways to make someone happy than sex,' Nick said drily, 'but at least that will be a good start, if we are going to be so frank.'

She swallowed. 'What about your mistresses?'

'Plural? I have never had more than one at a time and I do not have one at the moment. Anusha, look at me.'

She managed to lift her head. He was very serious, although his eyes were smiling. Perhaps this was going to be all right after all.

'I told you last night. Anusha, for some time now there has been no other woman but you and there never will be, I swear. I will be faithful to you, always.'

What Nick promises, he does. And he would promise that for me? To be faithful even though he does not love me? Oh, Nick. I do love you. Anusha managed to smile and was rewarded by the way he looked at her. 'I have not changed my mind. I will marry you.'

'Thank you. I am honoured.' He leaned forwards and kissed her lightly on the lips and she closed her eyes and let herself dream.

Chapter Nineteen

It took a month to be married, they told her. 'So short a time?' Anusha asked. 'But what of all the preparations and the feasting and the dancers?' Lady Hoskins laughed and Anusha blushed. This was a different world and she had forgotten.

The time seemed to flow past like water and as the day grew closer a panic closed around her heart like a fist. She had trapped him. She should have known when she had wept in his arms that he would always protect her, only this time it was not with his life, but his freedom, and he would grow to resent her, she was certain.

Ajit returned from Kalatwah with messages and news: everyone was safe, they missed her. The maharaja's spies had been eliminated, for the moment. He slipped back into Nick's service, a soft-footed, smiling shadow.

The horses arrived from Kalpi, tired, but unmarked by their journey. Nick took her to the *maidan* early each morning so she could ride Rajat astride in her Indian clothes, but she knew she would have to master the side-saddle soon.

Nick had been using part of the disused women's quarters as his bachelor's rooms when he was in Calcutta, although he had a house in the hills a day's ride away. Now her father had them turned into a self-contained home for the newly-weds with two bedchambers, dining room, drawing room, a study for Nick and a sitting room for Anusha and a wide veranda overlooking the gardens at the rear.

Except for these morning rides they seemed to see very little of each other. Nick was at the fort most of the day and when he was at the house he seemed remote and formal. It was expected that a bridegroom kept his distance, Lady Hoskins explained, and of course, she did not want to be a trouble to him, but she missed him.

'Do you mind?' Nick asked ten days after their betrothal as they sat on their veranda and watched the gardeners turning a small patch of tangled vegetation back into a garden. He had come back mid-morning and, unusually, seemed intent on spending time with her.

Anusha did not pretend not to understand him. 'Not having a separate house of our own in Calcutta? No, Papa would be lonely and so will I be when you are away.'

'You will miss me?' It was asked casually.

'Of course. And I will worry about you, now I know the kind of risks your missions lead you into.'

'Don't worry. I cannot imagine that any future commissions will necessitate escorting dangerous young ladies.' *He means it as a joke*, she told herself. 'How will you spend your time when I am away?'

'I shall help Papa and be his hostess. Lady Hoskins says that is the best way to learn to be a proper English lady. Then when you come home I will know how to… deport myself.'

'Comport.'

'I thought that was something for putting fruit in. And I will make the house nice and buy clothes and accustom myself to them.' Instinct told her to keep the conversation light. Like that she could almost pretend they were still on their journey. She flipped her skirts back and forth, exposing a bare foot.

'Anusha! Are you patterning your feet with henna?' Nick dropped to one knee and lifted her foot in his hand. 'Wicked woman.'

'No one can see under my stockings and shoes.' His thumb was stroking the top of her foot, following the complex twisting design. She glanced around, the gardeners had gone. It seemed a very long time since they had been alone together.

'So this is just for your husband?'

'No, of course not.' She tried to cover herself, but he bent his mouth to the bare skin and desire washed through her. 'Stop doing that!' But she twisted in the chair, tried to position her foot in the perfect place for his caresses. 'Nick!' He sucked her toes into his mouth and began to tease them with his tongue. 'Nicholas, that is very…very…'

Unable to speak, he waggled his eyebrows at her lasciviously and she collapsed into giggles. It felt so good to laugh, such a long time since she had. 'Idiot man, stop it at once or the servants will see.'

'How very European and repressed of you, my dear.' He released her foot and sat back in his chair. Anusha wriggled her wet toes and tried to look reproving.

'I am trying to learn to be good.'

'Well, don't learn it for the bedroom,' he said, his voice suddenly husky.

'No. I won't.' The silence that followed seemed to need a lot of filling. Anusha scrabbled for a safe topic. 'Lady Hoskins says that I am fortunate not to have to learn all the things that an aristocratic lady must know, like how to go on at court and how to wear the strange court dress, and being a political hostess and holding a salon in London and managing an enormous house in the country. She says that young ladies are brought up from childhood to know all that.'

'So I believe. I never saw much of it, with my father being estranged from my grandfather, but court life is a nightmare, by all accounts, and London society is a good match for the plotting in a *zanana*. Although I doubt rival heirs are ever garrotted by eunuchs.' He studied her face, suddenly serious. 'You can put that in the balance of positive things about this marriage—you will have nothing more to worry about than Calcutta society.'

'I do not need to find things to be glad about,' she said carefully. 'But I knew that I would never marry an aristocrat anyway. Lady Hoskins explained that, too.'

'Why not? There are a good sprinkling of lordlings around—younger sons, heirs-in-waiting, men doing a more-than-usually-adventurous version of the Grand Tour.'

'Because I would not be received at Court, of course.' Surely he knew that better than she did? 'My parents were not married and my mother was Indian. You only have to look at me.' She extended one arm, the lace around her sleeve falling back to reveal the honey-coloured skin. 'And Papa is in trade. It is a good thing—I would not want to have to balance an ostrich on my head.' Whatever that was.

'Just some of its plumes,' Nick said absently. He was frowning. 'Is that woman telling you that you are not good enough?'

'For the English Court? Of course.' It did not worry her—after all, she would never go to England, she accepted that now. 'I thought they would snub me here because of *Mata*, but they do not, so that is all right.'

Nick still looked troubled. 'Are you sure? If anyone says anything about your birth or your looks—'

He would fight them for me. I do love him. It made her want to cry, a little, so Anusha reached over and rubbed at the crease between his brows and scolded instead, 'Stop frowning. You do not look handsome when you frown. No one is unkind to me.'

'Good.' He leaned forwards and smoothed her skirts back over her bare feet and she gave an involuntary murmur of disappointment.

'Stop tempting me, you wicked woman. I am resolved to resist ravishing you until our wedding day.'

'Oh.' She tried to sound disappointed, and one part of her was, the part that ached and yearned and tingled when he touched her. But it was also…charming that he should respect her and should obey the conventions in order to do this properly for her. Unless it meant that he was not as eager for that part of their marriage as she was. But if he was not, then what did they have? Only his sense of duty?

'That does not mean that I do not intend kissing you until your toes curl. Kissing you all over,' Nick added, so softly that for a moment she thought she had misheard him. Anusha sat up sharply, but he was lying back in the wide rattan chair, eyes closed, apparently about to drift off to sleep.

Was he playing games with her? He must be. Or it was

her own longings that she was hearing? Anusha got up and crept bare-footed into the house and the shuttered gloom of the drawing room. There was no furniture here yet, only a pile of rugs, haphazard on the floor at her feet, their vivid colours spilling patterns like all the riches of the garden. The sight stopped her in her tracks, memory clogging her throat so she had to swallow hard against it.

'What is wrong?' Nick came in, silent behind her, and caught her by the shoulders to pull her back against his chest.

'Those carpets. There were rugs heaped like that in my rooms that day I was packing and you were the other side of the screens and we quarrelled. Or I tried to quarrel and you walked out on me. Very unfair.' Anusha took a deep breath and kept her voice light and amused. 'That was the last time I was in that room before everything changed.'

'Poor love,' he murmured, holding her close.

'What…what did you call me?' She could have bitten her tongue the moment she asked.

'Mmm? Oh. Poor love.' She could feel him listening to his own words properly for the first time. 'Just an expression,' he said lightly and so carefully that she winced. 'Do not worry, Anusha. I am not becoming starry-eyed and sentimental. I know you don't want that.'

'No, of course not. But I do want those kisses you promised me,' she said, fixing a smile on her lips so he would hear it in her voice as she turned and laid her cheek against his chest.

'Kisses? Ah, yes, I promised to kiss you all over. I'll just lock the doors.' She watched him as he padded across the room to secure the inner door, then slip the catch on the pair of doors on to the veranda. Nick was wearing loose *pa-*

jama trousers and a hip-length *kurta* in subdued patterns of brown and green that made the colour of his eyes seem more intense. His feet, brown and strong, were bare like hers.

The sight of him, his sheer physicality and grace, affected her as it always did, with simple, trembling desire. He must have seen it in her face for he coloured, just a little. That was another thing that she loved about Nick, the fact that he seemed surprised that she found him so desirable, that she wanted to look at him. He was so handsome and so masculine and yet he never seemed aware of it.

'What?' He lifted an eyebrow.

'It is so unfair that European men can lounge about in Indian clothes and yet I am trussed up like a fowl in these things.' She waved a hand at her chintz skirts and tight bodice.

'There is no reason why you cannot relax in your Indian clothes in private,' Nick said. 'You will just have to scramble into your corsets if someone comes to call.' His fingers were working on the long row of buttons down her back, his mouth kissing each inch of skin as it was exposed.

'No one scrambles into a corset!' Anusha protested, trying to stand still as he slipped her bodice free and undid the ties of her skirts. They pooled around her feet, followed by her petticoats, leaving her in her corset, chemise and very little else.

Her breath came out with a *whoosh* as he freed the laces: partly the loosening of the constriction, partly tension that was building too fast. 'Poor darling,' he said, rubbing her ribs lightly with the palms of his hands. *Darling, not love.* 'I'll kiss it better.'

He held her between his hands while he caressed each red crease on her skin with his lips, trailing down each side of her rib cage in turn until he reached her navel, then twirling inside it with the point of his tongue. 'Nick!' She wriggled, but his hands were firm on her hips as he knelt and kissed across her belly to the right, then down to her groin, his lips brushing the tangled curls. *'Nick.'*

She knew about this, of course. But the reality, the intimacy, was shocking. He trailed back up, across, down the other side, and her hands twitched with the effort not to take his head, press him close to where she ached and pulsed.

Nick came forwards on his knees, pushing her before him until her legs hit the pile of rugs and she toppled backwards, sprawled open to him on the soft silken platform.

His hands pushed at her thighs until she parted them, stiff with nerves for a moment. Then, when his tongue flicked out and found her, she collapsed back and abandoned herself to whatever he chose to do to her.

He chose to drive her to the edge of madness with slow, slow licks and kisses, each probing deeper and deeper into her quivering intimate heat until she was sobbing, pleading, for release. Then, as her hands grasped at the pile of the carpets and her back arched up, he parted her gently with his fingers, bent and stroked just one tiny spot with his tongue, again and again and she shuddered and cried out, reaching for him.

Nick lay with Anusha in his arms, and watched while she drifted back into reality as his frustrated body began to calm down. She was beautiful in the throes of passion: uninhibited, trusting, utterly sensual. Eighteen more days seemed an eternity to wait to make her his. But he *would* wait because she trusted him and because he wanted to do this properly for her. In this, at least, his second marriage would not be like his first.

Anusha desired him. Now she must abandon her dreams, and, he hoped, most of her fears, and marry him with only that unpredictable thread of mutual passion to bind her to him.

He had been right not to protest that he loved her, try to romance her. Anusha would have seen right through lies and he knew she did not want emotional involvement. He had heard the alarm in her voice when he had casually called her *love* just now. She needed to be herself, not emotionally tied to a man she did not love, he understood that.

It was a relief, of course. He could not cope with the clinging, needy, love of a woman. He had hurt Miranda by not being what she wanted in that way and he did not want to hurt this woman. At least he would *try* never to be cruel. His mother's sobs echoed down the years to the man who was once a small boy standing outside her bedchamber in the dark night listening, helpless. *Why can't you love me, Francis? All I want is for you to love me…*

'Nick?' The real woman in his arms stirred and smiled up at him, her eyes a little unfocused. Then Anusha's gaze sharpened and she lifted her hand to touch his cheek. 'What is it? What is wrong?'

'Nothing. Just an old memory from long ago.'

There was a knock at the inner door. 'Nicholas *sahib*?' The door handle rattled. 'Laurens *sahib* asks if you can come to his study to speak to him.'

'Tell him ten minutes, Ajit,' Nick called back. He stooped and kissed Anusha on the mouth, taking his time, gently exploring, and she curled her arms around his neck and responded with an ardour that had him as hard as iron again in seconds. 'I must go. Let me help you dress first.'

He watched as she walked to her clothes, not at all shy of his eyes on her nakedness. Why could she bring the heat to his cheeks whenever she looked at him with those gorgeous eyes heavy with desire or calculating feminine assessment? She was the one who should be bashful.

Then, as he stood over her helping with that confounded corset, he saw the colour in her cheeks and the way her eyes shifted a little, shy under his scrutiny, and something inside him twisted, almost painfully. 'There,' he said briskly. 'That's the last button.'

'Will you be here for dinner?'

'No, it is mess night at the fort. I'll be rolling back in the early hours, drunk as a lord.'

'Do lords get more drunk than anyone else? Why is that?' She was on her knees finding hair pins.

'Just an expression.'

'Even so, I am glad you are not a lord!'

He was still chuckling when he tapped on George's door and let himself into the study. The amusement vanished at the look on the other man's face. 'What's wrong?'

'A ship from England has just docked. There is post for you.' He reached across the desk and dropped half-a-dozen letters in front of Nick. 'It brought the newssheets, too. I glanced through the Deaths column first—a morbid habit. Nick, your uncle has died.'

'Which uncle?' His mother had three brothers, he seemed to recall, not that he could put a face to any of them.

'Grenville. Viscount Clere.'

It took a moment. His first thought was that his father would not care: there had never been any love lost between the two brothers. Then he realised. 'My father is heir to the marquisate. My God, losing Grenville and having to see my father in his shoes—it'll kill the old man.'

'By all accounts your grandfather is holding up remarkably well. The newssheets cover a month after the funeral and he was certainly alive and apparently in good health. What his state of mind is, one can only guess.' George nodded towards the letters. 'Those might be some guide, I would hazard.'

'These?' Nick lifted the topmost, its stained and dirty canvas cover bulging over the shape of a seal beneath. 'Why?'

'Are your wits wandering, Nicholas? You are now second in line to the marquisate of Eldonstone. Those will be from the lawyers and your grandfather. Possibly your father.'

To go back to England? To the grandfather who had washed his hands of him, the father who hated him, the stifling life of the English aristocracy, a mountain of responsibilities he did not want in a world that was alien to him now. He had made a new life for himself here, one he loved.

'No.' He found he was on his feet. Nick gave the stack of letters a push that scattered them across the desk top. 'No. Be damned to that. I can't... I cannot deal with this now. I have an engagement—mess dinner.'

He strode out, leaving the door swinging open. Behind him he heard George's chair scrape back. In the hall, as he headed for his bedchamber, he saw Anusha, her eyes wide and questioning as he strode past her without a word. How the hell could Fate do this to him?

Chapter Twenty

'Papa?' Anusha slipped into the study through the open door. 'What is the matter with Nick?'

'Eavesdropping?' He smiled, but his eyes were sombre.

'I heard his voice in here, then I saw him in the hall. I have never seen him look like that, as though Kali were on his heels.' Danger only made Nick more focused, more alive, but whatever this was had deadened something in him. She felt more fear than she had since he had taken her from the palace. 'Tell me what is wrong.'

'Most people would say there is nothing wrong at all,' he father said with a grimace. 'He'll tell you himself when he is over the shock, but his father's elder brother has died, which mean that Nicholas, God willing, will be the Marquis of Eldonstone one day.'

'That is good for him, is it not?' Even as she asked it Anusha felt the ground beneath her feet shift as realisation struck. A marquis was an aristocrat, a high-up one. Nick should be marrying a lady born and bred and trained for being a marquis's wife. Her stomach swooped as she clutched the edge of the desk. *Not me.* Not the illegitimate, half-Indian daughter of a trader, however rich and powerful her father was here.

'It is—if what he wants is wealth and vast estates, about six houses, and all the political power and influence he chooses to exert from a place at the top of English society.'

'And if he does not want it?' Perhaps Nick could give it up. He did not love his father, he did not seem to be pining for England. Hope fluttered fragile wings.

'There is no remedy for that. He cannot renounce the title, only death can free him,' her father said drily. 'If he does not take up his inheritance then all that he will become responsible for will be neglected, dealt with at arm's length by agents. I do not think that Nicholas could do that. There will be hundreds of people involved.'

The floor seemed to shift again. 'Then he needs a wife who is born of the aristocracy, does he not? One who knows what to do to help him, one who will be accepted.'

'He is marrying you.' Her father said it with a gentleness that only made the pain worse. *Pity. He understands what this means, he understands that once Nick has given his word he keeps it. He will insist on marrying me.*

'*Ha,*' Anusha agreed. It was as though suddenly she could only think in Hindi. And with the change of tongue came the realisation of what she must do.

The women of her family had walked down singing to the pyres, rather than lose their honour to conquering armies. She had inherited that sense of honour, too. In the agony of a broken heart she would sacrifice everything that she now treasured and hoped for—the reconciliation with her father, her love for Nick—rather than stand in the way of his duty and his honour.

'Anusha?'

She struggled to find the English words. 'I am sorry, I keep... I am keeping you from your work, Papa. I will see you at dinner time.' Four hours before dinner to plan and prepare, perhaps an hour or so afterwards. Nick would be coming home late, as drunk as a lord. She bit her lip to stop the sob of desperate laughter that threatened to escape. How right he had been in his prediction. Hysteria would not help, now she must be cold as ice. When he sobered up and started to think straight she must be long gone or she would have no hope of escape.

'Nicholas *sahib*. Lean on me.' Ajit stood by the step down from the carriage.

'I'm not that drunk, Ajit.'

'Yes, you are, *sahib*.'

Nick clutched the doorframe, missed the step and was neatly fielded by Ajit's wiry strength. 'So I am. Drunk as a lord.' He'd said that to Anusha, hadn't he? It had seemed funny then. It probably still was, but he seemed to have forgotten how to laugh. Still, this felt good—nothing was real, everything floated, he was feeling no pain whatsoever, except whatever was digging its talons into his heart.

'You are going to bed now, *sahib*.' It wasn't a question. Ajit pushed and pulled him up the steps and into the hall past the startled watchman. 'Quietly, *sahib*. Laurens *sahib* and the *memsahib* will be asleep. They do not want to hear your singing.'

'Al'right.' The corridor was bending oddly and the floor was swaying like a rope bridge over an up-country ravine, but Nick struggled on until a final shove from Ajit landed him neatly on his bed, head to the end, buckled shoes on the pillow. 'Go'way. Tha' you.'

'Shoes, *sahib.*' Ajit pulled them off, then started on his neckcloth.

'Go'way,' Nick repeated. 'Go'bed.' The darkness swirled dangerously when he closed his eyes, but he fell into it gratefully.

'Nicholas *sahib*! Wake up!'

Earthquake? Nick dragged his eyes open and squinted at Ajit's face. No, the room was still, the man was shaking him. 'What's the matter? And what the hell is the time?' It was still dark and his head felt like a bag of hot, wet sand.

'Half past three by the clock, *sahib.* Someone has stolen Rajat.'

'When?' Nick pushed himself upright and struggled against dizziness and nausea. He'd been back an hour and the blood in his veins was fighting a losing battle against the brandy.

'The groom saw when he stabled the carriage horses. The stall is empty, the saddle and bridle gone.'

'But—' Something was wrong with that. Nick tried to work it out. 'Rajat would kill anyone who tried to take him, so would Pavan.'

'I know.' Ajit clutched his turban. 'I think and think—perhaps he was drugged?'

'Or taken by someone who he was used to.' What little blood was circulating seemed to drain to his feet. 'Oh, no, she wouldn't.'

'The *memsahib*? But why?'

'I don't know, can't think. Find out if she is safe in bed.'

Nick got his feet on the floor and somehow made it to the washstand. The water was lukewarm, but he plunged his head into it and towelled himself dry. He was still in dress uniform and he struggled out of the tight jacket, the high stock and the fitted breeches and started to drag on civilian riding clothes and his boots.

'The *memsahib* is asleep,' Ajit reported from the doorway.

'Are you sure?'

'I opened the door a little and looked in. I could see the shape in the bed under the covers.'

The brandy was acting like a blow to the head, but his instincts for trouble had not deserted him and the hairs on the back of his neck prickled. He walked doggedly to Anusha's bedchamber, went straight in and pulled back the mosquito netting. Without its shrouding effect the bolster down the middle was obvious. 'Get her woman here *now*.'

Half an hour later, amidst a flurry of servants, Nick stood forcing down scalding black coffee while George paced up and down, the skirts of his silk robe flaring out with each agitated turn. 'What the devil is she doing? Her woman says she has taken several changes of linen, and the clothes she wore when she arrived have gone—this isn't a moonlit ride on the *maidan*! I know Anusha is upset, but—'

'What is she upset about?' Nick poured more coffee.

'She knows about the inheritance.'

So that explained it. 'She's run away,' Nick said flatly through the splitting headache that was making his eyes cross. 'She thinks she isn't good enough for an *aristocrat*.'

'It would not be easy for her,' George said. 'Or for you, perhaps.'

'I know that. But anyone who tries to tell me she isn't acceptable and refuses to receive her is going to be exceedingly sorry—and that includes the whole damned court of St James. She's been brought up to be a princess, her bloodline goes back into the mists of time, she's got more courage than most of the men I know. Hell, George, what am I going to do if I can't find her?'

'You will find her.' The older man gripped him by the upper arms and gave him a shake. 'You will. Now think—where would she go?'

Through the pain in his head and the fear in his gut and the ache in his heart the answer came to him. 'She's gone back to Kalatwah, the only place where she thinks she'll be accepted.'

'But how? If she's taken the horse she can't be going to try to find a boat.'

'Have you been in your study? Come on.' Nick strode out, George on his heels. 'Look at those map rolls—they've been disturbed. And the ledgers in front of your safe have been moved—she can pick locks. Check the money, I'll find which maps she's got. I have a horrible feeling that Anusha is intending to ride all the way back. If she's planning that, then she'll most likely find a group of travellers heading that way. My guess is that she'll start by going to Barrackpore.'

There was a groan from the other side of the room. George turned from the open safe and dumped a pile of gems on the desk. 'She's taken money and she has left her jewels in return.'

'Don't worry. I will get her back.' Nick realised he was the one offering reassurance now. His headache was ebbing as he sobered, but it was replaced with a knot of fear for Anusha and something else, an emotion he could not quite define, but which gave him hope and at the same time terrified him. 'Ajit and I will try the gates around the city—if nothing else, she's riding Rajat and he's distinctive.'

He strode to the door, calling for Ajit as he went. He would move heaven and earth to find her. Anusha was his, whether she realised it or not.

Sunrise. Anusha shifted in the saddle and looked back over her shoulder for the twentieth time, or so it seemed. The road behind the cavalcade of Bengali traders to which she had attached herself was clear. But of course it would be and she was fearful for no reason. Nick would have come home drunk, as he had threatened, no one would notice anything amiss until Nadia came with her morning tea and then there would be confusion and questions and it would take an age before they worked out that she had not slipped out for a morning ride, but had fled.

'You are sorry to be leaving Calcutta, my young friend?' One of the merchants who had given permission for her to join the party brought his horse alongside. 'You leave your sweetheart behind perhaps, eh?'

'Yes,' she agreed, keeping her voice gruff. The tail of her turban was pulled across her nose and mouth, as if to protect her from the dust of the road and the tight long-tailed jacket flattened her breasts and covered the curves of buttocks and thighs. If she did not get too friendly with anyone she had a reasonable chance of staying undetected, she hoped.

'That is a fine horse,' the man continued, apparently settling down for a long chat. 'It would not be for sale, I suppose?'

'No, I am sorry, but it belongs to my master who sends me on this errand.' *Hoofbeats behind.* Anusha twisted round as a troop of cavalry swept past, leaving the traders cursing in their wake and her heart thudding so hard that for a moment she thought she would be sick.

The dust cloud swirled in the early light and then settled, along with her pulse. 'You must have left in haste to have no provisions for the journey,' the trader went on. 'If your master has not given you enough money for a pack mule, you can put your supplies in my wagon if you wish.' He waved aside her thanks. 'We help each other on the road, or where would we all be? At the mercy of dacoits, that is where! Barrackpore is a good place to get supplies and we will be there for the noon meal.'

He talked on, quite content, it seemed, to have no response from her beyond a nod, or a grunt of agreement. Anusha felt her head begin to droop and pulled herself upright. There would be time to sleep tonight and at least the weariness might keep her unconscious long enough to give some respite from this heartache.

Why did I have to fall in love with him? I should have known it was impossible. There was the nagging worry that her presence in the palace might be a problem for her uncle, although her father had said that Altaphur was thoroughly chastened for the moment and skulking behind his frontiers. Might he still try to kidnap her if he knew she was back? If necessary, she would marry some prince of her uncle's choosing, Anusha vowed. Then she could not be a pawn to threaten Kalatwah or cause her father and the Company a problem.

If she could not have Nick, it really did not matter who she was with. It was strange that a breaking heart was physically painful. She had never believed that before…

'Wake up, young friend!' A hand on her shoulder roused her. 'You are swaying in the saddle. And here come more riders in a hurry—what is there in the air today that every-one must rush and cover innocent travellers in dust?'

Disorientated, she reacted slowly and the riders were in amongst them before she could gather her wits.

'*Sahib*, there is Rajat!' *Ajit*.

She wrenched the reins, turned towards the fields and the tangle of jungle beyond, but Rajat was reluctant, neigh-ing for his stable mate, as Pavan, his rider tall in the saddle, swept through the ox carts and horses towards her.

'Anusha!'

Hemmed in by a camel behind, she turned at bay. *How has he found me so fast? What can I do now?*

'Leave this young man alone! He travels with our protec-tion,' the burly Bengali trader shouted and forced his horse, with courage she could appreciate despite her anguish, be-tween Pavan and Anusha's mount.

'If you think this is a young man, my friend, you have need of spectacles,' Nick said without looking at the man. 'Anusha, why did you leave?'

'You are a woman and this is your sweetheart?' the Ben-gali demanded, looking from one to the other, amazement on his round, honest face.

'Yes,' she said. Nick was looking implacable—she did not trust him not to use force if her protector persisted and the poor man did not deserve that. 'Please do not agitate yourself. We had a…disagreement. I will go aside with him and discuss it.'

'Do you want us to wait?' The other traders had begun to gather around them, hands were resting on knife hilts.

'No. I thank you for your help.' It was hopeless: Nick would never allow her to leave. She would just have to con-vince him with words that they could not marry. 'Goodbye, my friends. Travel safely and with profit.' She turned Rajit's head and fell in between Nick and Ajit, who was mounted, she saw, on her father's favourite hunter.

'You should have let me go,' she said. Nick looked dreadful: his chin was stubbled, his eyes were bloodshot and his brow was furrowed as though he had a crashing headache. *I thought I would never see you again.*

'I will ride ahead, *sahib,*' Ajit said and spurred towards the road.

'Go back to Calcutta,' Nick called. 'Tell Laurens *sahib* that she is safe.'

Ajit raised a hand in acknowledgment and cantered off.

'Why the devil did you do it?' Nick turned in the saddle and searched her face. 'Your father is beside himself with worry.'

'I am sorry. You came because of him, then?' *Not for me.*

'I came for both of us! You were going to marry me, I thought you were reconciled to that. I thought you were happy.'

'I was. But I cannot marry a lord.'

'I am not—'

'You will be. You will be a marquis and I am no wife for you. You know that; we talked about what a wife of a lord must be, and a marquis is a very important lord, almost a prince.'

'Anusha, I do not want to be a marquis.' He sounded so violently miserable that she wanted to take him in her arms and kiss him.

'Papa said you could not do anything about it. That you would be one and that he knew you would do your duty, and I know he is right, for you would not do anything dishonourable.'

'Anusha… Damn it, I can't talk to you on horseback like this. Look, let us sit down there.'

There was a small shrine set on the edge of the fields, its stone platform so like the one where they had spent that first night that Anusha caught her breath. Silent, she let him lead the way, then slid down from the saddle and sat on the edge of the platform, her knees drawn up, arms tight around them as if somehow she could contain the misery.

Nick stood in front of her, hands clasped behind his back. Perhaps he did not trust himself not to touch her. 'I know I cannot avoid it. If I outlive my father, then it is my destiny to inherit.'

She nodded. Destiny—fate—she believed in that. It was her fate to love this man. And to lose him.

'But I cannot do it without you, Anusha. No—' he held up a hand to stop her protest '—I know what I said. I know how hard it will be for you, that I have no right to ask it of you, but I will fight anyone who tries to insult you, override anyone who tries to bar you from any privilege due to a marchioness. *I cannot do it without you.*'

Chapter Twenty-One

'**B**ut I know nothing! Why do you need me?' *He needs me?* Anusha hardly dared breathe.

'Because I love you,' he said, his eyes intense on her face. 'Because I do not think I can live without you.' She gasped, dizzy with disbelief and hope, as Nick pressed on, like a man fighting against odds to express himself.

'No, let me explain. I did not realise, I had no idea what love for a woman felt like. Who have I ever loved in my life except for Mary and George, my surrogate parents? It was not until we were searching, questioning everyone along the northern gates and I was so...so *afraid*, that I realised what it was, why I felt as if half of my being had been torn away.' His voice, usually so strong, so certain, shook with the emotion that gripped him.

'I know you do not love me, Anusha. I realise that you agreed to marry me because it was the only way out of your problems.' He turned on his heel and took a step away from her, looking out over the field as though he could not bear to see her rejection on her face, as though he left her free to tell him that she did not want him.

When, speechless, she did not answer, he went on doggedly, baring his heart and soul to her to be torn apart. 'But we have friendship and desire, surely? That is a start. We do not have to go to England now. My father is alive and well, by all accounts, and he will not want me back any more than I want to go. It may be years before we must return. Time for you to become accustomed, perhaps to grow to love me a little.'

Anusha slid down from the wall and crossed the dusty earth until she was standing by his side. 'You *love* me?'

'Yes.' He was still looking into the distance. 'I am sorry, I do not want to make you feel you have to stay, to marry me, because of how I feel. I won't ask more of you than you feel able to give. It is just that I—'

'I love you, Nicholas.' Unable to bear his pain any longer, Anusha took his hand and he looked down at her, green eyes blazing. *It must be true*, she thought, almost dizzy with joy. *It is not a dream. I can feel him, here, skin to skin, pulse to pulse.* 'I love you too, so much that it felt as though I was cutting out my heart when I left you. I thought that to leave you was the only honourable thing to do, because you had never *wanted* to marry me in the first place. *Oh!*'

He pulled her to him so fast that she lost her footing, was lifted and kissed until she was dizzy and then hugged so close that she could hardly breathe. 'Nick!'

'My love?' He set her on her feet again, but did not let go of her. 'Was I squashing you?'

'Yes, but I do not mind. Nick, tell me truthfully—will marrying me make things more difficult for you when you inherit this title?'

'Honestly? I do not know,' he said, tracing his index finger down her nose, along the line of her lips, as though he had never really seen them before. 'Will there be bigots and snobs who are too stupid to see your quality and your intelligence? Perhaps, but I will not let them rule my life and by the time it comes to it, you will be able to out-marchioness any lady you might meet.'

'Is that what I will be, a marchioness?' It was an unwieldy word on her tongue, almost as bad as the reality of the role would be.

'Indeed. And everyone, except members of the royal family, dukes and duchesses and marquises and other marchionesses, must bow or curtsy to you. That does not eliminate many people, so you will become very top-lofty, my lady.'

'Top-lofty? That is better than totty-headed, I think.' Anusha pulled his head down for another kiss and pretended not to notice a group of camel herders staring, wide-eyed, at the sight of a *sahib* kissing a youth by the roadside. 'Mmm. I thought I would never be able to do that again, never feel your arms around me, never taste you on my tongue.'

Nick appeared bereft of speech, something so unusual that she felt herself begin to gabble out of sheer happy nerves. 'You must have an heir now, as soon as possible.'

That made him smile and he turned his arm around her shoulders and began to walk back to the horses. 'Are you proposing that we go home and begin dealing with the matter at once?'

'Perhaps.' She cut him a glancing look and saw his lips twitch. 'Yes?'

'No, wicked woman. We wait until we are married, which is only seventeen days now, so you will have to behave.'

'So will you. Nick, do you remember that first night together at the shrine? Is it not a good omen that we find that we love each other at another shrine?'

'A very good omen. I think we should leave an offering. I have an oil flask in my saddle bags. Have you your knife? There is a flowering bush over there.'

Together they poured the sweet oil over the Shiva *lingam* and placed a spray of flowers at its base. 'I found a branch with fruit and flowers,' Anusha said, leaning against Nick, her head on his shoulder, their fingers entwined. Were there tears in his eyes? There were in hers. 'For the future.'

'This is your house?' Seventeen days later Anusha stared, delighted, at the sprawling white bungalow with its low sweeping roofs and the wide, shaded verandas all around it.

'It is *our* country house, Mrs Herriard. I thought you might not mind travelling all day after the wedding if there was peace and quiet and privacy at the end of it.'

'It is beautiful.' Grooms ran out of the compound to take the horses as she slid down from the saddle of the chestnut mare that was Nick's wedding gift.

'I wanted to find some height, and a view, and this was the best spot I could find within a day's ride of Calcutta. I come here when I can.' He pointed. 'See, there is the Hooghly over there, but the hills make it healthier and less humid, even in the summer.

'Come, let me show you your new home.' He bent and, before she could protest, swept her up in his arms and strode up the front steps. 'This is an English wedding custom: the bridegroom carries his bride over the threshold.'

'I like it.' Anusha buried her face against his neck, then wriggled to get free when she found herself being carried straight past a row of servants, all bowing a welcome over

their joined hands. '*Namaste!*' she called as her new husband simply kept walking whilst offering the same greeting. 'Nick, put me down!'

'Of course.' He shouldered open a door and set her on
her feet in a room that seemed to take up the entire width
of the back of the house.

White muslin curtains blew in a breeze that was cooled
by the dampened mats hung in front of each opening. A
marble pool had been set into the floor in front of the wide
double windows and, as well as a big European bed, there
was a wooden-framed Indian one swinging from chains attached to the ceiling beams.

'A proper bed,' Anusha exclaimed.

'I was hoping it would be a most *improper* one,' Nick
said. 'Shall we bathe?'

'In the pool? Oh, yes.' She remembered all the lessons
of the *zanana.* 'I shall undress you, husband.'

Nick had sat down on the edge of the bed to pull off his
boots. He raised one eyebrow, but stood and opened his
arms. 'If you wish. And then I will return the favour.'

'Oh, no, I must disrobe for you.' He was in Indian dress
and she began by untucking the end of his turban and coil-
ing it neatly into her hands.

'There are rules?' He shrugged out of his coat as she finished with the buttons and she folded it across a chair. Like
him she was wearing tight trousers and a long jacket and
had ridden astride, but today their clothes were cut from
luxurious silks and brocades to mark the wedding journey.

'Of course.' Anusha pulled Nick's shirt from the waist-
band of his trousers and over his head so his hair fell across
his face and he had to shake it back.

Has he any idea how magnificent he looks? Anusha ran

her hands over the flat planes of his chest, teased the tight knots of his nipples with the pressure of her palms, then drew her fingers down the hard muscles and over the flat stomach to the drawstrings of his trousers. Under her hands she felt his skin tighten and smiled.

'What is it?' She could smell the faint musk of aroused male, the tang of sweat from their journey, the spice of his skin.

'Do you remember, in the bathhouse?'

'I recall a rather incompetent attendant with cold hands and very little technique.' He sounded amused, but his breath caught when she pushed the trousers over his hips and let her hands run down his flanks. His erection sprang free and Anusha closed her eyes as she caressed it with both hands in one long stroke before pressing him back.

'My lord should lie down.' For a moment she thought he would simply seize her, but Nick took a deep breath and did as she bade him. Reclining on the swinging bed in arrogant unconcern for his aroused nudity, he took her breath away.

'I am sorry I was so clumsy in the bathhouse,' Anusha apologised. 'I had come out of curiosity and then I touched you and I was undone.'

'I think I was undone the moment I laid eyes on you,' Nick murmured.

'Truly?' She took off her turban and freed her hair, swinging her head so it fell free over her shoulders. 'I should not be wearing these clothes,' she added, suddenly aware that this was not how she should appear before her new husband.

'I could not agree more,' Nick said with a wicked chuckle that had her blushing and laughing as she shed her few garments. It was impossible to do so with the erotic expertise she knew she should display, but he did not appear displeased with what he saw. But then, Nick had seen her naked before, she thought, suddenly feeling more confident.

'My lord will bathe now?'

'My lord and his lady will bathe.' Nick got up, swept her into his arms—he appeared to enjoy doing that, Anusha thought with a smile—and walked down the steps into the pool. It was deep enough to cover him to the chest when he sat down, laughing at her struggles as the cool water washed over her hot skin.

His laughter died away as he looked into her eyes and she gazed back, drowning in the green depths and the love she saw there. Her love, her English gentleman, her *noble* man. It was her last coherent thought before he took her mouth and his hands began to move, sure and subtle, weaving magic out of water and oils as he caressed her and bathed her.

'I should be washing you,' Anusha protested when she had the strength and was floating, languorous and yet tingling with arousal.

'I am at your disposal.' Nick laid his arms along the marble surround and slid down until his head rested on the edge and his hair drifted around him, gold silk on the surface of the water.

Anusha oiled and stroked, her hands caressing over skin roughened with hair, puckered by old scars, smooth as polished stone. She massaged his long legs, then, greatly daring, took a deep breath and went under the water to take him in her mouth.

Nick shuddered, arched and she used her tongue and her lips while her breath lasted and finally surfaced, seeing stars and little else through a curtain of wet hair.

'Oh, my love.' Nick moved fast. She was wrapped in

towels and somehow he had flung some on the swinging bed, for she landed on thick cotton, as Nick fell full length beside her, setting the whole thing swaying.

'There are many subtle things we can do on this bed,' he said as he pushed the wet hair carefully from her face. Anusha nodded, hoping she could interpret the illustrated texts well enough to satisfy him whilst her legs were trembling and her heart was beating like a *tabla*.

'But I do not think,' Nick said between kisses as he bent his head to her breast, 'that I am going to attempt any of them today. I intend to be a straightforward Englishman and simply worship you.'

And he did so, with his mouth and his hands and his words, until she was mindless with pleasure and desperate with spiralling tension. Soothed and provoked, kissed and teased, she moaned his name and arched under him, begging for him in Hindi and English and soft, incoherent murmurs.

Anusha had no inhibition or fear left in her by the time Nick settled himself over her. She cradled him in her thighs, curled her legs around him and opened her body and her heart to him as he thrust, slow and strong, and made her his.

'Nick,' she said and opened her eyes on to his as he looked down at her, every strong line in his face refined by tension, his eyes full of love and desire.

'I am here,' he said, as if she could doubt it, and began to move, gentle at first and then with a rhythm that swept her with him, up and up until everything exploded and they were one and indistinguishable and she did not know where her body ended and his began, nor her mind either.

'Anusha,' Nick murmured and rolled over with her still tight in his arms. The bed swung wildly and she clutched at him and laughed, her wicked laugh that never failed to make him smile.

'I am here.'

'Are you happy?' It was a brave question to ask of a new bride who had just lain with her husband for the first time, he thought with a wry smile. What if she said *no*?

'I think perhaps it is not permitted to be this happy,' she said and came up on her elbows to smile at him. 'Are future marchionesses allowed to be so?'

'I have no idea,' he confessed. 'But we will make new rules and do as we will and I predict that we will laugh more than any other lord and lady in the whole of England.'

She curled down beside him and her hands began to explore. She was brave, a little tentative, and he realised she was putting her theoretical learning to the test.

'I also predict,' he said, trying not to gasp, 'that you will be the only aristocratic lady in England with an understanding of the Indian classical erotic texts. I am not sure what I have done to deserve it, but please, my love, do not stop!'

Anusha rested her arms on his chest and kissed along his collarbone. 'Oh, I do love you, Nicholas!'

'For ever.' He drew her up for his kiss and the two words that were a question and an answer and a vow all at the same time. 'For ever.'

* * * * *

Author's Note

In the early years of the East India Company's rule in India their officers and men were encouraged to marry local women or to take Indian mistresses, for that was seen as an important way to gain understanding and acceptance. Many officers had liaisons with ladies from the princely families and there was little prejudice—many British men became Hindu or Muslim, studied the languages and culture of the sub-continent and raised families in Anglo-Indian households.

It was only from around the 1820s, when English wives and missionaries began to settle, that attitudes changed for the worse and such liaisons were frowned upon. Company officials were expected to live lives as close to the English norm as possible and doors to advancement slammed in the faces of Anglo-Indian children.

I was first enchanted by the world of the eighteenth-century Anglo-Indians when I saw paintings of them in the National Portrait Gallery's exhibition *The Indian Por-*

trait 1560-1860. William Dalrymple's book *The White Mughals* tells the story of one such liaison, in this case between the Resident at the court of Hyderabad and the high-born daughter of the Nizam's Prime Minister. But that love story ended in tragedy and I was determined that my lovers would find their happy ending.

An amazing two weeks touring Rajasthan, staying in royal palaces, gave me settings and more fantastic memories than I could ever use. The states of Kalatwah and Altaphur are, of course completely fictitious.

Begums, Thugs and White Mughals, the Journals of Fanny Parkes, gave me essential information for the trip down the Jumna and the Ganges from the pen of an intrepid Company wife. From a very different point of view, but full of fascinating detail of such things as sugar production and the difficulties of travel, Bishop Reginald Heber's *A Narrative of a Journey Through the Upper Provinces of India* gave me a great deal of information.

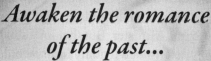

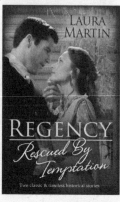